meet me on the bridge

SARAH J. HARRIS

LAKE UNI
PUBL

T0036183

Published by Lake Union Publishing, Seattle

www.apub.com

Amazon, the Amazon logo, and Lake Union Publishing are trademarks of Amazon.com, Inc., or its affiliates.

ISBN-13: 9781662518829
eISBN: 9781662518836

Cover design by Emma Rogers
Cover image: © ex_artist © Chipmunk131 / Shutterstock

Printed in the United States of America

PRAISE FOR SARAH J. HARRIS

THE COLOUR OF BEE LARKHAM'S MURDER

'A rich tapestry . . . distinctive and compelling'

—Observer

'A stunning whodunnit'

—Mail on Sunday

'A beautiful, original novel, at once funny and tragic and brave'
—Sarah Pinborough

ONE ORDINARY DAY AT A TIME

'A gorgeously quirky, charming and inspiring read'
—Beth Morrey, author of *Saving Missy*

'A perfect blend of light and dark with warm characterization and a lot of heart'

—Harriet Tyce, author of *Blood Orange*

'It's the best book I've read in ages. If you like Gail Honeyman, you'll ADORE this'

—Anstey Harris, author of *The Truths and Triumphs of Grace Atherton*

meet me on the bridge

ALSO BY SARAH J. HARRIS

For Mum, Dad and Rachel, with love

PROLOGUE
MARIANNE HOCKNEY
Sunday, May 9, 2004

'We're late! You're not going to make it, Marianne.'

Mum's voice is tinged with worry, and criticism, as we scan the destination board on the busy concourse at Euston station. A woman streaks past, pulling a large bulky suitcase. I swing Julia out of the way to avoid a collision, but she deliberately makes her knees jelly like and won't stand when I try to put her down. I scoop her up and plant her on my hip.

'Is there a later train you can catch?' Mum asks.

'No! I've told you already – I've booked the tickets and they're non-refundable.'

'Oh dear. You should have set off earlier.'

I stifle a sigh. Mum's rising anxiety – together with her talent for always stating the bloody obvious – isn't helping my own nerves. I'd slept through my alarm clock after yet another disturbed night, punctuated by terrifying dreams. Julia catches hold of a lock of my hair and plays with it, the way she did when she was tiny. She's been clingy ever since I told her I was going away.

Mum squints at the board. 'Glasgow Central is platform one! I don't think you have enough time. The train's already boarding.' She takes a deep breath. 'Perhaps you should ring and say you can't make it, love? It's not the best timing with everything that's going on.'

'No, Mum! I can't let everyone down at the last minute.'

I need this catering gig. It's cash in hand and could lead to more work at other music festivals and events across the country. A tiny part of me is also desperate to get away. I'm dying to let my hair down and have some fun. I feel like I turned forty-five two months ago, not twenty-five. I'm still processing everything Mum told me; it's a hell of a lot to take in. I should probably book another appointment with the psychiatrist to help get my head straight, as well as the sleep specialist. Maybe persuade my GP to refer me for another brain scan; the hospital *may* have missed a tumour during that battery of tests. I've never felt so unwell. But for the next couple of days, I can forget it all – a music festival on a remote site, miles from civilisation, in the southern uplands of Scotland, where no one knows me, has never sounded more appealing. I feel a small twinge of guilt at leaving Julia, but she'll be happy with Mum.

'I can make it if I run. The ticket barrier's only over there.' I point in the direction of the turnstile, which is blocked by dozens of commuters and tourists.

Mum bites her lip. 'We'll only hold you up. Go ahead, and we'll follow.'

I try to put Julia down again, but she plunges her hands deeper into my hair and holds on tightly.

'Can you let go, Pickle? Pretty please?'

'No!'

'Julia!' Mum tries to prise her fingers free from my tangles. 'Mummy can't miss her train.'

She buries her head into my chest. I pat my necklace, checking she hasn't accidentally pulled it off.

'It's okay. I can carry her if you take the suitcase?'

Mum nods, grabbing the handle. I lead the way through the crowd, my arm aching beneath Julia's weight – she turned five last week and is growing up fast. It feels like only yesterday when I could tuck her into the sling and take her everywhere with me. I jiggle her onto my other hip so I can grab the ticket from my pocket.

'I guess, this is where we'll have to leave you,' Mum says flatly as we reach the gate.

I feel Julia tense beneath my fingertips. I glance at the attendant standing on the opposite side of the barrier.

'Please can they come onto the platform to see me off?'

The fifty-something woman smiles and swipes them through. We lurch towards the platform. The train is only fifty metres away, but it may as well be miles. I'm exhausted despite nodding off twice at the breakfast table and again on the tube here. Luckily, Mum scooped Julia onto her lap; I was out of it for twenty minutes. I'll need another nap on this train. Shortly before my birthday, Mum had explained that the sleep attacks were a genetic condition and they would worsen, but I didn't think they would be *this* bad.

We're both out of breath by the time we reach the correct carriage. Most of the seats are taken; thank God I booked one, otherwise I'd be napping outside the toilet cubicle.

'It's time, Julia,' Mum says, gently. '*Now,* you have to let your mummy go.'

She sighs deeply and slithers down my long, turquoise dress. I'm tempted to snatch her up, turn around and go home with Mum. But haven't I earned some 'me' time?

'You've got everything?' Mum asks briskly. 'You didn't forget to pack your stimulants and other medication in the rush to get here?'

'Of course I didn't!'

She flinches.

3

'Sorry, Mum,' I say, softening my tone. 'Please don't worry about me. I just need . . . *this*.'

She nods. 'I can't help worrying. You and Julia are all I have now.' Her eyes moisten as she adjusts the belt on her favourite camel coat.

I feel another stab of guilt – Dad's death from cancer three years ago was bad enough, but her only sibling, Rose, was killed in a car crash last November, devastating her further. The pressure that comes with being an only child has never felt so intense.

'Let's talk more when you get back,' Mum continues. 'But please remember what I said and don't do anything silly. You need to look after your health.'

I'm about to hit back with a snarky remark when the announcer says the train is ready to leave. I heave my suitcase into the carriage and turn around.

'Time to go.' I pull Julia towards me, but she resists.

'Do you promise to be a good girl for Grandma?'

'No!' She folds her arms, glowering. She's still furious I'm not letting her come.

'Can I get a goodbye kiss?'

She shakes her head. I bend down and point to my chest. 'What if I let you play with my necklace as an extra special treat?'

Julia's eyes light up.

'For goodness' sake, Marianne!' Mum looks daggers at me.

'What's the problem?' I say, glaring back. 'It's just a lullaby and she loves it.'

I ignore her and sing: '*Spin the stone and make a change. Transform the world and rearrange.*'

Mum harrumphs disapprovingly as Julia reaches out and taps the gem, making it twirl around, gleaming red and black.

'See? You changed the stone's colour. You're making everyone in the world happy. Can I get a kiss now?'

She darts behind Mum and clings to her skirt.

'Never mind. Bye, Pickle. I love you.'

My heart shrinks a little when she doesn't reply. No doubt Mum will tell me I deserve that snub. Instead, she envelops me in her arms.

'Take no notice. You know she loves you more than anything in the world. Me too.'

I inhale her familiar rose scent. Tears prick my eyes; this is the closest I've felt to her in months after all our heated arguments.

'I love you, Mum.'

'Promise me, you won't keep running away. And you won't stay too long. You'll come back.'

I let go of her abruptly. 'Of course I'll come back. It's only a week!'

I manage to swallow the 'for fuck's sake' I'm longing to add and climb inside, shifting my suitcase further along.

'Remember, Marianne—'

I slam the door shut, cutting off Mum mid-lecture. It feels like a small victory until I attempt to pull down the window and it jams. I can't remind my daughter I love her. Mum puts her arms around Julia and pulls her closer. *Away from me.* They smile warmly at each other. We're separated by glass and something far, far bigger than I can ever begin to describe. The barrier feels solid, *permanent,* preventing me from reaching them.

I grab the handrail to steady myself as I'm hit by a wall of tiredness.

My vision shifts and softens. Mum and Julia are blurry like ghosts, but maybe it's me that doesn't exist anymore. I blink. My eyes fill with tears, obliterating them completely.

Who am I? What kind of mother and daughter can I ever be?

A rubbish one! I'm cracking up and failing them both.

I touch my pendant. I don't want it; *I don't want any of this*. I whip it off and immediately feel lighter, as though a weight has been lifted from my shoulders. I yank hard at the window, pulling it down far enough to dangle out the chain.

'Take it!'

Mum's face brightens as she springs forward. I drop the necklace into her cupped palms.

'Thank you!' she says, sighing with relief. She stuffs it into her pocket. 'Ring me as soon as you arrive, otherwise I'll worry.'

I nod. That's a given – I'll never hear the end of it if I don't call.

'Love you!' I mouth at Julia, but she's deliberately staring further down the platform.

I wave as the train pulls away. Suddenly, Julia breaks free from Mum and runs alongside the glass.

'Stop! I want to kiss you goodbye.'

Tiny daggers puncture my heart.

'Come back, Mummy!'

It's too late. Julia's cries become fainter.

Then she disappears.

1

JULIA

THURSDAY, MAY 9, 2024

'She's back!'

My eyes fly open. Where am I? Bright lights. The scent of garlic and tomato. A vibrating, loud noise. *Applause?* It ripples around the table, punctuated by laughter. More sounds: the tinkle of cutlery, the pop of a champagne cork, a woman's voice rising at the end of a sentence. Is she asking me a question? I straighten in my seat. Too late. I'm slipping away. My head nods forward.

'Julia!'

'Oh no! We've lost her again.'

Sounds and lights shrink, becoming a distant pinprick in a never-ending tunnel. I'm swamped by crashing waves of grey nothingness before plunging into ice-cold water. Splashing. Something's dragging me down. I'm sinking beneath the ripples, deeper and deeper. Now, I'm being pulled up and away from danger. An invisible thread draws me towards a handsome man with bluish-green eyes and curly brown hair. He's in soft focus, as if I'm staring at him through a blurred camera lens. Butterflies dance across my stomach as he smiles and reaches out his hand. Instinctively, I sense I'll be safe. I'm trying to reach him, but the background shimmers. Faint voices pierce the film-like bubble.

'Is she okay?'

The strangers' voices become louder. More insistent.

'Is she always like this? It must be difficult for you.'

Pain stabs my arm. Repeatedly. Red-hot pincers.

'Julia, for God's sake, wake up!'

I'm fighting my way to Ed's voice. My eyelids flicker open briefly. Sharp colours fade fast. Sounds drift from my grasp. I blink and blink.

Stay awake.

I gasp for air. A familiar hot, shameful heat creeps across my cheeks for falling asleep *and* imagining that man who isn't my boyfriend. I have no idea who he is or why he's been making fleeting appearances in my dreams recently, but I'm not complaining. It's far better than my usual nightmares. My lids droop. I widen my eyes, saucer like, trying to resist the invisible invader that wants to drag me to foreign shores. It's hovering on the edges of my brain. Waiting to claim me again. I can't let it. Tonight is important. I can't remember why.

Think.

I check the edges of my mouth for drool and attempt to concentrate. My eyes refocus on a sea of unfamiliar faces. A middle-aged man with black-rimmed glasses glances away. Two twenty-something women are talking behind their hands at the end of the table. They freeze.

Who are these people? What am I doing here?

My brain restarts. I'm in an Italian restaurant in Clapham with Ed's work colleagues and boss, Tony, a classic car enthusiast. I'd been talking to his wife, Sabrina, who was far less passionate about his hobby. Before we'd set off from White City, Ed admitted he'd researched famous old cars to impress Tony, ahead of next week's pay appraisal. He'd begged me to chat to members of the marketing company and their partners.

Unspoken words had lingered between us:

Please make a good impression.

Don't embarrass me.

Oh God. That ship has long sailed.

'I'm so sorry,' I blurt out. 'I can't help it. I have no control over when it happens. The tiredness just hits me.'

No one speaks. Someone a few seats down clears their throat. An uncomfortable silence lengthens. I wait for Ed to leap to my defence, the way he used to when we first got together, but his mouth is a tight, straight line. His hands grip the sides of the chair, his shoulders rigid.

'How long was I out for this time?' I whisper, leaning closer.

'About ten minutes *and* you were snoring,' he hisses. 'I couldn't wake you.'

'Sorry.'

That's a word I've used a lot recently. I feel for his hand under the table, but it's out of reach.

'Don't worry,' Tony says. 'My wife sends me to sleep with some of her stories. Don't get her onto the subject of her sewing group. You'll definitely nod off!'

Sabrina rolls her eyes dramatically. '*I* do that when you talk about restoring Jaguar E-Types!'

She flashes me a sympathetic smile but I'm dying inside. I'd asked Ed to explain my narcolepsy to everyone before we came tonight in case I had an attack, but it must have slipped his mind. Now I feel like the evening's circus act.

'It's not that, I promise. My brain can't regulate sleeping and waking properly. I fall asleep at inappropriate times.'

'*Very* inappropriate times,' Ed says, laughing loudly. 'Like at your birthday party last week when you fell off the chair! It was incredibly dramatic – worthy of an Oscar.'

I take a swig of Diet Coke; my throat is horribly dry. 'Thank you! Florence Pugh had better watch out. I'm after all her roles.'

I'm playing along, but my cheeks burn hotter. I shoot him a look – he could have picked a million better ways to lighten the mood.

Miranda, the firm's latest recruit, giggles, making her dangly star earrings shimmer delicately. 'Omigod. That's terrible!'

Ed has previously described her as annoying and loud, but he obviously forgot to mention she's also flirty and attractive. She tosses her long, blonde mane and nudges his arm. 'What happened? Spill the beans!'

I stare harder at Ed, silently begging him to stop, but he's on a roll and had too much to drink.

'The waiter almost tripped over her, but never spilt a drop from the beer glasses on his tray. He was a total pro!'

Miranda snorts with laughter, her hair brushing against his suit sleeve. 'God, I can't even begin to imagine what that must have been like.'

No, you can't.

'It was a shock.' Ed takes a large gulp of wine. 'Luckily, Julia wasn't hurt.'

I catch hold of his hand as it returns to the table and squeeze it gently. He knows I hate discussing my episodes with strangers, and my birthday party is an evening I want to erase from my memory *forever.*

'Yeah, but—'

I apply more pressure. He finally gets the message and gives me a brief, apologetic smile as the waitress returns to our table. He loosens his old Harrovian tie and takes off his jacket, slinging it over the back of the seat.

'How are we doing for drinks?' the young woman asks. 'Can I get anyone a coffee or a liqueur?'

Tony bangs the table with his fist, making his wife wince. 'I fancy a port. What about anyone else?'

I grab my handbag, seizing the chance to escape. 'I'll be back in five.'

'Sure thing,' Ed mumbles.

Miranda swishes her hair as I pass her chair.

'Will she be okay on her own?'

I don't hear Ed's reply. He reaches for another bottle of red and tops up their glasses. They clink them together. I want to tell Ed to slow down before he blurts out something he'll regret in front of Tony. But I can hardly lecture him when I've created a spectacle. I weave my way through the closely positioned tables to the bathroom and lock myself inside a cubicle. Tears slide down my cheeks.

Why is this happening to me?

I already know the answer. In some rare cases like mine, narcolepsy runs in families due to an inherited genetic fault. I'll thank Mum for the permanent leaving present if she ever bothers to get in touch with me or Gran again. The bathroom door creaks open as I tear off a piece of tissue and dab beneath my eyes. I hear footsteps, a tap turning on and water splashing into a basin. I breathe out slowly. I need to go back to the GP; the stimulants she prescribed aren't working. If anything, I'm getting worse. The episodes have been happening up to a dozen times a day since my twenty-fifth birthday. Ed is probably describing in graphic detail how I ruined my party last Friday. When I came round on the restaurant floor, I couldn't stop crying about Mum. It felt like she'd abandoned me yesterday, not twenty years ago.

I unlock the cubicle, praying one of the cold-eyed girls from the end of the table, or worse still, Miranda, hasn't followed me in. Thankfully, the elderly woman rummaging in her handbag by the sinks isn't from our party. I peer in the mirror. Jesus. I resemble Dracula's bride. My short-sleeved black blouse emphasises the ghostly pallor of my face. My eyes are bloodshot from crying and mascara is streaked beneath them for added gruesome effect. The humidity in the restaurant has curled my hair into tight, red corkscrews; it never stays straightened for long. I pull out my brush and make-up bag, searching for powder to fix my shiny nose before moving on to the rest of my 'raised from the dead' appearance.

'You have beautiful hair,' the lady remarks, dabbing at her face from a powder compact. 'Such a lovely colour and texture.'

She looks older than Gran – mid to late eighties – and has deep wrinkles engrained on her forehead and cheeks, but her blue eyes sparkle brightly, and her white hair is cut into a fashionable bob.

'That's kind of you, but *this* is the bane of my life.' I hold up an unruly tendril. 'Sometimes I think I should cut it all off.'

'No, you must make the most of everything while you can.'

Her voice is tinged with sadness. Her liver-spotted hands shake as she grips the side of the basin to steady herself. She's frailer than I first thought.

'Are you okay? *You* look fantastic by the way.'

'When you get to my age . . .' She coughs, clearing her throat. 'It hurts to remember things you took for granted in your youth. Your looks, career, friends . . . You don't realise how quickly everything can be taken away.'

She smiles but it doesn't reach her eyes. They've moistened.

'I'm sorry.'

She forces a brittle laugh and applies lip balm. 'Ignore me. I'm being maudlin. Don't let a tired, old woman ruin your night.'

'It's already ruined.' I sigh as I dab at the dark streaks beneath my eyes with a tissue.

'Boyfriend trouble?' She snaps her compact shut.

'Possibly.'

'I've had some bad boyfriends in my time too. You should dump him.'

My mouth falls open as I stare at her in the mirror. God, she's blunt, like Gran was – still is when she has brief moments of lucidity. They both come from an era when you could apparently say whatever the hell you wanted to people, including total strangers. Or, maybe, when you get to a certain age you don't care anymore and tell it straight.

I give my hair a quick brush and throw everything into my bag. 'My boyfriend's great. He'll be wondering where I am. It was nice meeting you . . .'

She hesitates. 'Patricia.'

I feel a tiny shiver down my spine as she stares at my arm. I glance down. Small crimson bruises have sprung up across my pale skin, the same as last week.

She sniffs. 'That's what your generation calls "a red flag", I believe.'

I gasp, remembering the shooting pain while I was asleep. Was Ed pinching my arm to wake me?

'Honestly, it's not what you think . . .'

'That someone gripped your arm tightly and left fingermarks?'

I open my mouth to argue.

'It can be scary to make the break,' she continues. 'But believe me, you're far better off on your own than stuck in a relationship with someone who doesn't respect you. I hate to . . .' She stops herself, shuddering. 'I can't bear to see a young woman treated badly.'

Omigod! This is embarrassing. She's completely misunderstood the situation.

13

'It's fine, honestly. Ed hasn't hurt me. Well, he didn't mean to. You see . . .' My voice trails off. I can't face explaining my condition again tonight. No one ever truly understands. 'Please don't worry about me. Ed's a good man. We're happy.' I pause. '*I'm* happy.'

Her eyebrows raise. 'You don't look happy. Good men don't make their girlfriends cry or give them bruises. Why don't you leave him? What are you afraid of?'

I glare at her. *How dare she?* I shouldn't have to defend our relationship to an interfering old woman. She's grasped the wrong end of the stick. She doesn't know anything about me or Ed, but she's judging us both. And she's crossed *way* over the line.

I grit my teeth, resisting the urge to tell her to mind her own business.

'Goodbye, Patricia,' I say, marching away. 'Enjoy the rest of your night.'

'Goodbye . . .'

The door swings shut.

Before it closes completely, I spin round.

I swear I heard a single word drift out.

Julia.

2

FRIDAY, MAY 10, 2024

'How did she know my name? It's weird, right?'

I've explained my encounter in the restaurant bathroom after slipping back into bed with Ed the following morning. Now, he's lying on his back, eyes closed and breathing heavily. I'd spent the night in the spare room again. He was too drunk for me to describe what happened when we arrived home. Tony had ordered yet another round of nightcaps and it was past midnight by the time we got in. Ed had collapsed face first onto the bed, spreadeagled across the duvet. Separate beds on weeknights were his idea, not mine – his alarm goes off early for work and he found it exhausting being woken by my screams during nightmares. Gradually, these sleeping arrangements have also crept into weekends. Breaking the habit needs to be added to my growing to-do list, along with finding a sleep specialist if my GP can't help. I miss the cuddles and late-night chats. And the sex. I miss that *a lot*.

I run my fingers through his short, blondish-brown hair and trace the outline of his face. Seriously, he has better cheekbones than me.

'Hello? I know you're still awake. Your eyelashes are fluttering. It's a giveaway.'

'Eeuuugh,' he groans. 'You're mistaken. I'm a dead person.'

'You deserve to be after that much port.'

'Don't say that word or I'll throw up.' He shudders. 'I'm never touching a drop again. Maybe it was corked?'

'Or it doesn't mix well with red wine and tequila?'

'Stop torturing me!'

I snuggle closer, moulding my body into his. Well, my warm, soft folds of flesh press against his lean, hard muscle, to be precise. It feels good. He must have regained consciousness at some point after I'd left him: he's managed to strip down to his boxers. My eyelids are heavy. I woke six or seven times during the night and struggled to get back to sleep after my regular nightmare: a faceless knifeman in my bedroom, poised to attack. Before I could scream, I was pulled towards safety. The good-looking stranger made another brief appearance. He was out of focus, as if standing behind thick, cloudy glass, but somehow, I *knew* it was him.

I open my eyes wide, blinking repeatedly. I don't have time to drift off or dwell on Dream Guy. *That* feels disloyal to Ed.

'How did the old lady guess my name correctly?' I touch the hairs that trail down his chest.

He manages to lift his hand a fraction of an inch before it flops heavily onto the crisp white duvet he picked out last month after complaining my faded floral one was 'old and mumsy'.

'You could have let it slip and not remembered.' He licks his dry lips. 'Or misheard what she said.'

'I'm sure I didn't though.'

'Or it could be . . .' He shivers as I run my fingers up the inside of his thigh. 'You're distracting me. I've lost my thread.'

'Sorry, not sorry.' I kiss his chest.

'What was I saying . . . ? She might have walked past our table and heard someone call you Julia.'

Something stirs beneath the covers as my hand travels higher. I smile to myself. That had the desired effect. We probably have time for a quickie before work. I'm squeezing in a visit with Gran before a shift at the *Gazette*, and Ed has a late start after last night.

'I only really spoke to Tony and his wife. I doubt many of your other work colleagues even know my name.' I climb on top of him, wrestling with my T-shirt. A button catches in my hair as I try to pull it over my head, ruining the sexy effect I'm aiming for.

'I wouldn't be so sure of that – you were pretty memorable.'

My cheeks sting as if I've been slapped. I peel off him and yank my top down.

'Thanks a million!'

'What? Shit. I didn't mean it like that.'

'Yes, Ed. You did.'

I flop down and turn my head away as he rolls onto his side. I don't want him to see my tears forming. I wish I wasn't like this. I want to be normal like everyone else. Why doesn't he understand? He used to be sympathetic.

He sighs heavily. 'I'm feeling rough. Please don't blow this up into something it's not.'

I shrug off his hand, which lightly brushes my shoulder.

'It is *something*,' I whisper. 'I embarrass you.'

He pauses. 'It's not that, it's . . .'

'What?' I glance across at him.

He hesitates, rubbing his stubbled chin.

'Go on. Say it. You obviously want to.'

'Well, sometimes it feels like an excuse.'

My body tenses. 'Come again?'

He takes a deep breath. 'You didn't want to come to my boring work dinner in the first place. You made that clear. You hate it when I talk about marketing and what's going on in the office. You think my colleagues are jerks.'

'That's because you claim most of them *are* jerks.'

I'm tempted to add he didn't appear to mind Miranda's flirting despite previously moaning about her poor work ethic – but he'll claim it's all in my imagination.

'I told you I was tired despite taking my meds. And you're right, I didn't want to spend an evening with strangers you've slagged off. I did it to support you!'

'Sure. Point taken.' His tone is sullen. 'But the endorphins from exercise are supposed to help you stay alert, yet you didn't bother coming to the gym with me on Monday morning.'

I open my mouth to point out I'd come off the back of another late shift at the newspaper, but he raises his voice.

'I bet if your friends at the *Gazette* plan something, you'll have a miraculous burst of energy. But when I arrange last night or your birthday party, it turns into a bloody disaster.'

'That's unfair!' I sit bolt upright. 'I can't believe you'd say that after all the times you've seen me . . .' I wipe my wet eyes with the back of my hand. 'Do you think I want to fall asleep in a restaurant? Do you realise how embarrassing that is for me? And how many times do I need to apologise for my party?'

'I'm just being honest.' His shoulders rise and fall. 'It's starting to feel one-sided – everything revolves around you. I'm the one making all the effort. You always come first, never me.'

His words wound like a knife. I remember the elderly woman's warning last night:

Good men don't make their girlfriends cry or give them bruises.

'I get it now.' I hold up my arm. His fingermarks have deepened into dark damson shapes. 'Is that why you pinched me? Because you think I don't appreciate you?'

His mouth drops open. 'I did that?'

'You tell me! I wouldn't know. Apparently, I wasn't making enough effort and deliberately slept through your crappy work dinner because I'm a horrible, selfish girlfriend who neglects you and wants to be the centre of attention.'

I throw off the covers and swing my legs out of bed.

'Hey! I'm sorry.' He wraps his arms around me in a gentle bear hug. 'Come back.'

'Let go, Ed! I mean it. I'm not in the mood.'

He loosens his grip. 'I apologise. Show me. *Please.*'

'Fine!'

I stretch out my arm. The marks are spectacular – Gran said I bruised like a peach when I was growing up. I'd look like I'd gone five rounds with a heavyweight boxer just from falling off my bike.

'God, this looks awful – as if I'm a wife beater,' he coughs. 'Not that we're husband and . . .'

I bite the inside of my mouth. We've never felt further away from *that* scenario. Ed's parents are divorced and he recently let slip he doesn't see the point of marriage.

'The old lady in the bathroom called you a bad boyfriend and I defended you. To be honest, I'm beginning to wonder why I bothered.'

He reddens. 'I swear I didn't pinch hard. I was trying to wake you. I panicked when Tony looked annoyed. Once you get on the bad side of him, you're finished.' He kisses the bruises one by one. 'Please forgive me. I was a jerk.'

'*Was?*'

'I *am* a horrible jerk with a horrible, horrible hangover who doesn't know what the hell he's talking about. I promise I'll never do anything like that again.'

'Or claim I'm falling asleep as a self-centred stunt to annoy you?'

'Or that. I'm a colossal jerk. Can you forgive your bad, bad boyfriend?'

'Hmm.'

19

He jumps as his phone vibrates with a message. I glance at the bedside table.

'Do you need to get that?'

'No. This is more important.' He presses my hand to his lips. 'I'll make it up to you, I promise. Where were we before I was being the world's biggest douche bag?' He pulls me closer, nuzzling my neck.

Seriously? Accusing me of faking narcolepsy is the biggest passion killer ever. 'I don't think so . . .'

'Hold that thought!'

His face pales as he pulls away, gripping the duvet. He leaps out of bed and runs to the en-suite. Violent heaving ensues. I hover on the other side of the door.

'Can you grab painkillers and an energy drink?' he calls. 'My head's exploding and I'm throwing up buckets.'

'Who said romance is dead?'

My frown dissolves as I enter the kitchen. The blinds are open and sunlight is streaming in, making the surfaces gleam. This is my favourite room despite its plainness. I'd wanted bright, sunflower-yellow paint, with a feature wall on the right, but Ed and his mum, Katherine, had argued that white would be timeless when he moved in with me. I'll win the battle of the décor in the bedroom – it's also painted white, but I've found a gorgeous teal colour that will look stunning. I tap the hanging saucepans, making them tinkle. Katherine gave Ed a cordon bleu cookery course voucher for his birthday. He spent hundreds of pounds on new utensils and is yet to christen any of them.

I take a bottle from his shelf of sports and energy drinks and stick the West Ham fixtures back on the fridge door. The Eiffel Tower magnet he bought on a Paris work trip has slipped off and gained another chip. After finding paracetamol buried at the bottom of my handbag, I return to the bedroom.

'You have another message,' I holler, grabbing his phone as it pings.

'Not now.'

Ed's slumped over the toilet, grey-faced, when I knock and walk in. I place the bottle next to him, along with the pills and back away to a safe distance. The locked screen lights up with a message before disappearing.

Call me? Need to talk. MM xx

'I think it's . . . Miranda? Does her surname begin with an "M"?'

His shoulders tense. He stretches his hand out without turning around. 'Let me check. It's probably about our pay appraisal.'

'She wants to discuss it at seven-thirty? After a big night out?'

'Hmm.' He examines the phone briefly. 'Yeah, that's her. She's stressing about her feedback. Uh-oh. What's with the kisses?'

'That's what I was wondering! Is she like that with everyone?'

'Oh shit!'

I beat a hasty retreat as he heaves into the toilet bowl. She could be checking in to see how he's doing as a pal, not in an I'm-after-your-boyfriend kind of way. But why add two kisses if this is about work? It's over-familiar. Is she his late-night texter? Ed is receiving messages at odd times; his phone pings through the wall of the spare bedroom. My heart sinks. So what if she fancies him and messages after 11 p.m. about a professional crisis? I trust Ed one hundred per cent. He was devastated when an ex-girlfriend slept with someone else behind his back. He swore he'd never cheat.

I turn on the radio and pad over to the mirror as an Ed Sheeran song blares out. I rub away the traces of last night's mascara beneath my eyes and brush my hair, attempting to detangle the knots. I push away the doubt that flickers at the corner of my mind. We've both been busy with work and fallen into a rut, but our first anniversary is imminent – a chance to reignite the spark. It was such a whirlwind in the beginning. Ed whisked me away on romantic weekends to the Cotswolds and the Lake District and booked tables at expensive restaurants and West End shows to help take my mind off worrying about Gran. He couldn't keep his hands off me at first and moved in within months when his lease came to an end. He'd argued it made more sense to live together as he spent so much time here. It was new and exciting, but stress, narcolepsy and the grind of daily life *have* taken over recently.

I'll make more of an effort to organise date nights.

We'll go back to the way we were.

I don't think he's planned anything yet anniversary-wise, but we could be spontaneous and go somewhere romantic, last minute, like Paris or Rome.

Everything is fine. We're happy. I have nothing to worry about.

I glance away as the old lady's observation reverberates in my head.

You don't look happy.

A strong breeze picks up along Chiswick High Road, whipping my hair into my face. I scrape it into a ponytail and turn left, weaving my way through the warren of double-fronted Victorian properties. I used to play a game on the way to the bus stop each morning before school – trying to picture the families who lived here. I gave them different names and faces, but one thing remained constant: I imagined a smiley, loving mum who adored her children in all the houses. I take a short detour; it's too painful passing Gran's old house on Airedale Avenue. After graduating uni I'd looked after her with the help of agency nurses, but that changed when she needed 24-hour care. Her Alzheimer's had worsened, and she'd suffered a mini stroke. It was impossible to keep the house *and* pay the fees at her nursing home, Ravensbrook. I had to use my power of attorney to put number 12 on the market two years ago, but guilt continues to gnaw at the pit of my stomach.

The familiar, tall building, with its modern glass façade that's so out of keeping with the nearby red-brick Victorian villas, looms in front of me. It looks more like a school than a care home. I tap the code into the keypad and let myself in. Peering through the hatch in reception, I spot fresh, steaming tea in a mug stamped with the word 'bossasaurus' and a picture of a dinosaur.

'You're here bright and early – the first visitor of the day.' A thin woman with a blonde Princess Diana-style haircut appears on the other side of the glass.

Everything Carole, the dragon duty manager, says sounds like an accusation. I immediately feel on edge.

'Hmm. I was . . .'

She approaches the hatch and pushes the visitors' book towards me. 'Sign in, Miss Hockney. You forgot last time. *And* you didn't sign out.'

'Sorry.'

'Please don't let it happen again. We must know exact numbers of visitors for health and safety purposes.'

I add my name, date, and time of arrival to the fresh, clean page. *9.30 a.m.*

'One more thing – your gran has been at the newspapers in the day room with her scissors again.'

'Ah, that's unfortunate, sorry.'

'We'll need to take them off her or scrap the paper service if this continues – she's upsetting other residents.'

The muscles in my shoulders tighten. Gran has her own set of papers and children's art scissors – the staff let her cut out articles that take her fancy. It's good for her concentration and coordination; she spends hours extracting stories. Even when I was at uni, she'd send envelopes stuffed with articles she thought would interest me. Gran mustn't lose this hobby, as well as the weekly hairdresser and nail technician – Carole has suspended their visits 'until further notice'. I can't face a stand-up row with her this morning; the battle can wait until another day.

'Thanks for letting me know. Hopefully, it won't come to that.'

Carole nods curtly and picks up the phone. I try to breathe through my mouth as I pass the row of faded seascape paintings on the wall. I hate the smell of disinfectant. It reminds me that, despite the pictures, potted plants, and soft, comfy green chairs in reception, this is a clinical place, like a hospital, not a real *home*.

A small, dark-haired young woman with a nose stud appears at the end of the corridor. It's Raquel, a young Spanish carer, who joined the staff three months ago and swiftly became one of the residents' favourites. Gran enjoys showing her photos of our family – her and Gramps on Hammersmith Bridge, where he got down on one knee and proposed; my mum as a little girl, and me and my best friend, Vicky, at Bristol University's graduation ceremony. Raquel frowns as she spots me. I pick up my pace.

'Is everything okay?'

'Sylvia isn't having a good morning,' she says as I reach her. '*Está enfadada*. She's upset.'

My heart sinks. Some days Gran sings and smiles while she looks through her photo albums, happily reminiscing about the past, or methodically cuts up her set of newspapers. Other times she insults fellow residents and nurses. Those are the worst visits, the ones I try to push to the back of my mind. I don't want to remember Gran angry and aggressive. She never swore or exchanged a cross word with anyone until her illness took a firm hold.

'Can I see her?'

Raquel hesitates, smoothing the plastic apron over her blue uniform.

'For a few minutes. It might help? *Por favor?*'

She sighs. 'Don't get your hopes up. She is confused and *frustrada.*'

I'm frustrated too. I follow her down the white-walled corridor. Raquel knocks on the open door and steps aside. Gran's room is usually immaculate, but this morning it's in disarray. Clothes have been ripped out of the wardrobe, along with shoeboxes, and drawers emptied. Photos, ripped newspapers, and cuttings are scattered across the green carpet. A pair of purple plastic scissors lie next to them. Gran is rifling through her bedside drawers. A hairbrush lands by her albums on the floor, followed by a paperback, creasing the cover.

'What is she looking for?' I whisper.

Raquel shrugs. 'I don't think she knows. She gets angry when I try to help. We'll tidy up while she's in the day room.'

Gran spins around, staring wildly. Her curled white hair is unbrushed, the pink cardigan hangs halfway down her left arm and her cream lace blouse is spotted with tea stains.

'Julia!'

She walks shakily towards me, tears streaming down her lined cheeks. Her mobility has worsened, but she recognises me. That's a good sign, right? Some days she mistakes me for another carer. She reaches out and grabs my wrist. She has a surprisingly tight grip for someone so small and frail.

'They don't believe me.' She lets go, her shoulders drooping. 'They all think I'm lying. But *you* believe me, don't you?'

I adjust the cardigan and pull her into a hug, inhaling her rose perfume.

'Yes! Please don't worry about anything.'

A tiny hand clutches my heart, squeezing it tighter, as she lets out a small sob. Our roles have long been reversed; she used to comfort me whenever I wept for Mum and begged to know when she'd come home and tuck me up in bed at night and walk me to school.

'I'm here and everything's going to be okay,' I say, my voice cracking. 'Shall we go to the day room and have a cup of tea? We can watch TV together before I go to work.'

'No, no, no! There's no time.'

'I don't have to be in the office for another couple of hours.'

'You're not listening,' she says impatiently. 'No one ever listens! I spoke to her a few minutes ago. She's back, finally!'

'Who?'

Raquel shakes her head and mouths: 'No one.'

The confusion clears in Gran's greyish-blue eyes as she meets my gaze. She stands taller, lifting her chin. Her voice is crisp and unwavering.

'Your mother. She was looking for her necklace – and she wants to see you.'

3

FRIDAY, MAY 10, 2024

'Marianne was standing right there a minute ago!' Gran beams through her tears as she points to the middle of the room. 'She wanted to see me before it was too late. I knew she would! I told her she'd taken her time and she laughed. Do you recall how she was always late? Trains, job interviews, nursery and school pickups, *everything*!'

I steady myself against the pale-yellow wall. Her words slice through me, reopening painful, old wounds that never fully heal. I don't remember because there's nothing *to* remember. Mum abandoned me when I was five without leaving a note. Gran had initially reported her as missing when she failed to return from her catering job at a Scottish music festival. Her mental health problems had worsened and the police were convinced she'd left willingly. Years later, Gran admitted Mum had been in touch – she'd moved abroad, working in bars across Spain, and had started a new life. It breaks my heart that she thinks Mum will return after all this time. She forgot us long ago.

'How was Mum?' My voice wobbles as I play along.

'Different, yet exactly the same.' Her voice rises as she looks around the room, almost losing her balance. 'Where is she? Where did she go?'

'Perhaps she'll come back later?' Raquel approaches and takes her arm. 'Let's make you comfortable in the day room. I'll put on the TV, and you can relax with your granddaughter. I'll bring in your photo albums.'

'Marianne won't come back,' Gran snaps. 'You scared her away, you fucking idiot! I'll never find her.'

'*Lo siento*,' she says softly. 'I'm sorry.'

I shake my head at Raquel, silently apologising. Gran would never have used that word when she was well. She hated swearing.

'Come on, Gran. Let's go.'

'Didn't you hear me? It's important I find it. I need to think.' She walks to the bed and eases herself down. Her arms wrap around her body and she rocks backwards and forwards.

'Did Marianne tell you what she's looking for? I've forgotten,' she says, looking up hopefully.

I raise my arms in a helpless gesture. 'No, sorry.'

'I'll fetch the wheelchair,' Raquel says. 'We can't let her stay in here – she could slip on the mess and fall.'

'Can you give us a few minutes? She might calm down if I find what she's looking for.'

'I'll be back in *cinco minutos*.' Raquel holds up five fingers before leaving.

I pick my way through the clutter and kneel beside Gran. 'What do you need me to find?'

I gaze at the photographic echoes from the past scattered on the carpet – me dressed as an angel in a school nativity play and, years later, blowing out candles on my eighteenth birthday cake; Gramps looking dapper in a smart suit, tipping his hat to the camera on Hammersmith Bridge; Gran and her late sister, Rose, with a cello; Gramps holding a small, red-headed child, cuddling an animal soft toy. *Mum*. My hand trembles as I pick up another old picture. I'm grinning and holding onto Mum's long, floral skirt next to a hedge.

Her hair is tied into a braid and a gold pendant hangs around her neck. I'm her mini-me with the same hairstyle, clad in a pink sun-hat and shorts. This looks like Gran's back garden. I only remember distant echoes from that day: the smell of suntan lotion, the sound of laughter and the promise of mint choc-chip ice cream. Mum is staring down at me with such a look of love. Was that a lie? Could she have been faking for the camera? But neither of us is looking at the lens; Gran had captured an unguarded moment. I stare at the little girl's innocent, trusting face. She had no idea her heart would shortly be broken in two.

'Is this what you were looking for? I think this is the last picture we have of Mum before she . . .'

Abandoned us. Discarded us like rubbish.

I clear my throat. 'Before she went away.'

I place the picture in Gran's hand, but it slips onto the carpet. The spark has disappeared from her eyes. She's mumbling incoherently and gesticulating at something in the middle distance, as if she's having a conversation with someone only she can see. It's like a light switch has been turned off. I swallow my disappointment. I've lost her *again*.

'I'll tidy up to save Raquel,' I say under my breath. 'She'll get it in the neck from Carole if she sees your room like this.'

Most of the faded newspaper scraps on the floor are from the *London Gazette*; I recognise the font. Gran was so proud when I gained my full-time admin job after two years temping in the City. She'd forget she left a saucepan on the stove, but she'd remember when I described the heart-warming stories that journalists were working on. She'd cut out the finished articles to paste into scrapbooks. I look closer and notice these cuttings are all crime-related. I scoop up an article from last year, dated May 12:

THE NIGHT PROWLER STRIKES AGAIN!

A 70-year-old woman was battered in her home last night by an intruder.

The pensioner was in bed, recovering from a hip operation, when a masked man armed with a knife broke into her house on Brackley Road, Chiswick, at 11 p.m.

The woman was badly beaten and robbed. She is now in a serious but stable condition at Ealing Hospital. Her attacker is believed to be the Night Prowler, a violent burglar who continues to terrorise London.

Police say he removed light bulbs in the kitchen and stole £200 in cash and jewellery, including an antique gold bracelet and diamond ring.

He reportedly left behind his signature calling card – a bunch of flowers stolen from a local graveyard – by the back door.

Breath catches in my throat as I notice articles about more attacks. I thought Gran had forgotten her old obsession! In my late teens, she regularly warned me about the Night Prowler – when I was little, he was suspected of breaking into her old next-door neighbour Ivy's empty house. It must have terrified Gran and preyed on her mind over the years, even though Ivy was away at the time. Gran had frequent nightmares about him, which worsened when she became ill. She once wandered outside in her nightgown during heavy rain and woke the family opposite by screaming that the Night Prowler was inside our house. She caught a chest infection and was hospitalised with pneumonia.

'How about we look for funny stories together? Or ones about wildlife. We could create another scrapbook. Ooh, I know, let's collect photos of Paul Rudd. You love him.'

When we lived together, I could distract her by cutting out pictures of Hollywood actors like Brad Pitt and Harrison Ford or watching classic old rom coms such as *When Harry Met Sally, Four Weddings and a Funeral* and *Sweet Home Alabama*.

Gran smooths the bed cover, singing under her breath. I collect the cuttings and notice a shoebox stuffed with faded, yellowing newspaper scraps – a quick rifle through reveals much older stories about the Night Prowler. He broke into a house in Acton in 2014 and beat the seventy-eight-year-old resident to death. I never saw her cut out these stories at home. I don't remember this box either, but agency carers helped pack up her house. It was a mammoth task – we had to sort out what came here, and what went into storage or to charity shops.

Gran reaches out and strokes my hair. 'Is that you, Marianne? Did you find your way home?'

I freeze. I can't pretend to be Mum. I won't walk around in the shoes of someone who abandoned their only child and loving mother and never looked back. What kind of person does that?

I dig my fingernails into my palm, leaving sharp indents. 'I'm not Marianne.'

'Oh, silly me.' Her hand presses against her lips, holding in a sob.

'You're not silly. It's the red hair – I look like her, but I'm Julia, your granddaughter.'

I hold my breath. If she says she doesn't know me, I'll run out of the room. I can't let her see me burst into tears.

She shoves her hand into her pocket, pulling out crumpled pieces of paper. Carefully, she unfolds them and places them on her lap. The scraps contain names and descriptions. These are the reminders about people's identities, which Raquel helped make last week. Gran holds one up and smiles warmly.

'Julia! I've told my neighbours you research and write brilliant stories every day.'

She passes me the note which reads: *Julia Hockney, beloved granddaughter, and journalist at the* London Gazette.

Raquel must have got confused by Gran's description of my job. It's supposed to be secretarial and usually involves sorting out journalists' squabbles about the rota, slashing inflated freelancer invoices, and being used as a general dogsbody by Rod, the news editor. He's now sent me to help out in the archives after a water leak, claiming that learning how to catalogue and preserve damaged records will be a useful experience. That's the spiel he'll give human resources if I dare to complain. Personally, I suspect he's surreptitiously punishing me for falling asleep while typing the news list for morning conference.

'Well, I work at the *London Gazette*, but—'

'That's what I said. Weren't you listening?' She tuts loudly. 'Do you think we'll have apple crumble and custard for pudding? I wonder if Ivy has any idea.'

She stares longingly out of the window. Is she seeing her old back garden at Airedale Avenue? She used to chat to Ivy over the fence. I put the lid firmly on the shoebox and sit down next to her, taking her hand.

'Fingers crossed. I'll ask Raquel.'

I'll also tell her to keep an eye on Gran's ghoulish hobby.

'Ed says hi. He couldn't come today – he's at work, but hopefully next time.'

Her forehead wrinkles. 'Ed?'

'My boyfriend.'

I point at our photo on her bedside table, next to a framed picture of me and Gran eating ice cream on Brighton Beach. The two of us had enjoyed a day trip, but that night five years ago was the first sign something was wrong. On the way back, she couldn't remember the name of the tube stop nearest to our house.

Gran nods but looks blank. She doesn't always admit to forgetting things.

'You like him,' I add.

That's probably stretching it – Gran tolerates Ed. She called him a moron the first time they met because he accidentally sat on her glasses. I wish he'd had the chance to get to know *the old* Gran properly, but she had another stroke shortly before we got together and deteriorated further. Ed has given up trying to get through to her and usually scours sports websites or watches football on his phone on the few occasions he comes along.

'I'm planning a city break for our first anniversary, like the ones you had with Gramps.'

'Promise me you'll watch the sunrise at Machu Picchu?'

'Erm, we probably won't go that far away. It's only a weekend and I've left it late to book.'

'Pity,' she sniffs. 'When will you live your life?'

I sigh. She and Gramps travelled the world in their twenties. Even in old age, she went on day trips by herself. She booked coach trips to Penzance and Bournemouth, whereas I can't risk falling asleep and waking up somewhere strange on my own.

'We might go to Paris or Rome.'

'*We*? How did you meet . . . ?' She frowns, her voice trailing off.

'Ed.'

Hopefully, retelling this story will jog her memory.

'I'd been invited to leaving drinks for one of the reporters at the *Gazette*. I was on the underground platform at High Street

Kensington, about to get onto a train, but a guy ran for the closing doors. He bumped into me, spilling his coffee. He missed his connection, and I was a mess! My dress was soaked, and I didn't go to the bar after all. I caught the next train back to White City to change my clothes. If I hadn't made that decision, I'd never have met Ed. It felt like fate.'

A smile hovers on her lips. 'Edward was at the bar? That's so romantic!'

My heart swells. She's trying to follow what I'm saying.

'No, Ed was in the same carriage on my journey home. I fell asleep and when I woke up, I found myself sitting next to this kind, lovely stranger miles away from my stop. Ed hadn't wanted to leave me alone. He was afraid someone might steal my handbag or do something worse while I slept.'

'Who was the man?' Her hand flutters to her throat.

'It was Ed.'

'The hero of the story!'

'Yes, like the romantic leads in the movies we watch.'

Gran giggles. 'I love a good film – one that makes me laugh and cry at the end.'

'Me too.'

I grip the edge of the bed. I wish I could ask her for advice about how to get my happy ending. I want to turn back time and meet the version of Ed from my story – the one who watched over me as I slept on the train. He did the same in a French bistro, a theatre, and during a picnic in the park. Back then, he was protective, instead of finding my narcolepsy annoying and embarrassing.

Gran taps my arm impatiently. 'Was it love at first sight with Edward?'

'Well, it wasn't exactly like you and Gramps.'

Her face falls even though I've fudged my answer. *Their* eyes had locked across the floor of a smoky dance hall in June 1966.

Gran had spotted a tall, thin man with a shock of black hair nursing a drink in the corner of the room. He didn't try to talk to anyone and appeared comfortable in his own skin. Gran had turned to her friend and said: 'Do you see that man over there? I'm going to marry him.' As a child, I used to ask how she knew he was The One. She claimed three words had popped into her head when she clapped eyes on him: 'There you are!' Nothing like that had ever happened to her with previous boyfriends. They were married for thirty-three years until he died from cancer when I was two.

I take a deep breath. 'We exchanged mobile numbers and Ed asked me out for a drink. I didn't get that immediate fluttery feeling, like you did with Gramps.'

Her shoulders sag with disappointment.

'But he grew on me! He was so persistent – messaging me dozens of times a day and buying me flowers and taking me places. He swept me off my feet and made me feel wanted. It was just what I needed at the time because . . .'

I don't finish my sentence. The truth is, I was lonely, and sad about Gran's ailing health and Ed appeared at exactly the right time in my life. He was the perfect distraction. *Still is,* of course. I can't admit this to her, or that I don't believe in love at first sight. She and Gramps were the exception. How can you know for certain someone is your soulmate after one meeting? It's no wonder divorce rates are high when people have such unrealistic expectations about love.

'I remember!' Gran stands up.

'You do?'

I'm getting through to her! Ed will be thrilled. He loves telling people the story about how we met because he says it makes him sound 'epic'. Gran walks over to the wardrobe and pulls out a long, camel coat, feeling along the seams.

'What are you doing?'

She ignores me and continues to grab handfuls of the silk tan lining.

Raquel returns with a wheelchair, eyeing the coat. 'I don't think you should go out for a walk, Sylvia. Remember how cold and windy it was yesterday? We have your favourite biscuits in the day room – custard creams! We should get there before Joe eats them all.'

'Come on, Gran. I'm hungry.'

She turns her back on us and tugs at the lining.

'Hey! Don't do that. You'll ruin your favourite coat. It's old – we can't buy an identical replacement.'

Too late! A large tear appears in the fabric, and something drops out, landing on the carpet with a soft thud. I'll need to find Gran's old sewing kit; it's probably in the kitchen drawer that Ed keeps nagging me to tidy up.

Raquel bends down and picks up a shiny object.

'*Qué es esto?* What is it?' She holds up an ornate gold locket, attached to a long chain. 'It's beautiful.'

'Oh my!' Gran clasps her hands together. 'There it is!'

'Is this yours?' I ask. 'Did you put it in your pocket by mistake?'

Gran gazes at the pendant quizzically as if the memory has slipped away as soon as it arrived.

'I don't think so,' Raquel says. 'She was searching for a handkerchief last night. I checked her coat pockets, and they were empty.'

'How did it get there?'

'*Quizás* there was a hole, and it slipped through?' Raquel suggests when Gran doesn't reply. 'Sylvia might have sewn it up without realising.'

'That would have been years ago when Gran could use a needle and thread. She didn't keep it in her jewellery box. I sorted through it before she moved here.'

'It's a lucky find.' Raquel passes the necklace to Gran. 'Look, Sylvia, it's a spinner locket.' She taps the ornate, gold pendant. It makes a gentle ticking sound as it rotates, flashing black and red stones on either side. 'A family heirloom, *sí*?'

Gran stares hard at the chain in her hand, before glancing nervously around the room. I can't tell if she's happy or not about the discovery.

'I have no idea,' I reply. 'I've never seen it before. Wait . . .'

I bend down and pick up the photo of me and Mum in Gran's back garden. 'My mum's wearing it in this pic.'

Raquel studies the picture. 'Such a beautiful lady. You take after her.'

'Thank you. Gran says we looked like peas in a pod.'

'Peas in a pod,' Gran repeats.

This explains why she was upset and thought Mum was hunting for her necklace – she must have noticed it in this photo and tried to remember where she'd put it. Maybe, deep down, she knows this weekend marks the twentieth anniversary of Mum leaving us.

'You could wear it, Sylvia. Let me put it on for you?'

Gran ignores Raquel's outstretched hand. She draws closer and presses the locket into my palm, curling my fingers over it.

She takes a breath and softly sings: 'Spin the stone and make a change. Transform the world and rearrange.'

The lullaby is vaguely familiar. Perhaps she sang it to me as a child. I can't believe she's remembered the words and my birthday! At the weekend, the catering staff made a chocolate cake for us to share, but the flickering candles made strange, frightening shapes on the walls, and she thought a man was lurking in the shadows. She screamed loudly until the cake was taken away.

'Are you sure you want me to have it, Gran?'

'It belongs to you. Keep it safe and never lose it.'

'I won't, I promise!'

This must be what she meant when I was little – Gran told me I was special and would inherit something important when I was twenty-five. She said she'd help me cope. She must have been referring to the clasp. She gestures to Raquel and I lift my hair as she fastens the necklace. I feel a tiny buzzing, like static electricity as the metal rests on my skin. It's cool and surprisingly heavy.

'Aren't you going to try it?' Raquel asks.

'What?'

'Spin the stone and transform the world!'

She's right. I should wish for something. I close my eyes and tap the gem. The stone continues to rotate as I take a peek.

'Dammit! I don't think I've managed to stop climate change or violence against women.'

'It was worth a try, *sí*?'

'Absolutely.'

Was this Mum's favourite necklace? If only it could give up her secrets and tell me everything I've forgotten. My childhood memories are fractured, like broken glass. Did Mum take me to play dates or push me on swings in the park? Did she kiss me one last time before leaving for Scotland? Did she ever say: 'I love you?'

My voice thickens. 'It's the best birthday present ever. Wearing it makes me feel closer . . . to both of you. I can't believe it's been lost all this time.'

'Lost,' Gran echoes. 'Where's Rose? She said she'd help you before your birthday. Is she here yet?'

'Not today.' *Or ever.*

Her younger sister, Rose, died in a car crash about six months before Mum left, but Gran still mourns both losses. I glance at the large, framed family photo on her bedside table, taken shortly after I was born. Aunt Rose had a shock of curly auburn hair and a wide grin. She's stood next to Gran and Mum, who cradles me in her arms. I can only be a week or so old.

'Everything is *bien*,' Raquel stresses. 'Everyone is happy!'

We both smile, attempting to jolly her out of the downturn in mood that accompanies any mention of Aunt Rose, but Gran's gaze is fixed on the shoebox. Her chest heaves up and down and her breathing becomes rapid and shallow.

'Come back, Marianne!'

I nudge the container out of her line of vision with my foot. 'Let's think about happy things. You found Mum's lovely necklace. Look how pretty it is!' I hold up the pendant against my dark blue collared dress, twirling the stone.

Her voice rises an octave at the ticking sound. 'No, no, no! Don't go, Marianne!'

I cradle her as she bursts into tears.

'It's me, Julia. I'm here. I'm not going anywhere.'

'We need to change her medication,' Raquel says quietly. 'These episodes are becoming more frequent. Let's get her into the wheelchair, *por favor*.'

Gran slumps as we each take an arm, all the energy draining from her body like a child's ball deflating.

'Promise me,' she says, glancing up, 'you'll come back.'

'Of course I will! I can visit you tomorrow and on Sunday.'

She pulls my head closer. I think she's going to kiss me, but her lips skim my cheek and hover close to my ear.

My heart shrivels as she repeatedly whispers the words:

Don't stay too long.

4

Friday, May 10, 2024

'Do we have a snapper free who can help find the have-a-go-hero?'

The news editor, Rod, a wiry forty-something, strides over to the picture desk. He's sporting his signature style – tie slung over his shoulder, sleeves rolled up and glasses perched on his head like sunglasses. He picks up a schedule and negotiates with Darlene the picture editor, a short, fierce woman with dark blonde hair. Salim grabs a notebook and pulls on his coat, while his colleagues talk urgently into their phones. I feel a vicarious thrill of excitement even though I'm only a bystander.

I skirt around the features department to avoid Rod. Merv, the chief reporter, has texted, asking me to swing by, and it's hard to refuse him. I sip my coffee as I manoeuvre towards his desk, which towers above the newsroom like Mount Everest. One of these days, he'll be found buried beneath an avalanche of files, books and papers. He's been at the *Gazette* forever and thinks the clean desk policy only applies to other people. I glance at Rod, but he's shouting at a trainee and hasn't noticed me, thank God. I quicken my pace and reach Merv, who is energetically pounding his keyboard.

'There you are,' he says, without looking up. 'Still in the doghouse with Rod?'

'Aren't I always?!'

'You should have a word with human resources about him. I'd back you up.'

'I'm not sure that would do much good. He's more senior than me and can argue his way out of anything.'

I watch as Merv bashes the keys like he has a personal grudge against them.

'Do you ever wonder why your "a" button jams and you regularly need replacement keyboards?' I ask, changing the subject.

'One of life's mysteries.' He frowns, stroking his greying beard. 'I need to ask you something – let me finish this first. I'm on deadline.'

I peer at the story on his screen:

A have-a-go-hero helped push a car off a level crossing in Barnes, south-west London this morning, averting a major disaster.

The man, who has not been identified, cleared the track with minutes to spare before the 8.30 a.m. to Waterloo sped past at 70mph. Almost 300 passengers were on board the train when the elderly man's car broke down on the level crossing.

A female pedestrian tried to restart the engine but couldn't shift the vehicle on her own.

A South Western Railway spokesman said: 'A male cyclist was passing and managed to push the car ten feet to safety. Thanks to the quick thinking and bravery of this individual, a tragedy was narrowly averted.

He presses the 'send' button, shooting it off to the news desk basket, and picks up his phone. Next to it, lie his three mobiles: work, personal and a burner, which he uses for God only knows what.

'That's all I have so far – I'll file quotes from witnesses and the police when we get them.' He ends the call without waiting for a reply from the deputy news editor.

'Do you know who the hero is?' I ask.

'Not yet. Salim's on his way to the scene to look for the guy. He's trying for an interview and pic.'

I check my watch – the longer I'm here, the higher the chance of Rod spotting me. 'What are you after? If it's to moan about the reporters' rota, I can't do anything about it, sorry. I'll be off news desk for a while.' I take a large gulp of coffee.

'No, it's about the archives. Rod sent you down there, right?'

'Yeah, it's the dream job – sifting through soggy newspapers. A careers advisor told me all about it at school.'

He shakes his head. 'Hopefully, you'll be back up here soon. In the meantime, I don't suppose you've come across any old cuttings about the Night Prowler?'

I almost choke on my drink. He's rifling through notebooks and doesn't notice.

'No, but building services made a mess when they fixed the burst pipe. They didn't move anything out of the way when they began work. We're sorting through all the files and finding what's salvageable.'

'Can you check? The library system was digitised in 2006 and doesn't carry many stories before that. This guy's been going for decades – I need the envelopes of old paper cuttings that go back further.'

My stomach shifts uncomfortably. 'Has something happened?'

'A man was arrested last night on suspicion of burglary.'

'Yikes. Where?'

'Clapham Junction. Police had an anonymous tip-off he was breaking into a house on Almeric Road.'

'Really? I wasn't far away. I was at a work dinner with Ed.'

'Dammit. If I'd known, I'd have sent you to speak to the neighbours.'

'I'm not a trained journalist, remember!'

I feel another twinge of excitement. Usually, I only get to type the interviews he records on his tape recorder. I've never had the chance to work on a 'live' news story or investigation, helping unearth new facts, working out the puzzle, and pursuing it to a satisfying conclusion.

'You'd be better than the public-school halfwits Rod hires.' He projects his voice loudly in the direction of a pimply, young male reporter. 'Anyway, the cops found the burglar inside the house, about to attack the fifty-two-year-old female occupant. It was his MO, flowers by the back door taken from a—'

'Graveyard,' I say, finishing his sentence. 'I read about it this morning. My gran has collected cuttings about the Night Prowler over the years. I found a container filled with them. She's a bit obsessed.'

He raises an eyebrow as I pull out the shoebox from my bag.

'She loves keeping newspaper clippings, but I wish she hadn't become fixated on this guy. I need to find her a new hobby that isn't so dark.'

'How is Sylvia?'

I feel a tug on my heartstrings as he opens the box. Merv always asks about Gran and remembers her name; his mum suffered from Alzheimer's too.

'Bad today. She'd lost something and was confused. I think she might have been upset about this case, among other things.'

'Well, the police are confident they've got their man – my contact says they're preparing to file charges dating back to 2005.' He scans the articles. 'May I borrow this while you look for the file downstairs? I'm researching a backgrounder about the attacks and want to find the missed opportunities to catch him in the early days.'

'Sure.' I notice Rod glancing in our direction. 'I'll text you if I find anything.'

'Thanks.' He shuffles more files, triggering a minor earthquake. 'Bugger!'

'I need more copy than this, Merv!' Rod shouts.

He strides across the newsroom towards us. Sleepy Hollow – the general news reporters' derogatory name for the specialists' department – provides my exit route. I burst through the double doors, and pass the site of the old library, where stories used to be cut out from each edition, marked up and put into brown envelopes. Now, the large room is part of the online news division, which is consuming the entire floor, amoeba like. I linger next to the full-length window by the elevators, my last glimpse of sunlight for hours.

Crushing tiredness washes over me as I step into the empty lift. I take another slurp of coffee and receive a text from Raquel, telling me Gran is asleep. She explains the different medication will make her drowsier. My chest aches dully. What if she sleeps through all my visits and no longer chats? I'll lose yet another piece of her, but what's the alternative? She's drifting away already. The old Gran would have begged me to stay longer, not wanted me to leave. I shouldn't take that outburst personally. It's the illness talking, not her. I touch my pendant. Her gift shows how much I mean to her – it connects us both to Mum.

I emerge into a labyrinth of grey, shiny corridors and glaring strip lights. This underground world is inhabited by invisible employees. The kitchen, IT and security staff all take breaks down here, as well as the cleaners and drivers. I zap my security pass, heading deeper into the bowels of the building. The scent of damp plaster assaults my nostrils as I push through the door into room 312b. It takes a few minutes to get accustomed to the mustiness and white noise. Industrial fans whir stale air around the room, making the pages of a newspaper stack flutter nearby. A dehumidifier is stationed in the corner, ready to be switched on by security after we've left tonight.

Floor-to-ceiling shelves line each wall. Most of the paper files were shifted down here decades ago and Jeremy, the chief librarian, is the sole survivor from those pre-digital days. The right-hand side of the room remains untouched by the recent flood, with neatly stacked boxes, folders and large red, brown and grey hardback books containing newspaper records dating back to the 1940s, but the rest of the room is a disaster zone. The burst water pipe brought down a large section of ceiling, drenching records, and newspapers that had been kept in a pristine condition. Building services emptied the shelves, dumping the contents in heaps on the floor. Files and books that escaped the damp are covered in a pervasive, fine black dust that also makes my hands and clothes smell.

I move around the printer, half-draped sheets, and an abandoned ladder, throwing my bag under the large wooden table. Sealed cardboard boxes are lined up alongside it. On the table lies a sheaf of papers and a laptop. Jeremy has stuck a Post-it on the lid.

In meetings all afternoon. Can you make a start on these boxes? Tick off on spreadsheet as explained. J.

My heart sinks as I sit down. Heavy blackness lurks behind my eyes: a thick, velvet curtain waiting to close. It will be harder to resist the urge to sleep doing such a repetitive task on my own: thoroughly checking each box, removing spoiled cuttings, and marking up on the inventory whether records are salvageable. Jeremy is compiling a list of the damaged 1940s and 50s books in a bid to persuade the managing editor's office to send them off to a specialist restoration company in Oxfordshire. No way will they fork out for the newspaper files and packs of cuttings envelopes too. If we can't dry them ourselves, they'll be binned.

I use a scalpel to slit open the packaging tape. My head nods forwards. Jesus. I'll need another coffee after I've finished this one. It feels like I've been awake for 48 hours nonstop. I walk up and down the shelves, pausing in the personals, which mostly escaped the flood. I check for the Night Prowler, but the burglar doesn't have a separate file in this section; it should be in crime, which took the brunt of the burst pipe and is now all mixed up.

I return to my seat and pull out a stack of brown envelopes marked 'drug deaths' and 'suspicious overdoses'. *What joy!* I empty them onto the desk and begin updating the spreadsheet. My shoulders droop and a grey mist descends behind my eyes.

No, no, no!

I stretch my arms above my head and flex my feet, widening my eyes until I'm forced to blink. The fans whir in the background. I play with my pendant, rotating the stone, and listen to its gentle ticking. I take another swig of coffee. I mustn't fall asleep. Jeremy is relying on me. I can't let him down. I'm fine. I'm alert. I'm present. I spin the pendant faster and faster.

More hazy fog falls beneath my eyelids. I'm being dragged away . . .

Spin, spin, spin.

Tick, tick, tick.

A murky, dense veil falls. Total darkness.

The room lights up, illuminating a bar. Merv is sitting at a corner table with Suki and other Gazette *journalists. A hen party is singing along to an old Harry Styles hit. Everything fades into the background apart from the man with the bluish-green eyes who looms above me. His black V-neck jumper hints at a taut body beneath. My stomach flips with excitement; I want to reach out and touch him. I mustn't do that. He'll think I'm weird. As he pushes his tousled, curly brown hair from his face, I spot cobalt blue paint smeared on his sleeve.*

That makes me feel slightly better about the stain down my favourite dark-blue collared dress – a guy with a cup of hot coffee knocked into me as he sprinted through the closing train doors at High Street Kensington tube station. Part of me wanted to give up and return home, or at least go and get changed, but now I'm glad I carried on to the leaving drinks.

A lock of hair flops onto the man's face as he laughs unselfconsciously, making his broad shoulders tremble. He has dark smudges beneath his eyes as if he's a bad sleeper like me, and a few freckles on his nose. In that split second, I catch a glimpse of what he must have looked like as a young boy. My heart thumps. I don't normally have such an immediate reaction to anyone, but Alex is different.

I really, really like him.

'Promise me you'll turn up, Julia,' he says, stretching out a tanned hand. Blue paint is embedded beneath his fingernails, which have the remnants of chipped red nail polish.

'W-w-what?'

Shivers run up and down my spine as he edges closer.

'Obviously, I don't doubt the word of a long-lost relative of David Hockney who doesn't use modern technology and secretly yearns to write long, Jane Austen style letters. But let's shake on it, so we know this is real.' His smile widens, as he gestures to the ever-decreasing space between us. 'That we're not imagining tonight.'

I reach out and his fingers encircle mine. I swear to God I get thunderbolts as our hands touch. A voice in my head says: 'I missed you.'

I'm not imagining it. I heard those three words. It feels like I've known him forever, which is impossible. Equally impossible is the expression on his face – as if he's thinking the same. Gran says she experienced love at first sight, but I never believed it could happen until now. However crazy it sounds, I think, I know, I was destined to meet Alex tonight.

I look down. Our hands remain clasped together.

I clear my throat. 'I've never done anything like this before in my life either. But I promise I'll be there – Hammersmith Bridge, May 12, at midday.'

'Just out of interest – why there?'

I feel a small twinge of disappointment as he releases my hand.

'Are you a secret bridge spotter with a closet interest in mechanical suspensions?'

I blush. He's teasing me, but not in a mean way.

'It's where my grandad got down on one knee and proposed to Gran.'

Why did I say that? He'll run a mile. I take a deep breath. 'Sorry. What I meant is—'

'It sounds like the perfect place,' he cuts in. 'It'll make a great story to tell our *grandchildren.'*

Omigod. How is this happening? I want to laugh or burst into tears or both. I've never felt so certain about anything in my life before – Alex is The One. I'm giddy with anticipation as his face lowers to mine. We're tantalisingly close. I know, without a shadow of a doubt, this will be the best kiss of my life. Our lips are almost touching. I'm . . .

'Julia!'

I ignore the gravelly voice shouting my name.

It's getting louder and louder, but I don't want to move towards it. I'm staying here with Alex.

I never want to leave him. This is where I belong.

'Julia! Are you here?'

The voice pulls me away from the bright lights of the bar, the hum of conversations and the smell of beer. *Alex.* I'm travelling at speed down a long, dark tunnel. A stale, fusty smell grows stronger. I hear the echo of a door banging shut. The noise is replaced by whirring. The door opens and closes again. Footsteps. A weight presses on my shoulder.

What is that?

'There you are! I've been looking for you.'

My eyes fly open. I gulp for air as the room spins. My brain races to keep up. I'm not standing in a bar, about to be kissed by a man called Alex who has cobalt blue paint smeared on his sweater. I haven't arranged to meet him on Hammersmith Bridge or planned to spend the rest of my life with him. I'm gripping a table with one hand and holding my necklace in the other. Newspaper cuttings flutter on the floor. A small, bespectacled man in his late fifties stares at me with a puzzled expression.

What is going on?

Think. Concentrate.

My cheeks warm guiltily. I've had the wildest fantasy about the man I keep picturing in my sleep. This time it felt different – my dream didn't have a strange, blurry, film-like quality as if I were watching it from behind a screen. It felt real, like I was *there* in the bar! I was even wearing this dark-blue dress with the Peter Pan collar. But, disappointingly, I'm actually in the archives with Jeremy, my temporary new boss and devoted Brentford fan. He'll probably complain about me to Rod.

Jeremy's hand drops from my shoulder. 'I could have sworn you weren't in here a minute ago when I popped my head around the door, but I came back and you were asleep at the table! I might need new glasses.'

It's a pity the floor doesn't open up and swallow me.

'I wasn't sure whether to disturb you, but you'd slumped to one side,' he continues. 'I was worried you'd fall off the chair and hurt yourself.'

'It's okay.'

Except it's not. I force myself to focus. Nothing about this situation is alright. In my head, I'm cheating on Ed with a gorgeous hunk who believes I'm related to the painter David Hockney. He wears red nail polish and thinks I'm a technophobe who wants to pen letters like Jane Austen. Why would Alex think that? Omigod, who the hell is Alex? More to the point, why do I keep thinking about him? He's been cropping up in my dreams ever since my birthday.

I wipe drool from the corner of my mouth, attempting to regain my composure.

'Sorry. I had a walk around but couldn't stay awake. My narcolepsy's terrible. I'm going back to my GP for new meds.'

Jeremy smiles reassuringly. 'No need to apologise – I'm glad of the extra pair of hands. Get some fresh air. I know it's hard stuck down here. You don't have to ask permission to take breaks. Do whatever you need to. It's not a problem.'

'Thank you.'

And thank you for being nothing like Rod.

He scoops up a file and tucks it under his arm. 'By the way, you've spilt coffee down your dress.' He walks away, leaving me gazing open-mouthed at the fabric.

How did that happen? Did I try to drink as I drifted off? Like most people with narcolepsy, I have automatic behaviour and continue to carry out some actions while asleep. I examine the empty coffee cup. I thought I'd finished it before my nap, but some liquid must have been left. I grab my coat and head to the lift, dabbing at the mark on my dress with a tissue and water from the bottle in my bag but the stain has already dried.

Up in the foyer, photos of present and former editors from across the news group stare at me – a long line of white men. The framed picture of Marc Campbell-Johnston, the *Gazette's* recent appointee, is nearest to the exit. A wide smile is spread across his thin lips. Piotr, the elderly security guard, gives his usual jovial salute with a newspaper as I push through the revolving doors. Cold air strikes my face as I step outside. The wind blows an empty coffee cup along the pavement and toys with my ponytail. I push a curl behind my ears, but it escapes. The guy in my dream fiddled with his hair.

What the hell?

Narcolepsy gives me terrifying hallucinations involving all my senses, particularly when I'm on the point of waking up or falling asleep. I'm drowning or about to be attacked by an intruder in my bedroom. I'm usually trapped inside my body, and unable to move due to sleep paralysis. Sometimes, I can smell smoke and believe the room is ablaze. I've woken up yelling at Ed to get out. But I've never experienced a romantic hallucination before this – especially not in high definition, and with such intricate detail. I smelled spilt beer, heard the cacophony of voices in the background and felt the warmth of Alex's hand in mine.

Instinctively, I knew he was The One. How is that possible? This morning I'd prevaricated about whether to order a flapjack or a muffin with my black Americano, but in my dream, I made a snap decision about who I wanted to spend the rest of my life with. *Alex.* Obsessing about another man isn't like me either. My face burns hotter, but why should I feel guilty? Sure, it might be emotional cheating, but I didn't *actually* get chatted up in a bar by a ridiculously handsome stranger. Perhaps I subconsciously conjured up a soulmate from another universe to punish Ed for flirting with Double-Kisses Miranda.

Horns blare as a bike courier weaves in between a taxi and another car. I step through the gates into Kensington Gardens and a weight lifts from my shoulders. The expanse of greenery is a hidden pocket of tranquillity away from the bustle of shoppers and noise of traffic. Women clad in expensive sportswear jog past. Up ahead are dog walkers, cyclists and elderly strollers. I linger next to the patch of gloriously bright daffodils, trying to soak up the joyful colours, but all I see is the man in my dream.

If only Jeremy hadn't woken me up, I'd have known what it felt like when his lips pressed against mine. Part of me is bereft that Alex isn't real. I sensed he totally understood me. What would have happened if we'd had that first date on the bridge? Would we have kissed? Would we have become inseparable? I think the answers to both these questions are a loud, emphatic yes. The pain in my chest grows stronger. This is insane. How can I miss someone I've never met? Or feel such intense agony for someone that doesn't exist? I definitely need another GP appointment – maybe see a psychiatrist, because my narcolepsy is messing with my head. I can't stop replaying our conversation.

I'd told Alex about Gramps proposing to Gran on Hammersmith Bridge and he hadn't run a mile. I swear Ed pales whenever I repeat Gran's proposal story, or when he hears the word 'babies'. But the man in my dream had claimed that meeting at the same spot would make a great story to tell *our* grandchildren. He'd made me shake hands on arranging our first date as if there could be the remotest possibility I'd back out.

I missed you.

Those were the words I'd heard when he took my hand in his. They rang out loud and clear in my head. Gran had said something similar when she first saw Gramps, but her three words were: 'There you are!' What does my dream mean? Does it mean anything? I grope beneath my coat and grip my pendant, turning the stone. I must have been thinking about how Gran and Gramps got together. My imagination came up with a love at first sight story to rival theirs. But if that's the case, why did I dream about *this* stranger?

A teenage cyclist, wearing a yellow high-vis jacket, hurtles towards me. She swerves, dragging her feet along the ground, and fixes me with a hard gaze.

'Watch where you're going!'

'Sorry!'

Why am I apologising? She almost flattened *me*. She pedals away without uttering another word. I power walk up the slope, keeping an eye out for deranged cyclists. Parakeets bicker in the trees and a squirrel nibbles on a pain au chocolat by the rubbish bin. That's Kensington for you – the wildlife receives a better class of snack. I rub the stitch in my side as I reach the glittering lake; the shallows are thick with ducks and swans competing for tourists' scraps. The sharp pain is a welcome relief from mulling over what this dream might mean about my relationship with Ed. I collapse onto a bench as a crazy thought strikes me.

What if this wasn't a dream?

Gran once let slip that some Hockney women, like my late Aunt Rose, can see the world differently to other people. She said something about it running in the family. She never explained what she meant, but maybe we get a sense of the future! I don't believe in that stuff, obviously. But say, for the sake of argument, I do have some sort of psychic ability, would I want to know what was going to happen? It could be terrible.

A small voice in my head whispers: *What if it's incredible?*

Perhaps I experienced a vision of a real-life event that *could* happen. If so, I should meet Alex tonight or tomorrow. Hmm. I've immediately disproved my theory since I'm a hermit who works in a damp basement that makes my clothes smell musty. I haven't been invited to work drinks and I don't recognise the bar from my dream.

But I do know *where* we're supposed to meet and the time.

The hairs on the back of my neck prickle.

Is there any possibility, however remote, that the man in my dream exists in real life?

Could Alex be waiting for me on Hammersmith Bridge in two days' time?

5

Saturday, May 11, 2024

'Do you have any idea how crazy this sounds?'

Vicky runs a hand through her glossy black hair and fiddles with the row of studs in her ear. Her lipstick is the usual, expertly applied trademark scarlet, matching her spotty dress, whereas I woke up late after another horribly disturbed night and only managed a quick smear of lip balm and a flick of a hairbrush before I left the flat.

'Of course I do. I think I've lost it. Strike that. I *know* I've lost it.'

She snorts loudly and attacks her Eggs Benedict. I've missed her laughter. I've managed to pin her down to brunch; our shifts have clashed for weeks, and we've struggled to catch up. She works unpredictable hours as a nurse at Chelsea and Westminster Hospital while I visit Gran each weekend and find evenings increasingly tricky. She came to my birthday party but barely ventured away from the bar. We hardly spoke all night.

'Help me. I need my best friend's advice, however harsh.'

She gazes at me for a beat. 'I'm no expert, but I'd say forget Imaginary Guy. Forget about your dream. I can't believe I'm having to explain this to a rational, intelligent woman: *It never happened. He doesn't exist.*'

'I know. But the dream was so detailed. He felt . . .'

'Real?'

'I was going to say "right", but that too.'

'Don't you have dreams all the time? Surely this is no different?'

I stab my poached egg with a fork and watch with satisfaction as the golden yolk oozes out. It's cooked perfectly.

'Except it *was* different. Massively so. I remember every single detail. The goosebumps when I looked at him, the Harry Styles song playing, the smell of beer on the floor of the bar and being showered with coffee earlier that evening.'

'That sounds more like a nightmare.'

I laugh. 'I wish I could relive it all over again. Last night, I tried to picture him before I fell asleep, but I dreamed that a masked man was standing over my bed holding a knife. He was about to kill me, and I couldn't move a muscle.'

'Remind me not to share a bed with you after a night out,' she says, through a mouthful of egg. 'But, like the guy in the bar, Mr Psycho wasn't real either.'

'Yeah, that was my regular sleep paralysis dream. It sucks.'

'So why are you obsessing about . . . Aaron?'

'Alex.'

'He's another figment of your imagination – an attractive one who isn't trying to remove your vital organs. That's healthier, right? It's progress.'

'I'm not sure my GP would agree.'

She reaches over and helps herself to smoked salmon from my plate; she's a terrible food thief.

'You don't even believe in love at first sight – unlike me. I totally get how you can fall for someone when you first meet them. It can be out of your control.' She pauses, her fork poised in mid-air. 'What am I saying? None of this makes sense. It was just another dream!'

'I know. I can't explain it.'

'It sounds like you've watched *Sleepless in Seattle* too many times with your gran.'

Instinctively, I reach for Mum's necklace. It feels comforting beneath my fingertips.

'Gran used to love that movie, but she can't follow the plot anymore. She doesn't understand why Meg Ryan would take a leap of faith to meet a stranger at the top of the Empire State Building when she has a lovely boyfriend who wants to marry her.'

'Your gran has a point.'

'She also thinks my mum has returned after all this time! Apparently, she had a good chat with her in the nursing home and told her off for being late.'

Vicky raises a bladed eyebrow, laying down her knife and fork. 'Has she come back?'

I frown at her. 'That's never going to happen. Mum hasn't given us a second thought.'

'Sorry,' Vicky mumbles.

'No, I'm sorry. I didn't mean to snap. I'm being an idiot – everything's getting on top of me. I hate this time of year.'

'Hey! Be kind to yourself. Your dream is a distraction from thinking about your mum and worrying about your gran. It's understandable.'

I feel my eyes moisten. 'Gran's getting so much worse. I'm dreading the day when I can't reach her. She won't recognise me; she won't talk.' My tongue feels too big for my mouth. 'I'll have no one.'

Vicky coughs, dabbing her mouth with the napkin. 'That's not true.' She reaches out and squeezes my hand.

'Thanks,' I say thickly. 'I don't know what I'd do without you.'

'You'd probably have wilder dreams!'

'I'm not sure that's possible.'

We both laugh. Vicky always manages to shake me out of low moods. We've been best friends ever since the Freshers' Fair at Bristol. I'd trailed around, attempting to summon up the courage to approach the student newspaper stand, but was intimidated by the third years behind the desk. I'd lurked around the next-door table: karate. I'd pretended to be interested in learning self-defence, whereas Vicky was totally upfront about hoping to find a hot black-belt boyfriend. We both took the flyer, and a stack of other clubs' details, abandoned the hot, packed hall, and went for a coffee. Neither of us went to any classes.

'Dammit. That's probably work.' She dives into her hand-bag, digging out her phone as it buzzes. She checks her messages, frowning.

'Do you need to run?'

'No! I'm not officially in for another hour and a half. They can wait.' She eyes the remainder of my smoked salmon. 'Is that going free?'

I push my plate towards her, sipping my coffee.

'What does Ed have to say about your sexy sequel to *Sleepless in Seattle*?'

'I haven't told him, obviously!' I mop up the spilt liquid in my saucer with a serviette.

'Why not?'

'Erm, hello? What should I say? "Oh, by the way, you don't want to sleep with me anymore, but I've conjured up a hot guy in my imagination who does."'

Vicky frowns. 'You and Ed aren't having sex?'

'It's tricky when we don't share the same bed.'

'What? That doesn't sound good.'

'It's temporary, I hope. We're both busy with work. Plus, Ed doesn't like the night-time drama – the screaming and being warned a knifeman is about to set our bed on fire. My narcolepsy is a turn-off.' I raise an eyebrow. 'I can't imagine why.'

'That's tough. I'm sorry, I had no idea.'

'I totally get it – Ed needs his sleep.' I sigh, screwing up the serviette into a tight ball. 'But I miss the intimacy – cuddling and talking late at night. It's like we're . . .'

'Brother and sister?'

'No! I mean, we still do stuff. Just not so regularly.' My cheeks redden.

I can't remember the last time we had sex. Was it a month ago? Six weeks? Longer?

Vicky studies my face. 'What is it?'

'I wonder if it's an excuse.' I take a deep breath. 'That he's using my narcolepsy to avoid sex.'

'Why would he do that?'

I glance away miserably.

'Julia? What is *really* going on?'

I hold up my hands. 'Who knows? Things feel different. *He's* different.'

'Things do change when you move in with someone – and it happened pretty fast with you and Ed.' She hesitates. 'Don't take this the wrong way, but might you have rushed into living together? Before you were both certain about each other?'

I run my hands through my hair. I don't want to consider I've made a mistake. It's too painful, especially now.

'I think he might be having an affair,' I blurt out.

'What the hell?' She leans closer. 'Are you sure?'

'No! That's the problem.'

I wait for her to scoff and say this sounds as crazy as my dream, but she stares back silently.

'What makes you think he's cheating?' she asks eventually.

'He's just acting off, distant. Plus, he slagged off Miranda, one of his new colleagues, but she was flirting with him at dinner on Thursday night and he didn't seem to mind. I think he enjoyed the attention.'

'Most men do – that doesn't mean he's being unfaithful.'

'True, but he's been receiving late-night texts for a while. I can hear the beep through the wall.'

'Excuse me, what?'

I burst out laughing again at her incredulous expression. 'This is what I've been reduced to – working in a damp, dingy basement and eavesdropping on my boyfriend from my own spare room. I'm approaching rock bottom. Actually, I hit it when I saw one of Miranda's messages. She signed it MM xx.'

Vicky shoves her coffee cup away. 'That's not good. What did Ed say?'

'He tried to play it down, obviously – in between vomiting for Britain. He said it was about work, but it didn't feel worksy.'

'It could be innocent.'

'Do you add kisses in messages to colleagues? To ones you're not dating?'

I'm joking, of course. Vicky's investment banker boyfriend, Giles, broke up with her at the end of March, and she remains resolutely single. She has a strict rule about not getting involved with anyone at the hospital, despite the hotness of the junior doctors; work romances get messy.

'You're right, Julia. It sounds shittily suspicious. You should confront him. I mean, properly – look him in the eye, and ask what's going on. Get it all out in the open.'

'I can't do that.'

'Why not?'

'What if he confesses something *is* going on?'

'Isn't it better to know?'

60

'Is it?'

I picture weekends passing without speaking to anyone except for shop assistants and neighbours. Birthdays and Christmases only shared with Gran. My voice bouncing off the walls of the empty flat, loneliness growing like mould in every crevice.

'Surely this uncertainty is worse? Not knowing whether he's seeing someone else?'

'Possibly. I bet the man in my dreams wouldn't cheat. He didn't seem the sort.'

Vicky rolls her eyes. 'You need to do something. I promise, you'll feel better if you know where you stand.' She pauses. 'I mean about Ed. I'm not suggesting you have a date with Dream Guy on Hammersmith Bridge.'

I flinch.

'Holy crap! Are you planning to see if he turns up?'

'No, that would be madness.'

I tap the spoon on the saucer. I can't admit I'm toying with the idea.

'Seriously, he won't be there. I repeat: *He doesn't exist.* Sort out your problems in real life, not your imaginary ones.'

'You're right.'

She takes the spoon from my hand. 'Talk to Ed. Ask him what's going on.' Her phone buzzes with another message. 'Aargh! Someone's called in sick. My boss is asking me to come in early. I'll tell her I can't.'

'No, don't worry. I should head to the office . . . I mean the dingy basement.'

She sighs. 'If you're sure?'

As she messages back, I call for the bill. We split it as usual.

'Are you around next week?' she asks, as we scoop up our coats and bags. 'I'm booking tickets for a comedy night on Wednesday.'

'I can't, sorry. My new boss prefers starting and finishing late. It's becoming a problem. I'm struggling to stay awake in the evenings at work and with Ed. He still hasn't forgiven me for what happened at my birthday party. He can't let it go.'

'You fell asleep?'

I nod. It's easier than explaining about cataplexy, another symptom of my sleep disorder. Experiencing intense emotions like surprise, love, stress and fear makes me lose control of my limbs. It's not the same as sleep. My eyes were closed but I was fully conscious on the restaurant floor, aware of everyone around me. I just couldn't move.

'Oh, sorry,' she says eventually. 'I didn't notice.'

I wonder if she's being tactful to protect my feelings – Ed had claimed all our guests saw the waiter step over me when I fell off my chair. Or she might still have been at the bar, chatting up the good-looking guy making cocktails.

'Things have got that bad?'

'I'm way, way worse than I was at uni.'

The symptoms felt far more manageable back then and during my school days. Now, they're controlling me, and not the other way round.

Outside the café, Vicky points at the pendant, which peeps through my coat. 'I meant to say earlier, I love this. It looks like it's part of an old watch fob.'

'It sounds like one when you do this.' I spin the stone. 'It belonged to my mum. I think it's been lost for years. We found it inside the lining of Gran's favourite coat.'

She pulls me in for a hug. 'It might be a priceless Victorian good luck talisman – and God knows, you deserve one.'

I close my eyes, inhaling the Chanel No 5 perfume, and remember her excitement when Giles bought a large, expensive bottle for her birthday. I feel a pang of guilt. I never asked how she's coping after their split – we spent most of brunch dissecting my dream and relationship with Ed. No wonder *he* thinks I'm self-centred.

'Can we do this again soon? Meet during the day? I've missed you. We didn't get a chance to talk much at my party.'

'Sure.' She disentangles herself from my wild hair and scarf.

'How about brunch next week? I'm thinking—'

'Remember, do something instead of waiting around, hoping things will get better. *You* have to make the change.'

Her boots make sharp clicking noises on the pavement as she strides off.

'What's the worst that can happen?' she shouts over her shoulder.

6

SATURDAY, MAY 11, 2024

The flat is shrouded in darkness when I let myself in at 10.30 p.m. I fell asleep again in the archives while Jeremy was in a meeting, but instead of seeing Dream Guy I had my regular drowning nightmare. Water closed over my head, and I couldn't reach the surface. When I woke up, I scrolled through Vicky's Instagram feed to see if I've accidentally fixated on one of her work friends, but no one looked familiar. I also discovered a text from Merv asking about the Night Prowler file. It wasn't among the boxes I've unpacked so far and could be buried in the bin bags. His story on the website today says police have been given more time to question a fifty-seven-year-old man from southwest London about burglaries and assaults, dating back to Croydon, south London, in 2005. Hopefully, Raquel won't let Gran cut out the latest development. It's a pity I can't distract her with the near-miss train story, but Merv said the have-a-go-hero has refused to be interviewed.

I flick on the light in the sitting room. Ed has returned all my novels to the shelf, including the one I'm currently reading, without its bookmark, and arranged the newspapers into a neat pile. His weights collection is slowly encroaching along the far wall; the metal glowers at me as the light bulb blinks. I hear his voice in the bedroom, he's probably on the phone to his mum. The door's ajar. I push it open and walk in.

'I know this isn't ideal, MM, but we should wait until the time is right,' Ed says softly. 'We need to—'

His tone changes abruptly when he spots me standing in the doorway. 'We should thrash this out before we give our presentation to Tony on Monday. He'll crucify us if it isn't properly costed.' He pauses. 'I need to go. Julia's home. Let's discuss this first thing in the morning.'

He hangs up without waiting for a reply. 'Hey! How are you?'

'Okay . . . Was that Miranda?'

'Yeah. I'm mentoring her.' He rolls his eyes. 'She's freaking out about her proposal.'

'Isn't this late for a work call? Did you have to take it?'

'I can't just ignore her! She'll tell Tony I'm not being supportive.'

I study his face. His explanation sounds plausible, but it didn't sound like he was talking to a work colleague when I walked in. His voice was low and intimate. I remember Vicky's advice to confront him.

'Why did you call her MM if this was about a presentation?'

'Because that's her nickname! Everyone calls her that at work.'

I swallow the lump in my throat.

'Wait – are you still upset about her message with the kisses? That isn't my fault!'

'I'm just asking . . .'

'No, you're insinuating . . . what exactly? That I'm shagging the most annoying person in the office?'

'That's not what I'm saying. It's just you seem—'

'Knackered? Hurt you don't trust me? You're imagining something that isn't there as usual. I can't deal with your insecurities tonight. I'm exhausted.' He thumps the pillow and rolls over.

'Ed!' I wait for him to turn back, but he doesn't move. 'Look, I'm sorry if I've got the wrong end of the stick. Please can we talk about this?'

'Not now! I have an early start. I need to get some sleep.'

'When?'

'Tomorrow,' he says in a muffled voice. 'I promise.'

I stifle a sigh. Lately, it's always tomorrow with us rather than today. I close the door behind me, my eyes welling up. Doubt creeps in as I head to the sitting room. Was I imagining the way he spoke to Miranda? I'm exhausted and my brain is scrambled. Ed *could* have been discussing work. I have no proof he's cheating, just a nagging feeling something's up, and he's pulling away. Why am I not good enough for him? *For anyone?*

I retrieve my memory box from the cabinet and rummage through the childhood tokens Gran kept: the hospital identity band taped to my wrist as a new-born, a baby tooth, and a lock of hair that Mum left behind. I have Gramps' cricket tie and pipe, but nothing from my dad; Mum never knew the name of her one-night stand. I leaf through her old journal. I've discovered no new clues about where Mum's living now after rereading it. It records the times of meetings with the psychiatrist she began seeing shortly after her twenty-fifth birthday, and appointments she had with a sleep specialist as her narcolepsy worsened. She'd also had a brain scan – she feared she had an undetected tumour after experiencing severe nosebleeds – but the pages from her final weeks are missing. Gran once told me that Mum had torn them out before leaving for Scotland; the reason why has vanished with her.

I study my old correspondence with a private investigator in Spain. While I was at uni I'd paid him to find a new address for Mum. He'd trawled the bars and clubs in Ibiza, where Gran said she'd last been working, but hit a dead end. I could hire a new one. Even if Mum refuses to visit me, it would mean the world to Gran to see her again. I should do it before she stops recognising people completely, even family.

I pick up the picture of Mum and me in Gran's garden which I brought back from Ravensbrook, tracing around her face with my finger.

Do you ever think about me at this time of year?

The dates are probably meaningless to her, she doesn't care. I hear Ed's phone beep with a message. Miranda, again! What should I do? I can't storm in and demand answers; Ed will deny everything. A relationship shouldn't be this hard – that's what my subconscious must be telling me when I picture Dream Guy in my sleep. Talking to him felt easy and natural; I didn't second guess myself and feel crappy.

I remember the old lady's questions about Ed on Thursday night: *Why don't you leave him? What are you afraid of?*

I can't face saying the answers out loud: *I'm a coward who fears being left completely alone in the world.*

We *will* face this tomorrow. I'll insist on a heart-to-heart with Ed about our future when I'm less tired and can think straight. We'll thrash it out. I won't let him fob me off or make me sound unreasonable. *Crazy.*

I rest my palms on the lid of the memory box. I'm strong. I can do this.

There's something else I must do tomorrow.

I don't care what anyone thinks, or how stupid it sounds. I have nothing to lose or feel guilty about when my life is in such a tailspin.

I want to find out how my dream ends.

I'm going to wait for Alex on Hammersmith Bridge.

7

SUNDAY, MAY 12, 2024

I lean over the faded wooden handrail and green iron trellis, staring into the murky, brown ripples of the Thames. A deflated balloon drifts past. I used to watch the Oxford and Cambridge Boat Race here with Gran when I was little. Today, the tide is high, submerging gnarled riverside trees. Protesting branches stretch out like hands, begging to be rescued from their ever-rising watery grave.

'Hard on the left!' A cox shouts through a loudspeaker at the four female rowers in the boat four metres ahead.

They're concentrating on maintaining the stroke rhythm as they pass under the bridge. Further along the footpath, tourists take photos of the sweeping landscape of west London. A couple of cyclists shoot by. My only other company is the family of mallard ducks at the far side of the bank. They repeatedly turn upside down, hunting for food. Dazzling sunlight warms my face and creates diamond-like ripples on the surface of the water.

'Hello! You made it.'

It can't be.

My heart leaps as I spin around, a smile hovering on my lips. A man in his thirties with short black hair waves at a pensioner who slowly approaches, using a walking stick. The young guy gives me a quizzical look as he jogs past. I return to staring at the ducks to disguise my flushed cheeks. Of course it's not Alex! I check my watch. It's 12.30 p.m. He's not showing up, *obviously*. How could he? *He doesn't exist.* My dream wasn't a sign of events to come. Apparently, the only special family gift I possess is being a total idiot. I'll never hear the end of it if I tell Vicky I dressed up for Dream Guy in my favourite green mini dress that brings out the colour of my eyes. She'll die laughing. I sigh heavily. I'm done wasting time on a dumb revenge fantasy. Vicky's right – I need to sort out my problems in the real world, instead of getting caught up in bizarre avoidance tactics.

I set off, gazing at the ornately decorated large arch; the parakeets and pigeons nesting in the towers are locked in open warfare. I imagine Gramps got down on one knee on this spot. A couple jog past, chatting. Up ahead, the guy has a protective arm around his elderly companion's waist. They're staring at something on the footpath.

'Terribly sad, isn't it?' the old man says as I approach. 'To die so young.' He jerks his head at bunches of flowers on the ground – yellow sunflowers, deep red roses and pale lilies. Dolls dressed in gold and blue gowns lie next to the bouquets. They're Disney princesses – I've no idea which ones.

'He was a brave man. Not many people would do the same.'

'Come on, Grandad. Let's go.'

His grandson nods at me, before leading him away, one hand under his arm for support. I'm about to follow when I catch a whiff of floral scent in the breeze. The bouquets are fresh. I crouch down and move the plastic wrapping, exposing notes:

Dear Alex,
Wherever you are, I know you're painting up a storm.

Love and miss you forever, Samira x

Alex, our lives will never be the same. Can't believe we'll never see you again. Miss you terribly little brother. We all love you so much. Zoe, Sally, and Hannah xxx

You'll be sorely missed by everyone here. An incredible talent, and an even more incredible man. Lizzy, Fatima and all your friends from the Acton artists' collective xx

Fluttering next to them are children's drawings of princesses holding hands with a stick man. The other notes have shorter messages: 'R.I.P. Alex' and 'Never forgotten, miss you mate' and 'In loving memory, from all your friends'. That's a coincidence – this guy has the same name as the one in my dream. My eyes well up. The elderly man was right – it *is* sad to see a life cut short, missed and mourned by loved ones left behind. *What happened to him? Was Samira his girlfriend?* Maybe this was a spot they used to visit together – Gran and Gramps loved walking along the Thames path. I stand up, steadying myself on the handrail. My gaze is drawn to a small, brass plaque next to my fingers:

IN LOVING MEMORY OF ALEX MARTIN WHO BRAVELY JUMPED FROM THIS SPOT INTO THE THAMES AT 12 P.M. ON MAY 12, 2023. HE DIED, SAVING TWO STRANGERS FROM DROWNING.

R.I.P. JANUARY 1, 1996 – MAY 12, 2023.

My knees weaken and my heart beats a million times a minute. Alex Martin died here at the exact time I had arranged to meet the Alex in my dream. He was of a similar age and painted, according to the note from a girl called Samira, and appeared to belong to an artists' collective. *My* Alex had paint on his jumper sleeve and mentioned David Hockney. Is it . . . *him*? It can't be! It's a bizarre

70

coincidence. A few weeks ago, I read a feature in the *Gazette* about real-life serendipity, pointing out that Stephen Hawking shared his birth and death dates with Galileo and Einstein. A Japanese man survived two atomic bombs – Hiroshima and Nagasaki, and Mark Twain's birth and death coincided with appearances of Halley's Comet. What are the chances? This is another strange event, which has no logical explanation. It doesn't mean anything.

Move on, forget about it.

I pass the seven coats of arms at the end of the bridge: sharp swords slice hidden enemies. A leaping ornate horse is frozen in time, waiting to break free. Once I've reached the road, the temptation is too great. I stop by the old graffitied phone box – the sprayed initials are mirrored on the nearby wall; an abandoned, tattered umbrella flutters nearby. I pull out my phone and google 'Alex Martin' and 'drowning' and 'news'. Headlines appear from local and national newspapers: *Hero Drowns Saving Couple, Tribute to Hero Swimmer, Man Dies After Attack on Bridge.* I click on a *Gazette* article dated May 14 last year.

HERO ARTIST DIED SAVING COUPLE FROM THAMES

By Mervyn Drury

The hero who jumped into the Thames to rescue a drowning couple has been named today as artist Alex Martin.

The 27-year-old, from Acton, west London, had been walking on Hammersmith Bridge when he witnessed an altercation. A man jumped, pulling his female companion into the river.

Mr Martin managed to drag the woman to the bank but got into difficulty after returning for the man and saving his life. He was pronounced dead at the scene by paramedics.

His friends have paid tribute to the talented, up-and-coming artist.

Samira Patel, owner of the Hidden Things gift shop in Brentford, said: 'Alex would never turn a blind eye if someone was in trouble. He'd try to help.

'He lived to paint and dreamed of holding his own exhibition. He was a doting uncle to his nieces. His family and friends miss him terribly. He will always shine brightly for us.'

His sister, Zoe, 30, the mother of 7-year-old twins Sally and Hannah, said: 'Alex had a heart of gold. We are utterly heartbroken by his death.'

Police have arrested a 41-year-old man on suspicion of attempted murder. His alleged victim was a 33-year-old married mother of two. She was treated in hospital for hypothermia.

A police source said: 'It appears the couple were in a relationship. When the woman attempted to break it off, her partner became agitated and leapt into the water, pulling her with him. Mr Martin jumped in, and sadly died after dragging them both to safety.'

Other articles refer to an art exhibition held in Alex's honour and a fundraising concert organised by his sister for an Alzheimer's charity. I bite my lip, noting we shared a mutual connection. The opening of his inquest also generated more articles – but it hasn't yet been heard in full. Dammit! Why don't these stories have a picture of Alex? What does he look like? My heart beats rapidly as I click on 'images'. My internet is crap. A photo painfully whirs before opening. A man with floppy brown hair and shining blue-green eyes stares back. His mouth is parted in a full, familiar smile.

An invisible thread tugs at my heart.

The air is sucked out of my lungs. I lean against the phone box, trying to remember to breathe in and out.

I can't believe it, don't *want* to believe it, but there's no mistake.

It's definitely *him*.

It's the man in my dreams.

I fell in love with Alex Martin.

8

SUNDAY, MAY 12, 2024

I sip my hot chocolate, shivering at the intense sugar rush. People drink this for shock, right? This cannot be happening, yet somehow, I have imagined meeting and falling in love with a drowned hero. Around the time of Alex Martin's death last year, I'd met Ed and already booked two weeks off work. I was swept up in a whirlwind of dates, which explains why I don't remember the initial flurry of headlines. I can't recall the trial of the man accused of attempting to murder the woman on the bridge either, but perhaps I've seen a photo of Alex somewhere, and it's buried deep in my subconscious. That's why I keep dreaming about him. It's the only possible explanation that makes sense. Nothing else does. If I tried to explain this to anyone, including my GP, I'd probably be referred for a mental health assessment.

A toddler wearing green dungarees and a large, floppy pink sunhat runs up to my table, waving a cuddly yellow lion.

I smile at her. 'Hello!'

She grins back and shows me her soft toy. I glance around, but the old lady in the corner, who *could* be her grandma, continues eating a teacake. The little girl lingers on tiptoes, staring at me with vivid blue eyes, her mouth opened in a broad, toothless smile. I catch a glimpse of strawberry blonde hair beneath her oversized hat.

'Where's your mummy or daddy?' I ask, bending down.

She strokes my cheek before throwing her arms around my neck.

'That's a lovely hug, thank you. It's just what I need.'

I check over her shoulder, but no one looks annoyed I'm touching their child. Everyone is preoccupied. I gently disentangle myself.

'Is this your biscuit, sweetie?' a woman calls from behind the counter.

I sigh with relief as she runs off. I scoop up a stray newspaper from the next table. My gaze rests on an advert for a gift shop. Where did Alex's friend, Samira, work? I call up the article on my mobile. Hidden Things in Brentford. A Google search reveals it's open until 5 p.m. I could take a detour en route to the office. Jeremy said he'll be late. As I pull on my coat, I realise the toddler has left her lion on my table. I look around but can't see her. No one has jumped up in a white-hot panic, shouting the name of a missing child. She must have left with her parent or carer. On the way out, I hand in the forgotten toy. The little girl will probably come back for it.

I pretend to choose a birthday card in Hidden Things, genuinely torn between pictures of balloons and cakes. I've browsed through the unusual handmade jewellery, ornaments and light, floral dressing gowns featuring exotic birds. Everything is gorgeous, but I'm not here for gifts. This seemed like a great plan in the café, but I have no idea how to approach Samira and talk to her about Alex. She's definitely the attractive thirty-something with the large hoop earrings and green nails unpacking boxes behind the till. I stalked her on social media on the way here. Samira doesn't have privacy settings on Facebook and she's a prolific Instagrammer, posting from her personal account and the shop's.

Oh crap!

I watch in horror as she comes over. I hurriedly grab two cards, a couple of postcards of Hammersmith Bridge, and an eye-catching abstract print of a girl's face constructed from aquamarine, cobalt blue and yellow diamond shapes.

'You're another journalist, right?' Samira pushes wavy black hair behind her quadruple pierced ear lobes. 'You want to ask me about Alex Martin?'

My cheeks warm. 'Erm . . .'

I'm flattered but equally panic-stricken by her assumption that I'm a reporter.

'I work for the *London Gazette*,' I blurt out. 'And yes, I'm here about Alex.'

Obviously, this isn't a lie, but it's not the absolute truth.

Samira nods. 'Thought so. Journalists pretended to buy things before they approached me last year – back when Alex was news. I thought most people had moved on. No one seems to be interested in him anymore, unfortunately.'

'I am.'

I follow her to the counter where she rummages in a box of postcards. I nibble on a ragged nail, debating what to say.

'It's the first anniversary of his . . .' She clears her throat. 'Are you writing another story? I didn't catch your name by the way.'

I bite the inside of my mouth. Rod will go ballistic if he finds out I'm pretending to be a reporter. I want to become a feature writer, examining subjects in depth, and finding a fresh perspective, even though Rod is disinterested whenever I suggest ideas for stories.

I can't give her my real name in case she rings the news desk, asking for me.

'Yep.' I lick my dry lips. 'I'm Tory Harper.'

Tory? What came over me? She might think I am one.

She stacks cards into piles without passing comment. 'Well, shoot, Tory. What do you want to know?'

'Erm.' I rummage in my handbag, playing for time.

What am I going to ask her? Only one question whirs around my mind on a loop: How can Alex Martin be the man in my dreams? I can't possibly tell her about my intense, life-like hallucination. She'll think I'm insane.

'Did you forget your notebook?' She drums her glossy, Shellac nails on the counter.

'Here it is!' I triumphantly hold up an old, torn pad I've discovered at the bottom of my bag, covered in dust and crushed Polo mints.

I forage for a biro until she produces a pen with a diamanté stud and price tag.

'Thank you.' I cough, trying to look professional, which is difficult when I'm clearly the most incompetent fake journalist ever.

'So . . . ?'

I take a deep breath. 'Why was Alex on the bridge? I couldn't find a reason in any of the stories I read.'

She shrugs. 'He'd arranged to go on a first date.'

The sparkly pen almost slips through my fingers. 'Really?'

'Alex is . . . *was* . . . a romantic. He thought he'd met the perfect woman in a bar the night before.'

My heart squeezes. 'What did he say about her?'

'He'd felt an instant connection – something he hadn't experienced with anyone else. He said they'd clicked and had agreed to see each other again.'

My hand trembles as I try to make notes. It's a good job she hasn't noticed I'm writing random words.

'Did she turn up? On the bridge, I mean?'

'I don't think so. The police said a couple of workmen called 999. If his date had shown up, you'd have thought she'd have tried to get help, and hung around afterwards.'

'She could have been running late.'

'More likely, she didn't come at all, otherwise she'd have spoken to the paramedics. She wasn't mentioned at the opening of the inquest.' Samira's lower lip quivers. 'I can't help but hate her. I know that sounds terrible, but if Alex had never met her, he'd be alive today. He'd be painting in his studio and visiting his nieces. He loved Sally and Hannah, and they miss him terribly. His sister, Zoe, says they still cry for him.'

Hot, guilty fingers claw at the back of my neck.

'I'm sorry,' I whisper.

'Are you alright?' Samira asks curiously. 'Do you want a drink of water?'

Why do I feel responsible? This isn't my fault. I'm not that girl!

'I'm fine. Just a dry throat.' I swallow hard. 'I could track her down and find out why she didn't turn up.'

She sniffs. 'What good would that do? It won't bring back Alex. Nothing will.'

'But what if the girl did plan to be there that day? Maybe she had an accident on the way and never knew what happened until it was too late. Or she had a panic attack on the bridge and ran away. She might regret leaving. It could help you both to talk.'

Samira inspects her glossy nails.

'I guess, but I don't know much about her. Alex never mentioned her name, he just said she had lovely long, flame-red hair and green eyes.' She fixes me with a hard stare. 'Like you.'

My heart beats faster and faster.

'Anything else?'

'I don't think so.' Her gaze flickers across the shop floor as the bell rings above the door. An elderly couple walk in followed by a teenage girl.

'What about where they met? I could start there. Someone might recall her in the bar.'

'I'm not sure I remember. Alex did say, but it was such a long time ago.'

My heart sinks.

'Shall I run this through the till for you?' She jerks her head at the cards in my hand.

'Thanks. I won't take up any more of your time.'

'That was Alex's last picture,' she says, placing my purchases into a white paper bag.

'Sorry?'

'The print you picked out. He'd started drawing the portrait with pastel pencils the night he met the girl. He rang on the way to the bridge to tell me about his date. He said he began sketching her as soon as he returned from the bar because he didn't want to forget her face. Alex worked until the early hours, but it wasn't finished. Some of the rhombus shapes aren't coloured in, and he'd have eventually painted a much larger version in acrylics. His sister found this when she cleared out his flat. Zoe loved my idea of making it into prints – we both thought it was a fitting way to keep his memory alive. It's comforting, knowing his artwork is loved by others. The proceeds go to the Alzheimer's Society.'

I gulp. 'Did he know someone . . .'

'His grandad suffered from the disease.'

'I'm sorry. My gran does too.'

'Hmm.'

Samira eyes my hair. Does *she* suspect I'm the girl from the bar? Or am I being paranoid?

The bell rings, and a tall, sandy-haired man walks in, carrying boxes.

'Did you find the missing order?' Samira calls out.

'Yep. It's all here.'

'Have I told you I love you, Hamish McLean?'

'About one million times.'

'How about one million and one? I love you.'

'Back at ya!'

He plants a kiss on her lips before disappearing through a door marked 'staff only'.

Samira's gaze switches back to me. 'When will your story about Alex be printed?'

'I'm not sure. I'll ask my news editor.'

'Let me know – we'll look out for it. Do you have a business card?'

Funnily enough, she doesn't appear surprised when I shake my head. I jot down my mobile number in the pad and rip it out. 'Text me if you think of anything else.'

'Sure.'

I've almost reached the exit when she calls after me. 'Hey! My pen.'

'Sorry!'

I double back and place it on the counter.

'The Swan in Chiswick,' she says loudly. 'That's where Alex met her. He'd been having drinks with old uni friends. They'd spent the day at the Whistler exhibition.'

I frown. The name rings a bell.

'You know, the nineteenth-century painter? There was an exhibition of his work in Piccadilly last year.'

I do remember. I read a profile about the artist in a newspaper at the time. The bar also sounds vaguely familiar.

'Yes, of course,' I say, colouring. 'I'll check out the pub. Thanks for everything.'

I return to the door, making the bell jingle as I yank open the latch.

'One last thing,' she shouts, as her boyfriend joins her at the till. 'I've no idea if this helps, but Alex said they were meeting at Hammersmith Bridge because it was a special place for the girl – it's where her grandad proposed to her grandma.'

I stumble onto the street. I steady myself against the glass and move blindly along the row of shops, out of Samira's line of vision.

What the hell?

Alex met someone who looked like me in a bar a year ago. Her grandparents became engaged on Hammersmith Bridge. He'd arranged to meet her at the exact time and date I remembered from my dream. How is this possible? It isn't.

I only imagined talking to him in my dream. It didn't happen in real life!

Hands trembling, I pull out the print from my bag – Alex's last ever piece of art. I examine the girl's face for similarities. She has long, wavy hair like me, but it could be anyone, to be honest; it's hard to tell with an abstract, made of diamond shapes.

I gasp as my gaze is drawn to the handwriting in the bottom left-hand corner:

An impression of Hockney, like the painter.

Alex Martin, May 12, 2023.

9

Sunday, May 12, 2024

Back in the empty archives, I sling down my bag and fire up the laptop, logging into my Gmail account. I retrieve the email I was cc'd into last year by Layla, the *Gazette*'s former health reporter, four months before she moved to New York with her girlfriend, Megan. I knew the Swan sounded familiar – it was the venue of the 2023 send-off she organised for Suki, the old education correspondent.

01/05/2023

REMINDER: Suki Whiteman's leaving drinks (May 11, from 7 p.m. at The Swan)

Dear all

As you may have heard, Suki is leaving us for a career on the other side of the fence — PR for an academy chain. I can hear your groans from here! Poacher turned gamekeeper etc.

Please join us next week for farewell drinks at The Swan in Chiswick on the evening of

Thursday, May 11. Apologies for the trek, but it's Suki's local.

Please do leave a message in Suki's e-card (to follow) or make a donation (both if you can!) via transfer to my bank account. Please send me your donation no later than FRIDAY, so I can buy the leaving gift over the weekend. Suggestions gratefully received. Hope to catch up with you all for a few drinkies!

Thank you,

Layla

That night, I was on my way to the Swan but turned back after being drenched by the commuter's coffee. The guy who'd bumped into me was furious about missing his train and I was equally peed off. I'd headed home, fallen asleep on the tube and met Ed. But in another life, maybe a parallel universe, the commuter made his connection, and I wasn't deterred by a soggy dress. We both continued with our onwards journeys. I met Alex in the bar and fell head over heels in love with him.

I shake my head. It's impossible! My mind is telling me none of this could have happened. It defies logic. Yet I'm staring at a half-finished portrait of a girl, with my surname printed at the bottom, and a reference to our private conversation. Our encounter was different to all my other dreams, including the ones when I saw Alex's blurry face. This one felt real. I even woke up with a dried coffee stain on my dress.

Something tugs at my chest – the invisible connection that repeatedly draws me to him. In my heart, I feel it's true. I was really *there* on May 11 last year, chatting to Alex. We had instant chemistry. He sketched this picture and travelled to Hammersmith the next day, where he heroically died.

Because I'd arranged to meet him for a first date on the bridge.

Samira was right. I'm to blame, or rather that version of me who went to the leaving do. If *that* Julia Hockney hadn't agreed to see him again, Alex would be alive today, bar another curveball thrown at him by a cruel universe. He wouldn't have seen a couple arguing and jumped into the water to save them.

How could I have met him when I fell asleep? It makes no sense and defies the laws of physics. Plus, I've had plenty of narcoleptic attacks, but never seemingly changed real-life events. *Or have I?* How do I know what I'm doing while asleep? Often, I don't remember my dreams, and those I can recall are usually horrific. Something must have happened during my episode in here, which was different to all those times before. *But what?* I remember chatting to Merv about his investigations; he begins with basic groundwork before attempting to fill in the gaps. I search for 'narcolepsy' and 'time travel' online. Articles about international travel and flying appear. I don't need tips for plane journeys unless it involves visiting a new dimension.

Logically, something must be happening to my brain when I fall asleep. I click on a scientific paper, which describes how narcolepsy develops due to changes in the brain's hypothalamus region. Many cases are caused by the reduction or loss of a chemical called hypocretin, which helps control wakefulness. But genetic mutations can occur within families, causing clusters of relations with the sleep disorder. I look up 'narcolepsy' and 'dreams' and find a support group blog. Other people report similar intruder nightmares during sleep paralysis, but I can't find any ultra-realistic romantic fantasies, and certainly nothing about events from the past being changed.

My phone beeps with a message from Jeremy:

On site visits – trying to find a new storage facility for the archives before basement is renovated. Taking longer than I thought! Won't be back tonight. Just get done what you can and go home. No need to stay late!

I message him back:

Thank you. Good luck with visits!

He's the best boss. Rod would have hung, drawn and quartered me for arriving late and leaving early. I must get through some of these boxes for him. The newspaper group is moving temporarily to another building in three months' time while this one is refurbished. Everyone at the *Gazette*, the *Herald* and *Sunday Herald* will have to clear out, so the archives need to be sorted, with all the salvageable documents packed up.

I turn on the fans, pull on plastic gloves, and sift through envelopes, spreading out cuttings that can be dried between pieces of blotting paper. After an hour of concentrating hard, waves of drowsiness lap over me. My eyes are dry and scratchy, my limbs heavy and uncooperative. I get up and do a few star jumps to prevent myself from falling asleep before WhatsApping Ed:

Hoping to leave soon. Can pick up takeaway if you haven't eaten? Will be great to have that chat x

Two blue ticks appear, but he takes his time replying.

Can we do it tomor? Have headache and want early night. P.S. Am sorry about yesterday. You're right – it's totally unreasonable. I'll ask Miranda to stop calling and texting after hours xx

Tomorrow, tomorrow, tomorrow.

Does he have a bad head, or is he avoiding a discussion about MM? He probably believes his apology draws a line under everything. Before I have a chance to reply, he messages again.

Do u mind sleeping in spare room? Will leave light on for you x

Irritation flickers inside me. *It's my flat!* I tap out:

I want to sleep in my own bed. I'll be quiet when I come in. Or you could go in there? X

Ha! He has no answer to that. I put my phone down. It's almost out of battery and I forgot to bring my charger. My conversation with Ed will have to wait until another day. I may as well press on with researching my dream – if I manage to stay awake long enough. I remember watching the 1980s movie *Somewhere in Time* with Gran. Christopher Reeve travelled back from 1972 to meet Jane Seymour in 1912 through self-hypnosis. He also immersed himself among items from the past. Could the cuttings I was looking at before I fell asleep have triggered something in my brain? I pull out the boxes containing the files I was working on when I had my strangely lucid dream – 'drug deaths' and 'suspicious overdoses'. An article could have had the same date as the bridge tragedy or involved someone connected to Alex. I leaf through both envelopes but can't find anything from May 12, 2023.

Perhaps I need more of a prompt? I print off the email inviting me to the leaving drinks, as well as photos of Alex. Most of the newspapers used the same one after his death: Alex grinning directly at the camera. But there's a lovely one of him with his sister, Zoe, and nieces, Sally and Hannah. They're stood next to a Disney princess, at the twins' seventh birthday party. I arrange them on the desk and place the abstract print in the centre, before continuing to search for a reference to Alex or Hammersmith Bridge in the old files.

Inky darkness claws ruthlessly at the back of my eyes. It's freezing in here, but that's not helping keep me awake. I feel like I've been hit by a bus and desperately need to sleep. I stare at Alex's photo before catching sight of the time on my mobile – it's 8.45 p.m.

My eyelids flutter and close.

I'm sinking faster and faster through cold, cloudy water, the light a small chink at the surface. A dark shape looms above. A hand stretches towards me. I can't grab it. I plunge deeper. My arms and legs turn to concrete; my lungs are bursting. I can't . . .

I jerk awake, taking a huge breath. I grab my mobile – it's 8.56 p.m. I've only nodded off for eleven minutes and haven't travelled back in time to the bar, despite being surrounded by images of Alex and stories about his death. I have no idea what I did differently previously. I return the cuttings to the boxes, rubbing my face. The nap hasn't left me refreshed; my brain is slow and fuzzy. Trying to think is like sifting through treacle. I need caffeine. I clip back my hair and pull on my coat. Before leaving, I turn off the fans and scoop up the papers. I'll look over everything in the canteen with a large coffee.

After a couple of minutes, I realise I've taken a few wrong turnings. I lean against the wall close to the underground car-park, dizzy and befuddled. Retracing my steps and reaching the elevators feels like a trek to Mount Everest base camp. I'm about to fall asleep again. I push myself off the wall and stagger down the corridor, trying handles. I need to sit down before I collapse. Eventually, a door opens into a storeroom stacked with cleaning products. I lurch inside and sink onto a stool.

I breathe out slowly, playing with my necklace. The stone rotates and ticks like a heart. Mine falls into the same rhythm until we're beating as one. My eyelids are hooded. I catch sight of the time before the battery on my phone dies. It's 9.24 p.m.

The room dims and softens around the edges. The email printout in my hand is blurry. The date briefly comes into focus: May 11, 2023.

Suki's leaving drinks at the Swan.

The words merge, cloud and fade away. My thoughts drift.

My eyelids flutter.

Spin, spin, spin.

Tick, tick, tick.

The sound grows louder and louder. The frequency changes and transforms into high-pitched squeals.

The world folds and collapses in on me, a fragile piece of origami closing.

A shroud of darkness descends.

My eyes close.

The deafening roaring sound obliterates everything.

10

THEN

May 11, 2023

Whoooaaa!

I shield my eyes from the bright, stinging light. A metallic blend of grease and dust fills my nostrils. My senses sharpen and send urgent warning signals to my brain: *Do something!* I'm swaying at the top of concrete steps, leading down to a packed platform. I grab the handrail, steadying myself. My gaze rests on the route planner to my left:

High Street Kensington.

I'm no longer in the basement storeroom; I'm at the underground station closest to work. A train has arrived and people are crowding on. Exiting passengers surge up the steps. I blink repeatedly. I'm still here. The rail is cold yet clammy beneath my touch. This all feels real. Am I having another incredibly lifelike hallucination? I lose my footing and bang my knee on the wall. Pain shoots up my leg. *Okaaay.* Usually, I'm not hurt in my dreams. I wake up just before the masked man attacks during my nightmares.

Have I done it? Have I travelled back in time? It's just after 7 p.m. according to my watch – almost two-and-a-half hours earlier than when I fell asleep. I dig out my phone but it's dead. I have no idea what day it is, or whether I can communicate with anyone. If I am *really* here, I could be in spirit form, invisible to everyone. A woman ignores the signs and climbs up the right-hand side of the staircase towards me, hanging onto the rail.

'Are you going to move, or what?' she snaps, glaring directly at my face.

She can see me!

'Oh, sorry.' I let go and move aside.

She tuts and her arm brushes against mine.

'I felt that!' I gasp. 'Did you?'

She gives me a withering you-are-completely-mad backwards look, but I don't care. I have no idea how I managed it, but I think I *am* here, in person. At the tube station, not in the storeroom. My vision swims as the steps appear to ripple and bend and I'm hit by a wave of nausea. I concentrate on trying not to fall as I make my way down to the platform, buffeted by commuters. A beeping noise reverberates.

This train is about to depart. Please mind the doors.

'Watch where you're going. Get out of my way!'

Someone thunders down the steps behind me.

Is this . . . ? Could it be the guy who . . . ?

I attempt to avoid the man by shifting left, but my movements are slow and heavy. He knocks into my arm, showering me with hot coffee from his Costa cup.

'For God's sake!' he mutters.

The drink soaks through my green dress and bra, finding bare skin. I stare, gobsmacked, as the brown stain spreads across the fabric. This is similar to what happened on the evening of May 11 last year, and when I fell asleep in the archives. I'm wearing a different outfit and we've collided on the stairs, not the platform, but it's the same outcome.

I glance up. 'Are we doing this again? Can I change—?'

The man ignores me and leaps down the final steps, charging towards the closing doors. A younger guy with a blond ponytail and a long black leather coat follows closely behind, clutching a violin case. Coffee Guy drops his newspaper and thrusts his briefcase through the gap. The doors crunch and grind. He waggles his bag determinedly, and they spring open. Both men jump on. A pre-recorded warning booms out about not obstructing the doors. I watch, open mouthed, as the man's copy of the *Gazette* flutters to the ground. It's dated May 11, 2023 and the headline reads: *Police Step Up Patrols in Acton After Night Prowler Attacks.*

My eyes widen. I'm definitely reliving the night I set off for Suki's drinks at the Swan. I can hardly believe it! I watch, stunned, as the twenty-something musician walks deeper into the carriage and finds a seat, laying the instrument case across his lap. Coffee Guy – late thirties with cold eyes, sharp features and thinning brown hair – stares from behind the scratched, smeared window. He gives me the finger as the train pulls away. My jaw drops. He hasn't done that before. The first time we collided, he missed the train and was angry. During my sleep attack in the archives, which appears to have changed Alex's fate, he made his connection but didn't make eye contact. I feel for my pendant. The stone has stopped rotating, but I can hear a gentle ticking noise in the background, beyond the other sounds on the platform. I'd been turning it when I fell asleep in the storeroom, *and* the archives. I remember Gran's song:

Spin the stone and make a change. Transform the world and rearrange.

Has the necklace helped me to travel in time to last year? It seems utterly mad to even consider the possibility. But something *has* happened tonight. Nothing odd occurred when I spun the pendant with Gran and Raquel in the nursing home, so is falling asleep the key to all this? I dab at my wet dress with tissues, my heart thumping with excitement. If I have gone back to an earlier date, can I change what is still to come? This could be my chance to transform Alex Martin's world and mine. I can rearrange events and prevent him from drowning at midday tomorrow, which would leave his family and friends bereft. Someone else will rescue those other people at Hammersmith Bridge – Samira had mentioned that workmen dialled 999.

I must decide whether to go to the leaving do or return to my flat without meeting Alex.

A pigeon stops pecking for scraps. The breeze dies down.

Time stands still, waiting for my decision.

I lift my chin. I'm not deterred by a wet dress tonight or the challenge ahead.

I'm going to meet my soulmate *and* save his life.

'Coming through!' A young woman with long, blonde hair and heavy, pencilled eyebrows manoeuvres past a hen party of glamorous 1920s flappers. 'Here you go!' She hands me a drink with bobbing ice cubes and a piece of lime.

'Layla! Thank you. It's so lovely to see you.' I give her a half hug and kiss on the cheek. 'It's been too long!'

'Er, how many of these have you had?' She nods at my glass. 'We spoke this morning. I asked you to swap my Sunday shift – I'm not supposed to work two in a row. It's Merv's turn, but he's trying to dodge it as per bloody usual.'

Shit. In this scenario, I'm still caught up in rota wars between the journalists and haven't been banished to the archives. Layla hasn't moved to New York with her lawyer girlfriend, Megan, and begun fertility treatment.

'Did we? Sorry. Am having a major brain blip.'

I scan the bar as I take a sip of . . . *gin and tonic.* God, this tastes good. It's what I drank on nights out before my narcolepsy worsened and I reluctantly switched to Diet Cokes. I definitely need alcohol to cope with the shock of tonight. I still can't believe I'm actually here, doing any of this. It's completely insane.

'How's Megan?' I ask, savouring the acidic tingle of lime on my tongue. 'How's the high-powered job?'

She gives me an odd look. 'She's keeping an eye out for open-ings after being made redundant.' There's a sharp edge to her tone.

Double shit.

'I'm sure something will come up,' I mumble into my drink. 'Soon.'

In New York. In four months' time.

I need to get better at this time travelling stuff or, alternatively, keep my big mouth shut.

'I hope so. She's moping around the flat and doing my head in.' Layla frowns, tapping her nails sharply on the glass of white wine. 'Are you meeting someone here tonight?'

'I don't think so, but I'm not totally sure. Why?'

'You're acting strange this evening – like you're nervous or something?'

More journalists join us, which saves me from coming up with a plausible excuse. It's hard to hear what everyone is saying above the shrieks from the bride-to-be and the thumping music. I take a large slurp of gin and make a mental note not to tell the industry correspondent, Brian, he will be sacked next month for an unknown misdemeanour.

It's past 10 p.m. I haven't spotted Alex yet. And where the fuck is Harry Styles when you need him? Not a single One Direction song has played tonight, let alone one of his glorious solos. I press the glass to my chest, almost spilling the contents as I sway along to Taylor Swift. I should leave. Oh God! *Can I?* How do I find home? Will I return to my flat in 2024 or am I stuck here in 2023, about to live every day forward from this night onwards? If so, I face another year of being used as Rod's personal punchbag ahead of an unofficial demotion. My head swims. This is a mistake. I have no idea what I'm doing. Earlier, I almost let slip my insider knowledge to Layla. I'm hopeless. I'll never manage to keep secrets for twelve months. Plus, I'll have to watch Gran deteriorate all over again.

I can't do this.

It was mad to think I could change the events of the past. Hopefully, this – whatever *this* is – will wear off soon and I'll wake up in the basement storeroom in 2024, debating how to pin down Ed into discussing the state of our relationship. I take another gulp of my drink. It feels as though weights are attached to my eyelids, and my stomach is churning. I half listen to the leaving speeches praising Suki's commitment to her work through my blurry gin haze. Merv helps her up onto a chair – she's one stumble closer to a trip to A&E than me.

'Yes, yes, yes,' she slurs, at the round of applause. 'I have a speech prepared.' She pulls out a piece of paper from her pocket, almost falling off. 'But screw it.' She throws it away. 'I'd love to say I'll miss the *Gazette* . . .'

I feel a punchline coming on. Hopefully, she'll say the exact opposite.

'But I've hated every fucking minute.'

Gin shoots up my nose. I'm laughing and choking, tears pouring down my face. The glass slips between my fingers. My arm flops to my side and my knees buckle. I feel myself falling, but I don't hit the floor. I'm hovering in mid-air. Someone's caught me.

'Julia!' *Layla.*

I feel wet. Please God, don't let me have peed myself.

'What happened? Did she faint?' A man's voice. 'Should we call an ambulance?'

I can't speak. My lips are frozen, my limbs have turned to jelly. I can't lift my hands or head. My heartbeat feels like it's stopped. Music drifts into my eardrums. Sounds change shape, sharpen and melt away. After thirty seconds or so, I can wiggle my toes and fingers again. I'm sitting on the floor, propped against someone. Harry Styles is singing 'Falling'. Oh, the bloody irony. God is definitely screwing with me tonight. Someone's arms are wrapped protectively around me. I stare up into familiar, blue-green eyes. A lock of longish brown, curly hair falls onto the man's forehead.

'It's . . . you!' I gasp.

Alex looks the same as before – the black jumper with the smear of cobalt blue paint on the sleeve and chipped red nail polish.

'Are you alright?' he asks, frowning. 'You scared the heebie-jeebies out of me.'

'I missed you,' I whisper.

'What did you say?' Layla crouches beside me, clutching my hand. 'I didn't catch that.'

I can't stop grinning, which must make me look deranged. Alex and Layla exchange worried glances.

'Does she need an ambulance? Or a doctor? Or . . . I don't know.' Alex runs a hand through his hair. 'Another drink?'

'Hell, no,' Layla says shortly. 'She's had enough.'

'I am here. I can hear both of you.' I take a deep breath. 'I'll be okay in a minute. It's cataplexy. When I laugh hard, I lose muscle tone and my knees buckle. I can't stand up.'

'Well, luckily for you, I tell terrible jokes, which no one finds funny.'

The skin around Alex's eyes crinkles as he smiles broadly. Butterflies dance in the pit my stomach. The way he's gazing at me . . . My heart flutters. There's a spark between us, like in my dreams. Layla looks from me to him.

'Do you two know each other?' she asks.

'No.'

'Yes.'

They both stare at me.

'Yes, but no,' I splutter. 'Not in this lifetime.'

'Did she hit her head?'

'No, I caught her.'

'Hello! I am here.'

Layla sighs. 'Can you stand?'

I look down and realise Alex's arms are still around me. A blush creeps into my cheeks. I don't want to move.

'Shall I give you a hand up?' he asks.

I feel a wave of disappointment but nod. 'I'll be wobbly.'

'Like me on Saturday nights.' He helps me to my feet, and I manage to stay upright. 'I couldn't save your shoes, sorry.'

'What?'

He points at my black suede flats. 'Unfortunately, a guy's pint went with you.'

This time, I caused the man to spill his drink and landed in the puddle of beer. But thank God, that's what the wet sensation was, and I haven't wet myself.

'I should buy him another drink, wherever he is.' I scan the bar, but no one catches my eye, apart from Merv and Suki, who are nursing pints at the corner table. Merv raises an eyebrow, as well as a glass.

'I wouldn't bother,' Layla says. 'He should have moved quicker – or helped catch you. Anyway, your shoes cost far more than a pint.'

'True. I'm a drinks magnet tonight.' I pull open my coat. 'Someone threw coffee down my dress earlier.'

Alex's gaze lowers, making my heart beat quicker.

'Interesting pattern. You're like a living, breathing piece of art.'

Layla giggles quietly.

'That might be the nicest thing anyone has ever said to me,' I reply.

Our gaze locks. I could lose myself in the beautiful shade of his eyes, green yet blue with golden flecks. I take in the dark shadows, evidence of a restless night, and the long eyelashes, the broadness of his chest. His hair is tousled as if he's only managed to run his hands through it after rolling out of bed. I can picture myself lying next to him, playing with a tendril of hair, and talking until the early hours. Doing other stuff . . . My chest tightens. I like him. I *really, really* like him. I can't stop staring. His cheekbones glow in the overhead lights. He looks vibrant and alive . . . Yet, within the next 24 hours he could be dead. *Because of me.* I kill him. I let out a small whimper. I don't think anyone heard.

'Tell me you're not going to drunk cry?' Layla hisses. 'Because that would be beyond embarrassing.'

I shake my head, batting away tears.

'I get it now – *this* is who you were waiting for!' She squeezes my arm. 'Shout if you need me but I doubt you will.' Her voice raises in volume. 'Bye! Lovely to meet you, er . . . ?'

'Alex. You too.'

I can't take my eyes off him. I pinch my hand, leaving a red mark. I'm definitely here in 2023. Alex Martin is standing in front of me, and he's even lovelier than in my dreams.

'Are you sure you're okay? You seem dazed. I could call your friend back?' His gaze trails after Layla.

'This happens a lot because of my narcolepsy. I mean, it will . . .' I stop myself from mentioning my worsening symptoms. 'I'm Julia. Julia Hockney.' I stretch out my hand, which quivers with anticipation.

'Like the painter,' he says, shaking it.

I missed you.

I shiver as I hear the words in my head.

'I'm Alex Martin – catcher of falling women in bars. It's terrible for my back, but someone has to do it.' He mock grimaces, rubbing the base of his spine. 'I warned you my jokes are terrible. I'll never make it as a stand-up comedian.'

'You were right. Don't give up your day job as an artist.'

He frowns. 'How did you know . . . ?'

I point at the paint splashed on his sleeve; I might be getting better at this foreshadowing business.

'I wasn't sure about the nail polish though.'

'My seven-year-old nieces gave me a makeover after their birthday party. I drew the line at their suggestion of pink hair dye.'

'The red varnish suits you.'

'I thought so.' He examines his hands. 'It's beginning to chip. I need to touch them up.'

'What do you paint, apart from your nails?'

'Mainly landscape and water abstracts, particularly storms. I'm working on a commission, but it's not going well. I can't capture the shades of the waves when lightning . . .' He gazes at me, making light tremors travel across my skin. 'Your hair is beautiful – the colours are incredible. I can see shades of purples, blues, yellows and greens, all shimmering like jewels. Even diamonds.'

I burst out laughing. 'Yellow and green? This is a horrendous light! It's not doing me any favours.'

He catches hold of my arm. 'Sorry. I shouldn't say things like that. You might fall. But seriously, you'd make a great subject if you ever fancy sitting for me.'

He blushes furiously as I raise an eyebrow.

'That's not a chat-up line, I promise. I mean it could . . .' He exhales, raking a hand through his hair. 'Sorry. I'm being an art snob or rather nob! I can't help it. I've been at the Whistler exhibition all afternoon. You remind me of Joanna Hiffernan, Whistler's woman in white.'

'Except, I'm wearing green, splashed with coffee and beer!'

He chuckles. 'True, but his muse had dark auburn hair, porcelain skin and beautiful green eyes, like you. There was an incredible seven-foot-high painting of her. I was debating attempting a portrait afterwards and meeting you has made up my mind.'

'Mission accomplished! I collapse in bars all the time – it's an act so I can find artists who are inspired to paint my luscious locks.' I flick my hair dramatically.

Who am I? I never joke about my sleep disorder, but my inhibitions have slipped away. Four gin and tonics, possibly five, may have helped, but he's also so easy to talk to. I've only known him properly for a few minutes, yet I sense I could trust him with anything.

He laughs, taking a step closer. 'I don't usually do this . . . Well, that's a lie. Sometimes I try to chat up gorgeous girls in bars and it goes disastrously wrong. I clam up and can't think of anything to say, but with you it's different.'

'Yes,' I say softly. 'It is.'

He thinks I'm gorgeous. He feels like home – a favourite song I've listened to repeatedly, a much-loved book I've reread.

'Can I get your number?'

I pull my phone out of my bag. 'It's dead, sorry. Probably broken.'

'Ah.' He studies my face. 'Is that code for saying you have a boyfriend?'

Do I? This is a year ago, which means I haven't met Ed. Technically, I'm single.

'Is that a no, but yes? Or a yes, but really a no?' The corners of his mouth twitch.

'It's a . . . I'm not sure what, if I'm completely honest. I was with my boyfriend, Ed, but now I'm not. I don't know if I can get back to . . . I mean, be with him. Or if I want to. I think he's cheating. Anyway, it's complicated.'

'Well, *a*, he sounds like a jerk, and *b*, it doesn't have to be complex – swapping numbers is simple.'

'My phone *has* broken. We could go down the old-fashioned route and write letters to each other – revive the dying art of paper and pen in the era of WhatsApp? That would be simple.'

'Erm, that sounds great, Jane Austen, but I was thinking more along the lines of arranging to meet tomorrow? Or is that too soon after your break-up?' He rubs his jaw. 'And too soon generally? Should I wait longer to show I'm interested?'

My heart leaps. *He's interested.*

'It's been a while since I've asked anyone out on a date,' he admits.

'Probably not as long as me! The last time I tried to take the initiative, I was at a bus stop, waiting to go to school. We got together, snogged, and broke up, before the number 267 arrived.'

'The joys of being a teenager! Modern-day dating is far more difficult to navigate with all the dos and don'ts . . . It's a minefield. Do I catch a girl who's falling, or will she think I'm mansplaining to her how to stand up? It's tough for guys.'

'My heart bleeds for you. Tomorrow's good. I have a day off from the *Gazette*.'

'You're a journalist?'

'I'd describe myself more as a caretaker of damaged, old newspapers and other people's stories—' I stop myself; I haven't been exiled yet.

'I also try to manage warring journalists – I'm secretarial, not editorial. I'm not important, in the grand scheme of things.'

'Oh, I wouldn't say that.' His eyes twinkle mischievously. 'So about tomorrow? Where do you want to meet?'

I need to completely change the place, and even the time, to shake things up.

'How about the lake in Kew Gardens at 12.30? You could get inspiration for your paintings.'

'Great idea! I haven't been there for years.' He stretches out his hand. 'Promise me, you'll turn up, Julia. Obviously, I don't doubt the word of a long-lost relative of David Hockney who doesn't use modern technology and secretly yearns to write long, Jane Austen style letters. But let's shake on it, so we know this is real. That we're not imagining it all.'

His fingers encircle mine and I hear those three words in my head again: *I missed you.*

This is the turning point, isn't it? I've saved Alex's life. He won't drown tomorrow at Hammersmith Bridge. He'll meet me on a first date in Kew.

His head lowers towards mine. Our lips are tantalisingly close. 'Alex!'

We spring apart. He glances at a guy further down the bar, who's waving. Standing nearby is a young blonde woman from the hen party in a long, red dress. She's watching Alex. Or is it me?

'I should go, sorry. I'm neglecting my old uni mates.'

'See you tomorrow, Alex.'

The bride's party departs from the pub in a blaze of sequins and raucous shouts. I was wrong – that woman isn't with them. She continues to stare at me. I look away first, unsettled by the intensity of her unwavering gaze. It's as if she can see right through me.

'Hey!' Alex doubles back. 'I can give you *my* number in case something comes up.'

'I'll be there tomorrow, I promise.'

He chews his lip, suppressing a sigh.

'We should take a leap of faith,' I insist.

'A leap of faith,' he repeats.

He flashes me a huge grin before walking away.

I hadn't expected to stay here this long. I thought I'd wake up in the present day after Alex left the bar, but I'm still in 2023. I've made it home to White City without having a narcoleptic episode. I feel a small twinge of guilt as I let myself in my flat. I'm half expecting Ed to confront me about flirting with Alex. But this is pre-Ed. I never met him tonight because I didn't catch the same tube. He's continued the journey to his basement flat in Wimbledon, without meeting a girl who falls asleep in strange places. He's probably made himself a spinach shake before watching football catch ups on TV – his old evening routine.

I glance around in wonder. My flat looks different but feels like an old record – forgotten beats strike familiar, comforting chords. Gran had given me a chunk of money from her savings before she became ill, and I'd used it for the shared ownership deposit when she went into the home. A year ago, I hadn't begun redecorating with Ed. The sitting room has the original, peeling magnolia wallpaper, which I'll soon strip off, while the kitchen is the matching, dull colour. My bookshelf is triple stacked – Ed hasn't persuaded me to give away my old paperbacks to the charity shop. His collection of weights has vanished. I've left out a sweater, mug, and last week's newspapers in a pile. Before Ed, I used to curl up on the sofa on Sunday mornings and read all the supplements with a cup of coffee.

The magnolia bedroom is undecorated; I'm in a state of indecision over the hues, painting small squares with primrose, teal and a delicate lilac. The furniture remains the same, but the framed pictures of me and Ed have vanished, and the photos of Gran have changed. We're on the sun terrace at Ravensbrook; her hair is freshly curled, and her fingernails painted shocking pink. The picture of Mum is new: she's sat in Gran's back garden, staring into the middle distance, lost in thought.

I pull on my old pyjamas, which mould around my body like a second skin. I regret replacing them with the expensive frothy lace number when Ed began staying over. The faded, floral duvet embraces me like a kiss. This might be an alternate reality but, despite my worries earlier, it feels like I belong here. I'm no longer worrying about being cheated on, my career taking a nosedive, or rather descending five floors to the basement, or whether Gran will sleep through all my visits. I have no idea what year I'll wake up in tomorrow, but I'm praying it's 2023. I pick up the pendant from around my neck. I can still hear a faint ticking noise, the same as in the bar. It wasn't coming from the stone there either. It's far beyond other sounds like the next-door neighbour's music and the hum of traffic beyond the window.

Is this 2024 calling me back? Do I just rotate the stone to return?

I drop the necklace and close my eyes.

My old life can wait.

For the first time in months, tomorrow brims with hope.

11

THEN

MAY 12, 2023

I'm still here!

I slept fitfully, dreaming I was sinking beneath an expanse of cold water, unable to get to the surface. I woke up struggling for breath, drenched in sweat. I stretched out, making starfish shapes beneath the duvet – an impossible feat on the single mattress in the spare bedroom. I went back to sleep around 4 a.m. and must have had a nosebleed; I found red spatters on my pillow. I keep checking the alarm clock and TV, but I'm definitely in the past. I can't remember what I was doing this time last year – pre-dating Ed I never did much on days off apart from clean the flat, read magazines, and visit Gran. But this morning, I can't do anything except lie down. The sitting room spins and I want to throw up whenever I try to stand. Gin hangovers are the worst.

I pick up my mobile from the side of the sofa. I've tried charging it, but the battery is completely dead. I can't ring Vicky and see what's going on with her. Perhaps that's for the best. I mustn't meddle. I only want to change Alex's life, not other people's. It's probably not a good idea to visit Gran later either. I've watched *The Butterfly Effect*, an old movie starring Ashton Kutcher. I could say or do something that will have an awful knock-on effect at Ravensbrook. My footprint should be kept to a minimum in 2023. I'll stick to meeting Alex in Kew Gardens, where I can't cause lasting damage to anyone else.

I'm late getting to Kew. I vomited repeatedly and had a bad nosebleed before leaving the flat, and the bus was delayed by a motorbike crash. I got off two stops early and sprinted, well jogged slowly, part of the way to Elizabeth Gate, but a coachload of OAPs delayed the queue when I arrived. It took ages to buy a ticket (*how much?!*) and get into the gardens. Sweat drips down my back and my chest hurts as I run towards the lake. It's 12.57 p.m. No time to brush my hair in the Orangery's bathroom. Has Alex waited or does he think I've stood him up? We didn't exchange numbers last night and even if we had, I couldn't have messaged or called. My mobile doesn't work at all in the past, but my watch is unaffected, perhaps because it's analogue.

I increase my pace but my chest and side hurts. I massage my stitch, gasping, as I force myself to make a final spurt past vivid flower beds and waddling ducks. The lake stretches out ahead, shimmering with promise. It's larger than I remembered. Frantically, I scan the visitors, realising I never said *exactly* where to meet on the banks. I spot Alex by the railings opposite the Palm House. He's wearing faded blue trousers and a denim jacket. A small, pigtailed girl is sharing her bag of crusts with him. Together, they toss bread to the ducks, seagulls and swans, making my heart twinge.

He's kind and good with children. As well as being ridiculously lovely.

'Alex!'

He spins around. A smile spreads across his face.

'Sorry I'm late!' I shout.

'No problem,' he calls back. 'Leap of faith!'

The girl, who's aged about five or six, also turns. Slowly, she shakes her head. I look over my shoulder, thinking she's spotted someone else, but she's frowning fiercely at me as if I've done something wrong. She mouths a single word:

Leave!

The magical moment shatters like glass. The sun pales. Shadows gather under the trees, draining colour from the grass. Dark shapes shift beneath the surface of the water, and wriggle in the recesses of my brain. Leaden weights are attached to both feet. I can barely lift them. The little girl backs away, as if she doesn't want to see what will happen next.

The ticking noise no longer lingers in the background, quiet and indistinct. It drowns out the chatter of a couple walking past but they don't seem to notice.

I glance at my watch. It's 1 p.m. The sound isn't coming from my wrist or necklace. It surrounds me. It's in the cloudless blue sky, the whispering trees, and the lake, pulsating and growing in strength. My heart pounds painfully and impossibly fast.

'Julia?'

Alex becomes smaller and smaller. Or I'm vanishing. I'm falling down a dark, cold tunnel. The ticking is unbearably loud. I clamp my hands to my ears.

'Help me!'

Alex is a tiny speck in the distance, his voice a hollow, hopeless echo.

Darkness surges over me in an unrelenting, unforgiving tide.

He disappears.

12

Sunday, May 12, 2024

Where am I?

The earth has turned on its axis, and I'm spinning in a Dorothy-style tornado. Colours twirl and bleed into each other like spilt paint pots before separating, solidifying and forming objects. *A bucket. A mop. A bottle of detergent.* Vomit rises in my throat at the sudden, sharp smell of disinfectant mixed with cheap soap. I'm in the basement storeroom. I cling onto my pendant, as the stone rotates and stops. My heartbeat slows.

My mind is splintered; memories stretch and distort into unrecognisable images. Random thoughts arrive – *leap of faith, the glittering lake in Kew Gardens, a scowling child*. Nothing is tangible. When I try to focus on what happened and where I've been, the explanation floats out of reach.

Concentrate.

I attempt to fit the broken images in my head back together, but only find more questions: *Did I travel back?*

It was too lifelike and detailed to be a dream . . . the arrival at High Street Kensington station, the Swan, my flat and Kew Gardens. It feels like I've lived every minute in the past. *Am I still there*? My watch says it's 10.15 p.m., but is this 2023 or 2024? Rummaging in my bag, I find my mobile, but it ran out of battery before I nodded off. Jeremy's laptop in the archives will have the time and date. I lean down to scoop up my printouts but almost fall off the stool. I snatch up the email inviting me to Suki's leaving drinks last year but can't find Alex's colour print or the newspaper stories about him. When my head no longer feels like it's falling off my body, I check under the shelves and inside my bag, but the papers aren't here. I was holding them when I fell asleep. I think. Or did I leave them on the table? I haul myself up, my hair falling loose over my face. I feel for the clip in the collar of my dress, but it's gone. Every part of me is unravelling.

The journey back to the archives is slow and painful; I lean against the walls when the dizziness and waves of sickness become overwhelming. I turn the handle to room 312b, but the door doesn't budge. I yank it harder.

Shit!

It must be late – security has locked up, with the laptop inside. I double back to the elevators, and barely manage to keep upright as the lift rises to the ground floor. In the lobby, I collapse on a sofa, my vision swimming. I focus on the portraits until the lines and shadows form faces. Marc Campbell-Johnston's picture is missing from the wall. It's doubtful he's been sacked in the last eight hours – he's far more likely to wield the axe on an underling's career. Someone must have forgotten to return the picture after spring cleaning.

A short, blond security guard approaches; Piotr has left for the night. Mike – according to the name on his badge – must be a recent appointee.

'Everything alright, love? You're as white as a sheet.'

'I need to take a minute. My phone's dead and I have to check something urgently.' I breathe out slowly. 'For Rod on news desk.'

He flinches. He can't be that new – he's already had an encounter with the tyrant.

'Here, borrow mine. Take your time.'

Mike taps in his PIN and thrusts the mobile at me, before returning to his desk. My eyes widen as I stare at the screen. It's Sunday, May 12, 2024 – around 45 minutes after I fell asleep. My heart aches horribly. Despite that invisible thread connecting me with Alex, we were never destined to be together in the present day. My time jump – if that's what took place – was disappointingly fleeting. What happened to him? I type 'Alex Martin' and 'London' and 'drowned' into Mike's phone. Nothing. I try different combinations, including 'Hammersmith Bridge', as well as 'Alex Martin' and 'artist', with zero success. No details of Alex's death, inquest, exhibition or fundraising concert appear.

A thought sears through me, making me light-headed. Did I manage to change the past? What if the cuttings in the cleaners' storeroom and the newspaper articles online no longer exist because Alex didn't die last year? He never went to the bridge. Alternatively, the papers were too far beneath the shelf for me to spot, and Mike has a dodgy, outdated search engine. I glance at him, but he's distracted by an incoming call on the landline. I can't find any Facebook or Instagram accounts for Alex, but he might not be on social media. Samira will know what's happened to him. I could swing by the gift shop tomorrow and pretend to be a journalist again. I walk unsteadily to the counter.

'Thanks.' I give the mobile back to Mike.

'No problem. Shall I call you a taxi? You look peaky and the weather's awful.'

He nods to the revolving doors; sheets of rain bounce off the pavement. I hesitate, debating whether I can face the short walk to the tube.

'I can charge it to the company account if you're ill.'

'That would be great, if you don't mind.'

He smiles sympathetically and picks up the work phone. After a brief conversation, he puts the handset down.

'You're in luck. A cab's here.'

'Great! Thanks, Mike.'

I push through the doors and step onto the pavement, clinging onto my umbrella. Inside the cab, the driver tries to strike up a conversation but gives up after a few attempts. I'm zombie like and can barely string a sentence together. I may have to call in sick tomorrow. Half of me wants to crawl into bed and never get out, but I'm also dreading returning home to my 2024 life. Not that I'll talk to Ed tonight. He'll be in bed, snoring, or faking sleep in a bid to avoid discussing Miranda.

I sink further into the seat, holding my pendant. I still can't believe I might have travelled into the past and potentially altered it. *Have I transformed Alex Martin's life, as well as my own?* Somewhere in London, he could be partying or reading a book in bed. Tomorrow, he may paint a new storm scene, meet Samira or his other friends, play with his nieces, and dream of becoming a famous artist with his own exhibition.

Hope grows inside me, a crisp green bud pushing through fresh soil.

He's alive, I'm sure of it.

The flat is dark as usual. I flick on the light and drape my wet coat over a hook. It looks like Ed's been shopping as a faded denim jacket hangs from another peg. It crosses my mind that he could be having an early mid-life crisis. He usually prefers sharp, designer suits or expensive blazers and chinos to vintage flea market buys. I dump my bag on the floor, my limbs growing heavier. I plug my phone in the hallway socket – the mobile lights up as it starts charging. It's not broken, thankfully. I head straight to the bathroom and grope blearily around the basin for my toothbrush. I close my eyes briefly and spin the stone in my pendant, listening to the ticking sound. I check my watch – fifteen seconds have passed and I'm still here, brushing my teeth with my forehead resting against the tiled wall.

This does appear to be somehow connected to my narcoleptic episodes. My mind flits to Mum. She owned the pendant before me and had narcolepsy. Did she know what it could do? And what about Gran? She was desperate to find this necklace on Friday and believed Mum was searching for it. But wouldn't Gran have told me before now that it's special? I'm too tired to figure this out tonight. I turn off the light and walk out, passing the spare room. Ed had asked me to sleep in there tonight, but I need to stand my ground. I tiptoe into our bedroom and undress in the dark. My pyjamas aren't at the bottom of the bed, and I stub my toe on a chair. I swallow a cry as I fumble towards the dresser. I promised to be quiet, but he's rearranged the furniture. I grope around the seat and find something that resembles a T-shirt, pulling it over my head. Within seconds of climbing beneath the covers, an arm slings over my waist. A warm body snuggles closer and I feel hot breath on my neck. For ages, I've been longing for Ed to cuddle me, but tonight doesn't feel right. He must be feeling guilty about Miranda's phone calls and texts. I wriggle from beneath his arm and shove him. Hard. He grunts and rolls over. I clamp a pillow to my ear to block out his snoring.

Smoke drifts across the bedroom, curling over the duvet, and crawling towards my neck with long, cadaver fingers. Something heavy crushes my chest. A dark figure hovers in the corner. He's started the fire. He's going to watch us burn to death and there's nothing I can do. I can't move. My eyes fly open. My breath is ragged, coming out in great gulps. Sweat drips down my back. Where is he?

Stop panicking. It's another dream.

I check the digital alarm clock. It hasn't magically reverted to 2023. It's 6.23 a.m., on Monday, May 13, 2024. The daily grind begins and nothing will change. Ed will postpone the chat about our relationship until tomorrow. I won't march into Rod's office and demand my old duties back. I won't stand up to Carole and insist she reintroduces weekly hairdressing and nail technician sessions for the residents at Gran's nursing home.

I glance across at Ed, who's buried beneath the cover. His bare arm has escaped. My gaze rests on a tattoo of a feather quill. Underneath is an ink birdcage. The door is open, and two swallows are in mid-flight.

'Fuck, fuck! FUCK!'

I throw myself out of bed, scrambling towards the corner of the room. I stub my toe on the chair, but don't feel the pain. My heart beats frantically. Am I still in my dream about to be murdered? Or have I woken up and a strange, tattooed man really is in my bed, about to kill me?

A head pokes out from under the duvet. 'Was it another nightmare?'

I gape at the man. He has tousled brown hair, stubble and bluish-green eyes. It can't be. I pinch my arm hard, until red marks appear, before lurching to the light switch. I turn it on and off – I can't do that in dreams.

Holy shit! This isn't a hallucination. It's Alex Martin. A half-naked Alex Martin. Here in 2024. A large compass tattoo stretches over his impossibly tight torso. Across his left shoulder are the inked words: *Leap of Faith* and the entwined letters: *A* and *J,* wrapped in intricately feathered wings.

He jumps out of bed in red boxers, taking me in his arms.

'It's another bad dream. I'm here.'

I breathe in his scent – an intoxicating mixture of salty hot skin, sandalwood and vanilla – as I melt into his body. *Whoosh!* I'm hit with a wall of air that knocks the wind out of me. I hang onto Alex's arm.

'Everything will be okay,' he whispers, stroking my hair. 'Take a deep breath in and slowly let it out.'

'Can't . . .'

I can't breathe.

The room spins. A year's worth of memories flood back:

I'm late for my first date with Alex. I'm walking towards the lake in Kew Gardens. He's feeding the ducks with a little girl. My heart beats quicker. I'm overwhelmed with emotion and my knees give way. Alex holds me until I regain feeling. We chat for hours in the Orangery until the staff say we have to leave because they're closing.

Our second date is at a Vietnamese street café in Soho, followed by ice cream and passionate kissing on the street. We return to my flat and talk until 2 a.m., falling asleep on the sofa.

The third date . . . An image of hot, tangled limbs flashes behind my eyes. The fourth too. And the fifth. Also, laughter. So much laughter. I'm gazing at Alex's seascape paintings in his Acton studio, his arm wrapped around my waist. 'What do you think?' he asks. 'I love, love, love them.' 'I love you,' he whispers in my ear. 'I love you too,' I reply without hesitation. We rip each other's clothes off and make love on the floor, laughing as we knock over a paint pot. I smear cobalt blue on his compass tattoo.

His sister, Zoe, hugs me, and arranges a girls' shopping trip. 'I'm so happy you're a part of our family.' Sally and Hannah let me play with their Disney Princess dolls.

113

I introduce Alex to Gran. He removes her glasses from the bed before sitting down. She kisses him on the cheek. 'You're like my Arthur,' she says. 'You're something special.'

We're on Hammersmith Bridge, taking goofy selfies at the spot Gramps proposed. We'll frame a picture and give it to Gran. Alex comes with me at least once a week to visit her. He gets a new tattoo – the words Leap of Faith are entwined with our initials.

'Surprise!' We jump out at Vicky, who walks into the Italian restaurant with Giles for her twenty-fifth birthday. She screams with delight and we hug. 'Best friend ever,' she slurs drunkenly.

We're celebrating Alex moving into my flat with a bottle of Prosecco; we make love in every room. We paint the kitchen sunflower yellow and cobalt blue and buy old bookshelves at a Chiswick car boot sale. We cook together, discuss books and enjoy lazy weekends, curled up together on the sofa. I nap during Netflix binges.

Alex holds me as I sob on Mother's Day. 'Why did Mum leave me? What did I do wrong?'

I fall asleep in a Thai restaurant during a party for Samira's first year since opening Hidden Things. Alex looks after me but is annoyed when Vicky flirts with Samira's boyfriend, Hamish.

We're with Oscar Simmonds, a private investigator and former detective who used to specialise in financial crime. We're at his office in Southall discussing how to find Mum. Oscar has told me to search for Mum's old bank details and cards, any records about her job at the music festival in Dumfries and Galloway, and the last known address in Spain. We visit Gran later that day and ask for help, but she's confused and claims Mum wants to surprise me at breakfast tomorrow. She'll be back in time to take me to school in the morning.

We're floating above Bristol in a hot air balloon – my twenty-fifth birthday surprise, followed by a picnic near Clifton Suspension Bridge. My narcolepsy worsens.

I find an old photo of Mum and me taken in Gran's back garden. Gran thinks Mum has returned and visited her. She can't find something important. She rips open the lining of her favourite coat and finds a pendant. She insists I have the necklace with the rotating stone. I weep as we leave. I thought she'd forgotten my birthday. Forgotten me.

I hug Alex's arm tighter. I can hardly believe what I'm remembering. Or seeing. The bedroom is blurry and shifting, but my vision finally clears and focuses on the walls. They're sky blue. Painting overalls are bundled in the corner; my duvet is faded and floral. Framed family photos are arranged on the bedside table: Gran sitting on a bench in the grounds of Ravensbrook; Mum relaxing in a garden chair, lost in thought; Alex and me with Zoe and the twins; the two of us hugging on Hammersmith Bridge and in a hot air balloon.

'It's incredible!' I say, gasping.

'What is?'

'Us. Our life together.'

'Of course it is,' he replies. 'It's perfect. I wouldn't change a single thing.'

13

MONDAY, MAY 13, 2024

I'm desperate to freeze frame this moment, capture it with a camera lens to prove it's happening. Somehow, I've gone back in time, changed the past and got together with Alex, not Ed. I've lived the evening of May 11, 2023 forwards, changing our lives in the present day. It doesn't make any sense, but I don't care that it sounds absurd. It's incredible! I don't want to blink in case Alex vanishes in a flicker of my lashes. *This* is the life I want, not my old one. Alex smiles reassuringly as if to say I don't need a photo. He's here with me in *our* bedroom and he's not going anywhere.

'We've had an amazing time,' I say shakily.

The corners of his mouth twitch. 'We're not over yet. Unless there's something you want to tell me?'

'No! I meant it's far better than—'

I bite my tongue. I was going to say 'with Ed'.

'Anything I could ever have imagined.'

My knees buckle as he pulls me up. Vomit rises in my throat, the room pitches and the walls close in. Furniture dances about like mischievous sprites, refusing to stay still.

'Whooaaa!'

Waves of competing emotions hit me square in the chest: pain and pleasure, passion and terrible loss. My grief for Mum and unhappiness over Gran's ailing health is heavy, unwanted baggage. I didn't leave it behind in 2023; it duplicitously smuggled itself back with me. I feel each rejection again like fresh knife wounds as more memories arrive: *I'm waking up in bed after a nightmare and crying for Mum, sobbing harder when I realise she's not here to comfort me. I wait for birthday and Christmas cards that never arrive and imagine Mum will sit down, late, in one of the empty chairs at my school concerts and parents' evenings. I scan crowds wherever I go, hoping for a glimpse of her face. Gran holds onto hope she'll return one day as her memory slowly fades.*

Energy drains from me, like blood from an open wound. I'm lightheaded yet heavy limbed, as if I've forced my body through a marathon. I press my temples and picture engorged, throbbing veins pushing back against my fingertips. My heart is beating at double time.

Alex helps me to a chair. 'This was a bad one, huh?'

He wraps his arms around me, nuzzling my neck. My shoulders curve self-consciously. We're both practically naked apart from thin layers of cotton. It's the first time 2024 me has felt his hands on my bare skin.

'Give me a minute.'

I can scarcely hold myself up. My body is refusing to cooperate, bones and muscles rebelliously declining to slot into place. Alex rubs my back gently as I bend over. A single spot of blood drips onto my knee.

'Take this and pinch the bridge of your nose.'

He passes me a tissue. After a few minutes, he re-examines my face.

'It's okay. You're all good.'

I can't find the words. His face glows, like it did in the bar. But this isn't a dream or a hallucination. *He's alive.* My gaze lingers on his tattoos; I've never dated anyone with ink previously. I hadn't dated many men before Ed, with just one serious relationship at uni. I love the designs covering Alex's body – he's a living, breathing piece of art, which is how he described me.

'How can I make you feel better? Does this help?'

He plants a trail of delicate kisses across my clavicle, making my skin tingle. I feel myself sinking into the body of the Julia Hockney who enjoys this and knows every inch of his body in return. He pulls away abruptly.

'By the way, I know you're fibbing.'

A rush of cold dread travels down my spine. Does he realise I've changed his life? He hasn't drowned and devastated his family. Or has he found out I left my boyfriend behind to find him in the past? But that's impossible. I never met Ed. I'd been single for years until the night of Suki's leaving drinks. I told Alex about Ed in the woolliest of terms in the bar. *I think.* My brain is sluggish, neurons refusing to fire.

'Erm, what do you mean?'

'If you're honest, you would change something about me.'

I gape at him. How can he possibly think that? Alex is everything I ever wanted from a partner – he's the loveliest, most caring and supportive man I've ever met. New images and sensations arrive: *Alex comforting Gran when she cries for Mum and begs to see her; waving a tea towel at the fire alarm after I fall asleep cooking pasta and the pan boils dry; scouring Mum's old journal for clues about where she might be living.* My energy ebbs further – I try to resist the urge to crawl back beneath the duvet.

'Seriously, there's nothing I'd change about you, Alex.'

'Apart from leaving my overalls and painting stuff lying around. You hate that.' He darts over to the pile of clothes in the corner and throws them into the laundry basket. 'Da-dah! Gone.'

I swallow my sigh of relief.

'Let's have a special breakfast since we couldn't do it yesterday. I could make pancakes.'

'Sure. Are we celebrating something?'

I manage not to fall over when he pulls me up, but my vision is fuzzy. My limbs are unfamiliar as if I've borrowed them temporarily from a stranger.

He cocks his head to one side. 'Very funny!'

I'm clearly supposed to know what's going on.

'Just kidding,' I add quickly.

'Your jokes are as bad as mine. Neither of us will make it as stand-up comedians.' He pinches my bottom. 'My T-shirt looks much better on you by the way.'

I manage a smile but I'm racking my brains about the importance of today as I follow him, distracted by his tight backside and muscular thighs. I try not to let the surprise register on my face as we reach the kitchen: it's painted sunshine yellow, with a cobalt blue feature wall. Ed's saucepans have disappeared, along with the West Ham fixtures. Upside-down paint pots and brushes sit on the draining board. A streak of red paint drips, bloodlike, into the sink. I shiver as goosebumps spring up on my arms.

'Blueberries or maple syrup?'

Alex opens the fridge and stares inside. The top shelf no longer contains energy drinks and is stacked with different pickles, sauces and jams. My yoghurts are randomly dotted around, instead of sitting in their allocated spaces.

'Julia?'

Nearby, a new blue vase is filled with sunflowers. Their broad heads are turned towards me, as if they're waiting expectantly to see what happens next.

'Hello? The pancakes?'

'I'm here.' I pinch myself again.

Am I?

'Are you still discombobulated?'

I burst out laughing. 'I've never heard anyone use that word before in a sentence.'

'What? I say it all the time. It's my favourite word!' He glances over his shoulder, his brow furrowed. 'Are you sure you're okay?'

'I feel like I'm playing catch up, as if I'm not completely in my body,' I say truthfully. 'It was a bad night with the horrors. I dreamed a man was watching us sleep. He had a knife and set fire to the bedroom.'

'Eeeugh, the usual one. You should have woken me. You don't have to go through that alone.'

'Thanks.'

'What for?'

I hesitate. 'Being here. With me.'

He winks. 'My medal's arriving any day.'

He pulls milk and eggs out of the fridge, kicking it shut with his foot. Whenever I did that, Ed's Eiffel Tower magnet fell off and chipped, but it's gone. I hold onto the counter, afraid to let go.

'Why don't you rest on the sofa? I'll bring in the pancakes when they're ready.'

He helps me to the sitting room. My mouths falls open as I walk inside.

'What is it?'

I shake my head. The rug has been replaced with a white bed sheet. An easel sits on top. Paints are stacked on the table, as well as sheaves of paper.

'Sorry, I meant to put all this away last night.'

He pads over to his painting corner, tidying up, but my gaze is drawn to the portrait hanging above the sofa. A woman's face is painted in acrylic using aquamarine, cobalt blue, burnt orange and purple diamond shapes.

It's me!

This is a larger, more intricate version of Alex's half-finished picture that Samira made into prints after his death.

'It's so big!'

'Thanks. That's kind.' He nudges me, readjusting his boxers.

I blush furiously. 'I mean the portrait. It's huge.'

He gives me a strange look. 'It's not that much different since you saw it in the early stages. The acrylic drafts in the studio were about the same size. Are you thinking about my early pastel sketches?'

'Yes!'

'You like it?'

'I *love* it,' I say emphatically. 'It's perfect. Like you.'

It's his turn to blush. 'I know we'd promised to wait and swap anniversary presents this Saturday, as the weekend was a work-fest, but I couldn't wait. I hung it up last night while you were at work. I wanted you to have it when you woke up.'

Of course! Yesterday was the one-year anniversary of our first date in Kew Gardens.

'Look, at this.' He taps the left-hand corner.

I step closer, expecting to see the words: *Hockney, like the painter*, but instead, he's penned *A Leap of Faith, Alex Martin, (Feb, 2024)*

Alex kneels on the sofa and points at unpainted shapes around my jawline. 'Can you see here? These diamonds are blank.'

'You have more work to do?'

'No, I deliberately haven't filled them in. That's because our story isn't finished yet. This is only the beginning.'

He pulls me onto the sofa. I quiver with excitement as he kisses me, his hands running over my body. My inhibitions slip away as we pull off our last remaining clothes. It feels like we're doing this for the first time, yet it's also wonderfully familiar.

I close my eyes as we make fresh memories together.

'Sorry,' Alex says.

We're lying naked on the sofa, our limbs entwined.

'What on earth for? That was amazing.'

'Ditto. It's my turn to be discombobulated.'

I laugh and trace my finger around the outline of his compass tattoo.

He shudders. 'What was I saying?'

'You were apologising for something. I have no idea what.'

'We've run out of time. I'll cook the pancakes tomorrow morning.'

I glance at my watch. It's only 6.55 a.m. 'There's plenty of time for pancakes or something else.' I plant kisses on his neck. 'I'm hungry and not necessarily for breakfast. I don't have to be in until 2.'

'You said yesterday you're on at 8.15 a.m.'

'Did I?'

'Have you forgotten?'

'I *am* discombobulated.'

I join in with his laughter to disguise my confusion. In this life, Jeremy must prefer day shifts. I don't remember anything new about the *Gazette*, apart from flashes of Rod's temper and my humiliation. That's a constant. I brace myself for reminders of fresh horrors.

'I should get moving.'

'Dammit. I wish I hadn't said anything!'

Reluctantly, I peel off him and head to the shower. I grab for my dressing gown on the back of the bathroom door, but it's no longer there. The hook has fallen off, and I find the robe at the bottom of my wardrobe in the bedroom. Beneath it is Gran's box of Night Prowler cuttings – I haven't offered them to Merv. He may have found the old file in the archives. I need to get up to speed with everything but when I return to the shower, I can't work out how to turn on the hot water tap. There's a delayed response from my brain to my hands. Cold water slashes at my skin like knives. Quickly, I wash my hair and towel dry it, listening to the dripping showerhead. I haven't gotten round to fixing it and Alex, like Ed, doesn't appear to be an odd job man.

Ed! I feel a small pang of guilt about leaving. Have I simply vanished, failing to come home from the *Gazette*? Or is his memory wiped and I never existed in his lifetime? He could be dating Miranda. She could be worrying that he's cheating on *her*. I ought to miss him, but being with Alex has shown me what a relationship should feel like – a series of small, kind moments rather than grand gestures that swiftly run out of steam. I should have asked Ed to leave long ago – never allowed him to move in – but the prospect of change had terrified the old Julia. The new me is apparently capable of incredible things.

I saved the man I love in the past and gave him a future. With me.

Rubbing the condensation away with the back of my hand, I gaze at my reflection in the mirror. I recognise the freckle on the side of my nose and my wet hair is making its way back into tight corkscrews. I find my first white strand and pull it out. Apart from that, I look the same. But something is off. It feels like I've slipped into someone else's skin, which doesn't quite fit. Regions of my mind remain sealed off and all my joints ache. This new life will definitely take some getting used to. Mum's pendant feels heavier when I put it on and adjusting the chain doesn't help, but it's safer to keep it close. Could Gran have done the same? Maybe she hid the pendant in her favourite coat so no one else could find it. Or it could have been an accident, as Raquel suggested. Gran may have stitched up the lining without realising it had fallen through. Will she remember anything about the necklace? It's tricky – I have so many questions, but she could get upset.

Alex looks like he's pondering his own problems when I walk into the bedroom, wrapped in towels. He's pacing up and down in his boxers, muttering to himself.

'Alex?'

He spins around, hiding something behind his back.

'What's wrong? Has something happened?'

He lurches towards me, collapsing at my feet.

'Tell me. You're scaring me!'

'I'm sorry. This was supposed to happen on Hammersmith Bridge.'

My stomach drops; the wind is knocked out of my lungs. I feel like I'm falling from a fairground ride, clutching at air.

'W-w-what? No, you're wrong. I couldn't let you die. That didn't have to happen.'

His expression clouds over. 'Erm . . . why do you think I'm about to kick the bucket?'

'Sorry, that was another dream,' I say, improvising hurriedly. 'What are *you* talking about?'

He whips out something from behind his back. Everything happens in slow motion. He flicks open the small, black velvet box, revealing a sparkling diamond ring. He plucks it out. Sunlight streams through the curtains and catches the gemstone, creating shimmering, fractured rainbows on the wall.

'I wanted to propose on the bridge, but I can't wait any longer. I don't want to waste a single second without saying this.' He clears his throat. 'Julia Hockney, long lost descendent of David Hockney, lover of my favourite word discombobulated and the love of my life, will you make me the happiest man alive by marrying me?'

124

14

MONDAY, MAY 13, 2024

'You won't believe what's happened – Alex has proposed!'

I'd dialled Vicky's number as soon as I emerged onto Kensington High Street. I frown as I spot an unfamiliar shop and look around. I've had a major brain blip and turned left out of the tube station instead of right. I double back, frowning.

'I said yes.'

'Of course you did!' she replies.

'You don't think it's too soon? That I've rushed into things like I did with . . .' I stop myself in time before letting slip Ed's name. 'This was sudden. It took me by surprise.'

'Really?'

'I woke up and everything felt different. Alex had planned to cook pancakes and . . .'

A young cyclist in a high-vis vest pedals down the road. I catch a flicker of recognition in the girl's blue eyes. It's the teenager who almost flattened me in Kensington Gardens. She slows down as she passes.

'What are you doing *here*?' she shouts.

I'm walking to work, obviously. What is her problem?

I spin around as the realisation dawns. She shouldn't be able to remember me; we haven't met in this life. Have we? I scan the traffic, but she must have turned off the high street. Even though I can't see her, my neck tingles. It feels like I'm being watched.

'And what?' Vicky says impatiently.

I was about to admit I've slept with Alex on a first date, but this isn't true. We've spent the whole year together.

'I was asking whether you think I've jumped into this relationship too quickly? You know – asking him to move in, getting engaged . . .'

'It's been twelve months! It was obvious to everyone from the start this relationship was different – that it would go all the way. You and Alex are meant for each other.'

'You could see that?'

'Erm, hello? I'm not totally stupid, whatever you might think.'

'No, of course not,' I say quickly. 'I'm being silly. I woke up this morning feeling weird and confused. You know what it's like with my dreams. They throw me out of kilter.'

'Yeah. You talk about them *all the time*.'

Is there an edge in her voice, or am I imagining it?

'Anyway . . .'

She sighs heavily. 'Tell me about the proposal. How did he do it?'

'He got down on one knee in the bedroom. It felt natural and right – much better than his original idea to propose on Hammersmith Bridge.'

'You always say that bridge is the most romantic place on earth because of your grandparents' story.'

I wince. I can't explain I now associate it with Alex drowning.

'But it sounds fantastic either way,' she says hastily. 'Many congratulations. Have you decided who's going to be your chief bridesmaid?'

'You! Who else would I ask?'

The line falls silent.

'Vicky? Are you still there?'

'That sounds great, but don't turn into a Bridezilla and decide the bridesmaids should look hideous in baby pink or lime green to make sure you're not outshone.'

I rub my brow. Vicky is decidedly off. I must have caught her on a bad day.

'I promise, I'll choose colours that suit you. *We'll* choose the dresses together.'

'Can't wait.'

Vicky sounds anything but excited about my upcoming wedding. My chest tightens and a buzzing noise in my ears grows louder. This should be one of the happiest days of my life, but I feel weightless. I grab hold of a lamp post to ground me, afraid to let go in case I float away, far above the street and over the shops, like an untethered child's balloon. No one else will get involved with my wedding preparations. I can't ask my mum for help; I have no idea where she is. She won't come to the dress fittings or beg me to go shopping for her outfit. She won't join the hen party, the rehearsal, or attend on the big day. Gran might not be well enough to come. No proud dad will walk me down the aisle, and my chief bridesmaid is turning passive aggression into a performance art.

I blink rapidly, forcing back the tears, as I continue walking. 'We'll have an incredible hen night. It'll be like old times.'

'Sure,' she says noncommittally. 'What's the ring like?'

I examine my finger, trying to remember what I've done in the last twelve months to upset her. The old Vicky would have been screaming with excitement and reeling off ideas for a debauched hen weekend.

'Alex said it belonged to his grandmother – it's a gorgeous diamond in a Victorian gold setting. He's engraved the underside of the band with our initials and the words: "Leap of Faith".'

'God, that's romantic! A man who wants commitment and babies – you must feel like you've won the lottery.'

Alex wants babies?

My cheeks flush with excitement. I want children, and they were out of the question with Ed. But then it hits me – Gran and Mum will miss this too. I'll become a mother without their support and have no one to ask for advice. Our son or daughter will miss out on having a grandmother, and their great-grandmother may never remember their name. I'm struggling to come up with a reply and an awkward silence grows between us.

'How are things with you anyway?' I say finally. 'What's happening in that department? You know – men, commitment . . .'

My voice trails away. I'm not sure if she's with Giles.

'You sound like an elderly aunt querying my lack of love life.'

'Sorry, becoming a soon-to-be-married woman means I've prematurely aged. Any shagging I should know about?'

'Lots, obviously.'

'That's great!'

'You didn't think so before. It's with Chris, the junior doctor I was telling you about. It's nothing serious – just a bit of fun.'

I hesitate. 'Sure.'

But what about your 'no work romances' rule?

'I can hear the disapproval in your voice.'

'I think it's the crappy mobile reception on the high street.'

'Stop bullshitting me, Julia. I know you hate that I'm seeing him, but he says his relationship has gone stale – all the spark has gone.'

'He's in a relationship?'

'You've made your thoughts clear on that subject already,' she says testily. 'But they're more like brother and sister than boyfriend and girlfriend. He'll break up with her when the time's right, but she's going through stuff at the moment. Her mum is sick.'

They're more like brother and sister.

Her words sting like a sharp slap. Vicky had assumed that about my relationship with Ed. *He* was probably telling Miranda on the phone that night he was waiting until the right time to end things with me. But Vicky had been appalled he might be cheating. She'd pushed me to confront him and expose his affair, yet in this scenario, *she's* the other woman.

'Why doesn't he finish with his girlfriend if it's so bad? Instead of doing the dirty on her and stringing you along.'

'I'm perfectly happy, thank you. And for your information, I'm not being strung along. I'm having fun.'

'And his girlfriend?'

'Jesus, you can be such a sanctimonious . . .' Her voice trails off. 'We can't all have the picture-perfect relationship, like you and Alex – Mr and Mrs Smug.'

Ouch!

I'm about to hit back but clamp my mouth shut. I should cut her some slack. It must be hard seeing me happy after Giles broke her heart. That must be why she's acting out of character.

'I hate to bring this up, but Giles . . . ?'

'He still won't take my calls.'

'Oh.'

'There's the judgement, Mrs Smug. Rubbing it in.'

'It's only a question!'

'Look, Julia,' she growls. 'I know I fucked up with him. But there's no point raking over it. I've apologised to you and Alex repeatedly.'

'For what?' I blurt out.

'Sure, have your pound of flesh.' She speaks slowly and in a monotone voice. 'I'm sorry I had a one-night stand with Samira's boyfriend. It was just sex – it meant nothing to me or Hamish. I'm even more sorry that Giles had to find out. He never had to know. But I have you and Alex to thank for that, don't I?'

Inside the *Gazette* building, I sink to my heels in the elevator, my mind whirring. Our phone conversation ended abruptly on the street before I swiped myself in. My best friend thinks I'm a smug, judgmental bitch and she may be right. It sucks that she cheated on Giles and broke up Samira's relationship with Hamish. It's also rubbish that she's currently hooking up with someone else who has a girlfriend. Worse still, this is my fault. If I hadn't gone back and got together with Alex, she wouldn't have slept with Hamish and gone on to break her rule about dating co-workers. *Attached colleagues.* I'm not sure if I like the new Vicky much and the feeling appears to be mutual. How can I fix this? We've known each other for years; our relationship must be salvageable. I'll ask her out for a drink to talk things through.

The lift pings. I stand shakily and pause outside the elevator; this must be what it feels like stepping off a long-haul flight. Slowly, I make my way through the empty, brightly lit labyrinth of corridors. I open the door to the archives, but close it, thinking I've made a mistake. I check the number above the handle. *312b.* I step inside and freeze. Jeremy's laptop has vanished, along with the table, chairs and printer. The shelves are completely bare and dozens of black bin bags and cardboard boxes are scattered across the floor. I catch sight of a red book peeping from the top of one of the sacks. Delving inside, I find albums from the 1940s and 50s. These books should have been sent to a specialist restoration company in Oxfordshire. All the cuttings have been dumped too, even though some of the envelopes aren't water damaged. Why hasn't Jeremy attempted to save anything? It's all being thrown away!

My phone vibrates with a message from Merv:

Where are you? Rod = ballistic.

He's added an emoji of a bomb. This looks worse than usual.

I hurry through the corridors, brushing my hand along the walls for support, and wait for the elevator. Inside, I hammer on the button. The doors close, the lift rises and more uncomfortable memories bubble to the surface:

My attempts to break into journalism are going nowhere. I gave Rod a list of ideas for features and in-depth investigations I'm keen to research, but he rejected all of them. Weeks later, I spotted at least three of my pitches in the paper, written by staff journalists. Rod laughed when I asked why he hadn't commissioned me to write the pieces.

My relationship with Vicky has never been worse. She hooked up with Samira's boyfriend after the first anniversary party for the opening of Hidden Things. Samira had stayed behind to clear up, and Vicky and Hamish went home together. Alex was furious and texted Giles, telling him what had happened. Giles dumped Vicky and she hasn't forgiven either of us. She's been partying wildly ever since to try to forget her devastation at losing Giles.

Alex has spent months painting my portrait in his studio and admitted it was finished in February. I'd secretly hoped he was holding it back as an anniversary present, but we couldn't celebrate at the weekend. I had to work both days and didn't have time to visit Gran.

I press myself against the wall of the lift. It's reassuringly solid, whereas everything else is shifting tectonic-plate-style beneath my feet. My face blurs in the mirror, smudging out my features.

Who am I?

What else has this Julia Hockney been doing over the last twelve months?

I'm tracing over this version of my life with a pencil, trying to colour in the gaps. But some parts are untouched, the memories strange and unfriendly, refusing to be filled in.

I lurch out of the lift as the door opens. It feels like I'm entering another time zone; I'll need a million cups of coffee today. I push through the double doors, anxiously scanning the newsroom for familiar faces. Merv's desk of doom is visible on the skyline. His chair is empty, but his favourite brown corduroy jacket is slung on the back, and three mobiles are lined up next to the keyboard. Layla is in the corner instead of being in New York with her girlfriend. This could be ominous; I make a mental note not to ask if they're still together. New faces are dotted around. I grasp hold of my pendant, rubbing the stone. I could beat a hasty retreat and call in sick.

'There you are!' Rod hollers as he spots me lurking in Sleepy Hollow. 'Get a move on! This news list isn't going to write itself.'

I scurry across the room and throw my coat over my old chair, hoping it's still my seat. 'Sorry. I was in the archives.'

'What the fuck were you doing down there? It's business services' job to clear up that mess.'

I grab a pen and notepad from the desk and follow him into his bunker. He throws himself into the chair behind his desk, scanning the computer.

'Do you know where Jeremy is?' I ask.

'Who?'

Seriously? Jeremy has been at the *Gazette* for more than twenty years.

'The chief librarian. He should be trying to salvage the files and books in the archives, but it's all being thrown out.'

'Oh, him! The IT department took over the online library six months ago, which meant redundancies. He's long gone. Didn't you know that?'

I shake my head numbly. 'But the old cuttings . . . Someone needs to—'

'What *are* you on about, Julia? No one gives a flying fuck. Everything's digitised anyway. The archives' room will be redesignated after the refurb so there's no point shifting stuff to the new site.'

My mind is racing. Clearly, the entire newspaper group is still temporarily moving out while this building is revamped. But with Jeremy gone, no one is fighting to preserve the records and find a new storage facility.

'Let's crack on,' Rod says briskly. 'Pavel typed the early news list, but we're updating the next edition. The Night Prowler has struck again – his fifth attack in twelve months.'

'No!'

Rod stares at me. 'Pardon?'

'I mean, I thought the police had caught him?'

The Night Prowler had been arrested before I travelled into the past. He couldn't hurt anyone else.

'Hardly! The detectives are a bunch of muppets. They don't have a clue. Merv says a new team could be brought in to review the investigation. He broke into another house last night and beat an eighty-eight-year-old woman in Hanwell. She's in a coma in ICU and may not pull through.'

'Oh God.' My throat constricts.

'Yeah, terrible. We'll list it as "Pensioner fights for life after Night Prowler attacks twice in four days".' He looks up from his computer. 'Are you going to write down the list line or are you hoping it will magically appear by osmosis?'

Shakily, I make shorthand notes in my pad. My fingers feel numb. A dull murkiness builds menacingly behind my eyelids. I long to close them.

'Next: "Families tell of sorrow after horror train crash on Barnes level crossing".' He hammers on his keyboard. 'We have pics of victims from Twitter. We're approaching the families for interviews and permission to use the photos.'

The pen slips from my hand. I reach down to pick it up, and almost slide off the chair.

The Barnes train crash.

I remember the story Merv was tapping out when he called me up to talk about the old Night Prowler cuttings, but that was a near miss on the level crossing. A have-a-go-hero had pushed a broken-down car off the track, avoiding a major disaster.

'The victims? I thought—'

'Police may start to formally release identities of dead passengers later. The relatives' stories will make a spread inside, as well as on the front. Features are doing a piece on the country's worst ever fatal train crashes – Lewisham etc.'

Fatal train crash. Dead passengers.

I cough to disguise the gagging noise in my throat. 'How many . . . died?'

'Good point. Add that to the list. We have a new tally since Friday morning: two more died in hospital over the weekend so it's 95 dead and 121 seriously injured. We'll change the list line to: "Horror for families with almost one hundred dead in England's worst train crash for 67 years".'

The room spins. My jaw slackens. I feel my body slump in the chair as blackness cascades behind my eyelids.

'For fuck's sake, Julia! You don't have time for a nap. We have work to do!'

I don't try to fight my sleep attack. I want to escape from all the pain and destruction I've caused.

I let go.

I fall into a gloomy, pitiless abyss.

15

MONDAY, MAY 13, 2024

My chest continues to ache with guilt after waking up in the empty bunker half an hour ago. I had to endure the walk of shame over to the news desk, where Rod glared furiously at me before resuming typing. After ten excruciating minutes sat in silence opposite him, he loudly announced I should go to the archives and check for salvageable records. 'Learning to catalogue and preserve files will be a useful experience for you,' he said.

I fled as he muttered darkly about me to the copy taster. I managed to make it to the bathroom before bursting into tears over the lives lost in the train crash. I don't need to check my compact to know my eyes are puffy from crying, my cheeks branded scarlet. I'm desperate to avoid the newsroom for the rest of the day, but I must speak to Merv.

'I hear you're in the doghouse.' He raises an eyebrow as I hurry towards his desk. 'How are you holding up? You look awful. I mean that in a non-sexist way – I attended last week's gender awareness and white male privilege workshop and passed with flying colours.'

'Rod will never admit it officially, but he's punishing me for falling asleep. I overheard him say that if I'm bothered about yesterday's news, I can sort through all the old records myself.'

'Someone needs to! I keep telling the managing editor's office everything must be saved because the digital library only goes back to—'

'2006 – the old paper cutting files date back much further.'

Merv nods. 'Rod and the other editors will never understand that the past matters – it's where the answers to most mysteries can be found.'

My hands tremble as I pick up the first edition from his desk. Three days after the fatal crash in Barnes, the front page is still dominated by photos of the wreckage. The story describes how the train hit a pensioner's broken-down car on the level crossing at speed.

'Talking of mysteries, why didn't the train stop in time?'

'No one knows,' he replies. 'It's possible the signals were faulty so the driver wasn't alerted to the obstruction, but South Western's investigation will take months.'

'Didn't anyone try to move the car from the tracks?'

'A passer-by attempted to push it off on her own, according to a witness. Salim's trying to track her down, but she may be among the fatalities, along with the elderly motorist. I haven't heard the latest though. Rakesh is working on it with Salim today. Rod, in his infinite wisdom, has reassigned me to another story.'

I wipe my watery eyes with the back of my hand.

'Is this personal for you?' Merv asks gently. 'Did you have a friend on board?'

'No, but I can't stop thinking, what if the car had been pushed out of the way?'

'You'll drive yourself mad wondering "what if?". There's nothing anyone can do now, apart from investigate signal errors and make sure something like this never happens again.' He puffs out his chest. 'God, I sound like an over-paid press officer. I should quit and find myself a cushy £150,000 salary in return for annoying reporters, and not answering my mobile after 5 p.m.'

I ignore his usual jab at non-journalists.

'Here's another "what if?" Do you know if there was a missed opportunity to catch the Night Prowler in Clapham Junction last week?'

'Not that I'm aware of – he broke into that house on Almeric Road and beat up a fifty-two-year-old lady, but she didn't manage to call the police until after he'd fled. Why? Have you heard something different?'

I chew the inside of my mouth. In my previous life, the police had received an anonymous tip-off, and the Night Prowler was arrested at this address on May 9, *before* he assaulted the woman. Her house was close to Ed's work dinner. But because the serial burglar wasn't apprehended that evening, he was free to strike days later.

'I just thought someone might have tried to raise the alarm,' I say feebly.

'I can put a call into the Met press office and check. I'll let you know.'

'Are you writing a feature about the Night Prowler?'

'Not yet. I'll only delve into this properly when they catch the guy. He's escalating – two attacks within four days. And he's getting more violent. His latest victim is unlikely to pull through.'

The cogs in my brain whir, trying to keep up. In this scenario, Merv hasn't asked for the cuttings file from the archives because the Night Prowler is at large, and I haven't offered him a peek at Gran's clippings. That's why I'm storing them at the bottom of my wardrobe.

'Why the interest if you don't mind me asking?' he asks.

'Gran's obsessed with the case. She's collecting stories about the Night Prowler.'

'Damn, that's dark. Can't you get her hooked on something else? Wasn't she into Brad Pitt a while back?'

'Yep, and Paul Rudd.' I steal a glance at the news desk. 'I'd better go before Rod sees me.'

'Catch you later,' he says as I walk away. 'Hey, hold on a sec. While you're in the archives, could you keep an eye out for any files on Hammersmith Bridge before they're binned? I want to look up historic drownings.'

My heart thuds loudly as I return to his desk.

'Sure, but why?'

A heavy feeling grows in my stomach as I wait for his answer.

'Just as background detail about deaths linked to that bridge. We're expecting the verdict soon from the inquest into the deaths of Andrew Marshall and his sons, Daniel and Oliver.'

'The names don't ring a bell, sorry.'

He gives me an odd look. 'Haven't you read any of the inquest coverage in the last few weeks?'

'I've been distracted with my gran.' That's a half-truth.

'Sorry.' He shuffles his papers. 'Do you remember the tragedy on the bridge this time last year?'

My heart beats furiously. 'Did a guy pull a married woman into the water when she tried to break up with him?'

'Exactly! Louise Marshall and Charles Fielding. They both drowned in the Thames.'

'No one managed to save them?'

'Nah, sad story. Louise's husband, Andrew, never recovered from her death and, presumably, learning about her infidelity. He drank heavily, lost his job, and spiralled.'

I grab the side of his desk as the newsroom pitches like an ancient, unseaworthy boat, throwing me off balance.

'Four months later, he downed a bottle of vodka and fell asleep with a lit cigarette, which set fire to the sofa. He died in the blaze in

Southall. His ten-year-old and eight-year-old sons died of smoke inhalation in an upstairs bedroom before firefighters could rescue them.'

He pulls out a newspaper from beneath his stack, causing a mini-earthquake, and shoves it towards me.

'Daniel and Oliver Marshall, bless 'em.'

Two little boys in Arsenal football strips stare back, with gap-toothed smiles. Their brown eyes twinkle mischievously. The bigger child has an arm around his brother, as if he wants to protect him. *From me.*

I clamp my hand to my mouth, attempting to fight back the rising bile.

'Julia? Are you feeling alright?'

I sprint across the newsroom and burst through the doors but don't reach the bathroom in time. Vomit spatters onto the carpet outside the elevators. I can't stop. I can't breathe. I need to feel fresh air on my face.

Hammering on the lift button, I cling onto Mum's pendant like a lifebuoy, the only thing that will stop me from sinking.

What have I done?

The doors open and I throw myself inside. The walls slide away beneath my fingers. My diamond ring glitters reproachfully as my knees buckle. I've been horrendously selfish. I'd wanted to save Alex and have a fairytale ending, but I'd never stopped to consider the consequences for others. Guilt sears through my body, draining away all the happiness and excitement from his proposal.

One thought goes round and round my head in a torturous loop:

Because of me, dozens of people have suffered and been horrifically injured.

Almost a hundred men, women and children have lost their lives.

I've single-handedly killed them all.

16

Monday, May 13, 2024

'I don't understand why you feel guilty,' Alex insists. 'None of this is your fault.'

I tap the code into the keypad outside the front door at Gran's nursing home while he uses his body to shield me from the driving rain. Predictably, the numbers have changed. As the umbrella blows inside out, I hammer out a second sequence and a third.

'Dammit!' I slam my hand against the panel.

'Hey, don't you remember the *Terminator* movies? The machines take revenge on humans.'

He pulls me towards him, and I bury my face into his damp coat. I've tried, *very badly,* to explain how it feels wrong to be happy about our engagement when terrible things have happened to others: the Night Prowler has struck again, the Marshall family has been wiped out and hundreds of train passengers have been killed or badly injured.

'It doesn't seem right to celebrate when other people are suffering.' I gaze miserably at him. 'I can't stop thinking what if the police had caught the Night Prowler last week, and a passer-by *had* managed to push the car off the level crossing?' I bite my lip. 'I'm also torturing myself about Louise Marshall. If someone had dived into the Thames and saved her last year, her little boys and husband would still be alive.'

His brow furrows. 'But that's out of your control. There's nothing you can do about any of it.'

I can't tell him the truth. I can scarcely comprehend any of this myself – it'll make no sense whatsoever to him. I remember our discussions over the last year. We've talked about everything – our families, hopes and dreams, jobs, politics, religion, Alzheimer's, and global warming, to name a few topics. We've shared our grief at losing our parents; his mum died of breast cancer when he was six, and his dad passed away four years ago from a heart attack. We haven't held back any secrets until now. But I can never tell him what I've done to save his life; it would be too heavy a burden for anyone to bear. He probably wouldn't believe me anyway. I don't think anyone will.

'This is what I love about you – well, one of the many things,' he says. 'You're empathetic and care about other people. But you can't carry the weight of the world on your shoulders.'

'What if I don't have any choice? What if I have to?'

'In that case, you don't have to do it alone. I'll always be here for you.'

Tears spill down my cheeks.

'Hey!'

'I'm sorry for ruining everything.' My words escape through huge, juddering sobs. 'You've made all this effort – the painting, our engagement, coming here tonight. I don't deserve any of this. I never put you first.'

'Don't say that!' He scrutinises my face. 'You don't have to apologise for feeling low. I figured you'd have mixed emotions today.'

I gape at him. He *can't* know what's tearing me apart.

'You want to share our engagement with your mum. It must bring old emotions and memories to the surface. It does for me – not having my parents around to celebrate with us. It's okay for us both to be sad but happy – in fact, we're shappy.'

I raise an eyebrow.

'That's totally a word. If it isn't in the dictionary, it should be.'

The corners of my mouth curl upwards.

'I'm trying to think of the word for that – almost a smile,' he says. 'We can find a pocket of happiness despite what's happened to us and all the horrible things going on in the world.'

'Maybe.'

'*Definitely.* If anything, it shows us that life is precious. We have to make the most of everything while we can.'

'I worry it could be taken away like that.' My voice breaks as I click my fingers. 'I could lose it all. *Lose you.*'

'You're stuck with me, I'm afraid. I have the proof.' He holds up my hand and examines the engagement ring. 'It was a non-negotiable, non-returnable "yes" to spending the rest of your life with me. Didn't you read the small print in the invisible contract I drew up?'

I laugh through my tears.

'That's better. You sound happier about getting old with me and seeing my wrinkly bum, long nose hair and false teeth each morning. It'll be such a treat.'

'I am excited. This . . .' I cup his face in my hands. '*You* are the best thing that's ever happened to me, I swear.'

I stand on tiptoes and pull his head towards mine. Our lips lock. I feel him shiver as I rake my fingers through his hair, and he kisses me back deeply.

'Snogging in the rain is very *Four Weddings and a Funeral*,' he says, when we break apart. 'Your gran will love our re-enactment – if I leave out the part about cold water running down my neck.'

'And my bra.'

'We can check that out later, but let's get inside before we drown.' He presses the button and leans closer as the intercom crackles. 'Hey, Carole. It's your favourite visitors – Alex and Julia.' He winks at me. 'Please can you let us into Noah's Ark?'

The door sounds like a sigh as Alex pushes it open. I hesitate. What if turning back time has created a terrible chain of events here? What if I've made Gran suffer?

'This isn't a good idea. My head is throbbing, and I must look a state.'

Alex dabs beneath my eyes at the streaked mascara, while holding the door with his foot.

'Da-dah! More beautiful than a Whistler painting.'

'As if!' I grasp hold of my pendant. 'Gran gets more confused in the evenings. It might be a better idea to come back in the morning?'

I'm clutching at straws, but Alex is having none of it.

'She'll appreciate the visit – you didn't get to see her this weekend with work. It's important we tell her our news tonight.'

I open my mouth to argue.

'Isn't she the first person you'd ring today if she didn't have Alzheimer's?' he asks.

'Of course.'

'She's still the most important person in your family. She should know about our engagement straightaway and share our good news. I've already told Zoe and the girls.'

I clear my throat. 'Gran is the *only* person left in my family – apart from you.'

'Until we find your mum. And we will, I promise. We won't stop searching for her.'

The determined look in his eyes fills me with fresh hope. Alex could succeed where I've failed in the past. I remember that despite the fact we're budgeting carefully to keep on top of mounting bills, he was the one who suggested hiring the private investigator in Southall.

'You're right. I want to share this, *us,* with Gran.'

I take a deep breath and follow him inside. Carole looms, her brows knitted together, as we step into the foyer.

'You're dripping water everywhere!'

I giggle. Some things haven't changed – Carole is *always* critical.

'Sorry.' Alex props up the umbrella in the corner and gives her a dazzling smile. It's wasted on Carole, who glowers back and turns to me.

'This isn't the best timing – we're clearing away dinner. Your gran refused to eat and is unsettled. It might be better to come back tomorrow when she's less tired?'

I'm ready to retreat, but Alex steps closer.

'We won't be long, I promise. We want to share our good news. We're engaged.' He points at my finger.

Carole's face almost cracks into a smile. 'Congratulations. But I want to warn you—'

'That Julia snores and overcooks pasta? I know, but I love her anyway.'

I jab him playfully in the ribs.

'Let's talk and walk. I'm heading in that direction.' She leads us away from reception. 'As I was saying, I should flag that Sylvia is upset about Raquel. You're both aware how attached she is to her.'

My stomach shifts queasily. Have I inadvertently hurt Raquel too?

'What's happened?' Alex notices I've fallen behind and doubles back. He gently propels me forwards.

'You haven't heard?' She frowns, waiting for us to catch up. 'Raquel's taking personal time – her boyfriend, Sergio, was injured in the Barnes train crash. He's expected to pull through but faces a lengthy rehabilitation – broken legs, pelvis, and ribs.'

'Oh God.' I cover my mouth with my hands. 'I'm sorry.'

Alex puts an arm around my waist. My knees weaken. I want to sit down, but we've passed the seating area.

Carole sighs deeply. 'We've arranged an agency replacement at short notice, but Raquel's unexpected absence has hit many of the residents hard. They don't like change. Neither do I, but we're doing our best to amend the rota.'

'That's good of you,' Alex says tightly. 'Under the circumstances.'

'Hmm.'

She fixes me with a steely look as if she somehow knows this is my fault, before turning her attention to Alex. I can't speak, but he's asking how Raquel is holding up, and whether we can send a card and flowers.

'We can't give out personal details, but we could forward something on if you wish,' she replies crisply.

Alex keeps a tight hold of my hand as we follow her. He keeps glancing at me, but I can't meet his gaze. I'm trying hard not to cry. We pass the familiar framed pictures; the décor is unchanged, along with the smell of disinfectant unsuccessfully masked by a pine air freshener. I recognise a few of the residents who drift past aimlessly.

Carole stops, smoothing her hair. She removes an out-of-date flyer about a family picnic in the grounds from the noticeboard opposite Gran's room and rearranges wayward drawing pins into a neat, straight line.

'Please prepare yourselves for how difficult this is for her. She may not be able to react to your news in the way you would wish.' She pauses. 'I'll speak to you another time about damage to the newspapers in the day room.'

She gives a curt nod and stalks off, without waiting for a reply.

'Ready?' Alex asks.

My mind screams: *No!*

I want to bury my face in his chest. He knocks and swings open the door. Hundreds of newspaper cuttings flutter like butterflies across the carpet in the draught. Gran's purple scissors sit alongside them. More clippings are stuck across the far wall and cover the dresser.

'She's been busy,' Alex remarks. 'I suppose no one's keeping her hobby in check with Raquel off work. We could take it up with Carole?'

'No way – she'll confiscate Gran's scissors.'

'Not necessarily.'

I know she will. I spot a few headlines about the Night Prowler among the newspaper scraps, but they're mostly about the train crash, the deaths of the Marshall family and the bridge tragedy last year. Cold dread washes over me. Why is Gran interested in *these* stories? It's freaky. And worrying.

On the bedside table are different framed photos: Alex and me on Hammersmith Bridge, Gramps holding Mum as a child along with her soft toy, and the picture of Mum and me in Gran's old back garden. The images of Ed, the day trip to Brighton Beach and the baby pic with Mum, Gran and Aunt Rose have vanished.

Gran is standing in front of the full-length mirror by the wardrobe, dressed in her favourite lilac trousers and top. Her hair is tightly curled, the way it used to look when the hairdresser visited, and her nails are neatly filed and painted shocking pink.

'Hello, Sylvia!' Alex says brightly.

She doesn't turn around and speaks animatedly into the glass.

'I'm worried too, but Marianne promised to come back.' Her reflection smiles and nods. 'The waiting is terribly hard, and tough for Julia. I can't tell her. How can she possibly understand when she's just a child? Impossible!'

'Gran? It's us.' My voice comes out in a croak. 'What was it you didn't think I'd understand? That Mum had left us?'

Her gaze remains fixed on the mirror. 'What did you say your name is?' She waits patiently. 'I didn't catch that, sorry. Are you friends with Marianne? Did she tell you where she's going? She should be back soon.'

'There's no one there, Gran,' I say, in a small voice. 'That's you.'

'No, this lady stopped by our house for a chat, which was nice of her. Who is she? I think she knows your mother.'

'She's called Sylvia too,' Alex says, before I can reply.

'The same as me? Oh my! What a funny coincidence.'

'Exactly! Isn't it a lovely name?'

I give him a warning look. I want to help Gran recognise herself, rather than go along with everything she believes to be true otherwise she'll drift further and further away from me.

She draws closer, taking Alex's hand in hers. 'You've a fine young man, like my Arthur. Kind too. I see it in your eyes. You're a keeper.'

'Thank you! I'm Julia's boyfriend. Well . . .' He looks at me expectantly.

I hold up my hand, pointing to my ring finger. 'We're engaged, Gran.'

She claps her hands to her face. 'Oh, how wonderful. A happy ending, like in the movies.'

'Yes, I'm incredibly lucky.' My voice cracks.

Confusion flickers across her eyes as she stares at Alex. She's trying to place him.

'You love Alex. We watch movies together, like *Sleepless in Seattle*, and he makes you laugh. Do you remember? Here's a picture of us.'

Something niggles at the back of my mind as I point at the framed photos, but I can't retrieve the memory.

'Yes, yes. I can't recall this lady's name.' She points at her reflection. 'Is she my next-door neighbour, Ivy Watkins?'

'That's Sylvia,' Alex prompts.

'Yes, you told me,' she says, nodding. 'I remember now. But where did Ed go? Is he watching football in the day room?' She shudders. 'I don't like him much, Julia. What an idiot! He sat on my glasses and never apologised. You can do much better than him.'

17

Monday, May 13, 2024

Breath catches in my throat as Gran pulls out the scraps of paper she made with Raquel from her pocket.

'I can't find his name. It was here the other day. Ed Slater, marketing manager and arsehole.'

Alex explodes into giggles.

'Gran!'

'He made quite the impression on her,' Alex whispers. 'How does she describe me?'

'I've no idea, but I don't understand . . .'

Alex has *definitely* heard of Ed. I'd mentioned him in the bar when we met, and we'd briefly discussed our previous relationships shortly after we started dating. But Gran shouldn't have memories of Ed because we never met on the tube. He hasn't sat on her glasses or ignored her to watch a West Ham match on his phone.

Perhaps I referred to him in passing over the last year, along with these news stories, and they stuck. Her brain is like a sieve, which keeps strange and trivial details, while more important recollections slip away, lost forever.

'Let me have a look.' I scoop up the notes from her upturned palm and unfold them.

Carole, duty manager. Dragon.

Raquel, my favourite carer.

Julia Hockney, beloved granddaughter, and journalist at the Gazette.

Alex Martin, talented artist, and the love of Julia's life.

My heart aches. Raquel has drawn a heart next to his name. Gran loves him. She never had such strong feelings for Ed.

'Why don't you say goodbye to your friend and sit down?' Alex suggests. 'We can tell you all about our wedding plans. Julia wants something small and intimate, but I may turn into a Groomzilla. I want the big day!'

My heart constricts as she waves at her reflection and slowly makes her way to the chair. Alex helps her, rearranging the cushions behind her back.

'Look, Gran. Isn't the ring pretty?' My hand shakes as I hold it up.

Her shoulders droop and she stares at the floor. 'Where's Raquel? Will she be here soon? She said she'd help me get everything in order.'

'She can't come today, sorry,' Alex says.

Gran rolls her eyes. 'What fucking use is she?'

I inhale sharply. She never speaks badly of Raquel.

'We can help.' Alex takes hold of her hand, stroking the papery skin. Her veins stick out like plump, green caterpillars, but he doesn't recoil the way Ed used to whenever he was forced to touch her. 'What should we do?'

151

'Oh, I don't know where to start with all this!' She jerks her head at the carpet. 'Such a mess. I can't make head or tail of anything.'

'Shall I have a sort through?'

Alex pretends he hasn't heard her muttered obscenities and kneels, picking up a handful of cuttings about the Barnes train crash.

'I'll put all the clippings about the accident together. Is that alright?'

She squints at his hand. 'Get off them! They don't belong to you.'

'Alex is trying to help,' I say reassuringly.

'He might swap them.' She drums her fingers on the side of the chair, sighing with irritation. 'I have to keep watch. Make sure they don't change again.'

My heart skips a beat. 'What do you mean, *change*?'

She leans forward in her chair, scowling. 'Young man, what did you do with the other cuttings? Where did you hide them?'

'What are you looking for in particular?' Alex sits back on his heels, surveying the scraps of newspaper. 'I'll try to find it.'

'I want to read the story about the Night Prowler arrest.'

My heartbeat quickens.

'I'm not sure . . .' Alex glances at me.

'The police haven't caught him yet,' I say shakily.

'Don't be an idiot! Yes, they have. I showed the cutting to Raquel the other day. We both said it was a relief. I knew Ivy would be ecstatic. She's been so worried about him returning. I remember telling Raquel this would finally put Ivy's mind at rest.'

Ants crawl beneath my skin. How is this happening? She shouldn't be able to recall meeting Ed or the capture of the Night Prowler. Neither of those events has happened in this life. Alex shuffles the papers and doesn't notice I'm hanging onto the chair, afraid my knees will give way.

'I'll tidy up and Raquel can help you sort them into piles when she gets back,' he says gently. 'Hopefully, her boyfriend recovers quickly. He was lucky to survive the train crash.'

Gran's eyes narrow. 'That's another thing! I keep telling everyone it didn't happen, but no one listens. They say I'm being silly and get upset.'

'You're not silly,' he insists. 'Unfortunately, a lot of people died and were injured, but Sergio is recovering in hospital. We're sending flowers and a card – we'll add your name.'

She bursts into tears. 'I don't understand! Did someone change everything while I was asleep? Did they move my pictures around?' She jabs an accusing finger at her bedside table. 'Who put them there? Was it you, young man?'

'No,' Alex replies softly.

My cheeks grow hotter. He doesn't appear to have any lingering, residual memories of what originally happened on Hammersmith Bridge, not even a niggling bad feeling, otherwise he wouldn't have considered proposing on it. Yet Gran has somehow retained shattered pieces from my previous life.

I put my arm around her. 'Don't worry. I'm going to fix this, I promise.'

'Can you find Raquel?'

'I'll see what I can do.' Alex hauls himself to his feet. 'I'll also rustle up some cups of tea and custard creams.'

'Oooh, thank you, young man!' Gran smiles gratefully.

She waits until he's left the room, before looking at me blankly. 'Who was that? Does he work here?'

'No, that's Alex, my boyfriend.' I kiss her forehead. 'I mean my fiancé.'

The word feels strange yet wonderful on my tongue.

I squeeze her hand. 'I'm sorry I've confused you. I never meant to hurt anyone. I had no idea it would turn out badly.'

153

She sighs deeply. 'Yes, you're right. It's been a bad day. Raquel didn't help and we never had apple crumble and custard for pudding. Hopefully, tomorrow.'

'Fingers crossed.' I squat beside her and pull out my pendant from beneath my cardigan. 'Isn't this necklace lovely? Do you remember Mum wearing it when I was little?'

Her gaze flickers around the room as if she's following an invisible fly.

'Look! It's around her neck in that picture.' I point to the photo on the bedside table. 'I was a little girl. We were in your back garden in Chiswick.'

'Did Rose tell you that? She likes making mischief and can't sit still. She flits about all over the place.'

'Please, Gran? This isn't about your sister. I'm trying to figure out what's going on.'

She turns her head and focuses on me. A rapturous smile spreads across her face.

'Oh my! You came back, Marianne. I knew you would. You haven't changed. You're beautiful.' She strokes my cheek.

My heart sinks. 'No. It's me, Julia. Your granddaughter.'

Her hand falls away.

'Oh, silly me! Where did Marianne go? She was here a minute ago, I'm sure of it. Stood right there.' She points to the centre of the room. 'Have you seen her?'

I shake my head. 'I need your help. I think you might be the only person who knows what's happening to me.' I hold out the pendant again. 'Can you tell me anything about this?'

Her bottom lip quivers but she doesn't reply.

'Do you know what it can do? Did Mum? She wore this necklace and was struggling with her narcolepsy, like me.' I twirl the stone, making it glint mischievously under the light. 'You once said some Hockney women see things differently to other people. What did you mean? You never explained.'

Gran's gaze remains fixed on the carpet.

'You're right,' I tell her. 'The pictures on your bedside table weren't there when I visited you *with Ed*. You don't have a piece of paper with his name, because you've never met him in this life. The newspaper cuttings are all different. I don't understand exactly how it's happened, but it's something to do with my narcolepsy and this pendant. You gave it me for my birthday.'

I stare at her. I need to say this out loud. Someone must hear my confession even if they don't understand my words.

'The train crash didn't happen originally, the Night Prowler was arrested, and Louise Marshall's sons didn't suffer fatal smoke inhalation because . . .' I take a deep breath. 'Alex Martin, *my Alex* died, on Hammersmith Bridge a year ago. I went back in time, saved his life and changed everything. But I never realised there would be terrible repercussions for other people in the present day.'

Gran breathes out heavily, sinking deeper into the armchair. I try one last time.

'Please tell me about Mum's necklace. The day you gave it me, you said she was searching for it. Was that before she set off for Scotland?'

'No, silly!' she snaps. 'Marianne dropped it out of the carriage window before her train left. I know I put it in my pocket. Stop confusing me. Stop changing things!'

'I'm sorry. Of course, you're right. We found the pendant in your coat. But I need you to explain something. You told me I would inherit something when I was twenty-five – was that the necklace?'

'Stop it, stop it!' she wails, clamping her hands over her ears.

'Gran—'

'You claimed you wouldn't stay long, Marianne. You promised me! What should I tell Julia? I don't know what to do. Someone help me! Help!'

Oh God. I've gone too far. I shouldn't have pushed her.

'I'm sorry!'

I try to embrace her, but she fights me off as Alex returns, accompanied by one of the carers pushing a tea trolley. A look of terror crosses Gran's face as she spots him.

'Get away from me! Leave me the fuck alone!'

'Don't worry, Sylvia,' the uniformed woman says. 'I've brought your favourite biscuits.'

Gran jabs an accusing finger at Alex. 'YOU'RE DEAD!'

He shakes his head in bewilderment.

The carer calmly taps the button by the door as Gran sobs loudly.

'It's better if you both leave while we calm her down,' she says.

Every breath hurts as I stumble towards Alex.

'I feel terrible. I upset her by asking about Mum.'

'Don't blame yourself,' the woman insists. 'It's the meds. We need to change them.'

Two colleagues arrive and I recognise Bernie, one of the nurses.

'Come on, Sylvia,' he says cheerfully. 'How about TV and a hot chocolate before bed? You like that.'

'I hate sodding hot chocolate. I want to see Rose! She'll help me find Marianne.'

'Let's go.' Alex helps me out of her room.

I notice a soft toy hanging from the noticeboard on the opposite wall, a pin stuck through its yellow mane, and a message saying a guest left it behind earlier today. Another new note has appeared alongside it:

The weekly hairdresser and nail technician visits have been cancelled until further notice. Also, apologies for the missing newspapers from the day room. We are reassessing continuation of this service due to regular damage caused to editions. Regards, Carole.

I rip off the piece of paper and throw it on the floor.

'I shouldn't have done any of this. It's all my fault.'

'It's not,' Alex insists.

I can barely hear him, scarcely walk, as he steers me to reception. My eyes are blurry with tears.

A crying child runs towards us, but I don't register her face. All I see are Daniel and Oliver Marshall, begging for their lives, the photos of the dead train passengers and the headlines about the Night Prowler's latest victim.

At the end of the corridor, Gran's indignant voice rings out.

'I'm telling the truth! Alex shouldn't be here. HE'S DEAD!'

18

Monday, May 13, 2024

Electric blues, turquoises, burnt oranges and mauves blur and merge, creating a whirlpool of pain and deceit. I blink and the colours slink away, re-forming into the diamonds that make up the painting of my face on the wall. But they no longer piece together seamlessly. Some are disjointed, jostling uncomfortably next to neighbouring shapes, sensing they don't belong.

Nothing fits because of me.

Gran is horribly confused and unhappy; people are dead and injured. I've ripped lives apart to be with Alex. I fiddle with my engagement ring; it winks complicity under the light and provides no comfort.

'Here you go. Sit down. This should help.'

Alex holds up two glasses containing a dark liquid as I sink onto the sofa. My legs are made of granite; my eyelids droop. The urge to sleep is sudden and brutal. His voice sounds unfamiliar, echoing from a faraway place.

'I found this in the cooking cupboard. I think I tried to make a tropical rum trifle circa 2016. I'm not sure what it's like but . . .'

My hand reaches out to take the glass. It flops down onto the cushion.

Dark clouds gather. Shadowy figures loom, poised to grab me.

My eyelids flutter.
The shutters close.

I'm falling from a huge height and plunge into dark, icy water. A faint light hovers at the surface. A hand stretches towards me . . . It yanks me out and throws me o   nto a dark landing inside a seemingly deserted house. But I spot a man hiding in the shadows, watching me. His knife shines malevolently as I run for the stairs.

My head jerks forwards. My eyelids spring open. I'm lying in Alex's arms on the sofa. He's scrolling through his phone. Memories of my dream cling on with long, bony fingers.

I sit up, rubbing my eyes. 'What year is it?'

'2024!'

'But . . . when? I mean how long was I asleep?'

He flicks a look at his watch. 'Twenty minutes. You were power napping.' He passes me one of the glasses from the floor. 'I thought we'd keep the champagne for another time.'

'What did you say this is?' I stare into the amber liquid.

'Rum. Consider it medicine after one hell of a day.'

I knock it back, gasping. My throat is on fire.

'Does it hit the spot?'

'It hit something,' I say hoarsely. 'And burnt a hole through it, like alien acid in Sigourney Weaver's spaceship.'

He tops up my glass and clinks it together with his. 'This isn't how I planned the evening, well your whole day, to pan out, but cheers.'

'Ditto.' I shudder as I take another gulp.

He nudges me. 'I'm sorry.'

'What on earth for? You're the only good thing about today.'

'Visiting your gran was a bad idea. I should have listened to you – Carole too. Those are words I never expected to say.' He takes a large slurp of his drink. 'I wish I could wind back time. I'd have swung by your office and told Rod he's a bullying dick, and I wouldn't have forced you to break the news to Sylvia tonight.'

'Would you though?'

'Tell Rod he's a total dick? Absolutely!'

'I mean rewind time and do things differently if you had the chance?' I call up a story about the Marshall family inquest on my mobile and scroll down to the picture of Louise Marshall's sons in their football strips. My heart contracts at the sight of their smiles, frozen in time.

'What if you could stop these little boys from dying? Or save the train passengers and the Night Prowler's victims – would you try?'

'Hold on a minute!' He slaps his pockets with his free hand as if he's searching for his wallet. 'I've misplaced my time machine. It was here a minute ago.' He sees I'm serious and takes my phone, reading the story about the brothers' deaths.

'In this time travel scenario, I'd wake up their dad before the sofa caught fire. Or I'd go back further and make sure the guy didn't fall asleep in the first place. Either way, I'd get the children out of the house.' He points to their red shirts, attempting to lighten the mood. 'I'd also warn them they have a lifetime of disappointment ahead for supporting the Gunners. What about you?'

'Sameish, apart from the football team advice!'

I'm playing along, but I trust Alex's opinion above anyone else's. I need to hear it.

'What if helping these boys meant you had to risk the life of someone you love? How do you choose who to rescue?'

He stretches his arms above his head, yawning. 'Isn't it late for philosophical questions? We're both knackered and wrung out after seeing your gran.'

'I'm serious, Alex. What would you do? Keep everything the same for you and your loved ones or risk losing it all to save the lives of total strangers?'

He falls silent, pondering my question. 'This reminds me of an awful game a teacher forced us to play during PSHE at high school. We had to pick six famous people and pretend they were in a hot air balloon plunging to the ground. It could only stay in the air if one person jumped or was thrown out.'

'Christ. Early childhood trauma – how did you turn out so well?'

'It's a miracle.' He squeezes my arm. 'We each had to argue our case for staying in the balloon basket – the contributions we'd made to history and how the world would be a lesser place if we died.'

'Who were you?'

'Adolf Hitler.'

I raise my eyebrows.

'I immediately jumped to save the others, and the whole world,' he explains hastily, 'but my teacher was cross I'd picked a murderous dictator. I was replaced by Nelson Mandela, which made everyone's choices far more difficult.'

'Definitely! Who was pushed off?'

'Marilyn Monroe. My class was full of budding sexists, who probably grew up to become members of parliament.' He pauses. 'I picked Hitler so I didn't have to play anymore. I lay on the floor, pretending to be dead until it was all over.'

'Why?' I stare at him curiously.

'I hated the game. Why should we decide whose life is worth more than someone else's? It brought out all the worst qualities in my classmates – they voted for the most popular kids, not for the people they represented. Marilyn Monroe aka Samantha had no friends and was bullied because of the thickness of her glasses. She was doomed.'

'Even more depressing than death by sexists.'

'I figured that someone always gets hurt unless you opt out of the game.'

I suppress a shiver as I fiddle with my pendant. Could I cause more damage if I attempt to go back in time and make amends? Will I lose Alex if I try? I don't know exactly how the time jump worked, and physically I'm not up to another attempt.

'In all honesty, I don't believe my life is worth more than the next person's,' he continues. 'The world won't stop rotating on its axis if I die. Life will go on. I won't leave a huge mark.'

I think of the plaque and bouquets of flowers on Hammersmith Bridge, of Samira's devastation a year on, and that of his sister and nieces. They hadn't moved on; they would never get over his death.

'That's not true. You do.' I take a breath. 'I mean, you would.'

'Sure, to loved ones, but not in the grand scheme of things. My life isn't worth more than those brothers' lives.' He nods at the phone. 'What if one of them had grown up to discover the cure for cancer? Or Alzheimer's? I'm never going to achieve anything groundbreaking that could change the world, but they might have if they'd been given a shot. Who knows how their lives would have turned out?'

'I hadn't thought about the repercussions from *their* deaths.'

'Every decision we make, however small, has repercussions. Sometimes the knock-on effect is huge, but we don't realise it yet.'

'God, you're wise.'

'And handsome.'

'That goes without saying.'

'Can we change the subject and talk about something cheerier? Like when you want to get married?' He puts his drink down and shuffles closer. 'Or where you fancy going on honeymoon?'

He draws in for a kiss.

'One last question,' I add. 'Could you live with yourself if you did accidentally change things for the worse, by saving people, like those brothers?'

His lips hover inches away from mine.

'More importantly, Julia, could you live with yourself if you didn't try to help?'

19

Wednesday, May 15, 2024

I've left it a couple of days before visiting Gran. I hadn't wanted to risk distressing her again but I'm desperate to make amends. Sadness washes over me as I step into her room, where she's asleep in the armchair. Her purple scissors sit on a large, untouched stack of newspapers on the floor. She hasn't cut out a single story since Monday. The whirlpool inside her mind is cruelly sucking away her favourite hobby.

I sit down beside her. 'It's me, Julia!' I gently squeeze her hand. 'I'm so sorry for upsetting you. I never meant to. I love you very much. Alex sends his love too.'

She doesn't open her eyes. My worst fears have come true: she's sleeping through my visit. On her lap are pieces of paper with people's names, including mine. I check each one before putting them back in her pocket. There's a new note for Seb, the carer who has temporarily replaced Raquel.

I freeze when I see a single word with a question mark.

Ed?

I screw up the notelet and stuff it in my pocket to prevent her from getting more confused. I've been googling her condition

– people with Alzheimer's develop tangles inside neurons in their brain, which block their communication with other neurons. Is it possible her memories of Ed, the Night Prowler, and the train crash have become caught in these knots? It may explain why she retains echoes of memories, while Alex doesn't.

I examine the final note:

Tell Julia.

'Can you remember what you want to tell me, Gran?'

Her eyelashes flicker. I'm sure she can hear me, but she doesn't speak. I retrieve a thick, red book from beneath the chair; it's her favourite photo album. It may trigger some memories.

'Shall we look at this together?' I flick it open.

My gaze rests on a colour photo of us wearing matching yellow raincoats. 'This is us on Hammersmith Bridge. Do you remember when we went for a walk in the rain along the riverbank, and you spotted a kingfisher?'

I turn the pages, describing what I'm seeing: her and Gramps together in Paris, and the two of us on Brighton Beach five years ago. This photo had been framed and sat on her bedside table before I travelled into the past and changed everything. I find the large picture of me as a new-born baby with Mum, Gran and Aunt Rose that was also on display previously. Mum's hair is tied into a long braid, and dark shadows are imprinted beneath her eyes. She's standing in front of a mantelpiece with brass candlesticks.

'I can only be a few weeks old in this picture. Mum looks exhausted! You and Aunt Rose are with us. Do you remember that day? Gramps must have taken the photo in your old sitting room.'

I study Aunt Rose's wide smile and unruly hair. My gaze lowers. Hanging around her neck is the pendant. I've never noticed it before! I catch my breath, and glance at Gran. Her eyes are still shut. I barely remember anything about my aunt, apart from the fact she was a talented cellist who toured the world with an orchestra. She had narcolepsy and should never have been driving home from a concert the night of her accident; she fell asleep at the wheel and crashed into a tree. Mum must have inherited the necklace from her.

I flick deeper into the album and find grainy black and white photos of Gran's parents: George and Violet on their wedding day, and later with their daughters. Violet is wearing the pendant – it's definitely a family heirloom. Interestingly, Violet gave it to Rose, the younger sister, not Gran. I turn the pages back to the photo of the three generations of Hockney women: me, Mum, Gran and Aunt Rose. Gran is the odd one out – she doesn't have narcolepsy. I carefully peel back the cellophane and pull out the photo to examine it more closely. I could frame it again for Gran as it clearly means so much to her.

I turn it over and excitement pinwheels inside me. There's a message from Aunt Rose! It's written in faded, spidery blue ink, and dated May 10, 1999 – the week after I was born.

I hear the blood pounding in my ears as I read on:

> *Dear Sylvia*
> *I know you only want to protect Marianne, but we*
> must *start preparing her for what lies ahead. Her*
> *narcolepsy gene* will *mutate aged 25 and she* will
> *inherit the family gift as I did. She will experience*
> *mini jumps in her sleep without realising what they*
> *are – but do not worry, they are perfectly safe. She*
> *will only flit between different timelines and dimen-*
> *sions as a bystander, never affecting anyone or any-*
> *thing. If she chooses to travel back in person, and*
> *potentially change the past, the family pendant will*

take her and bring her back. I promise I will teach Marianne to use it safely, and sparingly, to protect her health. The necklace is nothing to be afraid of, Sylvia. It has been used for good by generations of Hockney women.

I beg you not to leave explaining this until Marianne turns 25. It will be too much to take in all at once and we can help her adjust gradually. This is even more important now she has become a mother. Please consider this for the sake of Julia as well as Marianne. I will be there for all three of you, whatever you decide. Always.

Love, Rose.

I bend over double, gripping the pendant as heat rises in my neck and cheeks. Mum could go back and change the past, like me! I had my suspicions – she owned the pendant previously, had narcolepsy and suffered similar symptoms. This decades-old note from Aunt Rose to Gran confirms it. I'm not a freakish one-off, my condition is inherited. I can move through time – it's connected with the narcolepsy gene, the same as Mum and Aunt Rose, and our ability is somehow controlled by the necklace. But my joy at finally finding answers slips away like sand through my fingers. Is this why Mum left the necklace – and us – behind? She found it too much to take in, the responsibility too great. Perhaps Gran had delayed telling her the truth until she turned 25, by which time Aunt Rose had died. Mum couldn't cope with the news and her ailing health. She freaked out and fled to Scotland months later, dropping the pendant out of the train window, according to Gran, so she couldn't be tempted to use it at the music festival. Gran must have left it too late to explain the family legacy to me as well. Alzheimer's robbed her of the chance as my birthday approached.

Tears slide down my face. I've never felt closer – yet further away – from Mum. If only she'd stayed and tried to come to terms with her unique skill, the way I'm being forced to. At least she wasn't alone – she still had me and Gran. Why wasn't that enough? Why am *I* never enough?

I turn the photo over and stare at the faces of the Hockney women.

Aunt Rose. Mum. Me.

We're inescapably bound together. My mind races and red and black dots swirl in front of my eyes. I tug at the pendant, which bites into my flesh. Swivelling it doesn't ease the pain. History is slowly strangling me; there's no escaping from the trauma of the past.

Aunt Rose is dead.

Mum walked out on her life.

I squeeze Gran's fingers. She's vanishing too, leaving only the shell of her body.

Soon, only I will be left. What twisted fate awaits me?

I wipe my face with my sleeve. Mum ran away from this gift, and the responsibilities that came with it, but I'm not her. I must make amends. Start over.

I kiss Gran's cheek. 'I love you. I promise I'll come back soon.'

As I stand up, she reaches out and grabs my hand. Her eyes remain closed, but she refuses to let go.

I've called in sick and returned home, changing into a sweatshirt and jogging bottoms – the clear-up operation in the archives can wait. Alex is still in the studio and won't be back for hours. I need to work out how to use the pendant properly if I'm going to correct my mistakes in 2023. Aunt Rose had planned to teach Mum, but no one is on hand to tutor me.

I fell asleep on the tube on the way back from the *Gazette* and fatigue swoops again, claiming me as prey. My eyelids are hooded as I sink into the sofa. A sudden thought forces them wide open.

Can *I* use the pendant to find Mum? I could travel back to the day she left for Scotland and ask her how this necklace works.

Beg her not to leave us. Tell her we love and need her.

Transform the world and rearrange.

I don't have to grow up without a mum, feeling unwanted and not good enough. Gran won't be bereft, haunted by the past.

My mind races. It's risky. What if I get stuck in 2004? How do I return? I was dragged unwillingly out of Kew Gardens at 1 p.m. the day after I travelled back, as if I'd outstayed my welcome in the past. But I heard ticking the whole time I was there. Is it that simple – do I concentrate on that sound and turn the pendant? Aunt Rose didn't go into detail in her message to Gran.

I'm increasingly drowsy and can feel a sleep attack coming. This is my chance to find out. I was thinking about Alex the last time I travelled back. Now, I must concentrate on Mum. I find the photo of us together in Gran's garden and stare at her face.

May 9, 2004.

The date is seared in my memory – it's when Mum left for the week-long music festival in Scotland. Gran told me we travelled to Euston train station to see her off, but I don't remember. Afterwards, we returned to Mum's flat in Brentford. Gran said it was easier for school drop offs and pickups, rather than staying miles away at her house in Chiswick.

I don't resist the tiredness. I rotate the stone, my eyelashes fluttering.

Tick, tick, tick.

My shoulders sag, my head nods forward.

I'm engulfed by darkness.

My eyelids fly open. I'm standing at the top of concrete steps, wearing my sweatshirt and jogging bottoms. To my left is a journey planner. I'm at High Street Kensington underground station. A train has arrived on the platform below and commuters are climbing aboard.

No, no, no!

I forgot to put on my watch and dart over to the clock by the barriers. *7 p.m.* Is this May 11, 2023? Why am I here, instead of 2004? It's the wrong time and place. I hear the faint ticking in the background and grip my pendant. Do I move towards it? I need to return to 2024 and try again. I stumble backwards, colliding with someone holding a coffee cup. Our legs become entangled and we both land, sprawled on the floor.

'What the fuck?' The man clutches his ankle, his shirt spattered with a brown stain.

It's Coffee Guy. This time he's burnt himself, not me, and our encounter is up here in the ticket hall rather than on the steps or platform.

'I've knackered my ankle.' He glares fiercely at me. 'You did this. I can't get up!'

'Sorry! Is this May 11, 2023?'

'Of course it bloody is!'

I back away. I need to escape from this timeline. I can't go to the Swan where I'll change Alex's life forever and cause a disastrous butterfly effect. I disappear into the crowd, close my eyes and rotate the stone, praying my escape route works.

'What the hell . . . ?' someone blurts out.

Silence.

I feel a whooshing sensation. I'm being spun up and around. I open my eyes.

Vertigo grips me, and I can't see straight. Colours swirl before separating treacherously. I'm on the sofa in my flat. Alex's painting is on the wall behind me. I breathe through the waves of nausea and splintering pain in my forehead. I flick on the TV and check the date and time. I've returned to 2024! The pendant *does* allow me to leave the past as well as arrive. Hopefully, I won't have badly affected Coffee Guy's life beyond a twisted ankle. But why couldn't I travel further back than last year? Maybe twenty years was too far. I could try six years – before Gran became ill. She would be well enough to explain everything.

My brief nap isn't nearly enough to keep me awake for long.

I can make another attempt to visit Gran in the past shortly.

I wait for another sleep attack and rotate the stone as my eyelids close.

I'm at High Street Kensington tube station. Again!

I shouldn't have tried so soon. I feel like I've just stepped off a vertiginous fairground ride. I make a grab for the rail and miss. I'm swaying, about to fall when someone pulls me back from the drop.

'Are you okay, Miss?'

I can't speak. I stagger away from the steps. My knees buckle and I fall into the arms of a man with a blond ponytail wearing black leathers and carrying a violin case. He drops it, and the commuter behind him trips over us both, spilling his coffee.

'Shit!' Coffee Guy writhes around on the floor, gripping his foot. 'I've sprained my fucking ankle because of you two.'

'Julia! I'm back. Julia?'

My name booms around the ticket hall. Who is doing that? How . . . is . . . this possible? No one knows I'm here. Why is this voice so loud? I'm trying to grab my pendant, but I can't reach it. I've lost control of my arms. Oh God. I could be stuck in 2023.

'Where are you, Julia?'

I close my eyes and embrace the hot, rushing sensation sweeping over my body. Now all my nerves are on fire. Skin is being flayed from bone.

'Julia!'

My eyelids spring open. Inwardly, I'm screaming. I blink again and again, unable to speak. Eventually, words and images solidify in my mind and I'm able to piece together the puzzle. I'm lying on the floor in the sitting room, staring up into Alex's anxious eyes.

'Is it another cataplexy attack?' he asks.

My throat has seized up. I try to swallow but can't produce any saliva. Alex holds me in his arms as my heart beats faster and faster.

'Don't worry, I've got you. I came home early – I thought I'd cook a romantic candlelit dinner.' He pauses. 'I could have sworn you weren't in here a minute ago.'

My eyes swim with tears. 'I'm here,' I manage to say hoarsely. 'I'll always come back to you.'

20

MONDAY, MAY 27, 2024

The nosebleeds, headaches and exhaustion took days to recover from, but I'm almost ready for another potentially longer jump into the past. The GP had signed me off work until today and I've spent the time preparing and building up my strength. My experiment has proven I can't find Mum in the past or visit Gran pre-Alzheimer's. I can only potentially change the events of May 11 and 12 last year. Perhaps I'm just destined to alter what happens here on Hammersmith Bridge. That will have to be enough.

I lean over the side. The Thames unfurls before me, a story waiting to be told and retold. It has witnessed history and caught a glimpse of the future. It has killed the man I love before changing course and sparing him, taking the lives of two strangers in his place. But I refuse to flow like the water beneath this bridge. I won't yield to the vagaries of the current. I can shape the narrative. Or, as Alex said a fortnight ago, I must at least try.

I restart the timer on my phone and sprint to the opposite side of the river, away from the moored boats and dank, foul-smelling mud. A dawdling grey-haired woman in a green coat accidentally steps into my path. I lose vital seconds but reach the bank in just under two minutes. This is my quickest time so far.

I press two fingers on my wrist. See! I *can* change things for the better. The double beat has finally vanished; my pulse is back to normal.

When I return to 2023, I'll call the police and lifeguard ahead of time and warn them that people will fall from this bridge. However, I need to be prepared in case things go wrong. The river will be high at midday, approximately 4.78 metres, according to last year's data, which I found online. The drop is relatively small compared with other London bridges, but the tide is hellishly strong. Apparently, that's why rowers often go out in two boats; they have a backup if one capsizes.

I don't want to jump or wade in – I had a cataplexy attack in the sea in Devon as a teenager. But I've paid for a couple of private, advanced lessons at the Serpentine Lido in Hyde Park, to help me acclimatise to outdoor swimming. The instructor, Lydia, has taught me what to do in an emergency, and I won't be alone – I'll be with Alex on the day. We could be dragging two people from the river if I haven't managed to prevent the tragedy from unfolding earlier in the day.

The regular exercise is building my endurance and I'm hoping some muscle memory will start to kick in. It's also helping bat away the memories – the worst ones ambush me in quiet moments, inflicting fatal blows. I hear my sobs every time I returned from school, hoping to see Mum chatting to Gran in the kitchen, and only finding an empty chair. Crying harder when Gran stopped laying an extra place for her at the dinner table. Maybe this is punishment for confusing Gran. She's still sleeping through my visits, but I will do better next time. I will change *everything*.

I glance around – this is the most accessible bank, reached by concrete steps. I could wade into the shallows from the shingle and grab an outstretched hand. Overhanging trees will be submerged on May 12, and I can cling onto branches if I need to reach out further. The only problem is the lifebuoy – two are stored across the river, and I can't find any here.

I update the detailed notes on my mobile: *could borrow a buoy from further down the Thames or would that create another ripple effect? Buy rope on May 12?*

The undergrowth is an ideal hiding place if I stash anything that morning. I lean against the wall, a mosaic of broken, shattered bricks, and reread my research even though I've memorised the details by heart. Merv does this before big interviews, and says it helps drill the important details into his mind. But unlike his reporting jobs, this could be the difference between life and death – I cannot afford for anything to go wrong. I glance up and spot the elderly woman in the green coat staring down from the bridge. She must think I'm odd, repeatedly running short distances. I perform calf stretches, as if I'm preparing for a marathon. Come to think of it, I am.

Pigeons peck in the mud, their cooing overpowered by shrieks from the parakeets sitting on the bridge tower. In the distance, cranes dip like giant praying mantises capturing prey, and a train announcement echoes across the river. Traffic rumbles. Life goes on as normal. No one, apart from the pensioner, notices I'm here, carrying out my last, crucial dress rehearsal. I watch as a branch, entangled in a shopping bag, floats past and lands on a small mud island. A raven sits, king like, on top of a traffic cone, surrounded by a fortress of flotsam and litter. The plastic attempts to snare the bird's claws but it flies off, its glossy black wings beating slowly. The bag drifts down river, looking for a new victim to trap.

I'll take the bird's escape as a good omen.

In all honesty, I'll take whatever I can get.

It's past midnight when I let myself in the flat. Merv had begged me to try to save the old cuttings books. I could hardly tell him there was no point – I plan to rewind time to a year before the water leak. But I'd headed into the archives after my run regardless. I concentrated on last-minute prep for my journey back to 2023, without interruptions. Despite taking a few naps lying on my coat on the floor, I also fell asleep on the tube and missed my stop.

Alex has left the hall light on. I hang my coat next to his denim jacket and press it to my face, inhaling his scent. My stomach tightens. In my head, I hear the words: *I missed you.*

Oh God! Should I do this?

I can't bear to lose him. What if this goes horribly wrong and he dies again? I leave his jacket on the peg before my resolution falters but suffer another major wobble when I find Alex's Post-it stuck to the bathroom mirror.

Can we afford Australia for our honeymoon? Is that a no, but yes?! xxxx

I try to block out the faces of Daniel and Oliver Marshall, and pictures of dead train passengers, which are imprinted in my mind. I could back out. I don't *have* to do this tomorrow. It could be in a fortnight, possibly in a month or two – I'll have completed more practice runs and had extra swimming lessons. Gran's meds will have settled, and she won't be as drowsy. She might remember what she wants to tell me.

I creep into the dark bedroom and climb into bed. Alex rolls over, his body spooning against mine.

How can I give this up? I don't want to risk going back to my old life without him.

'Have you decided yet?' he asks sleepily.

'W-w-what?'

'The honeymoon. Where do you want to go?'

'I don't know . . . It's tricky.'

'Sorry, Australia was a bad idea. You don't want to be so far away from your gran.'

I exhale heavily.

'You're still worried about her?'

'That's a constant.' I bury my head in the pillow as tears form behind my eyelids.

'Are you crying?'

'No,' I lie.

I'm planning to throw our life in the air like confetti and have no idea where it will land, or who I could hurt.

He hugs me closer. 'I'm sorry about your gran – and the news. I had to turn off the radio in the studio. It was depressing.'

I lift my head from the pillow; I'd deliberately avoided looking at the newsstands when I walked into work after my run and didn't pick up any of the free papers in the lobby. I'd wanted to keep a clear head while I went over my plans.

'What did you hear?'

'Doctors turned off the life support of that old lady who was attacked in her home by the Night Prowler, and another train crash victim has died. He was only in his twenties and had just got engaged, like us.'

I press my knuckles to my mouth. I can't delay. I must stop this never-ending ripple of misery by withdrawing the grenade I've casually lobbed into other people's lives. My eyes are closed, and I see the smiling faces of Daniel and Oliver Marshall. They want their lives back. They're waiting patiently for me to save them.

'Are you ever afraid we're too happy and it could be snatched away?' I whisper, rolling over to face him.

'No! Why ruin our lives waiting for something that might never happen?'

'But what if it does? What if we lose everything?'

'We won't.' He kisses my forehead. 'Stop catastrophising.'

'I can't help it. I'm scared I'll wreck *us*.'

'You mean self-sabotage?'

'Something like that.'

'I won't let you. This is the beginning of our lives together, not the end.'

I sigh. 'I get that. I think our engagement must be making me jittery.'

His body tenses beneath my fingertips.

'I'm not having second thoughts,' I add hastily. 'But it's a commitment that should last for life and my mum didn't bother to stay for my childhood. It's hard to believe anything will continue forever after something like that happens.'

'In case you hadn't noticed, I'm not your mum.'

'That would be weird!'

'Don't worry about anything,' he says, kissing me. 'I'll never leave you.'

'Me neither.'

That's a lie, but he doesn't notice me flinching as he kisses me deeper.

I must go.

I promise I'll come back to you, Alex.

21

Tuesday, May 28, 2024

'I'm leaving! See you tonight.'

The door clicks shut. I throw it open and run after Alex in my pyjamas down the corridor.

'Hold on, don't go!'

He stops by the lifts, hoisting his rucksack over his shoulder.

'What did I forget?'

'This.' I throw my arms around him.

His body presses against mine as we kiss. I feel his heart pounding through his chest. I don't want to lose this memory. I need to preserve it in my mind forever. Never let it go.

'That's some goodbye!' he says, when we pull apart.

I shiver. 'Not goodbye. *Until tonight*. Can't you stay for breakfast? I could cook pancakes. Or try to, anyway. Or . . .'

I rack my brains, attempting to think of something to stop him from leaving, to delay what I'm planning to do by a few precious minutes or seconds.

'I want to get to the studio early while the light is good. If this commission goes well, it may lead to more work and contacts. It could help build up my collection, and lead to an exhibition, and gallery interest.'

I force the corners of my lips to form a small smile. I'm trying to share his excitement and avoid worrying about whether I'm about to ruin his career and, possibly, life.

He hugs me tightly. 'I'll see you tonight, I promise.'

My fingers loosen. I have to let him go.

I shower and put on a new purple dress and ballet flats. Alex is fired up about his commission and will stay late. My experiment proved that returning to the present day is not only dependent on spinning the necklace. I can be accidentally pulled back, at least in the initial hours in the past. Alex's voice in my flat and Jeremy's in the archives interrupted my journey. I mustn't be disturbed. I plan to change the events of May 12, 2023, and live that day forwards with Alex.

I check my watch. It's 7 a.m. I try to focus on the weight of my research, rather than the heaviness of my guilt for messing around with Alex's life. I've written down the sparse details I remember from the reports of his previous death as well as the inquests for Louise Marshall and Charles Fielding. I know what went wrong for the couple in the Thames, but Alex's inquest hadn't been heard in full. The coroner had just formally announced he would be investigating the death and released Alex's body to his sister. He was yet to hear evidence from eyewitnesses and the emergency services. I can only guess how Alex got into trouble after he'd rescued Louise and went back for Charles.

I hug my folder. It's comfortingly thick, something solid and tangible to cling onto as more doubts flood my mind. I push them away.

This can work. I'll return to my life with Alex after putting everything right.

I flick through the rest of my file. Merv has given me contact details for DCI Martin Fairweather, the senior investigating officer in the Night Prowler case. I've created a timeline of all the attacks over the last year, using stories from the *Gazette*'s digital library. The burglar strikes at 11 p.m. the evening I should arrive in the past: May 11, 2023. He'll break into a house in Chiswick and beat a seventy-year-old woman – an article reporting the attack was in Gran's shoebox. Merv says it happened at number 4, Brackley Road. I'll tip off DCI Fairweather and get the Night Prowler arrested there a year early. This will save his future victims *and* hopefully make Gran and her old neighbour, Ivy, feel safer. I'll also report a faulty signal box at Barnes level crossing to prevent the train crash.

My confidence grows. I make sure Gran's cuttings are in correct date order in the box before rummaging through my keepsakes. Memories crackle beneath my fingertips; ghosts stir and gather around. I reread love letters between Gran and Gramps; old birthday and Christmas cards; the Mother's Day cards I crafted at school and never delivered, and stare at pictures of Mum. I can't go back to the past and find her, but I don't want to forget her face.

My eyelids flutter. I try to keep them open for as long as possible. Just as I've become comfortable in my new skin and remembered everything from the last year, I'm about to slip out of this life and shed it, snake like. Will I recognise the new Julia? *Us?* I pick up the photo of Alex and me on Hammersmith Bridge and kiss him, tracing my finger around his face.

I can't imagine my life without you.

Sinking back into the sofa, I check my notes one last time. I'm ready, or as ready as I'll ever be. I readjust the acupressure bands on my wrists. I bought a pack in a pharmacy after browsing motion sickness aids – they might help with the nausea. As shadows gather and multiply beneath my lids, I rotate the stone in my pendant.

Tick, tick, tick.

My heartbeat mirrors the soothing sound, like water dripping from a tap.

I prepare for darkness to claim me.

It doesn't keep me waiting long.

22

THEN

MAY 11, 2023

'Leap of faith!'

Alex grins over his shoulder as he returns to his old uni friends at the far end of the bar. In our previous life, he'd admitted they were teasing him about our intense conversation, and his cheeks were a deep crimson. The hen party cheers as another round of cocktails arrives. I catch the scent of sweet, sticky coconut; it makes me gag. I take a swig of Diet Coke to get rid of the bitter taste. Despite my acupuncture bands, the nausea, dizziness and crushing exhaustion were even worse when I arrived at High Street Kensington station at 7 p.m. My reactions were horribly sluggish, and my purple dress ended up showered with the hot drink again. At least Coffee Guy didn't give me the finger as he jumped on his train.

'He's GORGEOUS!' Layla lurches towards me, shouting above the Harry Styles soundtrack. 'But he's a dick, right? It's impossible to be that good looking *and* a decent human being. It's a proven scientific fact.'

I shake my head. 'That's Alex Martin, my future husband.'

'OMG.'

She gapes at him. I follow the direction of her gaze, and notice the blonde woman in the long, red dress standing close to his group of friends. She stares hard, forcing me to break eye contact first.

'Stop gawping,' I urge Layla. 'He might notice!'

'Sorry. But you know he's The One?'

I nod.

'How?'

'I think we must have met in another life.'

'Holy shit!' She downs her drink. 'Can I be a bridesmaid?'

'If I'm still here. And you are.'

'Wait – are we going somewhere?'

In the morning I'm heading to Hammersmith Bridge, where I could change the lives of hundreds of people, and she may be in New York within months, supporting her girlfriend's burgeoning legal career.

'I'm joking.'

'We both need another one.' She nods at my empty glass. 'How about a gin and tonic?'

I've stuck to soft drinks so far tonight to keep a clear head – I can't risk a hangover on top of what feels like the worst ever jet lag combined with travel sickness.

'No, thanks. I have an early start tomorrow.'

'Anything exciting?' She glances hopefully in Alex's direction.

'It could change life as we know it.'

'Dammit. I'd hoped you'd at least got his number. But he hasn't left yet. Stay for more drinkies! We're going on to a club to pretend we're young and can keep up with the trainees. You could invite him?'

'Not tonight, sorry.' I kiss her cheek. 'Bye, Layla.'

Before she can protest, I manoeuvre through the packed bodies and search for Merv. I find him nursing a pint, lodged between Brian and Suki, at a corner table.

'Heading off already?' he slurs, trying to sit up straight.

My heart is thumping erratically. It has a double beat again, and my energy levels are depleting, like a car running out of battery. I was about to warn him about the threat to the archives and Jeremy's job, but my memory is fading. I can't remember everything or save everyone. I need to prioritise and make a note of all the Night Prowler attacks before I forget them.

'Can I quickly borrow a pen and scrap of paper?'

Merv fumbles in his jacket pocket and produces a battered notebook and biro. My hand quivers as I jot down the times, dates and locations of all the break-ins that are destined to happen over the next year. The first one is due soon. My phone is fried; it definitely doesn't work in the past. I'll borrow a stranger's mobile on the way home and report a man acting suspiciously outside number 4, Brackley Road, Chiswick. If something goes wrong and the police don't catch him tonight, I can tip them off about further chances.

'Are you okay?' Merv asks. 'You're shaking.'

'Yeah, it must be the alcohol! Thank you.'

I tear out the page and hand back his pen and pad. My head throbs as I lurch towards the exit. I've almost reached the door when the woman in the red dress steps in front of me. She has bright, sea blue eyes. Her hair is brittle and brassy and appears to be a wig, and her skin is smooth. We're probably about the same age. I smile, expecting her to move out of my way, but she stands firm. Her frown deepens.

'Stop it,' she says almost inaudibly.

'Excuse me?' I lean closer, wondering if I've misheard. 'I don't understand.'

'Stop coming back here.'

'The Swan?'

My stomach dips as she looks pointedly at my pendant.

She knows.

185

My heart beats even quicker. 'Can you time travel? How are we—?'

'You've left people behind who need you.'

'No, I haven't! I'm not staying here long, just until I've fixed things.'

She gestures to Alex. 'You can't have him in this lifetime or any other. You'll only hurt more people. You have to let him go.'

'That's not true.'

She shakes her head. 'I've seen what happens tomorrow. This isn't going to end well, for anyone.'

'What do you mean?'

'I'm warning you, Julia – leave now and don't ever return.'

She walks out, the tassels on the hem of her dress shimmering and rippling like running water.

23

THEN

May 12, 2023

'Come back!'

I've jumped off the bus in Putney and a guy in a suit is chasing after me. He could be working with the woman from last night, trying to stop me from saving Alex. I increase my pace, but he's faster. I scream as he catches up and grabs my arm.

'Sorry. Didn't mean to scare you. You fell asleep and left this on your seat.' He hands over my Oyster card, which must have slipped out of my handbag.

'Oh, thank you.'

My heart beats wildly as he strides away. My nerves are ragged after the ominous encounter in the Swan. The woman knew my name, and what I'm doing here in 2023. She claimed I could never be with Alex, but she's wrong. I *will* get this right today. Something else she said is preying on my mind.

You've left people behind who need you.

I said goodbye to Gran and promised to return. But what if each time I leave 2024, I vanish completely from her life? She knows Ed has gone. In those timelines, she could be asking after *me*, and wondering why I'm not visiting. *Mourning my loss.* Vicky could be searching for me, and even Ed. They could contact the police. I shudder. Hopefully, in those parallel universes, I never existed.

I check up and down the street for the blonde woman before dodging traffic to reach the bus stop on the opposite side. I napped for 20 minutes on the bus, missed Hammersmith, and am wasting valuable time by doubling back. There's no chance to shop for a rope or move a lifebuoy to the far bank before meeting Alex at midday. I'd planned to reach the bridge by 11 a.m. for last-minute prep but had seriously underestimated my recovery. The after-effects are far worse than last time. Severe stomach cramps, vertigo and nausea meant I spent most of the night by the side of the toilet, retching. I'm still wobbly.

I catch a glimpse of my ghost-like reflection in the bus shelter window. This isn't how I'd normally look on a date. I didn't have time to put on makeup and I've dressed for survival, rather than to impress Alex. I'm wearing leggings, a T-shirt, pumps, and a jacket and scarf – light clothes I can quickly shed or are less likely to drag me under if I'm forced to jump into the river. The pendant is tucked into my bra, where it can't get ripped off.

Shit, shit, shit. It's 11.30 a.m., according to my watch.

This isn't going to end well. For anyone.

I vividly remember that woman's warning, but not how I got home last night. I may have fallen asleep on the way. I definitely borrowed a passer-by's phone and called 999 just before 11 p.m. Did the police arrest the Night Prowler on Brackley Road? I nip into a newsagent before the bus arrives and buy a *Gazette*, quickly scanning through the pages. I can't find a story about his arrest, but there isn't any mention about another attack. The police could have scared him off and saved the victim because of my anonymous call.

If that's the case, I've proved the woman in the Swan wrong. I ignore the faint ticking noise in the background; I'm not returning to 2024 yet.

I'm only just beginning to put things right.

It's 11.51 a.m. I have nine minutes until I meet Alex, and Charles Fielding will drag Louise Marshall into the Thames. I join the sea of pedestrians surging across the road outside Hammersmith tube station and walk briskly to the bridge. As soon as the decorative turrets are in sight, I stop a young woman with a pushchair.

'Excuse me, can I borrow your phone? It's an emergency. I need to call the police and mine isn't working.'

A look of relief sweeps across her face when she realises I'm not asking for cash. Her little boy stares curiously at me, chewing his fingers, as she passes her mobile.

'There's an incident on Hammersmith Bridge,' I tell the operator. 'A guy is threatening to pull a woman into the river. You need to send the police and also a lifeboat. They're both about to fall in.'

I hang up before he can ask any questions. The woman frowns, staring at the bridge, and snatches her phone back.

'I can't see anything happening. Where's the man you're talking about?'

'He's over there, I promise. He's about to try to murder someone.'

'But—'

Her mobile rings. 'Hello?' she says, picking up. 'No, that wasn't me.'

'Thanks,' I mouth.

I wave at her son and run towards the ornate green and gold towers.

'Hey, come back!' she shouts. 'The operator wants to speak to you again.'

I ignore her and keep going. The police just need to get here, not ask more questions.

Alex is waiting for me close to where Gramps got down on one knee. He's leaning on the handrail, staring out at the views across the Thames. My heart thuds painfully. His fingers are almost touching the exact spot where his plaque sat. He's wearing the same denim jacket, faded blue trousers and white T-shirt from our first date in Kew Gardens.

Further along the walkway, on the same side of the bridge, a couple are locked in conversation. The man with the black goatee beard and navy shirt resembles a weightlifter; his chest is broad and muscular, and his biceps are huge. He gazes at a slight, bird-like blonde woman who could easily pass for a twenty-something rather than being in her early thirties.

Nothing would appear out of the ordinary to most people, but this is Charles and Louise. I recognise them from photos published in news coverage of their inquests. They appear to be consoling each other, not arguing. Could things work out differently today?

Alex turns around and waves.

'Leap of faith!' he shouts.

I grab the handrail, attempting to catch my breath. Regular jogging in 2024 has only helped marginally; most of the gains have been wiped out by the side-effects of the time jump.

'Hey, you didn't need to run!' he says as I reach him. 'I'd have waited if you were late.'

'I know you would. I mean, sorry. I must look a state.'

'You're as beautiful as a Whistler painting, if not more so.'

My cheeks warm and the tight knot in the pit of my stomach loosens when I glance at Charles and Louise. They're both calm. Hopefully, I've already inadvertently done something, which has created a positive ripple effect and stopped this situation from escalating.

Alex gazes at the river. 'This would make an incredible painting – all the shimmering diamonds where the sun hits the water. I usually prefer recreating the passion of storms, but there's a beauty in stillness.' He turns to me. 'I can see why your grandad chose this spot to propose to your grandma. Do they come back here much?'

'Gramps died when I was little, and my gran . . .' I clear my throat, 'she used to love walking along the bridge and riverbank, but she has Alzheimer's. She's in a nursing home in Chiswick and isn't well enough for day trips.'

'I'm sorry.' The skin around his eyes creases with concern. 'That's tough. My grandad had Alzheimer's – it's a cruel disease. It was far worse for him when he felt himself slipping away, but after a while . . . Well, you know what it's like.'

'It becomes worse for the people left behind, when their loved one is there, but not really present,' I say quietly. 'I try to see her at least a couple of days a week. I want her to sense I'm with her, even if she can't remember my visits afterwards.'

His eyes shine. 'Nothing is more important than family.'

'You're right. I'd do anything for mine.'

'Me too. My sister and nieces mean the world to me.'

Our eyes lock and my stomach flips. If this had been our first date, I'd have realised my gut reaction in the bar was right. I'd met the man I wanted to spend the rest of my life with. As he studies the river again, I steal another glance at Louise. She's hugging Charles. He nods in agreement and embraces her warmly. Now, they're holding hands at arm's length and saying goodbye. Louise takes one last look before walking towards the far bank.

Alex stares after her. 'Do you know them?'

'I don't think so. The woman reminded me of someone.'

Charles doesn't move. He watches Louise leave.

The tragedy isn't going to happen. Charles let Louise go, without trying to stop her. Everything is going to be okay! When the police turn up, they'll check the bridge and move on. If the woman with the pushchair points me out as the anonymous caller, I'll apologise and say I made a terrible mistake.

'Do you fancy getting a drink in one of the pubs down there?' Alex asks, pointing to the footpath along the river. 'It's a shame to move on when it's so beautiful here.'

'I'd love to.'

He takes my hand and smiles. Our fingers slot together perfectly. Tomorrow, we'll wake up happy and engaged. When Alex gets home from the studio in the evening, we'll pick up where we left off – planning our wedding and honeymoon. We pass Charles, who's rooted to the spot, wiping tears from his face. Louise has stopped further ahead, helping a howling toddler in a pink hat. She's toppled over, dropping her ice cream.

'Whoops a daisy. Where's your mummy or daddy?' Louise scans the bridge as we approach, looking for her parents.

We've almost reached them when a shout rings out behind us.

'Stop!' Charles cries.

My throat dries as I spin around. Charles has climbed over the side. He's facing inwards on a narrow ledge, standing on tiptoes. His knuckles whiten as he holds the rail tightly.

'No!' Louise screams, her eyes wide with panic. She abandons the little girl and runs. 'Get down, Charles. Let's talk!'

'Omigod!' Alex fumbles in his jeans and jacket pockets. 'I forgot my mobile! Can you ring 999?'

'My phone's dead.'

'Dammit!'

A woman jogs past on the opposite side, but she's wearing ear buds and doesn't hear our shouts. Panic claws at my throat. I can't hear sirens, but the police should be here shortly. Someone else will see what's unfolding and call them – possibly the toddler's mum or dad? But she appears to be alone. Tears stream down the child's face as she staggers towards us. A cyclist wearing mirrored shades and a vivid yellow jersey races along the road. He's timing himself on his watch and doesn't see Charles. I lean over the partition, waving frantically.

'Fucking move out the way!' He swerves and pedals furiously off the bridge.

Alex slowly approaches Charles, holding out his hands, attempting to placate him.

'Please, sir, don't do anything silly. Let's chat.'

'It's too late for that.' Charles's jaw is rigid as he loosens his grip and leans back.

The little girl stumbles, almost falling, as she reaches us. I have no choice but to scoop her up. She clings onto my neck. I feel hot breath and salty tears on my skin.

I catch hold of Louise's arm. 'Don't get any closer. He could pull you over with him.'

She shakes off my hand. 'Charles would never hurt me. He loves me. I have to help.'

'I don't think—'

'We can talk him down together,' Alex cuts in.

'I only want to talk to Louise,' Charles shouts. 'This is between the two of us. No one else.'

The child lunges for Louise with both arms outstretched. I lose my balance, almost dropping her.

'It's okay,' Louise says, gesturing for us to move away. 'It'll be fine.'

'No, it won't,' I insist. 'You shouldn't trust him.'

I try to put the girl down, but she's holding on limpet like. *Where are her bloody parents?*

Charles leans further from the railing, removing one finger and then another.

'Will the two of you get back?' Louise hisses. 'I can calm him down. This isn't *him*.'

Oh God. I don't know what to do. If either of us gets closer, he'll let go and Alex will probably leap in after him.

'We need the police,' Alex says quietly. 'We can't deal with this ourselves. He could fall at any moment.'

'Over there! I think someone's calling them.' I point at a workman in a high-vis jacket at the end of the bridge. A phone is clamped to his ear. His colleagues stare at us.

'Thank God for that. Let's hope she keeps him talking until they get here.'

I sigh with relief as I hear the distant wail of sirens. Louise stretches over the side and throws her arms around Charles's neck, pulling him to her. The toddler sobs harder into my chest.

'Please don't,' Louise begs. 'I'm here for you, I promise.'

'I'm sorry,' Charles cries into her neck. 'I don't know what came over me. I shouldn't be putting you through this. I love you so much.'

He looks broken as he weeps, enveloping her in a bear hug with one arm while his other hand grips the rail. She stands on tiptoes, leaning into him.

'I know, Charles. I'm sorry. I love you too.'

'Why are you doing this to us?' he asks tearfully.

'I can't lose my children.'

Something dark shifts behind Charles's eyes.

Oh no. I open my mouth to warn her, but he speaks first.

'I can't lose *you*.'

He lets go and heaves Louise over the side with him as if she's as light as a feather.

Her ear-piercing scream echoes as they both fall.

24

THEN

'No!'

Alex lunges at thin air. The little girl shrieks. I hear sickening cracks and splashes as the couple hit the water. I peel off the protesting child's fingers from around my neck and put her down. Leaning over the side, I spot Louise bob up first, but she's struggling to keep her head above water. Charles resurfaces, spluttering and shouting.

Alex pulls off his denim jacket and trainers.

'Don't! It's dangerous. We can reach them from over there.' I point to the bank below. 'We can hang onto trees!'

'This is quicker.'

He climbs over the rails and holds on with both hands, leaning away from the bridge. He looks back at me as the hysterical toddler hugs my leg.

'Leap of faith!' he cries.

'Alex, no!'

My heart contracts as he jumps. I watch him resurface, treading water as he acclimatises to the cold and tries to figure out who to help first. Charles is closest but he's paddling against the current, trying to reach the bridge's pier. Despite his gym fitness, the coroner had said he was a weak and inexperienced swimmer. Alex pivots towards Louise. His instinct is right – the inquest revealed she drowned first. She's managed to grab driftwood and is floating with the current, but the proceedings heard she was underweight and had little upper body strength. She tired quickly, suffering cramps from the cold, and swallowing water. Alex doesn't have much time to save her. Someone shouts for the lifebuoy, but it's on the far side by the Riverside Studios. There's no time to fetch it. Adrenaline, and my practice drills kick in. I pull off the protesting girl's hands from around my leg.

'Take her!' I yell at the workmen.

I reach the tree-lined bank in less than two minutes. Alex's and Charles's heads are above water, but Louise is in trouble. The branch springs from her grasp, and she goes under. Alex picks up his stroke pace and ducks beneath the surface. They're both underwater for what feels like minutes but must only be seconds. He emerges, clutching her, and scrapes along an island of debris.

'Alex!' I wave my hands frantically. 'Lie on your back!' I try to catch Charles's attention too. 'LIE ON YOUR BACK!'

Lydia, the swim instructor at the Serpentine, had explained you must go with the flow in a fast river, floating with feet flexed and pointed downstream. That way your head doesn't hit rocks, and you take in less water. But Charles ignores me. He's swimming slowly to the base of the bridge, while the current drags him in the opposite direction. Alex grabs Louise under the chin and tries to push her onto her back, but he's tiring. I shed my jacket, kick off my pumps and leap feet first into the water. The cold is like a punch, taking my breath away. I thought it would be relatively shallow here, but my feet can't find the bottom and my head goes under. My clothes drag me deeper, and my limbs turn to stone. The undercurrent drags me sideways. No lessons could prepare me for the ferocity of the Thames.

When I break through the surface, gasping for air, dark shapes are bobbing in the water. All three are in trouble. Charles is flailing his arms, using up energy battling an invisible foe, while Louise is barely conscious in Alex's arms. Her lips are pursed and underwater.

'Lift her head!' I shout.

Alex shifts position, jerking her chin up. I try to swim towards them, remembering what Lydia told me about breathing evenly to avoid taking in water, but gag on a foul-tasting mouthful.

'Lie on your back!' I say, coughing.

I swallow more water and my words don't reach Charles. He's scrambling around the stone pier, attempting to cling on. I'm barely making any progress, and Alex and Louise are further away. The undercurrent tears at my clothes, trying to pull off my leggings and top. It sweeps me into a maelstrom of debris and flotsam, tossing me into overhanging trees. Branches rip at my face and arms, but I'm too numb to feel pain. I swipe at a branch and cling on. Police sirens blare on the bridge overhead.

Alex screams and lets go of Louise. They both disappear beneath the surface.

'Alex!'

Louise thrashes up, her arms waving. I catch sight of a streak of blood on Alex's hand as he reappears. He grabs her elbow and yanks her above the waterline.

'Alex! Over here.'

Hanging onto the branch with one hand, I pull off my scarf and throw it. It lands in the water, curls uncooperatively, and is almost dragged away. I wrench it back. I can't lose it. I'll never survive the current if I try to swim after it, and Alex can't save two people. He's slowing and having difficulty keeping his mouth above water. Louise's eyes are rolling; her face is a ghastly corpse white.

'Grab this!'

As they float closer, Alex stretches out his hand. I toss my scarf. It's three feet away. I drag it back and try again. This time, his fingers curl around the wool. I yank them towards me. The Thames has other ideas, keeping a firm grip. Their faces dip in and out of the river. Alex's grasp is weakening.

'Hold on!' I scream.

Alex floats past, but lunges for a bough. He holds on one handed, blood dripping down his arm and tugs Louise closer. He's not going to manage it. I take a deep breath and let go, briefly allowing the current to claim me. I swipe for the branches and land next to him further along the bank. Together, we manage to drag her in. She gropes blindly through the bramble, spitting up water.

Alex shivers violently. 'Where's the guy?'

I point behind him. Charles is thirty feet away. He's attempting to reach the bank. The inquest heard that when he couldn't get a proper grip on the pier, he'd attempted to swim to the side, but had no energy left and hyperventilated. It's happening again. He's exhausted, and fear is etched on his face. Even the world's best indoor swimmer would probably die today.

'Help! Help me!'

He waves his arms, disappearing under the water with his mouth open. He bobs up, coughing and choking.

'I have to go back in,' Alex says hoarsely.

His teeth are chattering, and a huge gash is streaked across his hand. Blood drips down his arm.

'You can't! He's too far out. You'll never reach him – and if you do, you won't be able to get back.'

'The current's pulling him towards us.'

Charles has figured out he must stop fighting against the flow.

I cling onto Alex. 'He's not going to make it. If you let go, you'll get swept away. We have to wait for the lifeboat. It must be on its way. It'll be here soon.'

Charles's head vanishes. This time he's underwater for longer. He struggles up, but his splashing is feebler, his cries fainter. He's about fifteen feet away.

'I can reach him!' Alex cries.

'No, you can't! Let me try with the scarf.'

'That won't work. He's too weak to hold on.'

He tries to shake me off, as I clasp his arm.

'Alex, no!'

'Stop it! I have to try. He's drowning.'

He stretches out his hand. Charles reaches for it as he drifts past. Alex hangs from the tree, leaning closer. The branch groans. It's going to snap!

'Alex!'

'Grab my hand!' he shouts.

Charles's fingers almost graze Alex's. His eyes are wide and glassy before his head sinks beneath the surface. Alex lets go, attempting to jump in, but I desperately hang onto him. I know what will happen if he re-enters the water.

'No!' he yells.

I press my eyes shut, trying to wipe the final image of Charles from my brain. I feel terrible, like one of Alex's old classmates playing judge and jury during that hot air balloon game – but it was a choice between him and Charles. I couldn't sacrifice Alex, a decent, loving, selfless person, for someone who was prepared to kill his lover for putting her children before him. I had to pick Alex. I'd do it a million times over.

A humming noise grows stronger. At first, I think it's my pendant, but it's coming from the water, not my chest. An orange lifeboat roars towards us at speed. It slows, before two men lean over the side and pluck me from the branches. I flop onto the deck, exhausted. A couple of seconds later, Alex lands next to me. He struggles into a sitting position.

'Go back for him. *Please*. He was just there!' He points over the side of the boat. 'I almost had him.'

'We'll keep looking, I promise.'

The men exchange glances, but we all know the truth. It's too late. Charles is gone. The pair concentrate on helping Louise, who has lost consciousness. The crew work together to haul her on board.

Alex slumps down, white faced and shaking. Blood runs in channels down his arm.

I reach for his hand, but he shrinks away as if I'm a monster. Perhaps I am.

Later, when I'm trying to pinpoint where everything went so badly wrong, I'll torture myself by replaying this moment over and over again.

We're sitting on the riverside, silently shivering beneath foil blankets. Alex's hand was slashed by a broken bottle. It's bandaged but blood seeps through the white fabric. Neither of us speaks or moves. It's as if we've slowed down, and the world has speeded up, with the people around us working at double or triple speed. Paramedics are attempting to warm Louise, and stabilise her pulse, before she's taken to hospital for suspected hypothermia. Police officers have set up a cordon to keep back the ghouls who treat death as a spectator sport. People in the crowd might have witnessed what happened, but no one else jumped or waded in. Maybe they'll feel ashamed and leave without giving statements.

We both flinch as the humming noise grows louder. Two lifeboats are searching for Charles Fielding. The crews don't realise the hunt is futile. They won't find his body until much later this evening, at Putney Bridge. I catch a glint of orange as one of the boats speeds past. I blink but the vivid colour lingers behind my eyelids, reminding me of the traffic cone I saw yesterday – or rather, a year in the future. It was stranded on the island of debris while

I practised my rescue mission. Was I right? Was the freed raven a good omen for Alex and I and all those people in the future?

'I should have saved him.'

Alex utters the words so softly, I wonder if I've imagined them.

He shudders, wrapping his arms around his body as if he's trying to stop himself from spilling out and unravelling.

'Why wouldn't you let me go back in? At least try to help?'

The ambulance pulls away, the siren blaring.

'Because you'd have drowned, and I couldn't risk losing you again,' I whisper.

He blinks. 'What did you say?'

'You tried. We both did everything we could. An experienced river swimmer couldn't have survived the conditions today.'

'You don't know that for certain! He was almost within reach. If I'd stretched out further, I could have caught him – grabbed his sleeve or hair. Or if I'd let go, I could have pulled him in further along the bank.'

'I run around here before work and know the river. The current is a killer – you must have felt it.' I glance at his bleeding hand. 'You're injured, exhausted and the water's freezing – there's no way you could swim properly. You'd have been swept away, or your foot could have caught on debris, dragging you under. Either way, you would have died, along with . . . that man.' *Charles.*

He presses his hands against his eye sockets. 'I don't know. I keep thinking what if I'd done more? Tried harder. Swum faster to reach them both. Or—'

'You're being too hard on yourself. I could never have jumped off the bridge, the way you did. Louise Marshall would be dead if it weren't for you.'

'Who?'

'The woman in the water. I heard the guy call her name.'

I want to tell him he's done so much more. He's not only saved her, but at least three other people in the future: her husband, and two young children. My actions today, including the letter I posted this morning warning South Western Railway about the dodgy signal box, may have prevented the future Barnes train crash. Hopefully, the Night Prowler is also caught. I can never explain any of this to Alex. He won't understand and I'll never find the right words.

'I mean it.' I squeeze his arm beneath the blanket. 'No one else tried to help. Only you had the courage to act. You couldn't do anything else.'

He shrugs, staring into middle distance. I know how his mind works – he's launching another invisible rescue attempt in his head, this time where he succeeds, and everyone survives. But that can only occur in his dreams. It *couldn't* have happened today. The coroner had said the undercurrent was particularly treacherous, and the tide unusually high.

'You were lucky to survive, but it could easily have gone the other way – your friends and family could be mourning you today,' I persist. 'Instead, they'll be incredibly proud you saved a woman's life. You're a hero.'

He sighs heavily. 'I don't feel like one, but you're right about my big sister. She's called Zoe – she'll love you. My nieces, Sally and Hannah, too.'

'I can't wait to meet them.'

He gives me a small smile, but it doesn't reach his eyes. They're dark whirlpools of grief and reproach.

We're in adjacent beds in A&E, separated by a thin, flimsy curtain, but I've never felt further apart from Alex. His breath shortens with pain as a nurse cleans his wound, preparing to stitch it up. I want to hold his hand, but I'm hooked up to a monitor. After getting my tetanus jab, antibiotics, and being checked for hypothermia, I thought I'd be free to leave, but the doctor's refused to discharge me. He's detected an abnormal heartbeat. Now, I'm in a gown, naked from the waist up, and pads are stuck to my chest.

'I can't believe this is your idea of a first date,' the nurse says jokingly to Alex.

'I promise to do better next time.'

'So there will be a second?' She pauses. 'You need to pull out all the stops! Take her somewhere nicer than Casualty.'

'How about X-Ray? I've heard on the hospital grapevine it's a blast.'

She laughs, thinking he's playing along with her, but I know him better. His tone is flat. A few seconds later, I hear a muffled cry.

'Hey, handsome! Everything's going to be alright, I promise.'

I lean towards his bed as a ticking noise grows louder.

'Alex?'

The beat drowns out my voice. I glance at the clock on the wall above the nurses' station. It's 12.59 p.m. The sound is coming from my pendant.

No!

It's almost the time I left Kew Gardens. Why does this keep happening? I can't be pulled back. I'm not ready to leave. I have to reach Alex. I try to pull off the pads, but my fingers are numb. I feel a dragging sensation through every cell in my body, as if I'm slowly and painfully being sucked down a whirlpool, one vein, artery and skin cell at a time.

'I just . . .' Alex's voice melts away. 'I can't stop seeing his face before he went under . . .'

'There, there, love. You're traumatised by what's happened – that's not surprising, but we'll look after you. Don't worry about a thing.'

I reach for the curtain that separates us as he sobs loudly, but it's too late. I'm swept into a powerful rip tide. I can't escape its vice-like grip however hard I struggle.

My hand falls to my lap.

The curtain darkens horribly into a claustrophobic cloak, smothering me.

Alex's howl is loud and visceral, like an animal in pain.

It haunts me as I plunge into oily blackness.

25

Tuesday, May 28, 2024

Alex is suffering. His cries puncture the harrowing silence.

It's the first thought that enters my head. Next: *lights and spinning shapes*. They flash around me in vicious circles; unforgiving spirits give chase. My pupils are tiny dots, before widening into huge moons. They can't make sense of the images. My limbs cramp and shake violently, invisible daggers stab my chest. The room turns and flips.

I'm falling.

Scraps of paper flutter like moths.

Alex.

An expanse of white stretches above my head: a sky drained of colour. My fingertips press into something soft. Not grass or sand. Where am I? I blink. It's a white ceiling. I'm lying on carpet. On my sitting room floor. Did I pass out? I have no idea how long I've been here. It could be a few minutes, or hours. *Or days.* Is it 2024 or 2023? My forehead throbs. I touch it tentatively and find blood on my fingertips. I may have knocked myself out on the coffee table. My nose is bleeding too.

The peeling, magnolia walls are rigid and no longer press in on me; the furniture is stationary. *For now.* I sit up cautiously, bracing myself. The waves of nausea are brutal; I breathe out slowly through them until they subside. My memory box is on the sofa, along with Gran's cuttings container, and my research file, which looks slimmer. Dozens of newspaper clippings about the Night Prowler are scattered about. It takes another couple of minutes to register other things: firstly, I've returned wearing the hospital gown.

Secondly, Alex's painting no longer hangs above the sofa; his brushes aren't in the corner and the dust sheet doesn't protect the carpet. The room isn't being used by him anymore. I've turned it into a workspace, with a stack of files on the table, and a flipchart where his easel once stood. Across it, I've written in sprawling letters the words: *Night Prowler.* Beneath the heading is what appears to be a detailed timeline of his attacks. I look closer. They're the dates I jotted down in the Swan when I travelled back. Some are double underlined and marked 'important'. Why have I become obsessed with the case? I've stuck clippings on the wall and used red string to link different articles, like I'm an amateur detective, attempting to crack a cold case.

Who is this version of Julia Hockney?

I rub my face, willing my memories to return, but the cogs in my cotton wool brain grind excruciatingly slowly. Nothing comes back to me. I touch my heart. It's beating so loud I half expect the neighbours to bang on the wall and complain about the noise. Or maybe that's the pendant. The stone is still rotating. The chain is like a serpent, coiled around my neck and biting the skin. I crawl across the carpet and grab the remote control, turning on the TV. It's 7.45 a.m. on May 28, 2024. This means Alex left for his studio about an hour ago in the previous life, yet there's no trace of him here.

I grip the side of the sofa like the safety bar of a rollercoaster as I gingerly lever myself up. The walls appear to slide sideways. Lunging out the door, I manage to reach the bathroom before being violently sick. I grab my robe from the side of the bath and jump, startled, thinking a strange, dishevelled woman is standing by the shower. I spin around, but no one's there. Slowly, I turn to the mirror. A ghoul stares back with hollowed eyes, and grey, sallow skin. I splash water on my face and pull hair from behind my ears to disguise a couple of white streaks.

Reaching the kitchen, I lean dizzily against the door frame. This isn't right either. We haven't painted the room in Alex's favourite shades. The sunflower yellow paint and cobalt feature wall have both vanished; it's dull magnolia. My skin tingles with fear. The blue vase has been smashed and glued back together; the cracks are deep and unsightly. The sunflowers inside have shrivelled and died. I stagger to the bedroom. This is also magnolia, with familiar swatches of paint on the wall. I'm prevaricating between teal, primrose, and lilac again.

This room is pre-Ed, who favoured stark white, and pre-Alex's joyous sky blue.

My eyes focus on a motionless shape beneath the bed covers. Someone else is here.

'Alex?'

I tiptoe closer and lift the duvet. The muscular arm looks like Alex's, but the Leap of Faith tattoo is missing from his shoulder. Paint isn't engrained beneath his fingernails. The man shifts position. This *is* Alex, but his face is thin and hollowed, the unhealthy colour mirroring mine. My hand hovers, about to touch his arm when my knees give way. I collapse beside him as memories from the last year ambush my brain:

Love . . . sex . . . laughter . . . joy . . .

Happiness is tantalisingly brief. It's replaced by worry, grief, pain and illness.

Alex is lovely but subdued on our second date in a sushi bar. He's unwell on our third meet-up and leaves halfway through dinner. A few weeks later we make love on the floor of his studio, but he winces when he pulls his clothes on afterwards. I'm worried his hand has become infected despite the tetanus jab, but he puts off going to the GP because he's working on a new painting. He mistakenly thinks the muscular pain and chills are a bad case of flu. When he collapses, coughing up blood, doctors diagnose Weil's disease, caused by rat urine in the river. He's treated with antibiotics, but exhaustion and aching limbs linger.

Alex moves in shortly after the next diagnosis: chronic fatigue syndrome sparked by his body's reaction to the infection. It leaves him bedridden for days and unable to paint. He's being treated for depression and PTSD after suffering repeated flashbacks of that day at the bridge. My health has also deteriorated. I'm seeing a cardiologist for my irregular heartbeat and awaiting blood test results for the blinding headaches and sickness. My doctor hasn't said the 'C' word but, like Mum, I'm scared I may have a brain tumour.

Gran no longer recognises me and has lost her grip on reality; she claims Mum is back and visiting her regularly.

I grip Alex's arm as long-buried memories from my childhood return:

I see Mum baking cookies with me in our old flat in Brentford. She brushes my hair and pushes in slides and waits for me at the school gate each day. Now, we're playing hide and seek together in Gran's house. I search both bedrooms but can't find her. I'm panicking that she's left for Scotland without saying goodbye. I run outside and see Gran sitting beneath an umbrella with a camera – she nods to the garden shed. Mum is hiding behind it! Gran takes our picture, but I refuse to have another one on her lap. I wriggle off because she won't let me come with her to Scotland.

'Sorry, Pickle. I'm working. But I promise I'll be back soon. I'll ring every day.'

Gran sighs. 'Are you sure you're doing the right thing by going, love?'

The smile vanishes from Mummy's face. She places her necklace on the table. It sounds like a clock. Tick, tick, tick.

Snap! I take a photo with Gran's camera. Mummy is staring sadly at something behind me. I turn around, but no one's there.

I breathe through a fresh floodgate of pain. These are the photos I found in Gran's room! I wasn't imagining the look of love when Mum stared down at me. She *did* love me. She called me Pickle – that was her nickname for me. I'd forgotten! And she was thinking about leaving for Scotland in the second, wistful picture. More recollections flood in – Mum's favourite colour was cerulean blue, and she loved sweet-smelling peonies – but others have washed away. I don't remember which of Alex's nieces loves the Disney princess Belle, and which one Jasmine. I can't recall a single detail from my graduation, the day Gran moved into Ravensbrook, or the Harry Styles song playing in the bar when I met Alex. But I can reel off the names of his medications and how many tablets he should take each day.

My head hurts, like someone has lit a fuse and it's about to explode. Blood drips from my nose and onto the duvet. I grab a tissue from the bedside drawer. When the bleeding stops, I throw the rag in the bin and return to our bed.

'Alex?'

He shakes beneath my fingertips. His skin is layered with a thin film of sweat and his hands move in his sleep, as if he's fighting off an invisible enemy.

'Stop!' he mumbles.

'I'm here.' I kiss his hair and press my body against his, hoping he'll feel my support in whatever dark place his mind has dragged him to.

'No, no, no!'

'It's a bad dream.' I whisper the words in his ear.

'NO!'

Alex sits bolt upright, his eyes wide with panic. The compass tattoo stretches across his torso, but the eastern and western points distort and disappear as he bends over, panting.

I kiss his shoulder while he gasps for air. Sharp bones jut out.

'Take a deep breath and let it out slowly. That's it!'

Sweat beads on his brow. I wait for him to recover – I used to hate it whenever I emerged from nightmares and Ed fired questions at me, artillery style. I screw a handful of duvet into a tight ball in frustration. I can remember that useless piece of info, but not what's happening between Alex and me, or whether my time jump was successful. Have I saved those people on the train, the Marshall brothers, and the Night Prowler victims? I've lived through whatever happened on those days. I *must* know deep down, but it's deeply buried.

'God, that was awful,' Alex says faintly.

His breathing is more regular, but his eyes are bloodshot and circled with deep shadows.

'It's over.' I rub his back. 'It wasn't real.'

'You're wrong. It's never over.' He weeps into his hands. 'And it *is* real.'

'How do you mean?'

'I can't stop seeing his face.'

A knot tightens in my stomach. I don't need to ask – there's only one person he could be referring to.

'Charles Fielding haunts me in my dreams. I see him all the time. He was staring straight at me when I stretched out to grab him.'

He looks up at me, an anguished expression etched on his face.

'I saw the horror and shock in his eyes when he knew. He just *knew.*'

'What?' The word catches in my throat.

'We would save ourselves and watch him die.'

26

Tuesday, May 28, 2024

My engagement ring is missing. I only notice it's gone while I'm boiling the kettle to make tea. At first, I panic and think it must have slipped off in the river, or when I travelled back, but it hits me like a punch to the stomach: Alex hasn't proposed. We're nowhere near thinking about marriage after the trauma of the last twelve months. We missed Vicky's birthday celebrations as Alex was so poorly, and never hired a hot air balloon in Bristol for my twenty-fifth. It's been a difficult year due to his illness. We're taking one day at a time and not looking too far ahead.

Gran's old advice from my childhood rings in my ear: *Be careful what you wish for.*

She used to say this whenever I wished time would speed up and the school holidays would arrive sooner. Now, I have Alex physically here with me, but not the Alex from before. His body and mind are badly damaged from that day on Hammersmith Bridge, and the ordeal I've put him through.

I could return to 2023 and try again. Do it differently. Make him better.

I dismiss the idea as soon as it enters my head. I'm weak and my heart is beating like crazy. The palpitations are far worse than before, and God knows what's wrong with my brain. My headache is crippling. *What could happen next?* The ripples I inadvertently cause could potentially be even worse. I'm with Alex and can help him recover. The main thing is we're together and I've stopped the other terrible things from happening. *I think.* I haven't had the time or opportunity to check yet.

'Here you go.'

I pass Alex a mug as he shuffles into the kitchen. He slumps into a chair and stares at a pile of post on the table, his brow furrowed. I catch glimpses of red reminder notices, which look ominous. I sit down and open the top envelope, finding a late payment warning for our electricity. Beneath it are backdated bills for gas and council tax. We're badly overdrawn and behind on credit card payments.

'Don't worry,' Alex says. 'We can pay it all off when I finish this commission.'

I nod and take a sip of tea. I don't want to press him. I remember he's been leaving the flat early every morning in the last few weeks to finish his storm scene – the only ray of good news recently.

'It won't be long, I promise. I know I've fallen behind with the painting, but I'm heading into the studio later. I've almost finished it.'

'Don't pressure yourself. You don't have to work if you're unwell.'

I rest my hand on top of his, but he snatches it back. He scrapes his chair across the floor, creating more distance between us. The muscles around my jaw tense. I remember him shrinking away from me on the lifeboat when he realised our rescuers wouldn't find Charles in the water. Alex couldn't bear to feel the touch of my skin then or now.

'Of course I do!' he says hotly. 'How are we going to pay off our debts unless this picture is a success?'

I flinch. Alex has never raised his voice at me before.

'Sorry! I didn't mean to snap. You can't get a second job on top of your shifts. It all comes down to whether this guy likes what I'm creating.'

'He'll love it! You're a brilliant painter.'

His eyes mist up. 'I *was*, but I'm not sure what I am anymore, who I've become. Sometimes, when I look in the mirror, I have no idea who's staring back.' He yanks his hair at the roots. 'I wish it would stop. I want it all to stop.'

I pull his hands away, pressing them to my lips. 'Please, Alex. What can I do?'

His body sags.

'What about counselling?'

The words hang bubble-like in the air as I remember he's had sessions to help with his PTSD but stopped attending a few months ago. The nightmares have increased ever since.

'You could go back to the psychiatrist. Or find another therapist.' It feels like I'm grasping at sand, which slips through my fingers. 'Or we could ask the GP for new medication. Try different anti-depressants – find ones that suit you better?'

'It doesn't work. Nothing blocks out the nightmares. You should know – yours haven't stopped. If anything, your terrors have been getting worse since your birthday.'

'It's different for me. I've always had them, ever since I was a kid due to my narcolepsy. They'll never go away. But you've developed them due to the trauma of . . .' I can't bring myself to finish the sentence. 'There must be something I can do to help?'

I'm almost pleading with him to agree, but anger and resentment flicker across his face the way it did that day on the river. His eyes are ice and filled with hatred. The expression vanishes so fast I'm hoping I imagined it.

'Please, Alex. For us.'

'I can't think of anything, unless you're planning to rewind time and let me save Charles Fielding,' he replies coldly.

I've played and replayed the conversation in my head on the way to work but concluded Alex's comments are a horrible, jarring coincidence. He has no idea what I've done, which is for the best. He sure as hell won't forgive me – he can't absolve himself from guilt over what played out. I'd researched the tide, the location of the lifebuoy, the most accessible bank, and how to alert the police and lifeguard. However, I hadn't taken into account Alex's personality, and general decency. The clues were hiding in plain sight when he talked about his school's hot balloon exercise. He hadn't wanted to put someone else's life above his own and had even faked death to avoid taking part.

Someone always gets hurt unless you opt out of the game.

But *I* played. I saved Alex and accidentally wounded him deeply. I chew the inside of my cheek until I taste raw meat. What about everyone else? Once I've passed through the ticket barriers at High Street Kensington station, I google Louise Marshall and Hammersmith Bridge on my phone. Nothing appears. I double-check – her name wasn't made public when the inquest was opened into Charles Fielding's drowning. I try a search on 'Andrew Marshall', 'house fire', 'brothers dead' and 'Daniel and Oliver Marshall' but that doesn't produce any results. Does this mean they're all alive? I may have achieved one small success, but that's where it ends. My heart beats furiously against my ribcage as I pull up the *Gazette* website:

MORE VICTIMS NAMED IN BARNES TRAIN CRASH

The accident has happened again! The signal box was never fixed – South Western Railway couldn't have taken my anonymous letter seriously. I guess, why would they? They must receive plenty of crank messages. When I click on the website's crime section, it's clear my carefully laid plans have disintegrated further into dust:

OAP'S LIFE SUPPORT TURNED OFF AFTER NIGHT PROWLER ATTACK

An 88-year-old woman has died in intensive care after being beaten in her Hanwell home on May 12. Detectives are no closer to catching the brutal burglar who has terrorised London for decades.

The Night Prowler should have been caught a year ago! I'd rung 999 the night I arrived in the past and had written down the locations and dates of all his future attacks in the Swan to give to the DCI in charge of the investigation. Something sparks in my brain about this detective, but I can't remember his name, what's gone wrong or why I'm poring over the old newspaper cuttings at home.

My mobile vibrates, revealing Zoe's number. I vaguely recall her telling me: *You're like the sister I never had.* I found a WhatsApp exchange between us last week, discussing Alex's mood swings. Before getting on the tube, I'd messaged, asking if she could check on him at the studio later. She's replied:

Thanx for letting me know. Will try to drag him out for lunch! Let's all meet soon. Love you xxx

Relief washes over me and I send a kissing emoji back. I hadn't wanted Alex to be alone. I'd suggested calling in sick, but he'd insisted I come into work. *We can't afford for you to lose your job when money is tight.*

I've almost reached the office when a WhatsApp message lands from Merv:

Rod is on war path. I tried to explain you've had a tough time with Gran and boyfriend being ill, but it's out of my hands. I can't help, sorry.

I text back frantically:

What are you talking about??!!.

The double blue tick appears, and he's typing back. My grasp tightens on the phone as his answer drops.

Need to keep out of this. Hope you understand? Call me later if you need to chat.

No, I don't bloody understand any of this! I can't think or see straight, my eyelids are heavy, and I feel like I've been awake for days on end. I can't remember what's happening at the *Gazette*, let alone elsewhere. I screw my eyes shut, rubbing my temples but nothing comes back. My pendant weighs heavily, a tombstone around my neck, chaffing the skin. Memories collide clumsily in my brain, becoming entangled like weeds in a stream.

As the revolving glass doors into the *Gazette* building consume me whole, one thought becomes clear:

I'm almost certainly entering a trap.

27

Tuesday, May 28, 2024

I'm bypassing Rod's inevitable cold shoulder treatment and unofficial demotion by heading straight to the archives. Being in the doghouse with my mercurial news editor doesn't change in any lifetime. I don't need a compass – all routes eventually end five floors down. I'm not sure what I've done to upset him, but I've probably fallen asleep while typing the news list. I readjust my necklace, which is cutting into my skin. I'm desperate for a nap.

I open the door to 312b and my gaze rests on towering piles of boxes and bin bags. The shelves are completely emptied. Jeremy must have been laid off again!

My eyelids close, my knees crumble.

The ground disappears beneath me. I fall into nothingness.

I have another missed call from Oscar Simmonds, the private investigator. I've been dodging him for days. I close the bedroom door before listening to his voicemail. Oscar is usually upbeat but his tone is worryingly sombre this afternoon.

'Hi, Julia. It's me again . . . Are you there . . . ? I've tried you a few times and emailed but I'm not sure if you're getting any of my messages.

I didn't want to do this over the phone, but I think you should hear my findings ASAP. There's no easy way to say this . . .'

I feel a sharp stab of pain in my chest as he takes a deep breath.

'I've completed a forensic search of your mum's finances and I'm afraid she abruptly stopped using her credit cards in Scotland twenty years ago. I've found no trace of her ever returning to London or buying a plane ticket to Spain. I know this isn't easy to hear after all this time.'

I close my eyes and slump onto the bed, tears slipping down my face.

'There's no official record of her death, so we mustn't give up all hope. However, we should discuss potential scenarios in person. With your permission, I'd like to report my findings to the police and press for their missing person's inquiry to be reopened. Can you call me so we can set up a meeting at your earliest convenience? Thanks. Speak soon.'

I delete the message and resolve not to tell Alex. Receiving bad news on top of his ill health could push him over the edge. I'm not getting back in touch with Oscar. I can't face what he's trying to tell me – that something terrible happened to Mum at the music festival.

She's never coming back.

No! Mum can't be . . .

My eyes open and I wipe the corners of my mouth. I'm sitting, propped against a wall in the empty archives. My chest feels like it's been split open and my stomach is sick with dread all over again. Mum *did* love me – my previous recollections have proved that, but perhaps she couldn't cope with her unique ability and faltering health. She needed to get her head straight and thought I'd have a better life with Gran.

But why would she stop using her credit cards? She should have bought a plane ticket to Spain. She couldn't have been somewhere else in time – Gran had her pendant. She remembers Mum leaving it with her before she set off for Scotland.

Unless Mum had decided enough was enough . . .

I shudder.

I can't go down that rabbit hole. I won't get in touch with Oscar in this life; I'll just pay the outstanding invoice I've found buried among the other bills. Like Gran, I must cling onto hope Mum will return one day. She could have opened different bank accounts overseas and not touched her UK ones.

I can still find her. I haven't lost her forever.

I haul myself up and head to the elevator. I may as well get Rod's hairdryer treatment out of the way. The newsroom is unusually quiet as I walk through. Layla is missing, but Rakesh and Salim are here. Merv studiously avoids eye contact while battering his keyboard. An image of myself standing at his desk flashes into my head.

I'm asking about Louise Marshall after the opening of the inquest into Charles Fielding's death. He tells me her name hasn't been made public yet; I fudge how I know it. He says she's recovered fully and split from her husband. They share joint custody of their sons and are both refusing to give interviews to the press.

They're all alive!

A small smile flickers across my face. It vanishes when I see myself back beside his chair.

Merv is explaining that South Western Railway has ruled out signal problems contributing to the Barnes crash; it's believed to be partly due to driver error.

My letter was useless! I couldn't prevent the tragedy. My stomach flips as Rod beckons me into the bunker. The junior news editors keep their heads down. Jesus. This looks serious. What have I done this time? Rod closes the door behind me – he never usually shuts it. He says he likes staff to hear him yelling at colleagues 'to keep them on their toes'.

'Sit down.' He gestures to a chair.

'I'm sorry for falling asleep,' I say automatically.

'What? When did that happen?'

'Oh, I meant on the tube. I didn't check my emails before coming in.'

He sighs. 'Don't worry about that. Look, Julia. Enough is enough. You've done a good job on news desk, and we're grateful for your commitment to the *Gazette* over the last couple of years, but I'm afraid we have to let you go.'

'Why? What have I done?' I grip the sides of the chair.

'We've already discussed this issue – your hoax calls to the police and interference in the Night Prowler case are making things difficult for Merv and the crime correspondent. DCI Fairweather has lodged complaints about your behaviour and you could face further police action, which reflects badly on the *Gazette*. We want you to go quietly, with three months' paid notice, which is generous under these unusual circumstances.'

'Omigod,' I whisper.

The memories hit me in a giant, destructive tidal wave:

Police turned up to Brackley Road in Chiswick the night I travelled back to 2023 after I borrowed a passer-by's phone to dial 999. Officers chased a masked man but didn't catch him. The Night Prowler had escaped, but I knew there were other chances. I called the police shortly before the attack due to take place in Hounslow, but he never struck, nor the evening of the Northolt burglary. The police traced my phone and pinpointed my locations – proving I couldn't have witnessed any alleged break-ins.

I anonymously emailed DCI Fairweather, claiming I'd worked out the Night Prowler's next target – Clapham Junction on May 9 this year. He ignored my repeated messages, but I accidentally forwarded one from my work account. He complained to the Gazette, *and I received a fixed penalty notice for wasting police time after officers found a fifty-two-year-old woman alone in the house on Almeric Road. There was no sign of the Night Prowler.*

All my information was incorrect because I'd disrupted his routine on May 11 last year. He didn't strike for an entire year, until two weeks ago when he broke into the Hanwell house and attacked the eighty-eight-year-old. DCI Fairweather wouldn't take my call and the police didn't turn up when I rang 999 with the pensioner's address because I was labelled a nuisance caller.

Rod's voice echoes through an invidious, grey, curling mist.

'Do you want to add anything, or shall we leave it at that?'

His tone raises an octave.

'Hello? Earth to Julia! Am I boring you? For fuck's sake, wake up!'

28

TUESDAY, MAY 28, 2024

I can't account for the last forty-five minutes; I've lost so much more.

I'm standing outside the entrance to the underground station on Kensington High Street but can't remember how I got here. I have no idea whether Rod helped me up or left me in the chair to sleep. I wonder whether security escorted me out or I fled the building in tears. What's happening to me? I'm here, yet I'm not. Is this how bad Mum felt when she fled London? I'm a phantom watching other people's lives: cyclists zoom past, shoppers juggle their bags, and office workers grab takeaway coffees. A tourist in a peaked cap and sunglasses, holding two Starbucks cups, stops and says something. What does she want? Her face is a blank canvas. Her lips move, but the sounds drift away. Or am *I* disappearing? My eyelids droop.

I pinch myself. I'm Julia Hockney. I'm here in west London, in 2024. My heart is beating way too fast.

'Kensington Gardens?' the woman says, louder. 'Do you know how I get there?'

'That way,' I snap, pointing to the right.

She holds out a drink. 'I have a spare coffee. Do you want it?'

I gratefully accept. She flashes a smile I don't deserve and walks away. The space she left behind is filled with more bodies. Flesh and bone disintegrate, replaced by atoms and molecules. I shudder, picturing Mum alone and poorly in the middle of nowhere. Not coping with her nosebleeds and headaches, unable to carry on. Galloway Forest Park is vast and has deep, deep lochs. Could she have fallen in one? Or deliberately jumped?

My phone vibrates with a message from Zoe:

Left messages for Alex. Hasn't called back. Sally has tummy ache – had to pick her up from school early so can't swing by studio, sorry x

I text back:

No worries. Have been given half day! Heading over x

I thought I'd replied immediately, but the time stamp says ten minutes have passed. I need to get a grip. Stop thinking about the possibility Mum had an accident or took her own life twenty years ago. I sip the coffee – it's my regular, a black Americano – and message Alex, but he's offline. I call up the address of his studio from my phone, shivering as the hairs on my arms stand on end. It feels like I'm being watched, but that's impossible. No one can see me. I'm barely here. I'm evaporating into thin air.

I wake up abruptly as the cab driver pulls off the A40 near Acton. A lorry cuts him up and he's hanging out of the window, shouting obscenities. Images of me sinking in icy water and being chased by a man with a knife linger malignantly in my brain.

'Sorry about that, love. Am having the day from hell.'

Tell me about it. We're weaving through narrow, near-identical roads lined with grey, unremarkable, anonymous looking warehouses. Instinctively, I know the huge building at the end of this row hosts the collective of local artists Alex has belonged to ever since graduating from the University of the Arts London. I pay the driver and double-check my phone but there's still nothing from him.

I lean against the building, dabbing my nose, which is bleeding again. My head jerks forward as I nod off. I straighten up and finish my cold coffee. When I feel more human, I push through the front door. Familiar smells drift back: the mustiness of wet clay from the pottery; the blast of heat scented with beeswax and wet newspapers from the glass studio. I wander down the corridors, trying to get my bearings, holding onto the walls with one hand.

'Julia! It's been forever!'

A woman with a leopard print headscarf pokes her head around a door. *Lizzy.* I catch a glimpse of vivid stained-glass windows behind her.

'Hi, Lizzy.' I lick my dry lips. 'I left work early. I thought I'd surprise Alex.'

A deep furrow appears between her eyes. 'He's not here.'

Dammit. I should have told the taxi to wait.

'When did he leave?'

I'm trying to work out my journey home – there must be a bus stop around here somewhere. Hopefully, it's close by. My legs won't carry me far.

She rubs her hands on her denim dungarees. 'We haven't seen Alex for months.' She nods at the pottery studio opposite. 'Fatima and me have both been worried, but he isn't replying to our messages. How's he doing? Is he working from home?'

Lizzy and Fatima. I remember the note they left for Alex on Hammersmith Bridge to mark the first anniversary of his death.

'But he spends hours a day here on his commission,' I blurt out.

My mouth tastes of cold metal as she shakes her head slowly. In the distance, I hear the tinkle of fragile glass breaking.

'I don't understand. I can't . . .' I knead my forehead. 'He said he was finishing his painting today.'

'That's good news. The last time we saw him, he said the commission wasn't going well.'

'Why not?'

She looks at the floor, biting her lip.

'Please, Lizzy! He's not telling me anything. I need to know what's going on.'

She shrugs. 'He was supposed to be working on a storm scene but had started a portrait instead. The client wasn't happy and they argued. Alex backed down and promised to paint whatever the guy wanted. We figured he'd been given more time.' She gestures to his studio. 'Take a peek – he didn't lock up when he left.'

My legs feel soft and malleable but somehow take me to the door. Stepping inside, my hand flies to my mouth. Slashed, discarded canvases lie stricken on the floor like carcasses, ripped from easels and walls. I can't spot a single sea scene among them. They're all variations of the single painting on the far wall that's escaped harm.

The walls and ceiling press down, squeezing me into a tiny, oppressive box, as I walk towards the huge acrylic portrait that's drained of colour.

Thousands of shattered diamonds explode across the canvas, forming lethal white, grey, and black shards. They cluster to form features – eyes, a nose, mouth and beard – before dissipating.

The mouth has opened into a gaping, silent scream for help.

I recognise the man's face.

It's Charles Fielding.

29

TUESDAY, MAY 28, 2024

Pick up!

Alex isn't returning my calls. I ring him in the back of an Uber, but it goes straight to voicemail. My throat aches and I barely get out the words through my rising panic:

I'm worried about you. Let me know you're okay xx

Clearly, he's not. Alex is severely depressed and has lost the commission – his ticket to a potential future exhibition. He has pretended to come to the studio each day, which is far worse than admitting he's not well enough to paint. He's withdrawn from his work, from our relationship, and it's not hard to see why – he blames me for what's gone wrong. He hasn't sketched me in pastel or painted my face in acrylic. He's torturing himself by repeatedly recreating the image stuck in his mind of Charles before he disappeared below the surface of the water. *We both have demons.* I stare at my fingers, feeling Alex recoil from my touch in the lifeboat as he realised hope of finding Charles alive was lost.

When we reach our building, I leap out before the car has completely stopped and run, wheezing, to the front door. The lift takes forever to arrive, but I'm not strong enough to make it up five flights of stairs. I fumble in my handbag, the keys slipping through my fingers. I shove them clumsily into the lock. The door hasn't been double bolted.

'Alex? Are you here?'

The flat is eerily quiet. I check the kitchen and bedroom. The spare room is empty. Pushing open the bathroom door, my insides turn to liquid. Alex is lying on the floor, vomit pooling next to his blue lips. Pills are scattered around him, together with an empty bottle of spirits.

'Alex!' I scream. 'What have you done?'

His eyes don't open as I heave him onto my lap. His body is heavy, his face deathly grey.

'Stay with me!' I plead. 'Please don't leave!'

I grab his wrist and find a feeble pulse, before pulling out my mobile and dialling 999.

'My boyfriend's taken an overdose,' I tell the operator. 'He's barely breathing. Please come quickly.'

Everything else is a blur.

I'm sitting with Zoe outside the intensive care unit in Hammersmith Hospital, watching the girls play. Sally is feeling better. She and Hannah are skipping down the corridor in dress-up clothes, waving their dolls at an elderly woman in a cream coat at the end of our row of seats.

'Don't bother the lady!' Zoe calls out.

'It's no problem,' she replies. 'They're not disturbing me.'

Zoe couldn't find anyone to take the girls after school and bundled them into the car minutes after I rang. I'm glad of the distraction. Alex was transferred here after having his stomach pumped in A&E. He'd failed to regain consciousness and his pulse was weak. I'd brought along the empty painkiller containers that lay next to the bottle of rum we'd drunk the night of our engagement in our previous life. Doctors had exchanged worried looks when they calculated the number of tablets he must have swallowed.

Hannah climbs onto my lap, a bundle of sticky fingers, yellow tulle and lace. She's clutching her princess doll. I've finally remembered she loves Belle, while Sally prefers Jasmine. That's one of the ways I tell them apart. They both have dark-blonde hair and dimples, but Hannah is an inch shorter than her sister and speaks with a slight lisp.

She throws her arms around my neck and gives me a hug.

'That's what I need, thank you – a lovely cuddle.'

I remember saying something similar to the toddler with the lion toy in the café. That feels like a million years ago.

Hannah nods solemnly. 'I thought so.' She plays with my hair, avoiding eye contact. 'Is Uncle Alex going to die?'

My heart cracks in two. My voice dies in my throat.

'Aunt Julia? Tell me!'

Zoe pulls Hannah from my lap and onto her knee. Her face is taut with worry as she pushes her long, chestnut brown hair behind her ears.

'No, sweetie. The doctors will make him better. He's going to be okay.'

'Promise?'

Her blunt fringe flutters as she breathes out heavily. 'Yes. Go play with your sister.'

Zoe stifles a cry as she skips off, and gropes for my hand. 'I had to promise. What else could I say? But what if he doesn't, Julia? Oh God. What if he doesn't?'

I wrap my arms around her. 'We can't think like that. We have to stay positive.'

Except, I'm not. My mind is treacherous, forcing me to hideously dark places – a life without Mum, Gran *and* Alex.

'I'm sorry,' I mumble into her coat. 'This is all my fault.'

'Don't say that. We both tried to get him back to counselling and to see his GP, but he wouldn't listen. He thought he could fight his demons on his own.'

'But I should have prevented this. I should never have gone to work this morning when he was upset.'

'He was hiding his pain from both of us. That's so Alex, trying to protect *us,* instead of looking after himself.'

We clutch each other silently, too scared to speak, as a doctor pushes through the doors. His expression is grave.

'How's my brother?' Fear catches in Zoe's voice.

He sits down next to us, with one of *those* looks. I recognise it from the time the GP told me Gran's brain scans had revealed Alzheimer's. It's a mixture of sympathy and dread at being the one who must break bad news to relatives.

'Oh God,' Zoe whispers.

While the girls chatter to the white-haired visitor nearby, Dr Benjamin explains that Alex is in a coma, on life support.

'We're doing everything we can, but the overdose cut off oxygen to his brain and caused injury,' he says. 'We don't know the full extent of the damage yet, but you must prepare yourselves that it could be life changing.'

Dr Benjamin left twenty minutes ago, and Zoe hasn't stopped crying. She's turned her face to the wall to prevent the girls from seeing her devastation. My eyelids are heavy and drooping. I mustn't sleep. Zoe needs me. I have to stay here with her. I catch a glimpse of Sally's turquoise princess outfit, and a shimmer of gold, before my eyes close.

I'm on a train platform with Mummy and Gran. Mummy's wearing her pendant and her favourite turquoise dress. She lets me play with her necklace because I'm sad about her leaving for Scotland without me.

'Spin the stone and make a change,' she sings. 'Transform the world and rearrange.'

I tap the stone and try not to look pleased. I'm still cross with Mummy. I hide behind Gran's legs when she asks for a kiss.

'Never mind,' Mummy says. 'Bye, Pickle. I love you.'

Now, she's on the train and I still won't tell her I love her. She drops her necklace out of the window because she doesn't like it anymore. Gran catches it. The train pulls away and I run after it, shouting at Mummy to come back.

I wipe the tears from my eyes and the train magically stops. The necklace is around Mummy's neck once more but it's turned into a huge, glistening snake. Mummy's trying hard to pull off the serpent but it's squeezing harder and harder. She can't breathe! Mummy needs my help. I reach up . . .

Julia!

My eyes open, and I straighten up, checking the corners of my mouth for drool. I examine my hand; it feels warm as though someone was holding it. Zoe's vanished, but Samira is here.

'Sorry,' she says, offering me a coffee. 'I told her not to disturb you.'

I rub my eyes. 'Who?'

232

'The lady who was chatting to the girls earlier. She squeezed your hand, worrying you were about to slip off your seat. She's gone now.'

I gratefully take the cup. I check my watch. It's 10 p.m. I've napped for fifteen minutes, but it's not enough. I want to fall asleep again and remember more about Mum on the train platform. This must have been before she left for the music festival. I refused to kiss her goodbye. I never told her I loved her.

I bat away the memory; it's too painful.

'Thank you for coming, Samira,' I say, my voice cracking.

'Where else would I be? Or any of us, for that matter.'

She's closed her shop early to be here, and Hamish pulled out of a two-day work trip to Belgium to join us. He's pacing up and down further along the corridor. Lizzy and Fatima from the artists' space are dozing on seats close to where the elderly woman had been sitting.

'Where's Zoe?'

'Her friend arrived to take the girls for the night. She's walking them to the lift. One of Alex's mates will drop them at school tomorrow morning so Zoe can stay here.'

'He's lucky to have so many people who care about him, and rally around.'

'We're the lucky ones,' she says, touching my arm. 'But you know that already.'

Tears sting my eyes. 'I wish Gran could be here with me.'

'Can you ring the home?'

'Oh God no. I couldn't put her through that – if she did understand the news she'd be devastated. I mean, I wish the old Gran was here. She wouldn't have said anything; she'd have held me and let me cry.'

'I can do that.'

I sniff, desperately trying to pull myself together. 'Thanks, Samira. You're a good friend to Alex. And to me.'

I jump as my phone vibrates. Vicky has finally replied after the four messages I left earlier.

OMG. So sorry. Am at work drinks with Chris. Can't leave but will call you later. Stay strong xx

The old, original Vicky would have dropped everything to be here, wouldn't she? Not stay out with someone else's boyfriend. But I remember the time when Gran went missing before she went into the home, and I had to call the police. She'd wandered out of the house and climbed on a bus, which took her into central London. I was hysterical and begged Vicky to come over, but she never replied. She apologised by text the next day – she had tickets for a gig in Shepherd's Bush, which were non-refundable. I spent long hours on my own, worrying about Gran, until she was picked up in a patrol car by two PCs. She was crying about the Night Prowler, and insisting she wasn't safe at home while he was 'out there'.

'Anyone important?' Samira asks, as I study my phone.

'I used to think so, but now I'm not sure.' I put the mobile back in my handbag without replying to Vicky.

Zoe returns, slumping down beside us. Samira passes her a spare coffee. We all jump as a nurse pokes her head around the door.

'He can have a visitor,' she says, nodding at Zoe. 'Immediate family only for a few minutes.'

I stay in my seat as she stands up. She stretches out her hand.

'Come on.'

'Are you sure?'

'You're family, Julia. Alex would want you there. So do I.'

My heart contracts. We follow the nurse into the unit, our arms wrapped around each other's waists. I keep my gaze fixed straight ahead, so I don't have to see the other sick patients. We stop walking. For a split second, I think the nurse has brought us to the wrong bed. I don't recognise the man hooked up to all the tubes and equipment. But the compass tattoo on his torso doesn't lie. It's Alex. He's desperately ill because of me.

'Oh God, this can't be happening,' Zoe cries.

'It isn't,' I whisper. 'It won't.'

The doctor's words ring in my ears: *Life changing.*

Zoe reaches for my hand, but I'm already backing away from his bed.

Transform the world and rearrange.

'I'm sorry. I can't stay here. I have to leave.'

'But—'

'We won't lose him, Zoe, I promise. I won't let this happen.'

'Julia!'

I run out, bursting through the doors. Samira and Hamish shout after me, but I don't stop. I need to go home.

Do better. Change this. Make things right.

I turn left and run past a disabled bathroom, heading to the lifts, but double back. There's no time to waste. I won't let Alex, Zoe, and his friends, suffer for a minute longer than necessary. Inside the tiny room, I lock the door and lean against it. Waves of tiredness wash over me.

I grip my pendant, close my eyes and spin the stone.

I wait for the curtain to fall on this life.

30

THEN

May 11, 2023

Where is Alex?

His uni friends are at the end of the bar, next to the raucous hen party. The *Gazette* journalists are getting steadily drunker at a corner table. It's approaching 11 p.m. and the Swan manager has exhausted his collection of Harry Styles albums and moved on to Ed Sheeran, but there's no sign of him. I return to staring at the door, willing Alex to walk through it, healthy, happy and smiling.

'Are you waiting for someone?' Layla nudges me and offers what I'm guessing is a double gin and tonic. 'You're jumpy. You've been acting oddly all evening.'

'Sorry. I was supposed to meet someone, but I think he's stood me up.'

'Bastard. You deserve better.'

'I honestly don't.'

'What?' She leans closer, cupping her ear above the music.

I shake my head, which is a mistake. The bar tilts and pitches. I grab her arm so I don't fall over.

'Why don't you go home? You look unwell. Your nose is bleeding.'

I dab at it with a tissue. It was far worse at High Street Kensington station, where it took ages to stop the gushing. I almost threw up on the platform and was bent over, retching, as Coffee Guy raced past. This time, I escaped being showered with his drink, which I'll take as a good omen. The man squeezed onto the train before the doors closed, followed by the pony-tailed musician with the violin case who caught me when I collapsed during my brief jump into the past.

'I'll give it a few more minutes,' I say, shrugging. 'He never usually lets me down.'

'You deserve to be happy, Julia.'

Do I? Maybe this life – trying and failing to correct wrongs – is all I can look forward to. It's my punishment for meddling in other people's lives. My ability isn't a gift, it's a curse. Perhaps that's what Mum discovered. I push her from my mind. When Alex arrives, I'll explain what could happen to him tomorrow. He'll think I'm mad at first, but he's open-minded. I'll make him see I'm genuine. We have to persuade the lifeguard to come to the bridge sooner. We could pretend a group of drunken youths are partying and plan to jump into the river.

'Can I borrow your phone quickly? Mine's dead. I need to ring the nursing home about my gran.'

Another lie. They slip out of my mouth so easily these days, I barely notice.

'Sure.' Layla rummages in her handbag and thrusts the mobile into my hand, reeling off the PIN number. 'I'll be over there with Merv when you're done.' She points to the corner.

'Thanks. You're a lifesaver.'

I skirt around the women dressed in flapper costumes, scanning the group. The woman in the red dress isn't among them. Outside, I find an emergency number to report gas leaks and claim there's an urgent problem outside number 4, Brackley Road, Chiswick, where the Night Prowler is due to strike. The woman on the end of the line says engineers are in the area and will arrive shortly. I pretend I have a dodgy connection and turn off the phone. With any luck, they'll deter the serial attacker without spooking him. He'll stick to his previous offending pattern, which means I can help police catch him later this year.

This plan *could* work. But what about Alex? Why isn't he here?

I stare at Layla's phone. The urge to turn it on and dial his mobile is overwhelming. I want to hear his voice and sense the smile hovering on his lips, even if he thinks I'm a wrong caller and hangs up. I don't want to remember him sick and in ICU. That can't be the last image I have of him.

I lean against the wall, my eyelids drooping. My shoulders cave and my jaw slackens.

'How are you, Julia?'

Layla's phone slips between my fingers. I pick it up, dizzily, and catch sight of tassels on a red hem.

'It's you,' I say numbly.

The woman in the blonde wig shivers in her thin, flimsy dress. Her cheekbones are razor sharp; she's thinner, and paler, than last time.

'What do you want?' I ask.

She fumbles in her handbag for a cigarette and lighter. Her hands shake as she takes a drag, blowing out small circles of smoke.

'For you to see sense. You wouldn't listen last time.'

'I *couldn't.*'

'But you must. I know what you're going through.'

'How? Are you like me?'

She stares at my pendant. 'Yes.'

I let go of the brickwork again, which is a mistake and make a grab for it.

'But you don't have one of these,' I say, holding up the stone locket. 'How are you doing it? Coming and going?'

'There are other ways.'

'Such as?'

'Hopefully, you'll never find out.'

She drops her cigarette and grinds it hard beneath her silver-spiked heel. I shudder.

'Is this when you tell me you're from the future and know how this is going to end?'

'Something like that. You're not going to like what I have to say, but you need to accept it. Eventually, you will.'

'Tell me!'

She takes a deep breath. 'It doesn't matter what you do, Julia, someone always dies in the river tomorrow.'

'I don't believe you.'

'I've seen every possible variation. You ring the police the night before and tell them there's a suspicious package on Hammersmith Bridge in the hope they'll close it, preventing Louise and Charles from visiting the next day. They treat it as a prank call and do nothing.'

I open my mouth to argue, but she continues.

'You make an anonymous call to the lifeguards to warn them that youths have organised a party on the bridge and plan to jump into the water at midday. It's treated as malicious and another emergency takes priority – two children fall from Kew Bridge.'

The woman smooths her wig, holding my gaze. 'You borrow a passer-by's phone earlier than before to warn the police about possible jumpers as Charles and Louise make their way to the bridge. The patrol car is diverted to a robbery. The next time you try, all units are sent to reports of a suspicious package and possible terrorist attack at Earl's Court. Nothing works, Julia. Charles and Louise die, or Alex dies. Or a combination of the three. There's no

239

alternative ending to this story. It ends unhappily for many people, now and in the future.'

I shake my head. 'What am I supposed to do? Nothing?'

She waits for my words to sink in. This is *exactly* what she's suggesting.

'You're learning the impact this is having on everyone around you,' she continues. 'The smallest change in the past creates huge ripples in the future, which are often disastrous. Stop travelling back. As hard as that may be for you, personally, you must leave things as they are. It causes the least amount of damage to the fewest people.'

I cannot, *will not,* accept what she's saying.

'I'm saving people.'

'By condemning others to death. You don't get to be judge and jury.'

'But you do?' I pause. 'Who *are* you?'

'Someone who's been doing this for much longer than you. I've made my own mistakes – plenty of them over the years.' Her eyes glisten. 'I should have done better, but I can't change any of my errors. I have to accept they are permanent. So must you.'

My heartbeat quickens. 'Have you ever met my mum, Marianne Hockney? She could do this too. You'd recognise her – we look similar.'

She shakes her head.

'But there are others like us? What—'

'Leave here now,' she interrupts. 'It's as simple as that.'

'I can't. I've hurt someone I love. I need to do it over.'

'Before long, your body won't let you. You must be feeling the after-effects of travelling – the vertigo and sickness when you return to your present day, as well as the nosebleeds. What you can't see is the damage it's doing to your body – the repeated acceleration and reduction in cell growth will lead to fatal abnormalities.'

'What do you mean? Cancer? Heart problems?'

She doesn't reply.

'How many jumps do I get?'

'That's not how this works. I'm not here to give you a cheat sheet. The only way to protect your health is to stop right now.'

I check my watch. It's 11.15 p.m.

'Alex isn't coming,' she says quietly. 'You won't meet him tonight.'

The muscles around my mouth tense. 'Why not?'

She remains silent and won't meet my gaze.

'What have you done to him? If he doesn't come . . . If I don't meet him—'

I feel faint and hot as blood rushes to my head.

'Your present-day life will be changed,' she says firmly. 'If you leave now, you'll go back to the life you left behind when you fell asleep. You already know what to do – move towards the ticking sound, rotate the stone in the pendant, and return to 2024.'

Alex in a coma and brain damaged. Zoe, the girls, and Alex's friends devastated because of me.

'No, no, no!'

'Think of your visit to the past as being set by a clock, which is always set for 1 p.m. tomorrow. You can't change this. If you are still here by then, you will have a life going forwards from that point.'

My heart freezes. *I won't be with Alex because I haven't met him tonight.*

'Where will I be?' I gasp. 'Who will I be with?'

'You won't like that life either. You've already lost Alex in one way or another, Julia. You must accept it. Let him go and move on with your life before you create more pain for yourself and others. Before you hurt your family and friends all over again.'

I dig my nails into my palm as I think of Gran.

'You don't know me or my family,' I say, staggering away. 'You're a stranger. You know nothing about my life.'

I run down the road, clutching Layla's phone.

'Julia! Come back. You don't understand what you're leaving behind.'

Sure, I do! The love of my life critically ill and on life support in 2024.

I'm not returning to him hovering between life and death in ICU. And I can't live without him.

I have no clue why this timing matters, but I'm going to find him before the 1 p.m. cut-off tomorrow. I'll save his life in the future.

31

THEN

MAY 12, 2023

Time is running out.

This morning, it's taken even longer to recover from travelling into the past. I spent hours with my head over the toilet bowl before I was well enough to move from the bathroom, let alone leave the flat. On the way to Alex's studio, I kept the windows of the cab open, and fell asleep despite the fresh air. We've pulled off the A40 and are now weaving through the warren of roads on the industrial estate.

'Can you wait for me here?' I ask the driver.

I half run, half stagger inside the building, and find my way to his workspace, pushing open the door.

'Alex?'

The room is empty, and surprisingly neat. His paints are tidied away, and old rags discarded. The floor is newly swept and cleaned, scrubbed of coloured flecks. A series of paintings of storms at sea are arranged on stands in a semicircle, as if awaiting inspection. This could be his new commission.

Before leaving, I stick my head through the doors of Lizzy's and Fatima's workshops, but they're not here either. I check my watch as I return to the cab. It's 11 a.m.

'Where to?' the guy asks.

I can't remember Alex's old address before he moved in with me, and I've tried calling his mobile using Layla's phone, but it's turned off. I haven't memorised Zoe's and Samira's numbers. They're stored in my phone, which is always dead in the past. There's no time to head to north London to speak to Zoe, but Samira should know where Alex is today.

'Brentford,' I tell the driver. 'The Hidden Things gift shop.'

'I've not heard of that one.'

'I'll direct you.'

I pray Samira falls for my journalist cover story one more time. She's my last chance to track down Alex.

I'm standing outside the closed shop, clenching my fists in frustration. The note on the door states: '*Apologies. Teething problems! Closed temporarily due to power failure. Hopefully re-open tomorrow. Samira.*'

I have no hope of finding Alex before 1 p.m. I can't contact him on Facebook or Instagram; he hasn't started to experiment with social media to promote his art.

I open the cab door and sink, defeated, into the seat.

'Can you take me to Hammersmith Bridge, please?'

I close my eyes and concentrate as the driver turns the key, and grinds into gear. Beneath the purr of the engine, and the droning traffic outside the window, is that faint ticking again. It's hovering below the surface of this life and calling me back to 2024.

I can't leave yet.

There's one more thing to do before moving towards this hidden, but ever-present sound.

I must stop Charles Fielding from pulling Louise Marshall into the river.

On the way to Hammersmith, I've made an anonymous call from Layla's phone to the police and lifeguard to report potential jumpers. Now, just before midday, the driver's dropped me a short distance from the bridge to avoid a traffic snarl up. There's no sign of any police cars but, hopefully, they'll arrive soon. I lurch towards the green structure. The horse leaps on the coat of arms, frozen and waiting to be set free. The swords silently sweep at hidden enemies. Or are they threatening me?

Loud voices overpower the birdsong from the turrets. It's Charles and Louise. They're arguing furiously further along the walkway. A man wearing tan trousers, a smart blue jacket, and shiny brown shoes, is watching them. From the back he looks like Alex. He's the same build and has wavy brown hair, but it can't be him. Plus, Alex rarely dresses formally.

The man briefly glances at the river before his gaze settles on the couple. My heart freezes as I catch his profile. How? It's impossible . . .

'Alex?' I shout. 'Is that really you?'

He turns around, shielding his eyes from the sun with his hand. 'Hey. Do I know you?'

Tears spill down my cheeks. I've found him. He's alive! Seeing him healthy, and not hooked up to the tubes, is the most incredible sight.

He frowns deeply; he has no idea who I am. We've never met in this life.

The sun passes behind a cloud, and shadows gather. My happiness drains away, and my blood turns to ice. He shouldn't be here. I have to stop whatever's about to happen.

'What are you doing here, Alex?' I call out, drawing closer.

Confusion flickers across his face. 'Are you from the *Gazette*? Is the photoshoot cancelled?'

'What photoshoot?'

A loud scream pierces the air. *Louise.* Charles has clambered over the side and is standing on tiptoes, facing inwards on the narrow ledge.

'Charles, no!' Louise cries. 'Please don't do this.'

His face darkens as he clutches the rail and leans back.

'You haven't given me any choice! I can't live without you.'

Pain spikes in my chest, and I'm frozen to the spot as Alex runs towards them. I can't stop what's unfolding. I can't breathe.

A girl aged about five with pigtails steps onto the bridge, her mouth falling open into an 'O' shape. She waves her arms frantically. I recognise her. She was feeding the ducks with Alex in Kew Gardens, the first time we met for a date.

'Stop!' she cries.

'Stay away, it's not safe,' Alex hollers.

She ignores him, drawing closer.

'Go back!' he insists.

I'm doubled over and can't intervene. The pain in my chest is crippling. I think I'm having a heart attack.

Alex approaches Charles with his hands outstretched. 'Hey, sir. You don't want to do this.'

'You're wrong! I do. One hundred per cent.'

'We can talk,' Louise insists.

'Yes!' Alex nods. 'It doesn't have to be like this. You can take a breather and step away. Think about this more.'

'What do I have left? My life is over.'

The little girl steps in front of Louise, but she skirts past easily and bends over the side, throwing her arms around Charles. He clutches her waist with one hand, holding on with the other.

'Stop this!' she begs.

Charles gazes at Alex with a pleading expression.

'Forgive me,' he says, letting go.

He falls backwards, holding Louise firmly. Her mouth is open wide, frozen in shock, as she's dragged over with him. She falls silently off the bridge.

'No!' Alex swipes at thin air.

The little girl screams and covers her eyes.

I run towards Alex as he slings a leg over the side, and another. He holds onto the railings, leaning out above the water.

'Stop, Alex! You'll die.'

'Don't worry,' he says, glancing back. 'I'm a good swimmer.'

I lunge at him, but he's already let go.

'No!' I cry.

Fear ripples across the little girl's face.

'Behind you!' she cries.

I catch a glimmer of bright yellow and mirrored shades as I turn around.

Cyclist. On the footpath.

'Move, for fuck's sake!'

We collide.

Shining metal, spinning wheels.

Blinding pain rips through my body, setting my nerves on fire.

The child tries to catch me, her hand stretching out.

Her fingers graze mine.

I'm falling backwards, suspended in mid-air.

I've landed in Gran's house. I'm standing barefoot on green carpet as soft as meadow grass. The clock on the wall ticks loudly. I'm playing hide and seek with Mummy again, but she's not in the house or behind the garden shed. I can't find Gran either.

'Where did you both go? I don't like this game.'

The sun hides behind darkening clouds. Shadows creep across the grass, trying to catch me. It's transformed into night-time and stars wink spitefully in the sky. Monsters are everywhere. I creep into the house and lock the back door to keep them out.

'Mummy? Gran?'

A floorboard creaks above my head. I run upstairs and burst into Gran's bedroom. A heavy, sickly scent fills the air.

'Found you!'

A figure stands by the window, but it's not Gran. She's fast asleep in bed and doesn't know someone else is here. A man in a black mask stares at me. He picks up roses from the vase. They droop, shrivel and die in his hands. Maggots crawl over the rotting flowers.

I scream but Gran doesn't wake up. I run out, the buzz of flies in my ears.

Clomp, clomp, clomp.

His footsteps are heavy hammers as he chases me down the stairs.

Sharp talons dig into my shoulders.

I trip and fall.

Pain explodes in the back of my head.

The whole world ignites.

32

Wednesday, May 29, 2024

'She's awake!'

Blurred, dark shapes dance behind my lids. They flicker open. Lights sear my eyeballs; strange, sharp noises assault my eardrums. I'm trapped in a frightening world. I'm afraid to keep my eyes open but scared to sleep.

'Hello, Miss? Can you hear me?' *A woman.* 'Do we have a name?'

'The ID in her handbag says she's Julia Hockney,' a man replies.

'Julia? I'm a doctor. Can you try to open your eyes again for me, please?'

Brilliant white light chases shadows away. Two faceless figures stand next to me. I see their outlines, the space they fill up, but they're unformed. Unreal.

This is another dream. I'm not really here.

'That's great,' the woman says. 'I'm Dr Dolan. You're in Hammersmith Hospital. We're treating you for a head injury. You have concussion and a possible fractured skull. We're keeping you in for observation.'

The words float around me. Time slips from my grasp. Minutes or hours pass.

I try to focus on what the woman is saying, but the words distort and stretch around the room.

'You were found in a disabled toilet close to ICU. Do you remember what happened?'

Alex took an overdose. The doctor said his brain damage could be 'life changing'. Zoe and I were allowed to see him. He was unconscious, hooked up to tubes. I stood at the end of his bed and . . .

Terrible memories nudge at the corners of my brain, trying to push through. My eyelids flicker shut to keep them out.

Loud voices bounce off the walls.

'The police want to interview her.'

'Do we think she was attacked?'

'The porter had to break open the bathroom door – he said it was locked on the inside. It's possible she slid the bolt after being assaulted, but the wound is consistent with striking the floor. My best guess is she fainted and knocked herself out.'

'Quite a blow. Lucky, it might only be a linear fracture.'

I try to sit up. The movement ignites fireworks inside my skull.

'Hey. Don't try to move yet.'

Strange hands press me down. I feel cool sheets beneath my body.

'Julia? Is there someone we should call?'

I open my mouth, but my throat tightens.

'Who is your next of kin?'

Alex.

'Did she say something?'

'I don't think so. Can you give us a name?'

Alex, Alex, Alex.

The light dims, before brightening as storm clouds lift. I drift in and out of different worlds, never outstaying my welcome. Old nightmares return, and new ones are far worse. Gran is screaming for help, her arms outstretched.

'Julia!'

I can't reach her. She's jerked back into darkness. Swarming dots reform and create another disturbing image:

Oscar Simmonds is trying to tell me there's no evidence of life. Mum could be dead, possibly murdered in Scotland 20 years ago. He wants to pass his investigation file over to the police. I'd previously considered an accident or suicide, but murder . . . ?

Open your eyes.

My head throbs. *Where am I?* Blurry shapes become beds. They're dotted around the room, with curtains draped around them. I stare down at a hand. *My hand.* Attached to it are tubes, which drape across the stiff white sheet. I touch my head and feel fabric. A woman with long hair stands by my bed. Her features are blurry.

'Julia! How are you?'

She must be a nurse. I'm injured, but how? Before I can ask, I slip away into inky blackness.

I'm crying after another nightmare about the man with the knife and flowers. I hear the light tap of Mum's footsteps coming up the stairs. They enter my room, and the mattress dips. Mum tenderly strokes my hair.

'Don't worry, I'm here, Pickle. It's just a bad dream. It's not real. Wake up!'

I obey.

Another woman comes into focus. She's checking my pulse. This is a different nurse; she has short, ash blonde hair. My head is much clearer, but my mouth is painfully dry. I'm in a ward at Hammersmith Hospital. I feel for my pendant, but it's no longer around my neck. A toy lion sits on the pillow, staring at me with big glassy eyes.

'What . . . what is this?' I croak, holding it up.

'A present, I guess. One of the nurses said you had a visitor while you slept.'

'Who?'

'No idea, sorry. They're off shift, and I've just started.' She feels my wrist, monitoring my pulse. 'You're doing better. We have to keep waking you, sorry. We can't let you sleep with a concussion.'

I touch my forehead. A bandage is wrapped around my skull.

'When can I go home? I need to see my gran. She's waiting for me.'

'The doctor can tell you more when she comes through on her rounds.'

I lick my cracked lips. 'What time is it? How long have I been here?'

She checks her watch. 'It's 11 a.m. on Thursday. I believe you were admitted in the early hours of yesterday.'

'But what date and year?'

She frowns. 'You can't remember?'

I lift my hand. It drops heavily to the bed. I can't recall anything. How I got here. Where I've been.

'It's May 30, 2024.'

'Where's Alex? Alex Martin?'

'Is he a friend of yours?'

'Alex is my boyfriend, my . . .' *Are* we still engaged? 'He was in ICU and then he wasn't. He might be somewhere else, but I'm not sure.'

'He may have been transferred to another ward. I'll double-check and fetch your phone when I've finished. We've locked away your valuables for safekeeping.'

I touch my neck. 'What about my pendant?'

'Jewellery will be with the rest of your belongings. I can get it if you want?'

'Please.'

I examine the toy lion as she leaves. Vicky must have brought it, or Samira or Zoe. I glance at the empty table. Whoever it was didn't leave a card. When the nurse returns, I check my handbag; my pendant is inside. I scoop out my mobile. I can't remember the PIN number or who I would call in this life.

'Did people die in the train crash at Barnes?'

The nurse's gaze flickers up from her clipboard. 'There's been a crash?'

I rub my forehead. 'I thought a car had broken down on the level crossing.'

'I haven't heard anything about it.' She scoops up a newspaper from the chair in the next-door cubicle, and flicks through the pages. 'I can't see anything in yesterday's *Gazette*.'

'The crash would have been a few weeks ago. Are there any photos of the dead passengers?'

'Not that I can see. Are you sure it's happened?'

'I'm not certain about anything.'

'It might have been a bad dream. You were shouting out in your sleep.'

'Do you know if there was a drowning at Hammersmith Bridge a year ago? Or if children died in a house fire in Southall?'

She looks blank.

'Please can you check online? If you google "Louise Marshall and drowned and Hammersmith Bridge".'

She sighs and types into her phone, showing me the words: *No results*. I beg her to search for 'Andrew Marshall and house fire'.

'Probably another nightmare, sweetheart. No one with those names drowned or died in a blaze.'

I sigh with relief. 'What about the Night Prowler?'

'I don't need to type that up! We were talking about him in the break room earlier. Police caught him. Apparently, he worked as a volunteer driver at Ealing Hospital.' She shivers. 'I guess that gave him the perfect cover to travel across London, hunting for victims.'

'He's been arrested?' I gasp.

'Charged, thank the Lord.'

She calls up a story from May 13, 2024:

MAN IN COURT AFTER DECADES OF ATTACKS

A 57-year-old man was charged last night with dozens of offences ranging from murder, burglary and assault to causing grievous bodily harm, spanning almost 20 years.

Dennis Clements, from southwest London, appeared before Ealing magistrates accused of attacks dating back to December 2005 in Croydon, south London. He has pleaded not guilty to all charges. He was arrested following an alleged burglary at Almeric Road, Clapham, on May 9. The case will proceed to trial at Crown Court.

'Does none of this ring a bell? It's been all over the news for weeks.'

I shake my head. I'm trying to fit the pieces of the jigsaw together: the train crash didn't happen, and the Night Prowler is awaiting trial. I *think* I tipped off the police and got him arrested at this Clapham address – close to the restaurant where I originally met Ed's work colleagues for dinner. I vaguely remember his offending pattern had changed yet again, and this was the only chance to catch him over the past twelve months. Charles Fielding and Louise Marshall don't appear to have died at Hammersmith Bridge last year, which means that Andrew Marshall and the boys must be alive. That leaves Alex. My memories of him are lodged somewhere secure and unreachable. I no longer possess the key.

'I can't remember where my boyfriend is, or what happened to him.'

'I'll check for you. Don't worry. Confusion is normal after a head injury. You need to give it time. Your memory will come back eventually.'

Will it?

Am I friends with Vicky, or am I closer to Zoe and Samira? Is Raquel back at work instead of looking after Sergio? Have I vanished from Gran's life in yet another timeline? Has she been left on her own, wondering what's happened to me? I'm trying to work out the conundrum when the nurse returns.

'This is odd. I can't find anyone with the name Alex Martin on the system in ICU or any other ward. I've tried different spellings of his surname. Can you remember if he's still being treated at this hospital?'

Memories drift closer, like clenched fists reluctantly uncurling to reveal their dark secrets. Ghosts hover at the end of the bed, waiting to ambush me.

'No!'

'What is it?'

'I can't! I just can't . . . Please make it stop!'

My nose feels wet. I can taste blood in my mouth.

'Julia?'

'I need my pendant. I have to go back.'

I reach for my handbag, but the nurse holds my arm.

'Stay still. You have a bad nosebleed.'

I'm too weak to fight. I try to put up my guard as recollections from the last year return. I wish I'd never asked the nurse to check. I don't want to remember what I've done, how I've changed time, but the barrier comes crashing down. I'm hit with a tsunami of pain and grief.

It's impossible to bear.

One memory, the absolute worst, plays on an agonising loop inside my head:

Alex isn't in ICU. He jumped off Hammersmith Bridge and drowned a year ago saving Charles and Louise.

33

THURSDAY, JUNE 6, 2024

Sleep used to be my enemy; now it's my best friend.

I'm always drowning or being chased by an intruder, but even these nightmares are preferable to reality. I close my eyes. I can blot out hours, or days if I'm lucky. My phone vibrates with new messages, refusing to let me slip away again. I roll over and grope for it on the bedside table. Carole has left a voicemail, saying Gran is drowsy due to her new medication; she slept through my visits at the weekend. The private investigator, Oscar Simmonds, has called twice. He says he's come to a dead end in his hunt for Mum and wants an urgent meeting to discuss next steps. I shudder. I can't face what he wants to tell me in this life or any other. Vicky has left a few messages, along with Merv and Jeremy. Apparently, after Alex's death last year, I gave up on my dreams of trying to break into journalism. I finally realised Rod would never give me a chance and requested a move to the archives. I'd been packing up records with Jeremy, ahead of their transfer to a new storage facility in east London. But I was signed off sick a week ago after remembering Alex's death and experiencing it all over again like it had happened yesterday.

I bury my head in his pillow, searching for his scent, but it's vanished. No framed personal photos of us sit on the bedside table, only the pictures I've printed off the internet from newspaper and website reports of his death. None of his clothes are slung in the wardrobe or slipping off hangers. I can't pull out one of his old sweaters and hug it to my chest to help me get through the impossibly long days and nights. Nothing exists because he was never here. We hadn't planned to get married or support each other through illness and hard times. My chest feels like it's been cracked open, leaving a huge, gaping hole where my heart once sat. I cling onto the cuddly toy from the hospital, running my fingers over Alex's chilly side of the bed. I'd give anything for another day with him but it's impossible. I can't barter with time. I sit up, rubbing my eyes, which are puffy from crying. My stomach growls with hunger. Yesterday's half-eaten bowl of cereal on the bedside table doesn't look appealing, but I manage to force down a spoonful without gagging.

Someone raps on the door, making me jump. They've managed to get through the intercom on the ground floor. I pull Alex's pillow over my head to block out the noise. Dammit. They're not giving up. I throw it aside and roll out of bed. As I pad into the hallway, the person knocks again, and a voice rings out.

'Julia, are you there?'

I hesitate before opening the door a fraction. 'What are you doing here?'

Vicky has the same immaculate black bob, topped with a velvet hairband, glossy red lipstick, and a matching polka dot dress. A frown mark is carved between her bladed eyebrows.

'Can I come in?'

Reluctantly, I remove the chain and step aside, catching a whiff of her Chanel No 5 – the birthday present from Giles.

'Thanks.' She hangs her coat on a hook, her eyes narrowing as she turns around.

'What's happened to your hair?' She steps closer, her hand reaching out.

I back away, rearranging the white streaks beneath my curls. I lead her into the kitchen, which is a mistake. Dirty bowls are stacked by the sink and left on the table. I've forgotten to put the milk carton away, and the bin smells like something's crawled inside and died.

'Let's go to the sitting room.'

Vicky brushes past, her eyebrows raised.

'Jesus.' She peers inside the bare fridge and cupboards, before spotting the empty cereal packets on the table. 'Very nutritious. It's time to clean up and do a shop, don't you think? And have a shower and wash your hair. I don't mean to be rude, but you stink!'

'Gee, thanks. Did you come here to insult me?'

'No, silly.' Her tone softens. 'I wanted to see how you're doing. I've been worried. You haven't replied to any of my messages.'

I turn away, hiding my face. 'Sorry. I haven't felt up to seeing or speaking to anyone.'

'How are you? Any better?'

No. Babbling in hospital about how I'd changed time and helped catch the Night Prowler was a bad idea. It had freaked out the nurses and they'd alerted the psychiatric unit. I managed to get through the evaluation by claiming confusion from the head injury. Before being discharged last week, I received outpatient referrals to a cardiologist after heart scans showed irregularities, and to a neurologist due to my headaches and nosebleeds. I don't plan to see either. I'm not a medical mystery; travelling to the past is my illness, and there is no cure.

'Did you hear me? I asked if you're feeling any better?'

I turn around. 'Why do you care?'

'What do you mean? Of course I do!'

'You didn't return any of my calls. I attempted to meet for drinks, but you ghosted me.'

Vicky's jaw drops open. 'Hello? It's the other way round! I've messaged repeatedly, but it's been radio silence ever since you were discharged from hospital. I'm always here for you. You know that.'

Anger bubbles inside me, a dragon waking. No one ever stays. Everyone abandons me in one way or another.

'That's not true. You called me smug for being happy with Alex. You were horrible about the bridesmaid dresses and thought I'd become a Bridezilla.'

'What *are* you talking about?'

'You haven't supported me. You didn't come to the hospital when Alex was in a coma in ICU.' My voice breaks. 'You didn't care. You were out with Chris and wouldn't leave his work drinks.'

'Erm, you're getting confused. Chris is a junior doctor, and he'd never invite me to a work do. He's in a long-term relationship with his girlfriend. And I'm sure I've never called you smug. Anyway, who the hell is Alex and when was he in a coma?'

I stare at her, my heart beating rapidly.

'Alex Martin drowned at Hammersmith Bridge last year.'

'Wait . . .' She pauses, frowning. 'This is the guy you told me about some time ago – you met him in a bar briefly, and he died the next day?'

I give a small nod. I never encountered Alex in the Swan in this lifetime – but I couldn't explain how he'd been deliberately diverted away by the woman in red and sent to Hammersmith Bridge. It sounded crazy and Vicky wouldn't have understood or believed me. I haven't been truthful with her about how I recently ended up in hospital either, claiming I collapsed at a neurology appointment.

'Alex wasn't in ICU,' Vicky points out. 'You said he died on the riverbank before he could be taken to hospital.' She readjusts her hairband. 'I don't want to sound harsh, Julia, but you barely knew him, did you? You must have talked to him for a few hours, max, the night before.'

'I knew everything about him.' My voice is barely a whisper. 'I loved him. We were meant to be together for the rest of our lives. We had it all planned out: marriage, children, grandchildren.'

She shakes her head vigorously, making her earrings tinkle. 'You've romanticised Alex, and I get why – you're worried about your gran and unhappy about your mum, but you need to stop obsessing about a stranger. You don't even believe in love at first sight.'

'I do now it's happened to me. I'm not romanticising or making up anything. Alex was the love of my life. Nothing will ever change that.'

Vicky's frown deepens. 'I don't understand . . . Why are you raking this up after all this time? Did the head injury bring it all back?'

'New memories return constantly. It feels like we met yesterday, not a year ago.'

She inhales sharply, eyeing the white lock that has escaped from behind my ear. 'You have to move on, Julia. This isn't healthy or normal.'

'What's a normal way to get over losing someone precious? Grief doesn't have a sell-by date. I'll never get over this. It'll always be with me – how I loved and lost Alex. How it's all my fault that he died, and I can't ever bring him back. This is a part of who I am now. I can't shed it like an old coat.'

'Okay, now I'm worried. You're acting crazy.'

'Thank you! Just what I needed to hear.'

'Sorry, but you have to get some perspective. I know you were upset when he died last year, and after the jury returned that verdict, but I honestly thought you were over Aaron. You'd moved on.'

'He's called Alex!'

My cheeks sting as I vividly remember how she steered our chats over the past year to her nights out – a combination of cocktail happy hours, and clubbing – whenever I wept for Alex. How she never kept me company in the public gallery during Charles's trial for attempting to murder Louise. I didn't give evidence; I wasn't a useful witness. I'd lost my memory after being hit by the bike on the bridge and suffered a serious head injury. I had no recollection about what had happened for weeks. Vicky wasn't there for me through my physical recovery. She wasn't at my side, holding my hand, when a jury cleared Charles, as the prosecution failed to prove intent.

'I'll never move on from Alex. I stopped talking to you about him because you weren't interested. You changed the subject whenever I mentioned his name. All you want to talk about is . . .' I stop, remembering suddenly. 'Giles. You're still with Giles.'

'Yes, I'm with Giles! Is it wrong to want to be happy?'

I stare at her. It's as though a mask has slipped from her face, and I see her for the first time. *Really see her.*

'Yes – when it's at the expense of other people.'

I've closed the door on Vicky, as well as all my previous lives. I can never reopen it. The reason why lies on my bedside table, next to the vase of wilting 'get well soon' roses from Jeremy. He also dropped off the envelope of cuttings I'd asked him to pull together. I reread an old *Gazette* article about Alex's death last year:

May 14, 2023

DROWNED ARTIST WAS CATFISHING VICTIM

By Mervyn Drury

The drowned hero who saved a couple from the Thames had been catfished by a young woman as part of an attempted robbery, police believe.

Alex Martin, 27, from Acton, west London, was tricked into going to Hammersmith Bridge. He'd told friends he'd been intercepted by a blonde woman on the way to a reunion with university friends at the Swan in Chiswick the previous night.

She claimed to be a London Gazette *journalist named Tory Harper, who wanted to interview him as part of a feature about up-and-coming young artists. The woman had arranged to meet him the next day at the bridge for a photoshoot.*

Police say the reporter does not exist and believe Mr Martin may have been lured to the bridge as part of an elaborate plan to rob him. However, the attempt failed when he intervened to rescue a couple from the river.

Mr Martin died at the scene and a man was arrested for allegedly pulling his female companion off the bridge.

Charles Fielding, 41, from Shepherd's Bush, who is charged with attempted murder, has appeared before Hammersmith Magistrates' Court. No plea was indicated, and he was remanded to attend the Old Bailey on June 15.

Samira Patel, owner of the Hidden Things gift shop in Brentford, said: 'Alex should never have been on the bridge. We want the woman who tricked him to come forward to the police.'

The woman in the bar will never resurface. She tricked us both that night in 2023. She'd deliberately prevented me from meeting Alex and somehow knew the fake name I'd adopted the first time I visited Samira. She engineered a way to make Alex go to the bridge to help Louise and Charles. She must have wanted to save the Marshall family and all those train passengers. I pick up the cutting from a month ago, which seals Alex's fate and means I must leave him, dead, in the past. It's one of the last pieces in the jigsaw puzzle that has taken me so long to work out:

May 10, 2024

HAVE-A-GO-HERO PUSHES TRAIN OFF TRACK

By Salim Badawi

A man has told today how he heroically pushed a broken-down car off a railway track and averted a major disaster.

Charles Fielding, 42, was cycling close to the Barnes level crossing when he noticed an elderly motorist in difficulty this morning. A passer-by had attempt-ed and failed to restart the man's car. Mr Fielding pushed the Volvo off the track, with minutes to spare before the 8.30 a.m. to Waterloo sped past at 70mph.

Mr Fielding was cleared of attempting to murder married mother of two Louise Marshall, at Hammersmith Bridge, following a trial earlier this year. He had pulled Mrs Marshall over the railings as he fell into the water but told the court it was an accident.

Mr Fielding said: 'I was cycling near the level crossing when I saw the broken-down car and heard someone shout that a train was coming.

'I wasn't afraid for my own safety. I wanted to help the people on the train.'

He added: 'Last year, I suffered a breakdown and wasn't myself. That's no excuse though, and I'm sorry beyond words for what I did. I never meant for anyone else to die at the bridge, but my actions hurt many people.

'A stranger saved my life that day, which I didn't deserve. I wanted to repay his bravery and kindness and make sure he didn't die in vain.

'I will never forgive myself for causing his death and hurting Louise and her family. I will spend the rest of my life attempting to make amends for my terrible actions.'

I stare at the photo of Charles standing next to the crossing. His face is thinner, and his beard is shaved off. He's smiling to the camera, but his eyes have a sorrowful, pained expression. I screw the newspaper story into a tight ball and throw it across the room. Even if I was physically strong enough, and my heartbeat has stabilised, I can't try to change things again. Louise and Charles must *both* live to prevent horrific future tragedies.

Alex's death puts an end to everyone's suffering – except for his family's and mine.

I swallow a sob. The truth slices through me like a knife:

If Alex were alive today and given the choice, he wouldn't have it any other way. He would accept that he had to die to save others.

34

MONDAY, JUNE 10, 2024

My fingers glide across Alex's plaque on Hammersmith Bridge. The bouquets lying beneath it, left to mark the first anniversary of his drowning, have withered and died. My dreams and hopes for the future have disappeared with them. I've traced and retraced over different versions of my life, filling them in with varying shades, but have only been left with a blurry outline of myself. I'm no longer recognisable. I hear Gran's childhood warning in my head again:

Be careful what you wish for.

Travelling back has helped me collect a collage of forgotten images of Mum from my childhood. But they're so painful, I want to draw over them or, better still, rub them out completely. I can't cope with repeatedly discovering something terrible happened to her in Scotland. It brings fresh agony each time, because deep down I sense this is the end – Mum is dead. Perhaps she didn't mean to kill herself, but she could have travelled backwards and forwards through time too often and her body couldn't take it. A similar fate might await me if I don't stop, according to the woman at the Swan.

I kiss the sunflowers I bought on the way – Alex's favourite – and dangle them over the side. I half expect him to turn up and stop me from dropping them. He'll put his arms around my waist, nuzzle my neck and whisper he loves me, but it's impossible. I fell in love with a ghost.

'I'm sorry you met me, Alex,' I whisper. 'If you'd never asked me out, or I'd refused to go on a date, you'd be alive today.' I wipe the tears from my face. 'I miss you terribly. You're my first thought when I wake up and my last when I fall asleep, and every second in between. You were my happy ending. You've changed my life, but I can't change yours. I love you, Alex, now and forever. There will never be anyone else, only you.'

I throw the flowers into the Thames, at the spot where he jumped. I can't bear to see them float away. It brings back harrowing memories of our combined battle to try to save Louise and Charles. I back away before breaking into a run, almost colliding with a white-haired lady who is taking in the views.

'Sorry,' I say, panting.

I'm sorry for everything – the hurt I've caused to so many people. I've not only lost Alex, but also his friends and family: Zoe and the twins, Samira and Hamish, and Lizzy and Fatima. We can't share our grief; I can't approach them. They don't have a clue who I am. Our lives have passed each other's, rivers branching off a main channel and never meeting.

Approaching the roundabout, I slow down. My mobile rings and Jeremy's name flashes up.

'How are you?'

'Much better,' I lie.

'I'm sorry to bother you. I know you're signed off until the end of the week, but . . .' His voice disappears into a sigh.

'What is it?'

'The stuff of nightmares. You know that pipe you warned me about in the archives last month? Well, building services did a slap-dash job repairing the crack. It's completely fractured. I need help salvaging the records.'

'I'm on my way. I won't be long.'

I hang up and cross the road, walking briskly towards the tube. This is exactly what I need: distraction.

It stops me from thinking about all the people I've lost.

'Welcome to the disaster zone.'

Jeremy throws his arms up in the air, surveying the sodden mass of boxes. Building services has mopped the floor, but they've cleared shelves to reach the split pipe in the ceiling. A huge hole yawns like a mouth above our heads. Damaged containers and files are piled in heaps across the floor.

'I don't know where to start with the mess,' he says.

'We need fans and dehumidifiers to air the room and each box should be checked for water damage. Let's start with the crime section – that's the worst hit. We'll need gloves and blotting paper to help dry out the cuttings. But you should get on to the managing editor's office and see if they'll pay for a specialist restoration company to dry out the historic books and large bound journals. There's a firm we could use in Oxfordshire.'

Jeremy's jaw hangs open. 'You sound like you've done this before!'

He has no idea.

We work solidly for the next couple of hours, sifting through damp boxes, books and files, before Jeremy sits on his heels, rubbing his back.

'Why don't you take a break? Go stretch your legs in Kensington Gardens.'

'I'm good, thanks,' I say quickly. 'I'd prefer to keep working.'

Alex and I had never visited the park together, but it still contains painful memories of him. This is where I'd walked, replaying our meeting in my head, when I was convinced our first encounter was a premonition, not time travel.

'Well, in that case, how about a coffee?'

'I'd love one, thanks. A large, black Americano.'

'I'll take a stroll around the lake to clear my head and get a couple of takeaways on the way back if that's okay? I hate canteen coffee.'

'Sure thing.'

Jeremy hesitates after grabbing his coat and walking to the door. 'Thanks for coming in at short notice. I appreciate it, especially considering—'

'I'm fine, honestly,' I say quickly.

Any hint of sympathy, and I'll crumble.

'You're doing me a favour, Jeremy. I want to keep busy. It helps me to stop dwelling on things I can't change.'

He nods. 'That sounds healthy.'

I'm a good liar. It doesn't matter whether my eyes are open or shut, I see Alex everywhere. He's painting in his studio. Hugging Gran and holding her hand. Laughing at Zoe's jokes. Chasing Hannah and Sally. Mainly, I feel him kissing and embracing me.

While Jeremy's on the coffee run, I attack the pile of crime boxes. It's doubtful I'll be able to save much in here; dozens of mushy envelopes are stuck together. I rummage deeper and pull out a handful of damp files. I put three aside, which are salvageable. The fourth is soggy. A cold shiver travels down my spine as if someone's walked over my grave. The words printed in the top left-hand corner state:

Night Prowler

The file is surprisingly slim, considering the scale of his offending. I pull out the wet scraps and unpeel them carefully. Merv had been interested in these early crimes. He'd wanted to discover if the police had missed chances to catch him before the assaults escalated. The most recent story is from October 2006, a burglary in Brentford, and two other suspected attacks earlier that year, in west London. The stories don't refer to Dennis Clements' nickname – the press had dubbed him the Night Prowler years later. One of the former librarians must have gone back through the file and renamed it, adding in cuttings after police publicly connected the old cases. They all look familiar – I've read about them in the online library so there must have been some crossover during digitisation.

I tip up the envelope and shake it, but nothing else falls out. Merv will be disappointed; this won't help much. I grab a new envelope from our supplies as this one is wrecked and pen *Night Prowler: 2006* on the front. I'm about to chuck the damaged packet when I notice a small piece of white paper tucked inside. It disintegrates in my fingers as I pull it out, but I can decipher the blurred, looped handwriting: *See general burglary file.* Librarians used to cross-check cuttings into other envelopes when they shared similar topics.

It takes me another half an hour to find two bulky envelopes stuffed with burglary cuttings among the boxes, and thirty minutes to unpack them. They're damp, but easier to handle. My heart beats faster as I find stories about a break-in at a Croydon property in December 2005. A forty-five-year-old woman was left with broken ribs and suffering smoke inhalation, after a masked man broke into her ground-floor flat. He robbed and attacked her, cutting the telephone line, smashing light bulbs, and setting fire to newspapers in the kitchen on the way out. The report says that 'in a macabre twist', the intruder also left flowers, which were believed to have been stolen from a nearby graveyard, outside her broken window. It's the Night Prowler's first known attack – the one he's been charged with committing! I place the story between blotting paper and put it to one side for Merv, along with similar stories from other papers.

I work backwards, this time from December 2005, in case there's another violent robbery involving flowers left at a house. My eyelids become heavy. There were so many burglaries across London during this year, most only make a few paragraphs. Nothing jumps out, until I go further back. I catch my breath as my gaze rests on a *Gazette* story from May 14, 2004:

Burglar Escapes in Dramatic Police Chase

Police pursued a burglar armed with a knife who broke into a house in Chiswick, west London, on the evening of Tuesday, May 11.

A neighbour reported a break-in at an empty house on Airedale Avenue at 11 p.m., while the house-holder was away. Officers attended the scene and discovered a masked man in the kitchen, attempting to set fire to newspapers. They gave chase for two miles, but the intruder managed to outrun them. He had removed light bulbs from fittings and cut the telephone line.

Detectives say he dropped a bunch of roses taken from a vase in the householder's bedroom, together with gold jewellery.

Next-door neighbour Ivy Watkins, 59, said: 'As soon

*as I heard glass smashing, I dialled 999. It's terrify-
ing to think what could have happened if my friend
had been home. I wish the police had caught him
– such a wicked man to try to set fire to her house. I
won't sleep easy in my bed until he's caught.'*

*Homeowner Sylvia Hockney was unavailable for
comment last night.*

Gran and Ivy! But the story can't be right. Gran said Ivy's house
was broken into. She wasn't confused – she mentioned this burglary
years and years before her Alzheimer's diagnosis. I reread the story.
There's no mistake. Gran's house was burgled, not Ivy's. Perhaps
she hid the truth because she didn't want to scare me on top of
everything else. That evening, Gran was with me at our flat while
Mum was at the music festival in Scotland. The break-in had a
similar MO to the Croydon burglary, apart from the flowers coming from inside Gran's house, rather than a graveyard. I jump at a
ticking noise and look down. I hadn't noticed I'd started rotating
the stone in my pendant.

My chest constricts tightly. This probably explains Gran's
obsession with the Night Prowler over the decades.

Because if she *had* been home alone that night . . .

I feel sick at the sudden realisation.

Gran could have become his first victim.

35

MONDAY, JUNE 10, 2024

A masked man is standing at the end of my bed, holding flowers. I can't smell the roses, only smoke. He lunges towards me. I sit up in bed, wide eyed, and screaming. This isn't real. It's the same nightmare I keep having night after night. I hear slow footsteps plodding up the stairs. Gran pushes open my bedroom door. Her eyes are red and teary. Her hand is a tight fist. My tummy tightens. Something feels wrong.

'Gran?'

'I'm sorry, Julia, but it's Mummy. I don't think she's coming back.'

'No!'

She holds me in her arms as my sobs become louder. I feel like I'm being stabbed in the chest. Something heavy drops out of her hand, onto my duvet. Gran snatches it to her chest before I can pick it up.

'Julia!'

I jerk awake, grabbing for my necklace. I'm not a child in my bed, in our old flat in Brentford. I'm in the archives. It's 2024. I've lost Alex and Mum. Gran is sleeping through my visits. *Her* house was burgled twenty years ago, and she tried to protect me from the truth.

'Are you alright?' Jeremy passes me a Costa coffee cup. 'I wasn't sure whether to disturb you, but you looked like you were about to slip out of your seat.'

'Sorry. I must have drifted off.' I take a large slug of coffee. 'I might take you up on that offer of a walk? I thought I'd take a trip up to the third floor and see Merv.'

'Sure thing. I'll crack on here.'

I take photos of the Croydon and Chiswick stories on my phone, and head out the door, coffee in hand. I WhatsApp the pictures over to Merv and tell him I'm on my way as I step into the elevator. I slip my phone into my jacket, thinking about my dream. This is the first time I've remembered details about the morning I found out Mum was gone. Gran could have rung her in Scotland to tell her about the break-in, and she flipped out. That's what finally drove her over the edge. I rub my forehead, frowning. But why didn't she come home to check on Gran? Or was she too ill to catch a train back? My mobile burns a hole in my pocket; I've ignored another message from Oscar Simmonds.

A couple of suited execs step aside, letting me out of the lift. I catch the journalists' favourite word – expenses – as the doors close behind them. I make my way into the newsroom, through Sleepy Hollow. I catch sight of my replacement on the desk: a fifty-something secretary who's moved across from the *Sunday Herald*. She has a reputation for not taking any crap from reporters. Hopefully, the same goes for news editors.

Merv spots me approaching his desk of doom. 'How are you?'

I force a smile. 'Great. Much better, thanks.'

'Are you—'

'I thought these stories might be useful for any backgrounder you're writing on the Night Prowler.'

He rubs his beard. 'You read my mind. I'm pulling together a feature to publish after the end of the trial. Chiswick is interesting – you're suggesting it could be connected?'

'It's similar to Croydon with the fire, and flowers being involved, but both these break-ins are different to his later MOs. None of his other burglaries involved setting fire to newspapers as far as I can see. He usually flaunted his signature style, removing or smashing light bulbs and leaving the flowers.'

Merv studies the story on his screen. 'He may have been practising, or evolving, as criminologists say, since his first few offences. In those early days, he cut the telephone lines, but that became increasingly pointless with the use of mobile phones.'

'Could he have forgotten to wear gloves during these burglaries and wanted to destroy his fingerprints?' I suggest. 'Later, he might have learned from his mistakes and decided to go full-on theatrical.'

'It's possible. His fingerprints weren't found at most of the houses, according to my source. He left his DNA behind by accident once or twice after cutting himself on broken glass.'

I rotate the stone in my pendant, thinking hard. 'I don't get why the police didn't attempt to connect this case to the Night Prowler, as well as the Croydon one.'

Merv shrugs. 'They may have or it became lost in the mix. Different detectives would have been involved. Records may have been lost. But there's also the sheer volume of suspected crimes. Police may have prioritised cases with victims, rather than ones involving empty homes when it came to charging. No one was hurt in this burglary.'

'I guess that makes sense.'

'Why the interest in this particular crime if you don't mind me asking?'

'This was my gran's house. She never mentioned a break-in, but I guess she wasn't likely to – I was only five. We had to deal with my mum walking out at the same time.'

'That's tough. It's no good asking Sylvia?'

'Sadly not.'

'I'll put a call into the Met press office and see if they ever reviewed the Chiswick case. I'll let you know. Was there anything else downstairs about missed chances to catch him?'

'Not in the Night Prowler file – you have everything online for 2006. I'm going through the burglary cuttings. I can let you have them when they're dried out.'

'Great, thanks. My contact has already admitted a major cock-up from last year. It's likely to come out during the trial.'

'What was that?' I ask curiously.

'Police received a call at lunch time on May 12, claiming the Night Prowler was in an internet café in West Ealing looking up stuff online.'

'And was he?'

'They think so, but the operator took down the wrong details, and the unit went to a different address. By the time they got there, he'd fled. But CCTV showed he was a match for an e-fit circulated.'

'Would you—?' I stop myself.

'What?'

'I was going to ask for the correct address and time of call, but it's not important.'

'Are you sure?'

I shake my head. What's the point? I can't make a second attempt to get the Night Prowler caught a year early; I can never go back to 2023.

'I should get a move on. I've abandoned Jeremy.'

'Before you go, I wanted to give you this.' He slaps a piece of paper on the desk. 'The *Gazette* is starting a graduate trainee scheme. I thought you might want to apply.'

I snatch up the printout, scanning the page.

'It's a good way in if you want to become a journalist – on-the-job training on news, before a stint in features, online and investigations.'

My heart beats faster. This could be the ultimate distraction from Alex – long days and late nights, throwing myself into work.

'What do you reckon, Julia?'

I glance up as Rod shouts across the newsroom at one of the reporters.

'I'll think about it.'

'Don't let him put you off.' He shuffles his pile of papers. 'You could try to get a head start – impress him, by bringing in an interview.'

'Me?'

'Why not? It'll look good if you apply with an exclusive under your belt.'

'What do you have in mind?'

He hands me another piece of paper, with an address in Southall. 'Do you remember the tragedy at Hammersmith Bridge last year? A hero jumped into the Thames and saved a couple. Alex someone.'

The scrap falls out of my palm. Merv leans down and scoops it up.

'Alex Martin.' My voice sounds like it belongs to someone else.

'That's the one. Good memory! Rod was desperate to get an interview with the woman he rescued. He thought it would make a good human interest story – a wife caught cheating, almost dying, and finding a reconciliation with her husband. A happy ending.'

'Louise and Andrew Marshall,' I gasp. 'They stayed together?'

'Bingo.'

'Rod wanted her story after that guy was cleared of attempting to murder her – a sit-down chat about how she coped with the trauma. Mr and Mrs Marshall refused all interview requests after the trial, which isn't surprising after the verdict. But she might be prepared to talk to another woman a year on after the tragedy. Do you want to give it a try?'

'I don't think I can.'

'Why not? It's worth a shot. What's the worst that can happen? She slams the door in your face. You leave. No big deal. You can do this.'

I bite my lip, hard. He doesn't understand, he never will.

What if Louise lets me into her house and describes Alex's final moments in full, harrowing detail?

36

Tuesday, June 11, 2024

A football and a couple of children's bikes lie in the front garden of 40 Lancaster Road. I picture Daniel and Oliver Marshall laughing and kicking the ball together. They're probably inseparable, begging their parents to let them cycle to the nearby park themselves. Daniel will promise to look after his little brother. Oliver will beam at his mum and say: 'Pretty please!' They'll ride two abreast on the pavement, chatting about Arsenal matches and compete to see who goes the highest on the playground swings. Those are far better images than imagining the brothers' stricken faces at the bedroom window, beating on the glass and unable to escape, as fire ravages the ground floor. I glance away quickly.

Yesterday, I didn't think I could face seeing Louise, but I've found myself dropping by on the way to work this morning. Like swimming against a current, this visit was impossible to resist. It might be exactly what I need to help me come to terms with losing Alex – seeing the good that has emerged from his death, the young lives flourishing. It's a cheap form of therapy, but it may also get me arrested. An elderly next-door neighbour stares at me suspiciously as she empties her bins for a second time. If I don't find the courage to knock on Louise's door soon, she might ring the police. My phone pings with a message from Merv, which is a godsend. I can pretend I'm busy.

You were asking yesterday – anonymous 999 call at 12.46 p.m. on May 12 last year saying Night Prowler was at Digital Paradise, 154 Broadway, West Ealing. Patrol cars went to Golden Digital Paradise, 134 Ealing Broadway, by mistake after operator misheard address. Hope that helps? See you later!

I reply with a thumbs up icon and tell him I'm preparing to call on Louise. When I turn around, the neighbour has vanished, and the front door of number 40 is open. I can see the back of a man's head in the driver's seat of the Volvo parked outside. Two little boys wearing school uniform charge down the path carrying red bags and lunch boxes. I catch my breath. *Daniel and Oliver.* They're laughing and punching each other playfully on the arms. Oliver whacks Daniel with his lunch box and he howls with pain, attempting payback. The driver toots the horn and they file obediently into the car, pulling the door shut. A few seconds later, they drive away. Andrew Marshall must be doing the school run. This is my chance to speak to Louise.

I take a deep breath and cross the road, stride up the drive and knock on the door. In my peripheral vision, I see the curtain in the window of the next-door house twitch. Footsteps pad into the hall, and the door opens. A blonde woman appears. Her eyes are puffy and bloodshot and her face is tear-stained. Louise is smaller and more fragile than I remember. Her blue T-shirt reveals a sharp collarbone, and her jeans could be child-sized. Behind her are boys' trainers and muddy football boots, abandoned coats and toys. Normal remnants of family life. She was battling in the river to return to this.

'Hello. Can I help you?'

A roaring noise in my ears grows louder, and black dots buzz like bees before my eyes. I see Charles pulling her off the bridge. I remember her desperation as she clung onto Alex, sinking beneath the water, and gasping for air as she broke through the surface.

'I'm not buying anything, if that's why you're here.' Her knuckles whiten as she grips the doorframe.

'No. My name's Julia Hockney and I'm from the *Gazette*. I wanted to—'

'We're not talking to the press. We've made that clear already. Please leave and don't come back.' She's poised to slam the door shut.

'Wait! I knew Alex. The man who saved your life.'

Her hand flies to her mouth and she stares at me intently.

'I seized the chance to come today when I heard the *Gazette* wants an interview. I didn't tell anyone about my personal connection. The truth is I wanted to talk in private about my boyfriend.' A painful lump grows in my throat. 'Former boyfriend.'

Louise's eyes brim with tears. 'I thought I recognised you. Were you in the public gallery during the trial?'

I nod. 'I had to watch. For Alex's sake.'

'You'd better come in.'

I step into the hallway, which is painted a fresh lemon colour. It's decorated with framed pictures – two sets of baby handprints and feet, tiny fingers and toes dipped in paint and preserved forever. Further along the wall, I pass children's paintings, with the words 'For Mummy' and 'Love you, Mummy' scrawled across the top. My heart contracts. The Marshall boys are much loved; their childhoods cherished. They'll grow up supported, and happy.

Thanks to you, Alex. You saved them.

Louise leads me into the kitchen. 'Take a seat. Excuse the mess – I haven't had time to clear up after breakfast.'

I sink into a wooden chair as she boils the kettle. The table is dotted with sticky fingermarks and empty cereal bowls. A few Rice Krispies are stuck to the cover of a children's book.

'I'm sorry for your loss,' Louise says, as she brings over two mugs. 'It must be hard to live with all the "what ifs?"'

I burst into tears. I can't help myself.

Louise's cheeks pinken. 'I didn't mean to upset you.'

'It's okay.' I dab beneath my eyes with a tissue. 'I thought I could hold it together in front of you.'

'Why should you? You've lost someone you love. Why pretend it never happened?'

My tears flow faster. No one has properly acknowledged my grief until now.

'What would it help you to hear?' She pauses. 'You know what Alex was like – in those moments in the river he was utterly selfless and brave. He put the lives of others before his own. He wouldn't give up on me or . . .' She can't bring herself to say his name.

'Charles Fielding,' I finish.

She nods. 'The worst mistake of my life. Because of him, *us*, your boyfriend lost his life. The jury may have cleared that man, but I'll never forgive him. I'll never forgive myself that an innocent man died. If I hadn't arranged to meet *him* on Hammersmith Bridge that day, none of this would have happened.'

I bite my bottom lip. It sounds as if *she's* torturing herself with 'what ifs?'

'I listened to your evidence in court. You said you'd picked that spot because it was close to your office. You'd decided to break off the affair because you loved your husband and had chosen to stay with him.'

'Yes . . . that's the story I told the jury.'

'It's not true?'

'It's what Andrew ordered me to say, to help him save face. He claimed it was the least I could do after my affair.'

'You committed perjury for him?'

'I left out parts that would embarrass him. Is that perjury? I haven't a clue. I—' She hesitates.

'You don't have to tell me.'

'It's okay. You of all people should know the truth.' She takes a deep breath. 'Andrew discovered our affair the night before. He saw Charles leaving our house. I think he suspected something was going on and came home early to try to catch us. He went ballistic and threatened to kick me out unless I broke things off. He said he'd take the children and fight for full custody by claiming I was an unfit mother. I was deeply unhappy with Andrew and starting to have doubts about Charles. I'd lurched from one bad relationship to another, but I did as Andrew said, because I love my children. I arranged to meet Charles on the bridge in my lunch break the next day. I couldn't risk losing my sons. The rest, as they say, is history.' She covers her eyes with her hands.

'I'm sorry.'

She looks up, her eyes wide with surprise. 'Andrew says I don't deserve pity.'

'You didn't kill Alex. He died because of Charles's actions, not yours. Charles hurt you, traumatised you. You're not to blame for what happened that day, or for Alex's death.' I reach out and grip her hand. 'Please believe that.'

'You don't blame me?'

'You're a victim, as much as Alex.'

'Thank you, Julia,' she says, brokenly. 'It means so much coming from you. I've thought about Alex's family over the last year, and wanted to make contact, but I didn't know if they'd welcome me getting in touch.'

'It helps me, knowing your boys have a mum who loves them. I missed out on my mum growing up, and it leaves a huge hole. You never get over it; you never stop thinking about your mum, however old you are. Alex stopped your boys from suffering, and that would have made him happy. I saw the pictures they painted for you in the hallway. They love you.' I manage a smile. 'They're happy.'

She winces at the word.

I stare at her, aghast. 'Aren't they?'

'Andrew and I . . .' She sighs. 'We're not in a great place. Everyone says divorce is bad for kids, but no one talks about how children can be damaged from hearing their parents fighting all the time. It takes its toll. No one is happy, not even my husband.'

'Why don't you leave him?'

I wince at my own hypocrisy. I didn't ask Ed to move out because I was terrified of being on my own. We had no real ties, but she has children, the glue holding this family together. She has potentially far more to lose by walking away.

'I'm scared Andrew will carry out his threat. He'll cut me off from Daniel and Oliver, and I won't get joint custody. He's punishing me for my affair. I don't think he'll ever stop. He wants me to suffer.'

I take a sharp intake of breath, remembering what Merv had told me. In another life, she left Andrew and had shared access to their sons.

'He could realise separation is healthy for all of you.'

'You think I should leave him? I need advice, but don't know who to ask. All our friends sided with Andrew.' She takes a sip of tea, waiting.

I shake my head. I'm done interfering and messing up other people's lives.

'I can't tell you what to do, sorry. It must be your decision. All I can say from my own experience is that you shouldn't stay with someone simply because you're afraid of the unknown. Sometimes the unexpected is wonderful, and it can change your life for the better.'

Louise smiles through her tears.

'I should get going. I'll be late for work.' I push my mug aside, standing. 'Thank you for talking to me.'

'It was lovely to meet you. About the interview—'

'I'll say you declined and won't change your mind.'

She smiles warmly. 'You're different to the other journalists who've called round here. They were after the story at all costs.'

I think about the archives, preserving thousands of people's lives: their births, deaths, marriages, greatest triumphs and tragedies, all recorded in print.

'The people behind the stories are more important,' I tell her.

We hug each other and walk to the hall. Louise freezes as she hears a key in the lock.

'That's Andrew. Do you mind pretending you're a mum from school? We'll have a row if I tell him who you are. It'll rake up everything.'

The door opens and her husband steps inside. My jaw drops as I take in his sharp features and thinning brown hair.

'*You're* Andrew Marshall,' I stutter.

He frowns. 'Do I know you?'

'I don't think you've ever met,' Louise says breezily. 'This is Julia, Tracey's mum.'

It's a good job she's improvising because I'm speechless.

'I can't stop. I forgot my work phone.' He grabs it from the shelf.

'Thanks for the tea and chat, Louise.' I manage to nod at Andrew without completely falling apart.

I walk down the drive, and turn left, counting my steps. It's only when I'm safely out of sight, on a neighbouring street, that I stop. My heart pounds with excitement.

I don't believe it.

Andrew Marshall is Coffee Guy – the man who kept bumping into me as he ran to catch his train. Each time he pushed past me and got on board, he must have arrived home early and discovered Louise and Charles's affair. So . . . if I prevent him from making his connection, it will stop the fatal chain reaction. He won't see Charles leaving their house and get into a huge row with his wife. Louise won't arrange to see her lover the next day to break off their relationship. *No one will die.*

I can go back one last time to 2023 and change what's happened from the beginning, without ever going to the bridge.

I'll save everyone's lives by keeping Andrew on the platform at High Street Kensington station.

Most important of all, I'll bring back Alex.

37

TUESDAY, JUNE 11, 2024

This is important. Please can you return my call? Better still, swing by my office in Southall so we can speak face to face. Am free all day. Thanks, Oscar.

The private investigator sends a second text with his address as I walk to the bus stop. I check on Google Maps and it's only a short walk away. Half of me doesn't want to hear what he has to say, but I could pop in and tell him I can't afford to pursue the case. He should leave the past – *Mum* – alone. It will get him off my back while I prepare to return to the past. Anyway, if his news is traumatic, I can erase this meeting. In my next life, I won't visit him. I'll keep my hopes alive.

I message back:

Am nearby. There soon.

He replies:

Putting kettle on!

Ten minutes later, I'm climbing the metal staircase at the rear of a betting shop and being buzzed in. Oscar's office is across the hallway from a tiny, musty kitchen, which smells of old microwave meals, and a bathroom with a sign saying the lock doesn't work.

'Come through!' he hollers.

The door doesn't open fully, and I skirt around piles of papers, which make Merv's tower of doom look like a molehill. I remember coming here with Alex. He had to perch on the side of my chair as there wasn't room for both of us to sit down.

'This is a welcome surprise.' Oscar bounds over and shakes my hand vigorously. His hair matches the colour of the opened packet of Digestives on his desk. Glasses swing from a gold chain around his neck.

'Take a pew.' He scoops up newspapers from a chair and adds them to the humongous pile in the corner. If it collapses, we'll be barricaded in.

'I remembered how you take your coffee – black no sugar.' He passes me a chipped mug, with a big smile. 'Which is lucky since the milk's gone off.'

'Thank you.' I stare at the drink, which resembles hot toxic waste. 'I've guessed what you're going to say – you can't find Mum. There's no trace of her in this country, or abroad, which you find suspicious. She never bought a plane ticket to Spain.'

He opens his mouth and shuts it, goldfish style.

'Correct. I'm sorry to say my inquiries have hit a brick wall. I'd like to contact the police about my findings, or rather lack of them. It's a logical next step.'

'Thanks for all your work. Will you email me the final invoice?' I put the cup down.

'Hold on. Can you bear with me? I appreciate this must be hard to hear after all these years, and you want to protect yourself from further heartache. But I wouldn't forgive myself if you didn't hear all the facts. You are paying for my services, after all.'

I swallow a sigh. *Here we go again.*

'I have old contacts from my time in financial crime who helped analyse your mum's bank account. Her expenditure stopped abruptly on May 11, 2004.'

'In Scotland,' I state flatly, remembering our conversations in earlier lives.

'I thought so initially. But I dug deeper and found one more transaction I'd missed originally – she made a couple of purchases from a gift shop on Kensington High Street. It was 7.10 p.m. on May 11, 2004.'

'She came back to London early?' I say breathlessly.

'That's news to you? You definitely don't recall seeing her on the eleventh or twelfth? This location means she could have been travelling back to Chiswick from Euston. She may have got off the tube at High Street Kensington underground station and decided to walk or catch a bus to Hammersmith.'

'I wish I did remember something!'

'What about the break-in on the night of the eleventh in Chiswick? Did your gran ever talk about it?'

'You've heard about that too?'

He nods, perching on the edge of the desk.

'Gran never mentioned it at the time. She was staying at our flat in Brentford and managed to shield me from it. Years later, she claimed her next-door neighbour, Ivy Watkin's house was burgled. Gran probably wanted to avoid me having nightmares. I only found out it was *her* house when I discovered this old cutting.' I call up the photo on my phone and show him. 'Do you think this could have something to do with Mum being in London?'

'Your gran certainly feared so.'

My jaw drops open. 'How do you mean?'

'Don't ask me how I got this.' He picks up a file and puts on his glasses. 'I have a copy of the original command and control record from that night. It records the 999 call made by Ivy, reporting the sound of breaking glass. Police attended and gave chase to an armed intruder but failed to apprehend him, as your article states. Your gran was contacted, and she returned to her property later that night.' He checks over the document, glancing up. 'I'm guessing she found a babysitter for you?'

I shrug. 'No idea.'

'The log says your gran was hysterical. She told officers she'd received a telephone call from your mum earlier that day. Marianne was planning to return from Scotland and expected to arrive in London later that night. They'd agreed she should sleep at your gran's house and come over the next morning, on the twelfth, for breakfast.'

I dig my nails into my thigh as ice pierces my heart.

'Gran never told me! Well, not directly.' I pause, thinking. 'I once asked her for Mum's last address in Spain and she claimed Mum would be back in time to take me to school the next day. I presumed she was getting confused again.'

'Interesting.' Oscar rubs his face.

'Was Mum . . .' My throat dries. 'Was she in the house when the Night Prowler broke in?'

'The police categorically ruled this out – the officers had arrived on the scene swiftly. They'd thoroughly searched the house and no one else was present. They reassured your gran that the house was empty at the time and Marianne hadn't returned to her property.'

'Did Gran believe them?'

'Not initially. A gold pendant was found outside the back door – the burglar had dropped it as he fled. Sylvia had argued it was proof your mum *was* in the house. She claimed Marianne was wearing it when she left for Scotland, and that your mum was missing.'

My heart thumps as my hand flies to my pendant. 'Is this what the police found?'

Oscar readjusts his glasses and scans the notes. 'I don't have a description, unfortunately.'

It *can't* have been this necklace. Gran recalled Mum dropping it out of the window before the train pulled away. In my dream, I saw the same scene. It must have been another item of Mum's jewellery.

'I guess this is when the police launched a missing person's inquiry?'

He shakes his head. 'Unfortunately, that never happened.'

'Because of Mum's narcolepsy? Gran said the police didn't take the case seriously to begin with because of her mental health problems. She never pursued it as Mum eventually got in touch, saying she was in Spain.'

'Missing person cases were handled differently twenty years ago. Nowadays, an investigation would have been launched straightaway, especially considering your gran's fears. But Sylvia discouraged the police from probing further.'

I cross my arms. 'That can't be right.'

'I've checked and double-checked. Sylvia called Chiswick police station early the next morning, claiming she was mistaken. She said your mum hadn't taken the necklace to Scotland – it had been in her jewellery box all along, together with her own keepsakes that were stolen. She explained that Marianne had just rung – her plans had changed last minute, and she was still at the music festival. Again, nowadays, attempts would have been made to independently verify your gran's story. But it appears it was accepted unquestioningly. The log was closed, stating Marianne Hockney was safe and well in Dumfries and Galloway.'

'But she wasn't! You've proved she was in London.'

Oscar raises an eyebrow. 'Exactly so.'

I sink back into my seat, reeling. 'I don't understand . . .'

'Your gran never received that second telephone call. I've analysed your mum's and gran's old phone records. Marianne called her on the morning of the eleventh from Scotland, as stated, but there was no subsequent contact.'

I bend over in my seat as air escapes from my lungs. I can't believe it.

'It's a shock, I know.' Oscar passes me a cup of water.

I straighten up and take slow sips.

'None of this makes sense,' I say, when I can finally speak. 'Why would Gran deliberately mislead the police when she'd been so worried about Mum the night before?'

'It's deeply troubling, and that's why I think we should involve them now. I have old contacts I can approach on your behalf if you don't want to speak to them yourself, at least initially.'

'What good would that do? Gran won't be able to explain to me, let alone a detective, why she's repeatedly lied over the years.'

'There's no chance she's lucid enough to understand the questions put to her?'

'Definitely not, and I don't want to risk upsetting her. What would that achieve?'

'In that case, we must figure this out ourselves. I can think of only four possible explanations for your gran's behaviour twenty years ago, and subsequently.' He holds up a finger. 'One – she was involved in your mum's disappearance. They had an argument after Marianne returned home early – something happened in a struggle, and your gran panicked. She misled the police to throw them off her tracks.'

'Absolutely not. Gran has spent the last twenty years talking about Mum, and promising she'll come back one day.'

'The second possibility is that she covered for a third party who caused Marianne harm somewhere between Kensington High Street and Chiswick.'

'Gran would never do that. She loved Mum and me. She'd die to protect her family. We came first, no matter what.'

'She *could* have come to an arrangement with your mum – helped her stay off-grid all these years, to avoid someone, possibly the police. It would make sense if your mum was involved in criminal activity. They could have colluded and agreed a cover story.'

'Doubtful.'

'I found no evidence of that either, which leaves the last, only possible explanation.' Oscar holds up four fingers. 'Your gran deliberately lied to protect *you* from the truth. The question is, what could she have gone to such great lengths to hide?'

38

TUESDAY, JUNE 11, 2024

Gran peers blankly into the full-length mirror and doesn't turn around when I enter her room. Her eyes are teary, her shoulders hunched. The cardigan slips down her arm, revealing a tea-stained blouse.

'That's not her!' She jabs a finger at her reflection. 'I don't care what you say, that's not Marianne. Do you hear me? Marianne was here a minute ago, but now she's gone. This woman looks like her, but she's an imposter.'

'*Sí*, you are right,' Raquel replies calmly. 'That's not Marianne. *Eres tú*, Sylvia.'

'Don't be so bloody stupid! It's not. Why doesn't anyone believe me? Marianne is back.'

Raquel glances across at me. 'We're not having *un buen día*.'

I'm not having a good day either. I'm trying to get my head around the fact Gran has covered up Mum's disappearance for decades. Mum *could* have rung her on the morning of May 11, 2004, admitting she was returning to London, but not to us. Gran may have lied to cushion the blow of her crushing rejection. The alternatives make my skin crawl – Mum vanished on the way back from Kensington High Street, or Gran's initial hunch was right, and she made it to Chiswick, probably by around 8 p.m. Mum could have popped into Gran's house to collect something, possibly her pendant, using the spare key from beneath the flowerpot. I doubt Mum stayed there all evening on her own without ringing to say she'd arrived safely; Gran was always a stickler for checking in. And Oscar only discovered one telephone call from her earlier that day, made from Scotland. Mum must have left again without finding her necklace, hours before the Night Prowler broke in.

Whatever happened that night, Gran may have been protecting me from the fact that something terrible *did* happen to Mum twenty years ago – but it was here in London, not Scotland.

'Let's say goodbye to that lady and sit down,' I suggest.

Gran sighs deeply but allows us to lead her to a chair. Slowly, we ease her down, and she closes her eyes. Within seconds, her breathing becomes heavier and she's asleep. I can't ask her what happened all those years ago. I might never know. I blink back tears and straighten up, embracing Raquel.

'It's great to have you back at work. We've all missed you, Gran particularly.'

She frowns slightly. 'I haven't been anywhere. We spoke before you hit your head, *sí*?'

Of course! I'm getting confused, like Gran. In this timeline, the train crash never happened, and she didn't take compassionate leave to look after her boyfriend.

'Sorry, I'm being silly. How is Sergio?'

'*Bien*! He's starting night school, and training to be a lawyer.'

'That's fantastic news. I'm happy for you both.'

She nods. 'Sylvia was worried he was hurt, but I explained he is fine!'

I try not to register any emotion. Gran must also remember that Sergio was badly injured in the train crash previously: another memory that has become entangled in her brain.

'We must talk,' she says, clutching my hand. 'I want to explain what happened before Carole speaks to you.'

I gaze at Gran's stack of newspapers and scissors on the dresser.

'Has she been cutting up papers in the day room again?'

She sighs. 'No. Sylvia has no interest in her hobby. She gets upset when I suggest making a scrapbook. She thinks I'm stealing her cuttings, and photos.'

I glance at the bedside table. The only framed picture remaining is the one of me and Mum in Gran's back garden. All the others have vanished.

'I was tidying up while Sylvia napped,' she explains, pointing at the stack of albums next to her chair. 'My mobile must have slipped out of my pocket and fallen on the floor. An hour or so later, *sorpresa*! The police arrived.'

'Omigod. Why?'

'Sylvia had found my phone. She dialled 999.' Raquel touches my arm. 'She was worried about you. Said you had *desaparecido*, disappeared.'

'Oh no!'

Raquel nods. 'She wanted to report you missing. She said you'd stopped visiting her, and so had someone called Alex. She was worried about you both. She wanted the police to track you down.'

My heart thrashes loudly and my insides twist painfully. 'I'm sorry.'

'You are not to blame. I told the officers I don't know anyone called Alex, but you visit often! They left. We explained to Sylvia you are safe and sound. There is nothing to worry about. She was *confundida*, confused, but she understands now.'

A cold chill creeps over my skin. I remember what the woman in the Swan told me: *You've left people behind who need you.*

In the timelines I've messed with, Gran remembers splinters of the past. When I disappear, she misses me.

'You want to sit with her?' Raquel asks, checking her watch.

'Yes, please.'

I crouch down beside Gran as she leaves. I kiss her papery cheek. Her eyelids flutter but don't open.

'I'm here. It's Julia.' I hold her hand. 'I promise you this is the last time I'll go back. I'll never leave you after this. I will return.'

A small moan escapes from her lips.

'I'll bring Alex with me the next time I visit. We'll all be together.'

I emerge from High Street Kensington tube station, squinting in the sunlight. Going home to White City would take too long and I don't want to waste another minute. I've timed how long it will take Andrew Marshall to run down the stairs and try to jump on the train.

Twenty seconds.

That's my tiny window to save hundreds of people's lives, including Alex's. But I can do it. *I must.* I dodge shoppers dawdling along the high street. In the distance, I catch a glimpse of a teenager in a high-vis jacket cycling furiously down the road towards me. It's the girl from Kensington Gardens. She's not going to deter me.

I make it through the newspaper building's revolving doors, panting. I feel the cyclist's gaze penetrate the glass and scorch my back but I don't turn around. Piotr salutes me with his newspaper from the front desk, and I manage a wave as I travel up the escalator to the huge, airy foyer. Turning right, I pass the canteen and wait by the elevators, hammering the button.

'Hold on. Coming in!' A guy strides towards me as I step inside. 'Sorry!'

The doors slide shut. I can't stop for anyone.

In the basement, I head to the cleaners' store cupboard, steering clear of the archives. I jam a broom beneath the handle to make sure I'm not disturbed. I don't want to be pulled back before I'm done. I sit on the stool and pull out the pendant from beneath my blouse.

I'll save Alex.

I kiss the necklace, close my eyes and turn the stone. I welcome the drowsiness flooding my body like an old friend.

Tick, tick, tick.

My heart beats with excitement as it falls into the same rhythm.

The countdown has begun to my reunion with Alex.

39

THEN

May 11, 2023

I'm falling!

I grab the handrail at the top of the flight of concrete steps as the world pivots and shifts. The platform below rises towards me and retreats into the distance. Blood drips from my nose. My eyes refocus on the train. The doors slide open, and people form a moving, faceless mass.

Oh God. This is the worst I've ever felt in the past, but I must keep going. I'm losing valuable seconds before Andrew Marshall arrives. I force myself down the steps, hanging onto the rail as a woman ignores the signs and comes up the wrong way.

'Are you going to move, or what?' she barks.

'No! You should use that side.' I jerk my head to the right.

She tuts loudly and steps aside. I plough on and make it to the bottom as a beeping noise rings out, followed by an electronic message:

This train is about to depart. Please mind the doors.

Here goes!

I turn around and see Andrew flying down the stairs, hold-ing a newspaper, briefcase and Costa cup. He's followed closely by the man with the blond ponytail carrying his violin case. Andrew knocks into a woman and doesn't apologise. He's desperate to make his connection. Louise was right – he must suspect she's having an affair and wants to catch her. He leaps off the final step and runs towards the nearest carriage.

'Andrew!'

I step into his path and the musician overtakes him.

'Get out of my way!' Andrew barks at me.

'No, sorry. This is important.'

I catch his arm as the doors close. The younger man uses his violin case to lever himself through the gap.

'Shit!' Andrew exclaims.

He jerks his hand back violently, showering me with coffee. I wince as the hot liquid soaks through my blouse and bra. I'm scalded, but I've succeeded.

'You can't get on that train!'

'What are you talking about? Who the hell are you to tell me what I can or can't do?'

Another electronic warning sounds from the train carriage:

Please do not obstruct the doors.

They spring open, and the pony-tailed guy yanks the instrument inside. Andrew darts to the opening. I lunge, grabbing his sleeve. I hang on firmly. People are watching, but I don't care. I have to stop him.

'Leave me the fuck alone, psycho!'

He shakes me off and jumps aboard. I try to follow but he shoves me back.

'People are going to die tomorrow if you don't get off the train!' I yell.

'Are you threatening me?'

The doors slide shut. Andrew glowers as I hammer on the glass.

'Please, get off!'

He gives me the finger but I continue to pound on the window.

'Don't threaten to take the children away from Louise! Daniel and Oliver need you both.'

His brows knit together as the train pulls away. He definitely heard that. Is it enough? I've failed to stop him from making his connection, and I can't turn up at their house. Andrew would probably call the police and I'd be arrested, wasting my time in a cell. Maybe he won't threaten Louise with sole custody this time, and she won't arrange to meet Charles at the bridge to break things off. I'm clinging onto hope when another train arrives.

The carriage doors open. I could go home to prepare for the worst-case scenario – that Louise and Charles continue to the bridge – as well as work out how to stop the Night Prowler attack later tonight.

But deep down, I know there's only one option. I step inside, dabbing my nose as the bleeding resumes.

I need to find Alex one last time.

I have to say goodbye to the love of my life.

40

THEN

'I missed you. I've missed you so much.'

The words slip out of my mouth as I open my eyes. Alex is holding me in his arms, while our song plays in the background: Harry Styles' 'Falling'. I've collapsed in the Swan – this time due to dizziness from a bad nosebleed, rather than cataplexy sparked by Suki's funny leaving speech. I try not to blink. I don't want to lose a single second. I want this moment to last forever. I breathe in Alex's scent that has disappeared from our bed, a musky mixture of sandalwood, vanilla and salt from his skin.

'I didn't catch that, sorry.' His eyes crinkle at the edges. 'What did you say?'

'I want to . . .'

How do you tell a stranger we've already met and fallen passionately in love? He'll never believe we've planned to get married and have children but have ended up suffering and hurting other people. We've parted traumatically. He has repeatedly died to save others. I open my mouth, groping for the right words. I want to explain that our love affair is the most wonderful, most excruciatingly painful experience of my life. But despite the terrible grief and loss that burns a hole in my chest, I'd do it all over again in a heartbeat. I stare at him silently as the words jam in my throat.

'Let's get her up,' Layla says. 'The bleeding's stopped. Can you stand?'

I nod, dabbing my nose, and stuff the tissue into my handbag. Luckily, it's not spattered down my blouse, which is stained with Andrew's coffee.

He helps me to my feet. 'Are you sure you're okay?'

'I am now. Thanks, Alex.'

'Wait, you two know each other?' Layla asks, glancing between us.

'No.'

'Yes, but not in this lifetime. Or in any other. It's impossible.'

'How badly did you bang your head?' Layla asks.

Alex frowns. 'I caught her in time. She doesn't have concussion.'

He gazes down at me, and there it is: the spark of electricity between us that never fizzles out or dies in any life. The crease deepens between his eyes. He can't understand why this is happening, or how to explain it, but he's falling in love with me. A lock of hair falls onto his forehead. I stop myself from reaching out and brushing it away. I mustn't touch him. I can't bury my face into his black jumper and hold onto him. Can't kiss him or feel my way around his body. Can't ever be with him.

Hot tears slip down my face for the most wonderful life I've lived, lost and can never have back.

'FYI, drunk crying is a total turn-off,' Layla hisses in my ear. 'How many gin and tonics have you had? You need to pull it together. He's hot, and it's not totally beyond the realms of possibility that he might be into you.'

I wipe my face with the back of my sleeve, forcing the corners of my mouth to turn upwards. I have to make the most of this final meeting, capture it like a photograph and carry it around with me forever.

'Sorry. I'm not drunk. I think I'm having a severe case of déjà vu.'

Alex frowns. 'I must admit, you look familiar. You know my name. Have we met before?'

It literally kills me to shake my head.

'I overheard someone speaking to you over there.' I jerk my head in the direction of his old uni friends. 'You're an artist, right?' I point to the cobalt blue paint on his sleeve. 'In an alternate reality we could have crossed paths at an exhibition.'

'You like art?' His eyes light up, glittering like sapphires.

'I should do. My name is Julia Hockney – like the painter, except we're not related, unfortunately.'

'Great name! I'm Alex. Alex Martin.'

'I'll leave you both to it,' Layla says. 'Lovely to meet you, Alex.'

She slips away but his gaze doesn't leave my face. It's as if he's memorising every feature, freckle and line.

'What kind of art do you like?' he asks.

'Seascapes, storms – anything by a particular artist I love. He's the most incredibly talented painter I've ever met. He once created a girl's face constructed from hundreds of multi-coloured diamond shapes. It's the most beautiful picture I've ever seen. Looking at it made me want to cry. It changed my life in the best possible way – it's never been the same since.'

Alex nods enthusiastically. 'Art has the power to transform. Is the artist famous?'

'Not yet. But I'm sure he'll be big one day and have his own exhibition.'

He gazes at me. 'It's funny, I'm usually drawn to landscape and water abstracts, particularly storms, but I went to the Whistler exhibition this afternoon. His portraits are incredible. They've really inspired me. Your hair reminds me of his flame-haired muse, Joanna—'

305

'Hiffernan,' I finish.

'You've been told that before?'

'Once or twice. I thought it was a compliment, but I read about the artist after someone mentioned him recently. Didn't he once describe Joanna as having beautiful hair but also looking "supremely whorelike"?'

Alex's face pales. 'Oh God, did he? Sorry. I had no idea. You must think I'm a total jerk.'

'Yes, but no. *Possibly.* But I forgive you for an artistic lapse.'

He throws his head back and laughs.

'I'm doing you a disservice anyway – you're far more beautiful than a Whistler painting. In this light, your hair shimmers like brightly coloured jewels. I can see shades of purples, blues, yellows and greens, even white diamonds.'

'Perhaps *you'll* paint a redhead one day, like Whistler. Someone who inspires you.'

'I'd love to.' He takes a deep breath. 'I don't usually do this . . . Well, that's not strictly true. Sometimes I try to ask out gorgeous girls in bars, but I clam up and can't find the right words. This sounds insane, but it's as if we already know each other. Maybe we've met in another life – in the alternate reality you talked about, and we crossed paths at an exhibition.'

I curl my fingers into a fist and bite the inside of my cheek to prevent myself from crying out.

'Do you believe in that kind of stuff?' he asks.

'Why not? I've learned that anything in life is possible.'

'Can I get your number? We could meet for a drink or a walk or . . . whatever you fancy doing tomorrow. Or is that too soon? Should I wait longer to show I'm interested?'

I stare at him longingly. Hands shaking, I pull the phone out of my handbag. 'My mobile's dead, sorry. I'm uncontactable.'

His face falls. 'Ah, let me guess – is that code for saying you have a boyfriend?'

The pain in my chest is so intense, I feel like I'm going to pass out. I'm desperate to reassure him my phone battery really is flat. I'll make a joke about wanting to revive the lost art of letter writing and he'll jokingly call me Jane Austen. We'll arrange to meet up without relying on modern technology, somewhere like Kew Gardens – anywhere except Hammersmith Bridge. But I have to walk away. I must let him go.

'Yes.' My voice cracks.

I sense the fissure growing, cleaving my entire body in two.

'I have a boyfriend, a fiancé.'

'He's a lucky man.' Alex's voice is tinged with disappointment.

'No, I'm luckier. I fell in love with him at first sight. We've only shared the briefest of time together, but it's been the happiest and saddest experience of my life. Through loving him, I've discovered I'm strong enough to do anything. I'm a better, braver person.' I wet my dry lips. 'When you meet that person, everything falls into place. They feel like home. It's like returning to your favourite painting and loving each brush stroke all over again.'

'Wow!' Alex runs a hand through his hair. 'I wish I could find someone who talks about me the way you do about your fiancé.'

'You will, one day. You'll love her with every fibre of your being and for a while . . .' My voice breaks. 'Everything will be perfect.'

I stand on tiptoes and press my lips against his cheek for the last time.

'Goodbye.'

I'll never forget you, Alex Martin. You are my life.

'One last thing – if a woman in a red dress and blonde wig asks you to meet on Hammersmith Bridge for a photoshoot tomorrow, don't go. It's a scam.'

My eyes are blinded with tears as I turn to go.

'Wait, Julia!'

I pause.

He tilts his head, frowning. 'Will I ever see you again?'

'Not in this lifetime.'

'What? I don't believe that. I refuse to!'

'You must, Alex. I'm sorry.'

'But—'

I manoeuvre my way through the hen party to the exit without stopping to listen. My resolve will weaken if I glance back. Pushing through the door, I hear Alex shouting above the hum of voices.

'Take a leap of faith, Julia!'

I gulp for air, holding onto the wall outside the pub before crossing the road. I can't breathe. A knife is driving deeper and deeper into my chest.

I'm slowly dying inside, but I've saved him.

From me.

He'll enjoy a happy, long life if we never get together.

41

THEN

I'm doubled over across the road from The Swan, trying to breathe through my erratic heartbeat and tiredness, when I hear the tap of footsteps. I keep my gaze fixed on the pavement.

'Leave me alone. I'm doing this. You can't stop me.'

'Steady on. I'd never tell a woman how to behave – I passed my gender awareness and white male privilege training with flying colours.'

I sigh with relief at the sound of Merv's voice. I thought it was my unwelcome visitor warning me against heading to Hammersmith Bridge tomorrow.

'Layla said you're unwell, and without wanting to sound rude or sexist, you look bloody awful. She suspects the dashing young man you were talking to in there has caused upset. I could challenge him to pistols at dawn?'

I wipe away my tears, glancing at my watch. It's 10.45 p.m.

'Thanks, but I'd prefer an Uber. Could you call one? My phone's dead.'

'Of course. Where do you want to go?'

I bite my lip. This is my last attempt at rewriting the events of 2023. I don't know why this timeframe is important, but I have until 1 p.m. tomorrow. I must make sure every moment counts during this small window otherwise I'll lose Alex for nothing.

'Brackley Road, Chiswick.'

He frowns. 'Don't you live in White City?'

'I need to swing by on the way home. It's close, but I'm not up to walking.'

He taps at his mobile. 'All done. It'll be here in three minutes. Anything else?'

'I don't suppose there's any chance of using your spare phone tonight? I promise I'm not making long distance calls to Australia. It's in case of an emergency.'

He digs in his pocket and hands over his pay-as-you-go mobile. 'There's not much juice left in it. Don't do anything I wouldn't.'

'That doesn't leave much to the imagination.'

'Touché. Take this as well.' He gives me a rape alarm. 'They were given out at a sexual violence conference. I was planning to ask my daughter to distribute them to her uni friends. You never know when you might need one.'

'Thanks for looking out for me.'

'No problem.'

My jaw tenses as I catch a pop of red in my peripheral vision. A drunken middle-aged woman in a short dress lurches across the road. It's not *her*. The fellow time traveller who warned me that all my attempts to avert a tragedy at Hammersmith Bridge would fail.

It doesn't matter what you do, someone always dies in the river.

Is she right? Louise has to be stopped from meeting Charles tomorrow, but if I can't persuade her to walk away . . . She mustn't die in the Thames and neither can Charles, otherwise the future consequences will be horrific for hundreds of people. I've already saved Alex by preventing him from turning up, which means everything comes down to me. A heavy, foreboding sensation balloons in my chest.

I attempt to plaster a smile on my face to avoid worrying Merv further.

'This might sound over the top, but I appreciate all your support over the years, and how nice you've been about Gran. You're the only person who understood what I'm going through with her Alzheimer's.'

He frowns. 'This sounds like a proper goodbye. Please tell me you're not about to quit and go into PR like the other turncoats?'

'Sorry, it's the alcohol. It makes me over emotional.' He doesn't notice the lie.

'Me too. I can't watch sad commercials after I've had a few pints.' He glances down the road. 'Your Uber's here.'

I walk away but stop, turning around.

'One more thing, Merv. Can you make sure the archives and Jeremy's job are safe if I'm not around?'

He looks puzzled. 'Sure, but remind me in the morning. I'll probably forget.'

I sigh as I climb into the cab. Layla stumbles out of the pub with Suki and other journalists from the *Gazette*. They're going clubbing with the trainees to prove they're still young at heart. I wave goodbye as the vehicle pulls away.

If tomorrow goes badly, this is the last time I will see them in this life or any other.

Number 4, Brackley Road, Chiswick, is tomb-like, shrouded in darkness. Merv's Uber has dropped me off across the street. It appears no one is at home, but I know a seventy-year-old woman is asleep in the front bedroom, recovering from a hip operation. She'll be attacked by the Night Prowler in approximately four minutes if tonight follows the usual course. I lean against a pillar as I'm hit by another wave of drowsiness and nausea. I check my nose, but there's only a tiny smear of blood on my fingertips. I have to press on.

Calling the police tonight didn't work the first time as the officers scared off the Night Prowler, and he wasn't caught for another year. Ringing British Gas during my next attempt to thwart him saved this pensioner but didn't help his future victims. *Third time lucky.* I need to persuade the police to request the force helicopter rather than chasing him on foot.

I cross the road, clutching Merv's burner. A food delivery driver hoots, but my jelly-like legs can't move fast enough. I trip as the motorcyclist veers past, shouting abuse, and fall spreadeagled, grazing my wrist and knee. My handbag spills out, and I drop the phone. It shoots towards the gutter. I try to grab it, but it slips through the grille.

Shit and double shit!

Now what? My leg and hand are gritty and bleeding, but I don't feel the pain. I could hammer on a few doors, but it's doubtful people will respond to a late-night caller. Alternatively, I could wake up the elderly woman and persuade her to call the police before the Night Prowler breaks in. I stumble down her drive, glancing about. There's no sign of him; he may not even come tonight. I might have done something that's caused another butterfly effect and disrupted his offending pattern again.

I'll quickly double-check the garden to make sure before banging on the front door. I jangle the latch on the gate. My heart sinks as it swings open. No security light reveals my presence. I limp around the side of the house, supporting myself on the wall. Her property is a criminal's dream. My heartbeat spikes as I reach the patio. The door is open. A glass panel above the handle is broken. I catch the sickly scent of flowers. I glance down and my skin crawls. A bunch of gladioli lies by the side of the step.

I hear a muffled noise inside; it sounds like a chair scraping across the floor. The Night Prowler could be here already! My head tells me to run and bang on a neighbour's door, but that would take too long. He'll have attacked the woman upstairs by the time I persuade someone to call the police. She will suffer serious injuries.

Fear snatches my breath away as I step into the kitchen, glass crunching loudly beneath my shoes. I fumble along the wall in the dark; it's become deathly silent. I need to at least find a weapon. I find a light switch and flick it on. The room is illuminated, revealing an intruder in a balaclava. He's standing on a chair beneath an old-fashioned lampshade, hands poised to remove the bulb.

My throat contracts. I utter a short, sharp scream, my breathing shallow.

The man's eyes widen with shock as if he's seen a ghost.

'I know you . . .' he gasps. 'You came back!'

He topples and falls heavily, yelping in pain on the floor.

'How is that possible?' he says, wheezing. 'You're exactly the same!'

A mixture of fear and horror grip me as I realise his mistake.

He thinks I'm Mum.

She hadn't popped into Gran's house and left again. She was still there when he broke in twenty years ago! I trip, banging into a cabinet. China smashes, but the sound is far away. I grope for the table, trying to put something solid between us. I miss and grab a chair with both hands as my knees weaken.

'Who's there?' a voice calls out feebly from upstairs.

'Burglar!' I manage to yell. 'Call the police!'

The man staggers to his feet. I open my mouth to quiz him but no words come out. His body braces to leap catlike for the door, then the tension melts away, a coiled spring unwinding. Slowly, he turns and stares. His corpse-like eyes are pools of blackness, devoid of emotion and empathy. I could rotate the stone and escape to

2024, but I daren't let go of the chair even to pull out Merv's rape alarm from my pocket. I'm hanging on for dear life. If my cataplexy strikes, I'll end up lying helpless on the floor.

I force myself to speak, praying I manage to stay upright. 'The police will be here any minute. But I want to know about—'

'Tell me how you did it.' His voice is low and gravelly, with a slight south London twang.

My heart hammers loudly. 'What do you mean?'

'Show me.' He steps closer. 'I want to see you pull it off again.'

'What? Did my mum—'

'Let's play, bitch!'

He lunges forward, swiping for my pendant. I heave the chair, catching him in the groin. He groans as I manoeuvre further around the table, gripping the wood. He fumbles in his pocket, and I catch the glint of metal as he swipes the air between us with a knife.

'You're talking about my mum,' I say, panting. 'I look the same as her. Long red hair. Two peas in a pod. You met her twenty years ago.'

Something undefinable flickers across his eyes. A siren wails in the distance.

'You broke into a house on Airedale Avenue in Chiswick and *she* was inside. She came home early from a trip and surprised you.'

I stare down at my necklace, remembering my dream and how Gran was clutching something to her chest when she broke the news that Mum wasn't coming back.

'You took this pendant from her, didn't you? You accidentally dropped it outside the back door as you fled. What the hell did you do to my mum? Where is she?'

The noise grows in strength. A police car has turned onto the street. He limps towards the door.

'Did you kill her? Tell me!'

He pauses, staring back at me one last time.

'What happened to my mum? I have to know!'

'Why don't *you* turn the stone and find out?'

He disappears, hobbling off into the night. I try to follow him along the side of the house, but the air is squeezed from my lungs. My knees buckle and give way. My head strikes something solid. I'm lying on cold, hard concrete. Invisible fingers force my eyelids shut.

I'm silently screaming a single word: *Mum*!

42

THEN

'Are you sure you don't want to be checked over at hospital?' a paramedic asks.

I'm wrapped in a foil blanket and shivering in the back of an ambulance. The elderly woman has already been taken to hospital. She suffered heart palpitations after hearing the commotion downstairs.

'I'm feeling much better, thanks. The shock of seeing someone with a knife inside the house sparked my cataplexy. I'm okay now though.'

That's a lie, obviously. My head feels like it's going to float off my body, but I don't want to be admitted to hospital and miss my window to save Louise and Charles tomorrow. I'm already at a disadvantage – I've lost Merv's mobile and my watch smashed when I fell.

The police officer leans against the door, making notes on his phone. 'So, you were saying . . . the gate was ajar, and you decided to investigate?'

'Exactly! I heard a noise as I walked past. I thought I heard someone shout for help. I ran into the back garden. That's when I saw the shattered glass. I peered inside the door and saw a man about to remove the light bulb in the kitchen. He threatened me with the blade and escaped when he heard the police cars. That's when I collapsed.'

'You were lucky the watering can broke your fall,' the paramedic says, removing the blood pressure cuff. 'Otherwise, we'd be insisting you come to A&E.'

I nod gingerly to prevent more fireworks from exploding inside my skull.

'And you're certain you've seen this man somewhere before?'

'Definitely. It'll come to me soon.' I frown, pretending to rack my brains. I haven't disclosed he was wearing a balaclava.

'That's it! Ealing Hospital. I think he was a volunteer driver. Dennis something. He drove Gran home once from an appointment. I remember he was friendly to all the pensioners – he talked about how much he loved visiting internet cafés locally.'

That's another untruth, but I can't risk giving his full name, without raising suspicions. This should give the police enough to catch him.

'Do you think it was the Night Prowler?' I press.

'Possibly,' he replies. 'You may have saved the homeowner's life tonight.'

My bedroom is bare and impersonal, bathed in magnolia and a drab sadness. It's pre-Ed's stark white and Alex's sky-blue walls, waiting for me to decide my personal tastes. A policewoman dropped me home half an hour ago. My mind is racing. All I can think about is Mum alone in Gran's old house in Chiswick, fighting off the Night Prowler. If I hadn't made her feel so bad about leaving me behind in London, she might not have decided to return early from Scotland. I fight against my rising feelings of guilt for inadvertently putting her in harm's way; I was just a kid and didn't know better.

Did the Night Prowler hurt Mum badly? He couldn't have killed her – he didn't have time to hide a body. The police arrived swiftly and would have found her in the house.

A chill comes over me as I replay the Night Prowler's words:

I want to see you pull it off again.

Why don't you turn the stone and find out?

Of course! Mum must have tried to time jump to safety, but something went badly wrong. Did he snatch the pendant off her neck as she vanished? Or perhaps *he* turned the stone out of curiosity. He could have dropped it when she gave him a scare.

By disappearing into thin air in front of him.

But why didn't Mum come back when she was out of danger?

My insides twist into tight coils with horror as I finally realise her fate.

Mum lost the necklace – and her way to return to us.

43

THEN

MAY 12, 2023

I'm holding Mum's pendant and staring at the Thames from the footpath on Hammersmith Bridge. My grief for her doesn't ebb and flow like this river, it's constant through every single life. If anything, it feels worse the more I've travelled back and unearthed new memories. I spent most of my life believing she'd abandoned and forgotten me, and I was wrong. Mum called me *Pickle*, and loved me more than anything in the world, but I keep losing her. Where is she now? Travelling through time to escape from the Night Prowler may have killed her, or she could be stuck hundreds of years in the past or future. I want her back so badly it hurts, but it's been twenty years. She may never be able to return to us.

I tuck the necklace safely into my bra. Whatever happens today, I mustn't lose it. I've slept with it on each time I've returned to the past and haven't taken it off. Would I have vanished, like Mum, if the Night Prowler had ripped it off *me* last night? My mind wanders. Perhaps, if I throw the pendant off the bridge now, I'll be thrown backwards or forwards in time to where Mum is trapped. I'll find her. My heart flutters with hope, but my hands don't reach up to rip off the chain. I can't do that to Gran. She's lost enough in one lifetime. I watch debris slowly bob towards me. The rippling water mirrors the sombre, slate-grey sky. In the distance, it's hard to see where one begins and the other ends. Gulls screech at me to leave, but I ignore them. This is where I belong today, whatever my fate.

I hang onto the railing as my vision swims. My heart beats fast, and then sluggishly slow, as if it can't control the rhythm. The bleed from my nose was worse than ever this morning, and my head throbs painfully, but I've already had one success. Police have released a CCTV photo of Dennis Clements, saying they want to question him in connection with alleged burglaries and serious assaults dating back almost twenty years. They've advised the public to dial 999 if he's spotted, and not to approach him. The Night Prowler is one step closer to being caught – a year early.

I walk unsteadily to the Riverside Studios and wait for a woman to overtake before pulling the lifebuoy from its holder. The second one is a short distance away – if there's another emergency here, hopefully, I won't cause a catastrophic knock-on effect in the future. No one challenges me as I heave it to the opposite bank, stopping and catching my breath every couple of metres. I hide the rubber ring among brambles and nettles, close to the set of steps leading into the river and return to the bridge.

I haven't managed to fix my watch and ask a jogger for the time.

'11.45,' she says, flicking a glance at her wrist.

I'm hoping the warning I shouted to Andrew Marshall on the platform last night got through to him. He might not have issued that fateful ultimatum, meaning Louise didn't arrange to see Charles today. But if this plays out as previously, I have fifteen minutes to prevent their meeting. I couldn't get to the Marshall house before they left for work, as I'm too dizzy. Charles joins Louise on her lunch break so if she's coming, I'm guessing it will be from the direction of Hammersmith. I head to the graffitied phone box, scanning the approaching people. There are only a few men and no women.

I'm too weak to walk closer towards the tube station, and I need to call the police from here. Minutes tick by. I check the time with a man walking his dog. It's almost midday. Something's wrong. I double back. As I pass the green coats of arms, I spot her approaching from the other side of the Thames. She's taken a stroll along the river before coming. Standing close to the halfway point on the bridge is a tall, burly man. Charles's biceps bulge as he crosses his arms impatiently. I half walk, half run, and reach him before Louise.

'Don't do this, Charles.' I'm wheezing and gripping my side. 'You'll hurt more people than you can ever imagine.'

He frowns hard. 'What the hell are you talking about?'

'You're about to argue with Louise. You think you can't live without her, but you're wrong. You can have a fulfilling life on your own, without hurting anyone. If you walk away now, you won't spend the rest of your life trying to make amends.'

'Who the fuck is this?' His dark eyes glitter dangerously as Louise arrives, out of breath. 'Have you put your friend up to this? Or was it your shitbag of a husband?'

She cowers. 'I've never seen her before in my life.' She turns to me. 'Can you leave us alone?'

'I can't, sorry.'

'Clear off, before I call the police,' Charles snarls.

'Go ahead. Do it now. That's exactly what needs to happen.'

'Just leave, *please*,' Louise begs.

I gasp for breath as my heart races freakishly fast. White-hot pain flares in my head.

'Are you alright?' she asks.

I can't speak.

321

'Come away from her. She's nuts.' Charles grabs Louise roughly. 'We need to talk.'

She wrenches her arm away. 'We can't just leave her – she might be having an asthma attack. We should call for an ambulance.' She pulls out a mobile from her handbag.

'Unbelievable! You'll find any excuse to avoid having this conversation. Clearly, I mean nothing to you, Louise, so fuck it. Fuck both of you.'

He climbs over the railings and stands facing us on the narrow ledge. Gripping the bar, he leans backwards and hangs on by his fingertips.

'What are you doing?' she gasps.

'Focusing your mind. This is about *us*, not her.' He jerks his head at me.

I stretch out my hand. 'Come away, Louise. This doesn't have to happen.'

'No! I can't just leave him.'

'Yes, you can!'

I might be able to save one of them in the water, but not both.

She ignores my plea and walks towards Charles. I take a large gulp of air as my heartbeat returns to normal. It's too late to change anything, this script is already written.

'I'm leaving,' I say hoarsely. 'I can't stop you, Charles – but remember, the only way to survive in the water is by lying on your back and floating with the current. Don't try to fight it, or swim to the nearest pier – you won't get a footing. Head for the bank.'

'It won't come to that.' Louise glances at me, her eyes shiny with tears. 'He doesn't mean this. We can work it out.'

'Can we?' Charles asks. 'Will you stay with me?'

She hesitates for a fraction and he pulls himself back to safety, pressing against the trellis.

'I can't go on without you, Louise,' he says, weeping.

'Don't say that!' She throws her arms around his shaking shoulders.

I'm wasting valuable time. This is happening again.

I spot workmen further along the footpath, phones clamped to their ears. They're calling the police. Clutching my chest, I force my legs to break into a run. I hear a scream and two splashes as I reach the end of the bridge. They're both in the river.

I drag the lifebuoy out of the brambles and yank it to the edge.

'Louise!' I wave my arms.

She bobs beneath the water and comes up as a branch floats past. She grabs it and holds on while Charles ignores my advice and swims against the current to the pier.

I jump, holding onto the lifebuoy, bracing myself for the paralysing shock of the cold. Breaking through the surface, I take a huge gulp of air and kick my legs, forcing the buoy closer to Louise. Charles yells and thrashes around. He swallows water and goes under. He re-emerges, eyes bulging and spluttering.

'This way!' I call.

He pitches and turns over, lying stretched out on his back. He's floating. *This can work!* We can all survive. I stretch out and grab Louise's hair as she sinks, yanking her up. She flings her arms over the buoy, coughing and gasping for air.

'I'm s-s-sorry,' she says, teeth chattering. 'I should have listened.'

'It's okay. Kick your legs.'

The current pushes us past a floating island of mud, studded with jagged pieces of broken glass. We both grab for a branch overhanging from the bank, pulling ourselves out. Louise scrambles onto the mud.

Charles is two metres away, and floating closer. I set off again, kicking my legs, and using the buoy to reach him.

'Here!' I call.

He flips onto his stomach and throws himself onto the ring, crushing my fingers. I lose my grip and go under.

'Stop it!' I gag as my mouth fills with water. 'We can both make it. Push it and kick.'

He doesn't listen and tries to clamber on top of the safety ring.

'Charles!' Louise shouts. 'Don't climb. Just hold on!'

He makes another attempt to use it as a mini bodyboard, and I sink a second time, the weight of my shoes and leggings pulling me down. When I come up, Charles and the ring are out of reach. He's moving closer to the bank, but my arms and legs are tiring. My chest feels like it's cracking open, and I'm making no progress however hard I kick.

'Come back!'

Charles grabs for a tree bough, hoisting himself out of the water. He lands a short distance from Louise.

'Throw the buoy to her!' she shouts.

'Can't move. Cramp in my arms.'

'Let me do it.' She hangs onto a branch, trying to join him.

'You'll fall in.'

'Charles! Give it to me.'

He lets go, and the ring drifts down the river. It snags on debris.

'No!' I cry hoarsely.

'Go after it,' Louise urges Charles, as the buoy comes loose and bobs away. 'You can reach it.'

'I'll drown. I'm not risking it.'

My legs aren't working. I can't kick. It's a struggle to keep my head above water. My body's shutting down. I'm losing control of all my muscles. I try to shout for help but choke on foul-tasting water. Panic sweeps over me. I'm not going to make it.

'We have to help her! She's drowning.'

Louise stretches her hand out, but it's a million miles away. I try to lift my arm, but it doesn't move. My head goes under. I bob up further from the bank. The current is dragging me to the centre of the bridge. My cataplexy has taken over and I can't call for help or paddle.

'Swim!' Louise shouts encouragingly. 'Kick your legs!' She hangs one handed from the tree. 'You can make it. Reach for me!'

'Stop it, you'll fall in.' Charles scrambles through the bracken towards her.

'We can save her.'

'She's too far out. The current's powerful – you'll be dragged away if you fall in.'

'I can almost reach her!'

Charles pulls her back. 'I can't risk losing you. It's you or her, and I choose you.'

I hear her shriek, but their voices fade and become distant. My limbs are leaden. I've lost all feeling, and my eyelids droop.

This is it.

I disappear beneath the surface. The light is a pinprick at the end of a distant tunnel.

I hear a ticking noise in the distance – my escape route into 2024. I try to reach for my pendant, but my arms won't obey. They're floating helplessly.

Nothing can save me. I'm sinking deeper and deeper.

My lungs are bursting. My ears are buzzing.

Suddenly, the surface above my head shimmers, and splinters into thousands of deadly diamonds.

A hand stretches towards me, the way it does in my dreams.

This isn't real. I'm imagining it.

No one will save me.

I close my eyes and stop fighting.

44

THEN

Someone grabs my arm. I'm travelling upwards. I feel a body pressed against mine. Louise must be trying to rescue me, but I can't hold my breath any longer. I open my mouth. Water fills my lungs.

Suffocating darkness falls beneath my lids.

Bright light. Chest pain. Hands pressing down. My ribs are cracking. I unpeel my gritty eyelids. A face looms above me. It's featureless. This is still my dream.

'Breathe, Julia!'

Hands roll me onto my side. I retch and water spews out of my mouth. I'm lying in sticky, sour mud on the riverbank. Someone's kneeling next to me.

'That's better. You'll be alright.'

I cough, bringing up a vile mix of water and vomit. Unfamiliar hands hold me in the recovery position.

'Wait until you've brought it all up.'

I vaguely recognise the voice, but it's not Louise.

'Thank you,' I say, panting. 'You saved my life.'

'*You* saved everyone else's.'

I turn over and look up into bright sea-blue eyes. The young woman's dark red hair is scraped back into a bun. Her thin, haunted face is familiar, but I can't place her.

'Have we met somewhere before?' My words come out in gasps.

A low, guttural moan escapes from her bluish lips. She clutches the sopping wet material around her bony chest. I catch a flash of colour before my vision blurs. *Red.* It's the woman from the Swan except she's not wearing the blonde wig!

My eyes sting painfully. I rub them, willing my sight to return. I force my lids open. My vision is fuzzy around the edges, but her features sharpen and come into focus. I must have hit my head on a rock because I'm wrong. My rescuer is far older than I initially thought. An elderly woman scrapes away the dripping white hair that's plastered to her forehead. She helps me into a sitting position, her arm cradling my shoulders. This time, I definitely recognise her.

'You're the woman in the restaurant bathroom! You warned me about Ed. You said he was a bad boyfriend. You're . . . Patricia.'

'I hoped you'd remember me, that something would stay with you from that night,' she replies hoarsely.

'What do you mean? What are you doing here?'

She breathes in sharply, her face etched with pain.

'Are *you* okay?' I blow on her hands, trying to warm her. They're as cold as marble.

'I am now you're safe,' she says, panting. 'I knew you'd come back after Alex died. Forgive me! I had to send him to the bridge that day, and figured you were clever enough to work out a way to save him. One last chance for us both to put things right.'

I wipe my smarting eyes with my wrist.

'That's not right. *You* didn't trick Alex. You're not the woman from the Swan. I banged my head and imagined you just now.'

'Are you sure about that?'

'Yes!' I rub her back vigorously. 'I have no idea how you know her, or why you're here. But you're freezing. Me too. I think we might both be hallucinating due to hypothermia.'

I glance at the bridge as the wail of sirens draws closer.

'Don't worry,' I reassure her. 'An ambulance is coming. The paramedics will take good care of you.'

'It's too late.' She collapses into my arms. 'We don't have much time left together. I came back for you, Julia. I did everything for *you*.'

'I d-d-don't understand, sorry. Who are you? How do you know me?'

I hear footsteps running towards us, and voices shouting.

'They're over here!'

'Get the stretchers.'

'This is important,' she whispers. 'Do you remember what I asked you in the restaurant that night?'

'You wanted to know why I wouldn't leave Ed. You asked me what I was afraid of.'

'You never replied.'

She coughs violently, her eyelids fluttering shut as two paramedics kneel beside us, firing questions. I'm wrapped in a foil blanket, and they check the woman's vitals and place an oxygen mask over her mouth. Her face is chalk white, her breathing shallow.

'Let's get her up, carefully,' the younger man orders.

'We're going to lift you onto the stretcher, love,' his colleague says. 'One, two, three. Gently does it. That's it.'

'Wait!' I stagger to my feet. 'You need to hear my answer, Patricia.' I take a deep breath. 'I didn't want to be alone. I was terrified I'd have no one left, after Gran slipped away and Mum didn't come back. I knew I'd be all on my own.'

She removes the mask. Her hand reaches out and touches my chest.

'You will never be alone, Pickle,' she says softly. 'I'm right here.'

'What did you say?' I gasp.

She doesn't reply, but her fingers find mine and slot between them. They're ice cold but familiar. I close my eyes and see Mum holding my hand on the way to school; swinging me in the air with Gran as we walk three abreast on the pavement; playing hide-and-seek in Gran's house; brushing hair from my face and kissing my forehead as she tucks me up in bed. Saying farewell before she leaves for Scotland. *Bye, Pickle. I love you.*

'Mum . . . ? Is it you? Is it?'

The edges of her mouth turn up. 'Always, Pickle.'

The yawning hole in my heart shrinks as she's carried away on the stretcher.

I hold Mum's hand all the way to hospital and won't let go. The paramedics let me ride with them when I explain I'm her daughter. One of them raises their eyebrows, but never asks how this woman could be so old. I can't explain it either; Mum should only be forty-five, not in her late eighties. I will her to speak and for her eyes to reopen, but she remains deathly pale and motionless in the ambulance. After being assessed in A&E, she's now on a coronary ward, hooked up to a heart monitor. I've torn myself away briefly while a nurse checks her pulse and heartbeat. My gaze flickers to the clock on the wall. It's 12.45 p.m. I'm running out of time in 2023.

I stop one of the elderly visitors who's leaving the ward.

'Can I borrow your phone? It's a quick call, I promise. It's an emergency.'

The man gives me his mobile. I move a short distance away before dialling 999 and ask to be put through to the police.

'I've seen Dennis Clements – the man wanted for all those bur-glaries. He's in an internet café in West Ealing. It's Digital Paradise, 154 Broadway. Please make sure you get the right address. It often gets mixed up with Golden Digital Paradise at Ealing Broadway.'

'I have the correct West Ealing address on the screen,' the oper-ator replies. 'You definitely think it's him?'

'Yes! Please come quickly before he leaves.'

'I've dispatched a car. Officers are on their way.'

I hand the phone to the man and return to Mum. She's alone. Her heart monitor beeps in a regular pattern. Wires are draped across the bed, and an oxygen mask covers her mouth. She's tiny and frail, as if she could snap in two with a single touch.

'Mum?' I grasp her hand, tears welling in my eyes. 'Is it you?'

I can scarcely believe it.

Her eyelids flutter and open. She removes the mask. 'Always late. Sorry.'

I'm groping around, trying to find the right words. 'How . . . ? Why . . . ?'

She stares at my pendant.

'The Night Prowler ripped this off your neck that night in Chiswick, didn't he? That's how you got lost. You had no way to come back without it.'

'I thought I was ready for him, but he knocked me unconscious.'

I frown as she takes another gulp of oxygen through the mask. I'm about to ask what she means but she continues speaking.

'When I woke up, I didn't have the pendant. I couldn't move towards the voices I heard in the background, calling my name. It felt like I was locked behind a screen, millions of miles away. I was lost in a time free fall.'

'What does that even mean?' I say, shivering. 'Where have you been?'

'My past and future. I had no power over where I travelled to in my life, or when. I couldn't get back to you and Gran, however hard I tried.'

Her eyes brim with tears.

'You're here now. That's what matters.' I kiss her hollowed cheek.

She smiles weakly. 'I managed it – in the end. I found you.'

'But how? What changed?'

'You turned twenty-five.'

'My narcolepsy gene mutated! I inherited the ability to travel into the past like you and Aunt Rose.'

She nods gingerly as if every tiny movement causes excruciating pain.

'I was drawn back to you but had no control over how long I stayed. I vanished into my childhood, adulthood and future old age. I returned in those forms. You never recognised me.' Her thin shoulders shake as she draws breath.

I swallow hard. 'So, you *are* the woman in the Swan? That was you on the riverbank earlier? I wasn't imagining who I saw?'

She nods. 'The ageing process speeded up dramatically after I saved you. I couldn't stop it.'

Her breath becomes ragged, with every word appearing a huge effort.

'I was the teenage cyclist in the park. And the child in Kew Gardens. I asked you for directions on Kensington High Street. I watched your practice runs on Hammersmith Bridge . . . and saw you throw sunflowers into the river for Alex.' She pauses briefly. 'I comforted you when he was in ICU. I held your hand while you slept on the chair. I was with you *always*. Everywhere.'

I sit back, reeling.

'I tried to help you on Hammersmith Bridge, but I was just a child.'

I remember the distressed pig-tailed girl who ran towards me.

'You warned me about the cyclist and attempted to catch me when I fell!'

'Yes.' She inhales, wincing in pain.

'Mum?'

She lets her breath out slowly. 'I wanted to stop Louise approaching Charles on the bridge. But I was even younger. Just a toddler. Too little to do any good.'

'That was you? The little girl I held?'

'I didn't want to let go. Or when I hugged you in the café.'

My eyes fill with tears.

'You gave me your lion toy! You left it for me again when I was in hospital after I found out about Alex's death. I slept with it every night.'

She smiles. 'It comforted me as a child. I wanted you to know I hadn't forgotten you. I *never* forgot you.'

The old photo on Gran's bedside table flashes into my mind and I see Gramps holding her in his arms. She was clutching the lion.

'You visited Gran in her nursing home, didn't you? You were the little girl running down the corridor. You dropped the toy lion and Carole stuck it on the noticeboard. I never realised what it meant. Or that you were there . . .'

'I had to see Gran. I don't know how much she took in. Or understood.'

'She did! She knew it was you. She said you were searching for your pendant. Now, I understand!'

A smile hovers on her blue-grey lips.

'I didn't believe you were back. It felt impossible. Gran had never explained about the time travelling or what happened the night of the break-in. She said you'd left us all those years ago and started a new life abroad.'

Mum coughs and puts the mask back on.

'Gran was protecting me, wasn't she? She'd guessed something had gone wrong with your time jump after the police found the pendant. She couldn't tell them or me the truth. She clung onto the hope you'd come back one day.'

The anguished look in Mum's eyes tells me my guess is correct. My chest twinges with pain. I don't blame Gran for shielding me. How could she say: *Your mum has disappeared into a time travelling black hole and may never return.*

After a few minutes, she's able to speak again.

'Better for you to accept I was gone. Let you move on. With your life.'

'But I couldn't. I never did.' I press her hand to my wet cheek. 'Everything stopped when I thought you didn't want me, that you'd walked out and left us.'

'Sorry. I'm so sorry. The Night Prowler . . . Changed all our lives.'

I frown, replaying our conversation. 'What did you mean when you said you thought you were ready for him? You didn't know he would break in – it was pure chance you came home early from Scotland to surprise me the next day.'

'You travelled back in time to save Alex. We'll both do anything to protect the people we love.'

My mouth falls open. This didn't happen by accident? You deliberately time jumped to Gran's house, knowing the Night Prowler would be there? But why? Why did you risk everything – our family – to confront him?'

Mum's eyes shine with tears. I glance at the clock. It's 12.55 p.m.

'Please tell me. I have to know.'

'Your nightmares,' she says falteringly. 'You've had them since you were five. The man with the knife, smoke, flowers . . . Not dreams. They're fragments of memories from that night. Trapped

333

in your mind, same as Gran. It's in our DNA. Some Hockney women can see things . . . but we *all* remember things differently to other people.'

'What do you mean?'

'I had to save you both from the Night Prowler.'

My ears buzz and my heart feels like it's stopped. 'We were there?'

'The *first* time . . . I went to the music festival. I gave my necklace to Gran before the train left the station.'

'I remember that! She did too.'

'You each retained tiny slivers from that timeline. *Before* it changed.'

I inhale sharply. Gran recalled how I altered previous events such as the near miss at Barnes level crossing after my journey to the past, but I never suspected I'd done something similar as a child. My stomach tightens as she takes in more oxygen. The line on the monitor leaps up in a jerky movement. Numbers in the right-hand panel are decreasing, as if a countdown has begun.

'Things were good in Scotland,' she continues breathlessly. 'I felt better. I'd stopped a little boy from choking. I pulled a fish bone from his throat. But a policeman called in the early hours of May 12. He had terrible news from London. You were both asleep in Gran's house. The Night Prowler broke in . . . He attacked Gran and beat her badly . . . He set fire to the kitchen to cover his tracks . . . I had to save her life. Bring her back.'

'Omigod!' My eyes widen. 'The Night Prowler killed her?'

'She died before the ambulance arrived,' she rasps.

Tears fill my eyes. I can't bear to think about my lovely gran deliberately hurt by someone. *Murdered.*

'Next time, I wanted to save *everyone*. I still went to Scotland to help the boy. I took the pendant with me. I made you both stay at our flat. I rang Gran and said I was returning early – that I was planning to stay in her house overnight and would come over for breakfast.'

'I knew you'd returned! I hired a private investigator. He said you bought something just after 7 p.m. on Kensington High Street. He thought you were trying to get home to Chiswick from Euston.'

'The trains were bad. I was diverted there. I checked the clock in the tube station's ticket hall. *7 p.m.* That time stayed with me. Twelve hours until I saw you the next morning. I couldn't wait! I bought presents for you and Mum and walked to Hammersmith station.'

This time it takes far longer to regain her breath.

'Back at Airedale Avenue, I prepared for the break-in. I wanted the police to catch the Night Prowler. But *he* changed this time. He turned up hours earlier. The landline phone didn't work. I was forced to confront him alone.' Her hand makes a jerky movement as she attempts to lift it.

'And he attacked you,' I say, my voice breaking. 'You were badly beaten, like Gran.'

'I recovered but was lost in time. I tried to catch him over the years. I tipped off the police and got him arrested in Clapham. That was the night we met in the restaurant bathroom. The address was a short distance away. But you went back, and he was free again.'

Mum gasps. I glance at the monitor, which makes another spiky pattern. The numbers continue to get smaller.

'I'm sorry, Mum,' I say, sobbing. 'So sorry you've gone through this. I think he'll be caught today. I've rung the police. They're on their way to an internet café in West Ealing. They'll arrest him a year early.'

I remember Merv's tip-off about this missed chance to catch him. 'You previously rang the police and told them he was in the café, and they got the addresses mixed up! But now, we've saved all his future victims together.'

She lets out a deep sigh. 'We're a good team.'

'Now what happens?'

'You were caught in my time loop, May 11 and 12. I think we've broken it. The clock will reset.'

'To when?'

'Where it all began.'

I rub my brow, thinking. She must mean my first time travel attempt in the archives.

'I understand 7 p.m. on May 11 – that was when you looked at the clock at High Street Kensington station and thought of me. But why 1 p.m. the next day? What happened at that time?'

'That's when I lost someone else I love,' she says, wheezing. 'The most important person in my life, my whole world.'

My heart beats quicker. My mouth forms the word 'me' but it's not audible.

'You tried to escape from the Night Prowler. The police thought you'd tripped, or he pushed you as you ran down the stairs. You fell and suffered a terrible head injury.' Her hand gropes for mine. '*You* died in hospital at 1 p.m. on May 12, my darling. I could never let that happen. I had to save my little girl. I was willing to do anything to bring you back to life.'

'Oh, Mum!' I press my lips to her hand, as tears roll down my cheeks. 'I'm so sorry I doubted you. I thought you'd abandoned me . . . I blamed you for everything that was wrong in my life – all the bad decisions I made, and opportunities turned down. But you sacrificed yourself to save me and Gran.'

'I would do it all over again in a heartbeat.' She takes a couple of short breaths. 'I need you to do something for *me*.'

'Anything. Name it.'

'Don't come back. Let me go.'

It takes a couple of seconds for her meaning to sink in.

'No! Let me help you.'

'Look what this has done to me.' She lifts her other gnarled hand a few inches before it drops heavily to the bed. 'You must stop. Don't change anything else whatever happens. You won't survive another jump. This is my last. I held on to save you one more time.'

The monitor beeps loudly and the numbers drop rapidly.

'What's happening?'

'Promise me, you won't change this, Julia. It's time to say goodbye.'

'No! I've only just got you back. I can't lose you again. Gran needs you. *I* need you.'

I hang onto her hand, kissing it repeatedly.

'Tell her I've returned. That I love her. Move forwards, Julia. You can't change what happens to me, or anyone else.'

'Yes, I can!' I clutch my pendant.

Tick, tick, tick.

It's 12.59 p.m. I try to block out the sound.

'Don't change the past again. Please, Julia – it's the only thing I want.'

The pattern on the screen changes and a piercing alarm rings out.

'Mum!'

'Get on with your life,' she whispers. 'Take a leap of faith.'

'But I need you with me.'

She places her hand over my heart. 'I'm here. I never left. I love you, Pickle.'

'I love you too, Mum. So much.'

Nurses run up to her bed and push me out of the way. They pump her chest, shouting for more staff.

Mum!

337

The ticking grows louder and builds to a crescendo.

But it's not the pendant making the screeching noise. It's the heart monitor.

A velvet curtain falls heavily behind my eyes.

I'm dragged away as she flatlines.

45

FRIDAY, MAY 3, 2024

A disc of light buzzes in the air like an angry firefly. It fixes above my head, expanding and growing stronger, scorching my eyeballs. Strange, moving shapes loom. I catch a glimpse of a hand brushing hair from a girl's face. The image burns brightly and fades. The world tilts. I snap my lids shut. Voices stab my eardrums.

'Wow! That guy's a total pro,' a man says. 'He didn't spill a single beer as he stepped over her.'

'She opened her eyes. Do you think she saw anything?' A woman's voice.

'No, she's totally out of it. Fast asleep.'

'Should we do something? She seems worse than usual.'

'I guess I should try.' Red-hot pincers jab my arm. 'Wake up, Julia!'

Lights stab my retinas. I see a glint of glass, a pop of vibrant hues, and inhale a heavy, rich floral scent. Nothing is familiar. This isn't 2023. I'm not in the hospital ward with Mum. Or on the platform at High Street Kensington. Or in the Swan with Alex. I'm lying on the floor. Roundish, luminescent objects hover above me. What are they? I have no idea where I am, what's happening or who I'm with. I must go back. I don't care what Mum says. I'll save her, even if it kills me. *The way she saved me.* I turn the stone in the pendant and listen hard for the ticking sound. I can't hear anything. Slowly, I unpeel my eyelids and look around. Faces loom and evaporate. Fuzzy shapes sharpen. I'm still here, wherever *here* is, on my back. Pink helium balloons, with trailing ribbons, jostle each other across the ceiling.

A man in black trousers and a white shirt strides past, holding a tray of drinks. The stark colours linger, mix and form grey shadows, slinking into the walls. This isn't right. Why haven't I returned to the past? I stare at my hands, and my insides churn. In my mind, my fingers are gripping the pendant, rotating the stone faster and faster, but my arms are resting helplessly by my side. The necklace isn't around my neck. Where is it? Oh God. Did I lose it?

'Shall we get her up?' a woman asks.

No.

'Yep. She's in the way down there.'

'Okay.'

Strange hands force me into a sitting position. Tables and chairs tilt and overturn; lights catapult and pictures spin. Dust motes defy gravity, floating upwards. I clamp my lips tightly together to prevent myself from throwing up.

'Can you make more effort?' the male voice hisses. 'It was hard to get a booking here. We need to get you off the floor, FFS.'

His tone lightens and grows louder. 'She's back!'

I'm rising in the air, a body raised from the dead, and land in a cushioned seat at a table. My hand jerks forward involuntarily. Red liquid spills, blood like, over an expanse of white.

'There goes my glass of wine!' the man says. 'Thanks a million.'

'Where am I?' The words are thick and heavy on my tongue.

'The restaurant we both fancied trying. Hey – you've got a nosebleed.'

Fingers clamp a tissue to my nostrils, pinching hard. I can't breathe. Black dots twirl before my eyes.

'Nothing to see here!' he says loudly. 'She'll be embarrassed if you all sit there gawping.'

Faceless people turn away from me as if I'm contagious, but I sense a few lingering stares.

Who are they?

I try to focus on this guy who's sitting next to me, but all I see is Mum. She never left me. She sacrificed herself twice to save my life.

'Mum.' The word jams in my throat.

'What did you say?'

Tears slip down my face.

'For God's sake, Julia,' he says, sighing. 'How much have you had to drink?'

'I'm not drunk. I lost Mum. Really lost her this time. For good.'

I cry harder in huge, gulping sobs that hurt my ribs.

'You lost her twenty years ago. Can't you at least attempt to pull it together? Everyone's watching.'

His fingers release my nostrils, and I inhale deeply. Something wet drips onto my arm. The tear pools next to a small red spot. Is that a bruise? I look up. The face comes into focus. High cheekbones. Neatly trimmed blondish-brown hair. Cold, grey eyes.

Ed!

'What are you doing here?'

He makes a sharp clicking noise with his tongue. 'Well, I'm hardly going to miss your birthday, am I?'

'My birthday,' I repeat numbly. 'Are you sure?'

I hear the drum of his fingers on the table. Behind him are pink and white streamers. A Birthday Girl banner is falling off the wall.

'How old am I?'

'Did you bang your head on the floor? You're twenty-five today! This is your party, but you decided to take a nap and fell off your chair. Luckily, the waiter didn't spill the drinks on his tray. Our guests are pretending they didn't see him step over you.' His lips almost brush my ear. 'But they're still looking so you need to get a grip.'

He throws his arm out expansively, a rigid grin fixed on his face. A woman with a black-velvet hairband and red polka dot dress is standing by the bar. *Vicky.* I catch a flicker of alarm in her eyes before she forces her scarlet lips into a smile and waves. Half a dozen journalists from the *Gazette* including Merv and Salim are also ordering drinks. Layla and her girlfriend, Megan, are here – they haven't moved to New York. I recognise most of the people sitting around the table and chatting nearby – Ed has invited friends and work colleagues. I spot a woman with long, swishy blonde hair. *Miranda.*

'Are you happy everyone came tonight?' Ed asks abruptly.

I'm back to where it all began: the day I inherited the ability to travel through time from Mum, Aunt Rose, and great grandmother, Violet. The time loop – created by Mum's intense love for me – has been broken.

I hold onto the table tightly as a rush of adrenaline overwhelms my body. I don't try to fight off my memories when they arrive.

Charles Fielding and Louise Marshall survived the bridge jump. Charles was cleared of attempting to murder Louise. The train crash never happened because Charles didn't drown in the river. He pushed the broken-down car off the railway track a year later. The Night Prowler is standing trial for murder, and dozens of burglaries and serious assaults.

Alex never met me for a first date at the bridge. He's alive.
Mum . . .
She sacrificed herself for me and Gran all those years ago.
Now, Mum is dead. Mum is dead. Mum is dead. Mum is dead.

I cry harder. The pain is unbearable. I want to curl up in a ball and grieve for the people I've loved and lost, but cheers ring out from around our corner table. A waiter strides towards us, carrying a birthday cake. A lone candle is stuck in a melting buttercream rosette. It flickers feebly as if it doesn't want to be here either.

'I can't do this, Ed, sorry.' I rise unsteadily from my chair. 'I have to leave.'

'No way! I've paid extra for the cake. I want to get my money's worth.' He catches hold of my arm and I reluctantly sink back down. He throws an arm around me, and I catch another whiff of the floral scent.

'Smile and look happy,' he says, through gritted teeth.

Happy birthday to you, happy birthday to you . . .

The chorus is deafening. My gaze flits to Vicky, who doesn't come over or join in the singing. She's staring at Ed and anxiously biting her bottom lip.

'What do you think?' he asks, pointing at the cake.

My stomach churns at the sight of the oily frosting, with garish pink streaks.

'Make a wish!' someone says loudly.

I close my eyes and blow out the candle to get it over and done with. My hand reaches for the pendant and finds air again. I hear clapping, but the sound is hollow and distant, as if someone else is receiving applause for their performance.

'What did you wish for?' Ed asks.

'Something that can never happen,' I say quietly.

I no longer have the necklace and I can't save Mum's life. I have to let her go. More tears spring to my eyes.

'You could at least pretend you're enjoying yourself.'

I glance down and notice red marks on my arm.

'Did you pinch me?' I ask, turning towards him.

'Sorry. I didn't know how to wake you.'

'Well, not like that! It isn't okay. None of this is.'

I stand and shove back my chair. I want to speak to Vicky before leaving, but Miranda is blocking my way. She thrusts a phone in front of my face.

'Smile for the camera!'

Ed gets up, clutching a fresh glass of red wine. 'Can you take one of the two of us?'

'Sure thing!'

'Sorry about your arm,' he whispers. 'But let's make the most of tonight, yeah? You said you wanted to show your gran some piccies from the party.'

He produces a dazzling smile for our photo, which vanishes as quickly when Miranda wanders off.

'Oh, I forgot to say – I can't come with you to the nursing home tomorrow. I'm watching West Ham and they're playing away.'

Another brilliant, white light flashes. People crowd around.

'Happy birthday, Julia.'

'Have a good one!'

I want to disappear – leave this restaurant, and this year. Return to the past, and never live this day over again.

Vicky finally approaches, tightly gripping a glass of bubbly. 'There's the birthday girl! Are you on the Prosecco? You look a tad worse for wear.'

Her tone is flat and she avoids making eye contact with Ed. She must be hating the party as much as me.

I inhale her Chanel No 5 perfume as she envelops me into a hug. I stiffen beneath her arms. Ed's shirt has the same scent.

Incriminating images sear my brain. Vicky and Ed were talking when they thought I was asleep. They never did understand that I'm fully conscious during a cataplexy attack.

'Do you think she saw anything?'

Ed readjusted Vicky's hairband as she laughed – an intimate gesture no one else noticed or understood before she headed swiftly to the bar. Finally, I see the full picture in technicolour.

I step back. 'How long?'

'Sorry?' Vicky gapes at me.

'How long has it been going on between the two of you?'

Her face pales.

'Don't be daft!' Ed says dismissively, swooping into the conversation. 'You're imagining things as usual.'

'I see everything clearly, thanks. You're cheating on me. I suspected you of sleeping with Miranda. I thought her initials were MM. But that's your nickname for Vicky, isn't it? Minnie Mouse, because of her hair and polka dot dresses . . . The hairband.'

His face blanches and he looks uncertainly between me and Vicky.

I turn to her. 'This is why you've been distant with me recently and tried to avoid meeting up – you felt guilty. Or were you afraid I might work out what you've been doing behind my back all this time?'

Her hand flies to her mouth. 'Oh God, Julia!'

Ed won't meet my gaze.

'Nothing? Either of you?'

'I don't know what to say,' Vicky blurts out. 'I never meant for any of this to happen. I'm sorry.'

'That's all you've got? Have you any idea how lame that sounds? Did you regret it when you broke up Samira and Hamish, or that junior doctor, Chris, and his girlfriend? Let me guess, you've justified this to yourself by saying Ed and me are more like brother and sister than boyfriend and girlfriend? You might not have owed anything to Samira, or Chris's partner, but you owed me. We're best friends. *Were* best friends.'

'I feel awful about *us,* I swear.' She steals a glance at Ed. 'But I don't know what you mean about those other people. I have no idea who Samira and Hamish are, and I've never slept with anyone at work. I was devastated by the break-up with Giles, and Ed comforted me. We became close. Neither of us planned this. It was out of our control. We didn't mean to hurt you.'

I roll my eyes. 'Was it love at first sight?'

'You know I don't believe in anything like that,' Ed says quickly.

In my peripheral vision, I catch Vicky wincing.

'Can we do this later, somewhere else? Really talk it through in private?' Ed nods at his work colleagues who are pretending not to eavesdrop. 'Maybe tomorrow when we've all cooled off?'

'No! We're doing it here and now.'

'Fine then.' Ed sighs and takes a large sip of wine. 'We haven't been good for a while, Julia. Everything was about your narcolepsy, and how we lived with your illness. I tried my best to understand, but I never came first. Your needs always came above mine. Is it so bad to want to be happy?'

'It is when it's at the expense of other people,' I hit back.

'We were planning to tell you soon, but we didn't want to ruin your birthday party.' Vicky reaches for my arm, but I shrink away.

'Is that why you want me to confront Ed about my suspicions? You're planning to encourage me to bring things to a head and save *you* from coming clean. That's cowardly, Vicky.'

She frowns. 'I don't know what you mean . . . We haven't discussed this.'

Not yet.

'We were waiting for the right time,' Ed cuts in. 'But you were upset about your gran and the anniversary coming up of your mum walking out. We weren't sure how you'd cope.'

'Mum didn't leave me voluntarily,' I say loudly. 'She saved me. Twice. And for your information, I can cope perfectly well without either of you. I have all this time. I know what true love and friendship is – and it's not this. It's never been *this*.'

I notice Layla edging closer. She's debating whether to intervene and break this up. I shake my head and she backs off. The other guests are watching but I don't care. I'm not done yet.

'I want you out of my flat,' I tell Ed. 'You're not coming back tonight or sleeping there ever again. You can make an appointment to pick up your stuff another time.'

He kicks away a deflated balloon that's fallen from the ceiling. 'Be reasonable, Julia! I know this is a shock, but when you've calmed down, you'll see this is for the best.'

'Yes,' Vicky adds eagerly. 'I hope we can all be friends again one day.'

'Not in this lifetime – or any other, thanks. You've shown your true colours, Vicky, and you're welcome to Ed.' I glance at the bruises on my arm, before facing him. 'You are a gaslighting, controlling piece of crap. Don't flatter yourself by thinking you ended "us" – I left you long ago.'

I ignore the row of gaping spectators and spot my birthday cake on the table.

'One more thing,' I say, turning back. 'I forgot you paid extra for this. You should definitely get your money's worth.'

I pick up the cake and shove it in his face.

46

MONDAY, MAY 6, 2024

'You're not going to throw a cake at me, are you?' Merv asks.

He pretends to cower behind the towering piles of paper on his desk.

'Only if you annoy me.'

I've spent the weekend recovering from my final journey into the past, and it's the first time back in the newsroom since my now infamous birthday party.

'I guess this isn't a good moment to ask you to swap my shift on the rota?'

'Afraid not. I need to speak to Rod. But I thought you might like these for your backgrounder.' I pass him the shoebox of Night Prowler clippings. 'Gran doesn't need them. We're collecting cuttings about Paul Rudd.'

He rifles through. 'This is great! The online library—'

'Doesn't go back that far, I know. When will the trial finish?'

'The jury should be sent out later this week. I'm trying to pull everything together about his arrest twelve months ago.'

I stare at his computer screen.

Dennis Clements was arrested last year in an internet café in West Ealing, googling 'time travellers', the court heard.

*Police received an anonymous tip-off he was using a com-
puter inside Digital Paradise in West Ealing, on May 12,
2023, and raided the property.*

*He told officers: 'I've been visited by time-travelling
aliens. They can appear and disappear whenever they
want using a necklace.'*

'Time travel!'

'I doubt he actually believes it's real,' Merv replies. 'His defence lawyer used his claims to argue he was unfit to stand trial on the grounds of insanity, but the judge dismissed the plea after listening to psychiatric assessments. There's no way the jury will acquit. The evidence against him is overwhelming. I'd bet my house on him being convicted on all charges. He'll probably die in prison.'

'Let's hope so.'

'Julia!' Rod shouts across the newsroom.

'I'd better go. Good luck with the court case. Thanks for everything.'

Merv nods, hammering at his keyboard. 'Dammit. Why doesn't this button work?'

'It's a modern mystery.'

I clench my fists as I walk slowly over to the news desk.

'Wakey, wakey, Julia!' Rod shoves back his chair and stands, sticking his glasses on his head. 'Get a move on. I need you in the bunker. This news list won't write itself.'

'It'll have to because I'm not typing it.'

'Sorry?' Rod flicks his tie over his shoulder. 'What was that?'

'You're wrong about the archives. We should preserve people's stories – their lives and deaths – and learn from them, not throw them away. Who are any of us without that shared history and experience? It's what binds us together. Without that, we have nothing. The answers always lie in the past.'

'Thanks for the inspirational lecture, Greta Thunberg, now do your bloody job or I can arrange a permanent transfer down there if you like it so much.'

'You can't demote or punish me – I quit.'

His mouth opens and shuts as a hushed silence descends across the newsroom.

'And to borrow Suki's leaving speech, I'd like to say I've enjoyed working with you, Rod, but I've hated every minute. You're a bully, and a misogynist, and an all-round terrible human being. Goodbye.'

As I stride away, Merv bangs his fist on a desk. Other journalists stand and follow suit, giving me a traditional Fleet Street send-off. I burst through the door and don't look back. On the landing, I jump into the elevator as the doors close and head down to the archives. I enter room 312b for the last time.

No fans whir, and the ceiling is intact. The room is spotless; the floor shines and the air smells fresh. Books line the neat shelves, which have been dusted. Crisp files are stacked in alphabetical order.

'I recognise you from the newsroom,' Jeremy says, glancing up from his laptop. 'Can I help? Does someone need a file?'

'I want to help *you*. There could be a major leak in here unless you do something about that dodgy pipe.' I point towards the ceiling.

He frowns, staring up. 'How do you know?'

'I overheard someone in the lift saying all the old pipework down here needs replacing,' I say, quickly improvising. 'But the records will be ruined if it bursts before it's fixed. The managing editor's office could use the cost of restoration as an excuse to bin everything before the office relocation. You need to find a permanent home for all the cuttings and books in case that happens. I've researched online – a few university journalism departments would probably agree to take them if no warehouse is available. That would be better than losing them completely. But you need to act quickly – isolate the cold-water supply pipe, and call building services, insisting this is an emergency. Don't let them get away with doing a shoddy repair themselves – make them call out a specialist plumber.'

Jeremy's brow wrinkles, as he fiddles with the large brass valve on the wall.

'Why are you doing this? No one from the newsroom usually cares what happens down here. The majority of what reporters need is online.'

'Because the past matters. It always has.'

Piotr gives me a final salute with his newspaper as I push through the revolving doors and leave the building. I hail a taxi – I can't face retracing my steps down to the platform at High Street Kensington tube station. I arrive at Ravensbrook and tap the code into the keypad. Peering through the hatch, I spot the dreaded dinosaur mug. Carole appears, looking like she's chewed a wasp.

'Good morning, Miss Hockney. This is a surprise. Your gran's not having a good day, I'm afraid. It might be best to come back tomorrow?' She walks over to the door, holding it open.

'No, thank you. I wasn't well enough to visit over the weekend, and I need to see her today.'

Annoyance flickers across Carole's eyes. 'Of course, you know what's best for her. You forgot to—'

I sign the visitors' book, adding the time and date.

351

'Thank you. Let's walk and talk.' She gestures down the corridor. 'Your gran has been at the newspapers in the day room with her scissors. We may need to take them off her, or scrap the service for the other residents, if this behaviour continues.'

I stop walking. 'Let's be clear about something, Carole. I won't let you confiscate Gran's scissors, and you're not going to stop the newspaper service. And on that note, I want you to reintroduce the weekly hairdressing and nail technician visits.'

She opens her mouth to argue.

'You might not think it's a big deal to stop the sessions because the residents can't remember having their hair styled or their nails painted afterwards. They don't necessarily notice their hair is unbrushed or they've spilt tea down their blouses. Yes, you take care of their basic needs – feeding, washing and toileting – but how they look also matters. Gran always took pride in her appearance. That's who she was – she still *is* that person.'

'Unfortunately, the usual hairdresser and nail technician are unavailable,' she says huffily. 'But if you think your gran would benefit from these extras, I'm sure I can look into finding replacements, for an additional surcharge.'

'I checked our contract last night and it's included in the monthly fees.' I raise an eyebrow. 'Unless you're planning to issue refunds?'

Carole's face tightens; her eyes glitter.

'I'll investigate this matter straightaway. Good day, Miss Hockney.'

I smile to myself as she stalks off. Mum would be proud of me.

Clothes, photos and newspaper cuttings are strewn across the floor of Gran's room. She's rifling through drawers in her bedside table as I walk in. A hairbrush lands on the carpet, followed by a book. Raquel picks them up.

'It's here, somewhere,' Gran cries.

'Let's search for it later after you've had a rest,' Raquel replies.

She helps her into a chair. Gran closes her eyes; her cheeks are tear-stained.

Raquel walks over. '*Ella está confundida*, she is confused.'

'Can you give us a few minutes?'

She hesitates.

'Please? I know what she needs.'

'I'll be back in *cinco* minutes.'

I pick my way through the clutter to the wardrobe and pull Gran's favourite camel coat from the hanger. I run my fingers around the lining and feel something hard. Carefully, I rip open the stitches and retrieve Mum's pendant.

'Here it is, Gran.' I place the necklace in her small, cold hands. 'This is what you were trying to find. I think you hid it in your coat lining years ago after that night in Chiswick and forgot where you put it when you became ill.'

Her eyes open, and a smile spreads across her face. She dips her hand into her pocket and pulls out her name prompts. Carefully, she opens the notes.

Marianne, daughter. She'll come back soon.

Julia, beloved granddaughter. Loves Alex.

Alex Martin, talented painter, and the love of Julia's life.

Her fingers waver between mine and Mum's note. She looks up, frowning.

'Is that you, Marianne? Did you find your way home?'

I hold my breath until it feels like my lungs will burst. Each time she's asked me this previously, I've corrected her. But not this morning. I'll tell her what she's waited decades to hear. It's the least I can do.

I give her a watery smile. 'Yes, it's me.'

It's a lie, but a kind one.

'Oh, Marianne!' She pets my cheek, weeping. 'Thank God for that. I've been so worried. I thought I'd lost you forever!'

'I'm sorry. I promised you I'd come back.' She feels frailer than ever as I hold her in my arms. Her thin shoulders judder.

'I stayed longer than I planned. I had to stop a bad man.'

She tenses beneath my fingertips and pulls back.

'The Night Prowler?' she whispers.

My voice thickens. 'Yes, but you don't have to worry anymore. He'll spend the rest of his life in prison. He'll never hurt anyone else again.'

'Thank God! When the policeman gave me your pendant, I guessed you were in trouble. I remembered you taking it to Scotland . . . at least, sometimes I think I did.' She frowns hard. 'I stayed up all night, worrying, and realised the police couldn't help; they'd never find you in the past. The next day I told them you were safe and your necklace had been in my jewellery box. I was trying to buy you time to get home. It felt like you were gone for years and years. When did you leave? Silly me. I can't remember!'

Gently, I wipe away the tears from her face. 'I came back as soon as I could. I wasn't gone too long.'

'That's good,' she says, nodding. 'It's been so hard to lie to the police and, particularly, Julia. But I couldn't tell anyone the truth. Who would believe what you can do, except me and Rose?'

'I understand how you've tried to protect Julia over the years.' I pick my words carefully. 'But when you thought she could cope with knowing everything, it was too late. You couldn't explain because of your Alzheimer's.'

'Too late,' she agrees. 'Don't stay long, Marianne. That's what I kept saying. You and Julia are the people I want to see most. And Alex. I haven't seen him for ages. I miss him.'

My heart contracts at the mention of his name. 'Me too.'

'But not Ed. He's awful.'

'I agree.'

Gran looks at me wistfully. 'You'll be proud of Julia. She's grown into an incredible young woman. So clever and kind.'

'Thank you for looking after her while I was away.'

'Oh, it was a pleasure. She's wonderful, but . . .' Her voice trails off, and she rubs her temple.

'What is it?'

'Her twenty-fifth birthday. Is that soon? Or have I missed it? I can't recall. We'll have to tell her about the family gene. Make sure she can handle it.'

'I'll keep her safe, I promise.'

'Hide this.' She passes the pendant, pressing it into my hand. 'Put it somewhere Julia will never find it until the time is right.'

'Won't she need it if she accidentally time travels when she falls asleep?'

Gran shakes her head. 'Rose boasted she could flit between worlds in her sleep but never change anything. Only the pendant can do that. But you must stop playing with time, Marianne. It's making you ill and look what happened to Rose!' She shudders.

'She crashed her car,' I say slowly.

'She was poorly after coming back from the past and lost control at the wheel.' She squeezes my hand. 'I can't bear to lose you again, Marianne. Promise me you won't leave us a second time.'

I swallow the lump in my throat. 'I promise.'

'Thank you.' She folds into my arms. 'I love you, Marianne.'

355

I stroke her hair and whisper: 'I love you, I love you', the way she used to whenever I cried for Mum as a child.

Marianne, Marianne, Marianne.

She repeats the words under her breath, and I don't correct her. Today, I'm whoever she needs me to be.

47

Sunday, May 12, 2024

The sky's the colour of faded denim; the pale sun is attempting to hide behind tattered clouds. I run my fingers over the handrail on Hammersmith Bridge. Yellowish-green lichen grows undisturbed where Alex's plaque used to sit. The old, lined wood is untouched by nails or tears. Alex's sister and friends never cried at this spot nor left bouquets and tributes. Hannah and Sally didn't abandon their favourite dolls to mark his memory. They haven't visited the bridge to mark the first anniversary of his death, because he is carrying on with his life, somewhere out there. I gaze out across west London, inhaling the scent from my flowers. Builder's cranes dip in the distance, ducks peck in the mud and boats drift closer and pass by. The gulls join in an argument with the pigeons and parakeets. Traffic hums and tube trains arrive and leave. Life goes on, unaltered by my presence – the way it should in the natural scheme of things.

I haven't tried to track down Alex or engineer a meet-up, hanging around outside his studio or favourite bars. I haven't browsed in Hidden Things or found a way to bump into Zoe. I've meddled in enough people's lives for one lifetime, leaving chaos in my wake. Who knows what further damage I could inflict on him or his family and friends if our paths cross? It's selfish to take the risk.

I toss a large bunch of sunflowers over the side.

'I love you, Alex,' I whisper. 'I always will. You made me feel truly loved. I'm sorry I've caused you so much pain. I want you to be happy and successful. I don't think you can do that with me. I hurt the people I love. I've taken more from you than I've given back, and you deserve better. *You* deserve that fairytale ending, not me.'

I pinch my eyes to stop the tears from forming. My next goodbye is even harder.

Mum.

'You loved me even more than Alex and Gran, which I never believed was possible,' I tell her. 'You were prepared to travel through time to save my life.'

My bottom lip trembles, but I force myself to go on.

'I thought I'd missed out on so much growing up. But we've shared something precious that no one else can: I've met you in each phase of your life. I've seen your first steps, childhood pigtails, teenage confidence and wrinkles in old age. You stroked my cheek as a toddler and wept on my chest. You were barely five when you tried to stop me from colliding with a cyclist on the bridge. In your middle age, you gave me a coffee on Kensington High Street because you knew I needed one. As an old lady, you tried to make me see the goodness and worth in myself. You watched over and comforted me in my darkest hours. I wish I'd spent longer with you, but I cherish every moment we spent together, however you looked. You were still *you*. My kind, brave, wonderful mum.'

I throw a bunch of her favourite sweet-smelling peonies into the water. They drift towards the sunflowers, and travel down the river together.

My fingers curl around something hard and shiny in my pocket. I pull it out.

'You were right, Mum. I can never go back. I can't do that to Gran. I know how much pain it caused her each time I left, and how she suffered when you were gone all these years. I promise, I'll look after her, and never leave.'

I dangle her pendant over the side. The sun emerges from behind the clouds. The birds stop singing, and the traffic noise fades away.

'Gran never meant to give me this for my birthday. She'd hidden it years ago. The more I think about that first morning at Ravensbrook, the more I'm convinced she believed she was helping *you*, Mum. She wanted Aunt Rose to explain how it worked.'

The necklace glints knowingly. I turn the stone, listening to the ticking noise for the last time.

'I'm strong enough to do this because of you. I'm not afraid. I'll never be alone.'

I let go.

The pendant hits the water, creating thousands of shimmering tiny diamonds on the surface before sinking. The ripples disappear as quickly, and the water continues to flow.

'Goodbye. I love you, Mum, and Alex. You'll both be right here.'

I touch my breaking heart.

48

A year later

MAY 11, 2025

Rain strikes the pavement in great sheets. Gutters are overflowing. I leap over a huge puddle in the road and miss spectacularly, soaking my shoes and tights. My feet are cold and wet as I dart across the pavement to the newsagent's and scan the magazine rack for *Grazia*. I shift a couple of copies of *Closer* and find the latest edition of the glossy hidden behind *OK!* My heart thuds with anticipation as I approach the counter, fumbling in my purse for change.

'I've had my first feature published in a magazine!' I tell the woman behind the till.

'How clever. Congratulations! I was never good with words at school.'

'Thank you!'

I steel myself for re-entering the storm – and possible disappointment. I could be celebrating prematurely. The article might not have made the cut. The editor said dozens of features compete for space every fortnight and even experienced journalists face disappointment. I toss my umbrella on the floor in the doorway and skim through the pages.

There it is! My photo stares back from beneath the headline:

The Girl Who Can't Stay Awake.

I've written a feature about living with narcolepsy, and how it's affected my daily life, and those around me – ex-boyfriends and bosses who didn't care what I was going through, and wouldn't make allowances, and one person who did. I reread my words:

> *This boyfriend was special. He never made me feel like a freak show or circus act. He never laughed, judged or made fun of me in front of his friends. He adjusted his life willingly and without resentment. He loved me for who I was, and accepted every part of me: the bad, as well as the good. He never let me down.*

I explain that I'm a stronger, braver person for knowing him. I've stood up for myself, challenged bullies, changed careers and ditched toxic relationships. I've fixed the leaking tap in my bathroom instead of waiting for someone else to do it and painted my bedroom wall the colour I love most: teal. I've travelled abroad on my own, watching the sun rise at Machu Picchu – a spectacle my gran had always wanted me to see. I'm no longer with this boyfriend, I explain, but he didn't leave because of my narcolepsy. I let him go. I had to learn to live on my own and come to terms with my condition and being parentless.

My heart aches dully for Mum and Alex. I see their faces vividly in my sleep and regularly dream about them both, revisiting our time together. Those first few seconds when I wake up are wonderful; they're both still with me. But their presence soon slips away and I remember they're gone. It's a pain that never disappears, but I'm learning to live with it. I don't have any choice. The GP has prescribed new stimulants, and I've had the all-clear from my cardiologist and neurologist. With the help of Raquel, I've taken Gran to visit where Gramps proposed on Hammersmith Bridge. I've made new friends through my narcolepsy support group. It's not the same as having Vicky, but she's in my past – I'm not sure she'll ever be in my future now she's moved in with Ed. That betrayal still stings, but it's a footnote amid my grief. I've tried to keep busy, retraining as a journalist, and I'm beginning to carve out a career as a freelance writer. I can work around my sleep disorder and never have to sit in an office. I feel a surge of pride as I scan the article, spread across three pages, and illustrated with photos of me at the top of Machu Picchu. This is just the beginning, a fresh start.

I pop back into the shop and buy a scrapbook so Gran can collect my articles; I've plenty more feature ideas. I put up my flimsy umbrella and run down the street towards the bus stop. Shop lights are reflected in shimmering orange, white and yellow puddles across the pavement. Ahead, the watery hues transform into a glistening rainbow of aquamarine, cobalt blue, and bright, acidic lemons. I glance at the window. My umbrella slips from my grasp. Water plasters hair to my forehead, and drips down my nose. I can't take my eyes off the portrait in the gallery window. A girl's face made of diamonds.

Me.

I admired this image as an unfinished print in Hidden Things, and as an anniversary present, hanging on my sitting-room wall in a previous life. But this new version is far more accomplished, and beautiful. I study the violets, electric greens, azures, teals and aquamarines that make up my face and hair – each diamond shape lovingly painted bar four left untouched on my right cheek.

I can't complete it. Our story isn't finished yet.

I shiver as I remember Alex's words. I can almost feel his lips on my neck. My gaze lowers to the bottom left:

He spent three months painting me after our meeting in the Swan. Another picture hangs next to it, crafted from the same rhombuses. It features two faces: me and Alex. I see every experience and emotion in our shared shapes. They're a mirror image of each other – when he laughed, I laughed. When I was sad, he was too. We loved and suffered together, as one.

Tears spill down my face, indistinguishable from the rain. My eyes are blurry. All the colours merge into one unforgettable, heartbreaking pattern. I see a life loved and lost repeatedly, and a new one rising phoenix like from the altered palette. Alex died for me and went through hell and back. I would have willingly sacrificed myself for him. We've kissed, made love, wept, argued, and made up, and started over. Because that's what life is, isn't it? Carrying on, continuing loving, no matter what cruel curveball is thrown at you.

A sob escapes from my lips. The pain is intense, a dagger to my heart. If I walk into Alex's exhibition, I'll be another bystander, someone on the periphery of his existence and no longer the centre of his universe. He won't realise that once we meant the world to each other. I'm the woman who briefly passed through his life two years ago and claimed I had a fiancé. Alex probably has a girlfriend. He could be engaged – he was ready to settle down and start a family. I can't face finding out. I turn to walk away.

'Are you coming in?'

I glance down at a girl with dark-blonde hair who's flung open the door. Another lump forms in my throat – it's Hannah. She's clutching her princess doll, Belle.

'I don't think it's a good idea,' I mumble.

'Why not? You're wet.'

'I haven't been invited.'

'I'm inviting you. I'm Hannah. I have a twin called Sally. She's annoying. Come and see my uncle's art. It's epic.' She tugs my hand, pulling me into the gallery.

A hot flush creeps up my neck. This is such a bad idea. I feel like a convict revisiting the scene of a crime. This is obviously Alex's opening night and he's here, somewhere, mingling with his family and friends. I often see his face in my dreams, but I'm not prepared for meeting him in person. This is too sudden and potentially traumatic. The times I've imagined encountering him have also never involved me looking like a drowned rat.

'Is my mascara smudged?' I ask, dabbing my eyes.

'Yes, it's messy and running down your face.'

I laugh. I'd forgotten her brutal honesty.

'I need to fix it quickly. I don't want to ruin Alex's show by looking like a vampire.'

I pull out my compact mirror and attempt to mop my face. My hair is curling into tight corkscrews.

'Do you know my uncle?'

'Yes, but no. Definitely no. Well, in another lifetime, perhaps.'

Hannah frowns, placing her hands on her hips.

'Sorry. I mean I don't know him. I should leave.'

'Let's go and meet my mum. I need to show her I'm a good hostess – she's promised to give me extra pocket money if I bring visitors into the gallery.'

I clutch my aching chest as she drags me past more diamond-shaped versions of Alex and myself. I can't bear to look at them. I focus on Zoe. She still has long, chestnut hair but has grown out her blunt fringe. I've missed our chats, and her fierce loyalty. She was the sister I never had but always wanted as a child.

'I've found another guest,' Hannah says loudly, interrupting Zoe's conversation with an elderly man.

A smile hovers on her mum's lips. 'Did you drag this lady off the street in the hope of earning one pound?'

'Yes, but no. Definitely no. Well, in another lifetime.' She winks at me. 'Perhaps.'

God, I've missed this. Missed *them*. Being part of an extended family.

'I'm sorry,' Zoe says. 'You're not a prisoner, I promise. You're free to leave at any time.'

'I'm good. Well, apart from being soaked to the skin.'

'Here. Use these.' She leans over the catering table and passes a handful of serviettes. 'Or you could dry off in the bathroom. It's over there.'

She points towards the back of the gallery. I spot Samira laughing and talking to Lizzy. Hamish brings over a drink and kisses Samira. Sally is running around and almost trips up Fatima. I recognise Alex's friends, his life. God, I miss everyone.

Suddenly, the crowd parts and I see *him*. My heart thumps wildly. I can barely breathe. My ears are buzzing. I automatically step closer but stop as Alex whispers in the ear of a gorgeous blonde. She laughs and plays with a tendril of hair. Is that . . . his girlfriend? Panic rises in my throat. I edge back.

'Sorry, it was lovely to see you and the twins again, Zoe. But I should go. This was a mistake.'

She frowns. 'Have we met? How do you know my name?'

The room is spinning. The lights stab my eyes.

I push my way through bodies and reach the door, throwing it open. A hand catches my arm.

'Is it you?' a familiar voice asks.

I turn around slowly. Recognition flickers in his eyes. The invisible thread, which links us together, tugs painfully at my heart. I remember the thrill of electricity as our lips touched and the butterflies dancing in my stomach.

A broad smile breaks out across his face. 'I remember you, Julia Hockney, like the painter.'

My chest pounds. He looks exactly the same. I feel like I'm floating out of my body and gazing down at myself. I watch his fingers encircle mine as we shake hands.

I missed you.

I hear those three words in my head. I lick my lips. My mouth is painfully dry.

'That wasn't my girlfriend.' He jerks his head towards the exhibition. 'In case you were wondering, which you probably weren't.'

He runs a hand through his hair, and his cheeks warm.

'Have you had a chance to see my paintings?'

'They're amazing, Alex.'

'You gave me the idea. You were my muse.'

'Like Joanna Hiffernan to Whistler?'

'I thought we'd agreed that could be an unflattering comparison?'

'You remembered!'

'I never forgot . . . *you.*'

I feel my heart quicken as he stares at me.

'I couldn't stop thinking about you. I might even have sent out vibes to the universe that you should break up with your fiancé.'

I laugh but Alex looks serious. 'Have you? Split with your fiancé, I mean?'

'Yes. I stayed with him for all the wrong reasons – mainly because I was scared of being alone. I'm not anymore.'

'You don't strike me as the kind of person who's afraid of anything.'

'I've conquered my fears. I'm not the same person you met in the bar. I've lost my mum, I've changed jobs. I'm different.'

'I'm sorry about your mum.'

Tears sting my eyes. 'I'm sorry she never met you, not properly, anyway.'

'Wait – did we meet?'

'I should go,' I say, turning to leave. 'I mustn't monopolise the artist. This is your big night, Alex. You need to share it with your friends and family.'

'No, wait. I can't let you walk away again – I'd prefer you to think I'm a madman than have a lifetime of regret.'

I open my mouth, but he cuts in.

'This might sound corny, but I'm going to say it anyway. I've never felt the same about anyone else as I did when we met in the bar. Come back inside and get to know me. Please? Give me a chance. Don't ask me why, but I have a feeling deep down we're supposed to be together.'

I stare at him, reacquainting myself with every inch of his face.

'How about it, Julia? Will you take a leap of faith?'

I smile and reach for his hand.

'I missed you,' he says, his fingers encircling mine.

ACKNOWLEDGEMENTS

I feel extremely blessed to have such a wonderful team working on this book at Lake Union. A big thank you to my editor, Victoria Oundjian, for loving my novel from the start and being such a huge support throughout the publishing process. I was very lucky to have two wonderful editors by my side – Victoria and Mike Jones. Their insights, suggestions and editing have made this a better book. Thank you to copy editor Antonia Maxwell, proofreader Frances Moloney, and Emma Rogers for the beautiful cover.

Thank you also to Alice Lutyens at Curtis Brown, who encouraged me to finish writing this book, and for helping bring Julia's story to readers. It wouldn't have been published without your support.

I always love carrying out research for my books and this one was no different – as usual, Graham Bartlett, a former chief superintendent, helped me with the policing aspects. I'd highly recommend his consultancy services to authors.

Thank you very much to Jonathan Bain and Peter Logue, who gave me a tour of the archives at Associated Newspapers' Northcliffe House and spent so long discussing the old library system, pre-digitisation. I had some memories of this from my early days in journalism in Fleet Street, and at the *Western Daily Press* in Bristol, but they filled in many gaps in my knowledge. Thank you to Anna Davis at the *Evening Standard*, a former colleague on the education beat, for answering queries about deadlines on a daily newspaper.

Narcolepsy fascinates me, and I read up widely on the sleep disorder. Thank you to Henry Nicholls, a trustee of Narcolepsy UK, for answering all my questions and being so generous with your time. Our discussion was incredibly helpful, and I'd highly recommend Henry's book, *Sleepyhead*, along with *Wide Awake and Dreaming* by Julie Flygare. I also follow Belle Hutt on Instagram, who shares her experiences of narcolepsy, and is very inspirational. I'm grateful for all the help I received with my research, and any mistakes are my own.

Julia's gran developed Alzheimer's in old age, but my father-in-law, Ken, had early onset of the disease in his fifties and has now, sadly, passed away. Hopefully, one day soon there will be a cure to prevent other families from suffering.

Thank you to author Sarah Govett for reading my book in its early stages and giving valuable feedback. As always, a huge thank you to my family – my mum, dad and sister, Rachel, and mother-in-law, Maureen. Mum always reads my drafts and I'm grateful for all her advice. I'm lucky to also have a supportive husband, Darren, who reads my drafts more times than he cares to remember, and two wonderful sons, James and Luke. One day they may read this book too!

ABOUT THE AUTHOR

Sarah J. Harris is an award-winning author and freelance education journalist who regularly writes for national newspapers.

Her debut novel, *The Colour of Bee Larkham's Murder*, won the Breakthrough Author award from Books Are My Bag in 2018 and was a Richard and Judy pick in WHSmith. Her second adult novel is called *One Ordinary Day at a Time*. Sarah also writes Young Adult thrillers under the pen name Sarah Wishart. (*Four Good Liars* was published by HarperCollins in November 2023).

Sarah grew up in Sutton Coldfield, West Midlands, and studied English at Nottingham University before gaining a post-graduate diploma in journalism at Cardiff University.

Sarah is a black belt in karate and a green belt in kickboxing. She lives in London with her husband and two sons.

Follow the Author on Amazon

If you enjoyed this book, follow Sarah J. Harris on Amazon to be notified when the author releases a new book!

To do this, please follow these instructions:

Desktop:

1) Search for the author's name on Amazon or in the Amazon App.

2) Click on the author's name to arrive on their Amazon page.

3) Click the 'Follow' button.

Mobile and Tablet:

1) Search for the author's name on Amazon or in the Amazon App.

2) Click on one of the author's books.

3) Click on the author's name to arrive on their Amazon page.

4) Click the "Follow" button.

Kindle eReader and Kindle App:

If you enjoyed this book on a Kindle eReader or in the Kindle App, you will find the author 'Follow' button after the last page.